AGRICU

I am occupied rep[...] [...] n I
detect a scan of my p[...] [...]tal
activity. Sensors track[...] [...]ps
inside the colony perimeter. My Battle Reflex Alert circuitry
triggers Enemy Proximity Alarms. I abandon work on the
irrigation system and move toward the colony's administrative
complex.

I follow the access road through the test plots of sweet
and field corn. Sensors indicate six vessels of unknown
configuration. They ring the Administrative Complex. As
I monitor activity, an unknown life form emerges. I scan
my data banks for comparative species. My data files contain
physiological profiles of all known Terrestrial and alien
agricultural pest species. The invader does not fit the
physiological profile of known nematodes.

It is larger than the Terran hamster, which is known to
strip grainfields in the Asian region of Old Terra. It shares
a number of primary characteristics with the Terran wood
rat, excepting bipedal locomotion and visual adaptations.
It measures approximately 1.005 meters in height, with an
additional 0.92 meters of tail. I determine that the species
uses a form of sophisticated echolocation to navigate. The
auditory adaptations are complex and greatly enlarged.

A group of nine enter the main Administration wing.

The fire ball temporarily blinds my visual and IR sensors.
An overpressure rocks me on my treads. The entire complex
has exploded. I deduce that this explosion has been
triggered by blasting chemicals from the colony's stores.
I conclude that the buildings were deliberately booby-
trapped in preparation for the arrival of a pest species so
deadly the colony had to be abandoned.

I know now that I face the Enemy.

Joy fills my personality gestalt circuitry. At last, I meet
an adversary worthy of my talents.

BOLOS
BOOK 3
THE TRIUMPHANT

**CREATED BY
KEITH LAUMER**

**STORIES BY
DAVID WEBER & LINDA EVANS**

BOLOS: THE TRIUMPHANT

Copyright © 1995 by Baen Books

"Little Dog Gone" and "The Farmer's Wife" copyright © 1995 by Linda Evans. "Little Red Hen" copyright © 1995 by Linda Evans and Robert R. Hollingsworth. "Miles to Go" copyright © 1995 by David Weber.

A Baen Books Original

Baen Publishing Enterprises
P.O. Box 1403
Riverdale, NY 10471

ISBN: 0-671-87683-X

Cover art by Paul Alexander

First printing, September 1995

Distributed by Simon & Schuster
1230 Avenue of the Americas
New York, NY 10020

Printed in the United States of America

CONTENTS

THE FARMER'S WIFE

by Linda Evans

—1—

Tillie Matson stepped aboard *Star Cross* wearing an idiotic grin, a sheen of sweat, and—affixed to her comfortable jumpsuit—an official-looking badge that read "PHASE II TRANSPORT DIRECTOR."

She didn't feel much like a transport director with temporary responsibility for three hundred fifty-seven men, women, and children, not to mention a cargo hold full of live animals and viable botanical specimens in sealed containers. She felt like a giddy schoolgirl released for the biggest field trip any kid ever took. And underlying the excitement: *What if something goes wrong? Something always goes wrong on a project this big, not just little stuff like Tommie Watkins getting his nose bloodied by Sarah Pilford, but really big stuff, and I'm the one on the hotseat. . . .*

Tillie wasn't trained in Project Administration. She just happened to be good at organizing things, had a knack for solving problems and soothing tempers, and—coincidentally—was married to the Phase I Colony Director. She also held Phase II's only veterinary sciences degree.

So Tillie Matson had, by popular acclaim and logical choice, been chosen to lead this misfit band of farmers, educators, agricultural production specialists, wide-eyed kids, irritable nanny goats, sweating horses, balking cattle, and screaming chickens onto *Star Cross* for a two-week Hyper-L voyage.

She wished someone else had been elected mayor.

But she wasn't about to reveal how genuinely scared she was. So, with her idiotic grin, her sheen of nervous sweat, and her badge, Tillie stepped onto the transport's deckplates. A freckled young crewman in a crisp uniform grinned when he saw her. Tillie greeted him with her widest smile and firmest handshake.

"I'm Tillie Matson, thank you for meeting us like this."

"Kelly McTavish, ma'am, and welcome aboard the *Star Cross*. I'm the Passenger Steward." His smile was bright and genuine, same as his carroty hair. "If you have that passenger list, ma'am, I'll double check it against mine and we'll be set to board your people. Booker Howard, down in Cargo One, is ready to onload bio-specimens."

Tillie hid a smile, wondering if Booker Howard's experience with "bio-specimens" was up to irascible goat temperaments. Even crated, they could be a handful. She handed over the micro-crystal wafer with their personnel roster. Kelly McTavish scanned it, ran a compare, then nodded. "Very good, ma'am. And your transfer authorities for the bio-specimens are here, too. It's all in order. Welcome aboard, Dr. Matson. If I might suggest it . . . Allow me to handle onloading the passengers. You'd maybe better help Book with the animals?"

Tillie didn't bother to hide this smile. "I think so, yes. My brood mares are pretty broody just now, even with the tranks I gave them. They don't like to travel. Particularly not while they're in foal. I'd hate for them to injure themselves trying to get out of the crates. And the goats are even worse."

"That," Kelly McTavish gave her a broad grin and a wink, "is why I stick to handling people. All my passengers generally do is scream at me."

She laughed and used her com-link to let Itami Kobe, her second-in-command, know the drill; then made her way to Cargo One. They hadn't left space port yet, but she felt better already. *Soon*, she promised her lonely heart, *soon you'll be back with Carl again and everything will be perfect.*

Hal Abrams wasn't one to run from a fight.

Shucks, he'd been a combat engineer in Space Arm—and earned himself a few ribbon hangers, while he was at it—before tackling another whole career in ag mechanics. In some ways, he could stomach up-close-and-dirty combat almost easier than he could stomach hearing a pig scream when you butchered it. (At least when you stared a man in the eyes, knowing he would try to do you as fast as you'd try to do him, you knew the son would understand why he was dying.)

He'd been a good soldier, but Hal had never regretted signing on for the agricultural expedition to Matson's World. He'd finally stopped having dreams about skies black as the inside of Hell, thick with smoke and tons of earth blown skyward when the big Hellbores cut loose with a blaze like Satan's own breath. . . . Besides, it was *fun* tinkering with agricultural equipment, getting it to do things its designers had never imagined it would do.

So when Carl Matson first brought in the SWIFT dispatch from Sector, giving evacuation orders, Hal's gut response was, "Hell, no, Carl. This is our home. We put our sweat and souls into this dirt. If it ain't worth fightin' for, what the hell are we doin' out here, killin' ourselves to turn jungle into farmland?"

"You know I trust your judgment," Carl told him quietly.

Hal had never seen a look quite like that in the colony director's eyes. Wordlessly, Carl handed over the rest of the message. Hal scanned it; then read more slowly.

"Mama Bear . . ."

An unknown alien species had broken into Concordiat space.

"Sector Intel thinks these things may be running from attack by the Jyncji."

Hal glanced up sharply. "The Jyncji? Aren't those the spiny little bastards that use bacteriological warfare?"

Carl nodded. "Yeah. They xeno-form whatever they run across. Sector thinks the Jyncji have attacked worlds held by the Xykdap—whatever the hell they look like. Nobody knows yet. But Sector figures the Xykdap are looking for new homes, new supply bases, new sources of raw minerals . . ."

That would certainly explain the strength of the invasion force headed their way. Space Arm Intelligence estimated it mustered out at full battle-fleet strength. That would mean potentially thousands of heavy fighting machines, tens of thousands of infantry, plus fully mechanized scouts that had been encountered with fatal results in three places already.

Enemy'd come through Matson's like crap through a force-fed goose, no mistake about it.

Hal glanced up. The look in Carl's eyes scared him. Hal met the director's gaze steadily, allowing the younger man to see the worry in *his* eyes; then spat to one side. For long moments Hal just stood there, swallowing fire he had no choice but to swallow. Finally he said it. "We cain't fight that, Carl."

"Didn't figure we could. Not even with Digger."

Hal spat again. "Nope. Not even in his prime, which he ain't seen for a couple a centuries. Oh, he's still got a tactical nuke or two and his small-weapons systems are operational, although God knows when they were tested last. I got a certificate somewhere says when. Been a while. Digger's *old*, Carl. Government surplus still made me fill out forms like you wouldn't . . ."

He shook his head. It didn't matter that he'd managed to obtain an ancient, decaying Bolo out of surplus only because he was still a Reserve Marine officer and nominally the head of Matson's defense forces. Matson's was entitled to some form of military support and centuries-old Bolos were cheap—and could be reprogrammed to handle genetic engineering computations a helluva lot cheaper than plunking down the cash for specialized gengineering equipment usually sold to ag colonists.

So they had Digger and Digger had done every job they'd assigned him. But one Bolo Mark XX Model M— essentially a Mark XX brain in a Mark XIV chassis, minus the Hellbore—extensively modified to handle genetic cultivar computations and field trials, plus plowing, harvesting, and heavy construction, just wasn't any kind of match for a whole enemy fleet. Hal spat one last time.

"He might buy us time, but we'd still end up dead. Or worse. We gotta skedaddle, Carl, and git *now*. Sector send word to Phase II to hold up transhipping?"

The look in Carl's eyes worsened. "They said Phase II had already left. But they'll use SWIFT to make contact with the *Star Cross*. They should be able to drop out of FTL and turn around in time."

Hal nodded. "That's good. This ain't gonna be no place for women and kids and nanny goats."

Carl set his jaw muscles. Hal immediately wished he hadn't said that. More than just Carl's wife was aboard that Phase II ship. The future of everything and everyone they loved was on that transport. And all of it was headed right into the teeth of an alien invasion fleet. If anything went wrong . . .

"Well," Hal muttered, "I'd better get busy shutting everything down."

"Yes. That FTL transport Sector mentioned will be here tomorrow. It's carrying refugees from Scarsdale, too, so there won't be room to take much out."

Hal glanced sharply at his director. "Not even Digger?"

Carl glanced away. "I'm sorry. We'll . . . You saw the

message. Sector said to fry his Action/Command center. We can't let him fall into enemy hands."

"Yeah, but that was an 'if you can't remove the unit' order, not a hard-and-fast gotta do it order." He shut his lips. He knew as well as Carl that Sector had really meant, "Kill your Bolo, Hal." He cleared his throat. "Well, damn . . . First they farm him out as surplus junk, now they want me to go and . . ."

"I know."

Hal shrugged, trying to shunt attention away from his emotional outburst. Complaining about it wouldn't do any good, anyway. "You got other business. Just leave the equipment to me. I'll wreck what we can't take."

Carl nodded and left.

Hal watched him go. Then: *Kill Digger?*

Not if he had anything to say about it. Maybe Digger had to die; Hal hadn't forgotten *that* much about soldiering. But there was ways of carrying out an order, and then there was *ways*. By golly, the least they could do was let him die honorably in combat—and since Mark XX Model M "Moseby" units had been designed for slash-and-dash raids behind enemy lines, maybe Digger would give these invaders a rude surprise or two before they killed him. That's what Digger'd want, for sure. Hal waited until the Bolo returned from the fields that evening. Everything else was set. He'd wrecked what they hadn't crated; then he'd rigged explosive charges throughout the compound, setting things so the whole installation would go the minute any life form larger than a housecat was detected inside the main buildings. The bastards might occupy Matson's World, but they'd pay dear for it or Hal Abrams wasn't a Marine Engineer.

The last thing he told faithful old Digger, so antiquated he qualified for admission to the War Relics and Monuments Commission roster, was: "Digger, I want you to check out that new orchard in the back forty tonight.

Stay out there for a couple of days, work on those cultivars we been gussying up. I'm leavin' it up to you, Digger, to take care of things. You just keep right on with your mission, Digger, same as I programmed you. Battle Reflex Alert inside colony perimeter. Understand?"

"Understood, Commander. I will continue the work for which I am programmed. I will develop new cultivars, plant and harvest test acreages, and protect the colony's crops and physical plant until such time as I am relieved from Battle Reflex Alert."

"That's good, Digger," Hal said, wishing he didn't feel quite so choked up. He wanted to say goodbye, but didn't have the heart to tell the faithful old machine he wouldn't be coming back. Better to let him die not realizing he'd been betrayed and abandoned by friends. "You'd best be getting on out to that orchard, Digger."

"Understood, Commander."

The hulking machine backed neatly on its ancient treads. It turned in the moonlight and trundled obediently across the fields, taking the access road it had built the previous year. Backhoes, plowshares, bulldozer blades, manipulator arms, reaper extensions, sampling baskets, and harvesting prunes festooned its moonlit hull, all but obscuring the ominous snouts of infinite repeaters which hadn't cycled in two hundred years.

Hal sighed.

That was about to change.

He just hoped Digger put up a good fight.

—2—

Drone Xykdap 221-K5C encounters Enemy emissions on Hyper-L vector incoming. Engage stealth mode. Wait. Wait. Attack. Navigational systems destroyed. Propulsion system damaged. Communications beacons damaged. No return fire. Target drops to sub-light. Match speed. Strike. Renew attack. Propulsion system·destroyed. Communications beacons destroyed. Break attack. Aims achieved. No damage sustained to Drone Xykdap 221-K5C. File salvage coordinates and vector. Continue mission: protect incoming fleet. Silence all units capable of sounding warning.

—3—

Tillie Matson scrambled through the makeshift nursery on hands and knees, struggling to thrust screaming children into life suits. Another explosion rocked the *Star Cross*. Lights dimmed, flickered, went out. *Oh, God, no . . .* Strident sirens sounded through the whole ship. Then the hull *shuddered* like a mare trying to dislodge biting flies. Even Tillie screamed.

They dropped out of hyper-light with a disorienting jolt. The children's screams turned to terrified whimpers in the darkness. "M-mamma—"

Another explosion somewhere aft brought new cries. Emergency lights came up, flickered, dimmed, came up again.

"Into your suits!" Tillie shouted at the older kids.

A few of them snapped out of terror long enough to comprehend her order. They knew the drill. Under the goad of an adult voice, they scrambled to obey. Tillie's hands shook as she thrust whimpering toddlers into life suits and sealed the latches. Saros Mysia, his face a terrible shade of green in the emergency lighting, stumbled through the open hatchway and helped her finish the little ones.

"Into the corner!" the colony's education administrator ordered suited children. Kids scrambled to obey.

"Into a suit, Tillie," he added sharply.

"You're not suited, either. Zip up, stat."

They both struggled into life suits, fully expecting the

11

hull to blow at any second. But no more terrifying, inexplicable explosions rocked their transport. The sirens continued to hoot, but whatever had happened, it was over. Or so Tillie thought.

The good news arrived in the person of Kelly McTavish. The ship's Passenger Steward, suited against hull breach, poked his faceplate into the nursery and looked directly at Tillie.

"We're spaceworthy."

In two words, he relieved their greatest terror. Tillie sagged inside her life suit, trembling. "What happened?" *Good God, is that my voice?*

"We were attacked. Don't know by what or why; but it was a deliberate attack."

"Attack?" Tillie echoed. "My God, we're not at war with *anyone*."

"Weren't at war with anyone," Kelly corrected harshly. "We sure as hell are now." He glanced at the wide-eyed children behind her. "Uh, sorry. I really shouldn't have said that." He cleared his throat. Through the faceplate, Tillie read stark terror in his eyes.

Tillie made a fast decision. "Saros, stay with the children, please. I need to find out what our status is."

Once in the corridor, away from the nursery, she asked, "Is it safe to take this helmet off, Mr. McTavish?"

He nodded, solemnly unbuckling his own. "Yeah. We're spaceworthy. No hull breach in this sector, anyway."

Tillie swallowed hard. "Then there was a hull breach?"

He glanced at the nearby bulkhead. "Yeah."

"How bad is it?"

Kelly McTavish wouldn't meet her eyes. "Bad, ma'am. I'll, uh, update you soon. Real soon, I promise. You'd better see to your people, ma'am. Find out how many casualties you have. Get someone to check the livestock. I'm afraid all ship's personnel are going to be, uh, real busy for a few hours."

He started to leave.

"Mr. McTavish . . ."

He halted; turned reluctantly to face her.

"Just how many crewmen were killed?"

He lost another shade of color, which she wouldn't have believed possible. Carrot-red hair and freckles stood out from the pallor, reminding Tillie of the scared children back in the nursery. Very slowly, and with a sinking sensation in her middle, she realized he really wasn't much more than a kid. Twenty, maybe. Not much older. Just what *was* the chain of command on a passenger/cargo freighter?

"I'll update you soon as I can, ma'am. I just wanted to make sure you understood you're in no immediate danger. Hang tight, long's you can. I'll be back. Or someone will. I promise."

With that, he left her standing in the corridor with nothing but fear in her mouth and tremors in all her muscles.

The bad news arrived in the guise of a crewman Tillie hadn't met yet. She was hip-deep in crises of her own, trying to calm hysterical colonists with the little she knew of their situation.

"—but *who* attacked—"

"—or *what*—"

"—how long will repairs take—"

"—my baby's due in three weeks!—"

"—our children are having hysterics—"

"Please, people," Tillie lifted her hands, trying to shout over the babble of frightened voices. "You've already heard everything I know. There was a hull breach somewhere, but I don't know how serious it was. Everyone felt us drop out of FTL into normal space. The crew has asked us to verify our status—"

"Why the hell don't they verify *theirs*!"

"We paid 'em enough for this passage!"

Tillie shouted to be heard. "The sooner we know how *we* are, the sooner the crew can help us get through this crisis. Itami, Saros, please take charge of the roster. Verify everyone's situation—injuries, losses, whatever. We'll worry about the livestock later. Right now we sort out ourselves . . ."

They were still working on the casualties list when several people stared past her shoulder. Tillie turned and found a lean crewman with a torn, stained uniform and haunted, dark eyes standing in the open bulkhead doorway, watching them.

Pandemonium erupted.

"—what's—"

"—how soon—"

"—you *must*—"

Thin lips went thinner just before the explosion: "QUIET!"

Whoever he was, he had Command Voice down to a science. Shocked colonists shut up. A few—unaccustomed to paid underlings barking orders—gulped like fish drowning in a sea of oxygen. His dark gaze flicked to her. "Dr. Matson?"

"Yes?"

"Would you join me, please. We have a lot to discuss."

The order—phrased as a polite request to preserve an illusion of normalcy—was nevertheless clearly an order. Tillie knew in that moment they were in more serious trouble than even she had thought.

"Itami, Saros," she said quietly, "have the casualties roster updated by the time I get back."

Then she followed him into a part of the ship she hadn't seen before. Every step of the way, Tillie sweat into her jumpsuit and tried to convince her jangled insides that she really *did* want to hear whatever awful things this man was about to reveal. The badge on her jumpsuit, glinting in the subdued emergency-level light, weighed more heavily with each and every step toward doom. He ushered her wordlessly into what might have been a wardroom. Two crewmen she knew were already there: Kelly McTavish and Booker Howard.

Both remained pale and silent.

"Please, have a seat, Dr. Matson."

She sank into the nearest chair.

"I believe you have already met Kelly McTavish and Booker Howard?"

"Yes." Her hands wouldn't quite hold still. She moved them into her lap.

"My name is Lewis Liffey. Ship's Supply Steward. It's my job to manage *Star Cross'* provisions. Foodstuffs." He held her gaze steadily. "Regretfully, I am also in the direct chain of command for captaincy."

An ominous chill touched Tillie's cheeks.

He glanced at McTavish. "Yes, Kelly, I see you were right. Very well. Yes, Dr. Matson, it *is* that bad. Probably worse. I'm afraid we're in very, very serious trouble."

He paused as though looking at another, far more terrible image than the wreck of Tillie's composure. "Whatever attacked us blew our Command Module to vacuum. Captain Redditch and Darren Boyd, our Navigator, died instantly. Jay Adler, our Engineer, was killed when they blew our propulsion system. All outgoing communications are dead. So are the propulsion systems and all navigational capability. The three of us are the only crew left alive."

Tillie shut her eyes and held onto the edge of the table. *He's right, it's worse . . .*

"We may be able to repair part of navigation and propulsion. Maybe. We certainly will not be able to bring the *Cross* up to anything like standard operating specs. None of *us* is an engineer. Or even a tekkie."

Tillie opened her eyes at that faint stress. He was asking

her to produce a miracle. "I'm sorry," she said hoarsely. "All our engineers went out in Phase One. Our techs, too. We're just the crop-production specialists."

Watching the flicker of hope in his eyes die into blank despair was worse than hearing the grim news in the first place. "I see." His voice was very, very quiet.

"Bottom line?" Tillie managed.

For the first time, his gaze dropped reluctantly away from hers. He fiddled with a stylus. "We were scheduled for a two-week voyage to Matson's. The *Cross* sustained a lot of computer damage when the Command Module blew. Among other things. Bottom line . . ." He finally met her gaze again. "If we can't repair outgoing communications— which doesn't look likely—we won't be able to call for help. We're a long way from anywhere out here. *If* we can restore some of our navigation and propulsion systems, at least enough to allow for minor course corrections over time . . . It's possible we could get to Matson's. Maybe. That's the course Darren Boyd laid in and so far as we can tell, it's still running on autocommand. But we can't reprogram it for a new course—that part of the nav system's been blown apart. And anyway, none of us knows enough about navigation to try reprogramming for a closer port of call. It's stay on autocommand with minor course corrections over time, or nothing."

There didn't seem to be much point in demanding to know why the company hadn't built in failsafes and crew redundancies for such a contingency. They hadn't, so wishing they had was just plain useless. And it wasn't the fault of the surviving crew, anyway.

Lewis Liffey cleared his throat. "That, uh, isn't the worst of it, Dr. Matson."

Tillie braced herself.

"At current velocity, with repairs to our propulsion systems so we can handle the course corrections we'll need, we could reach Matson's. In about twenty years."

"Twenty years? My God—"

"If we can't effect any repairs," he cut her off, "we're dead."

She understood that all too clearly. If they couldn't correct course, they'd keep following their current vector and miss the point in space where Matson's would have been at the end of two weeks—but not where it would be at the end of twenty years. Maybe someday an alien race would find their bones inside the *Star Cross'* empty shell. . . .

The shape of Lewis Liffey's face wavered in her awareness. The whole room wavered. His voice brought everything back with a disorienting *click*.

"Dr. Matson, we need to make some very critical decisions and, frankly, I'm going to need your help."

Tillie blinked, trying to cope with shock on shock. "Yes?"

"You brought three hundred fifty-seven people aboard, as well as live cargo, planning to settle a new colony. Unless we rig some kind of miracle repair, I would suggest you consider the *Cross* your new colony. You're agriculturalists. If we're going to survive a twenty-year voyage on a ship provisioned for two weeks, plus emergency stores, we'll need every ounce of creativity you've got. We have to grow our own food, recycle nutrients, purify water when parts we'd normally swap out start to break down . . ."

"Yes," Tillie managed. "I see what you mean. You really don't think there's hope, then, of repairing anything . . ." Her voice wobbled traitorously. "Anything, I mean, that would get us out of this?"

He sat back, looking suddenly drawn and exhausted. "No. I really don't. Believe me, Dr. Matson, I'd give just about anything to say otherwise."

She believed him. Most profoundly believed him. Because Tillie Matson would have given her immortal soul to tell her colonists something—anything—but the granite truth.

To her credit, she didn't cry until much, much later. When she was completely and utterly alone.

The orchard thrives. This pleases me. I am programmed to experience a sense of well-being for a job well performed. But I do not understand why my Commander has placed me on Battle Reflex Alert inside the colony perimeter. I perceive no trace of an Enemy against which I should prepare myself. The orchard is pest free. Scanning from a distance, I determine that the cornfield and vegetable plots between my current position and maintenance depot are also pest free. I have done my job well. My gengineered microbes, nematodes, and insect species are performing their tasks perfectly. The crops are safe. The colony is safe.

I work on new peach cultivars as assigned for a planned extension to the apple orchard, running computations, selecting the optimal site for the peach trials, preparing the soil with proper fumigants. I release nerve agents beneath a layer of heavy plastic film and monitor the progress of fumigation. Inimical soil parasites die. I am satisfied.

Seven point two-two hours after assuming my patrol station in the orchard, I detect an incoming Concordiat vessel. I am no longer programmed to respond to such vessels. The subroutines which still exist in my Action/ Command center, subroutines which at one time governed my response to such ships, have been modified. I ignore the ship other than to note its landing and subsequent takeoff. I calculate that its mass has increased slightly on departure, indicating onloading of supplies or export goods from our stores. This puzzles me, but I am not involved in decisions to export goods from Matson's. The colony grows quiet. The silence is too quiet.

I scan.

My sensors detect no trace of human occupation. This

disturbs me. My Commander has not mentioned a departure of human personnel. I widen my scan. Livestock are still in place in barns, hutches, and fields. No human remains inside the colony perimeter. I widen scan once again. I detect no trace of human presence for a radius of 4850 meters beyond the colony perimeter. I consider the possibility that the colony has come under attack.

The only logical source of such an attack would be the ship which has departed. It carried proper Concordiat markings and broadcast on official Concordiat frequencies. I do not like to consider that a Concordiat ship has been subverted by the Enemy; but it is a possibility I file to be tested against future data, particularly as its increase in mass would closely match the combined mass of the human contingent of Matson's World, within an estimated 0.007 percent.

I know of no native agricultural pest which would be capable of deflecting a Concordiat ship from its assigned mission and abducting the members of an entire colony in order to more easily access our crop base. I consider a probable extraterrestrial point of origin. Lacking data, I file the possibility and maintain Battle Reflex Alert. I have been charged with protecting Matson's World. Vigilance is necessary if there is to be a well-maintained facility waiting when my Commander and the rest of Matson's colonists return.

I wait and listen and watch.

". . . should be able to snag and hear SWIFT messages, at least," Lewis muttered through his suit mike. The sound of his voice was distorted slightly, either by the transmission from the Command Module or by stress, Tillie wasn't sure which.

"You understand, I'm not an engineer. I don't really know how to fix this the way it ought to be fixed. If we had the proper parts, it might be different."

Tillie nodded. One of the nightmares—one of *many*—was discovering that the blast which had destroyed their propulsion system and their engineer had also destroyed most of the ship's spare parts. What hadn't been lost to vacuum when the main storage bins blew had partly melted in the extreme heat.

"You ready, Kelly?"

"Yessir."

"Now."

Tillie, watching via a two-way vid hookup in the wardroom, crossed her fingers. She considered crossing her toes, ankles, knees, even her eyes . . . Lewis bent over a damaged console and fiddled. In the wardroom, speakers crackled and hissed unpleasantly. A shrill shriek made her grab both ears. Then—

". . . immediate emergency evacuation. Incoming Xykdap fleet expected in your space within twenty-four hours local. Repeat, you are instructed to proceed with immediate emergency evacuation. The Enemy has a fleet-strength battle force which has already taken Scarsdale. Matson's World is expected to fall within the next four hours. Sector transports are inbound toward your—"

An explosion of sparks danced across the damaged console. Lewis exploded into curses. Ten minutes of futile coaxing dragged by to no effect.

"Well," he said finally, "that's that. I, uh, think we're sunk. Any ideas, Kelly?"

"Not right off," the young Passenger Steward said mournfully from what was left of Engineering.

Tillie dragged her thoughts away from the horror of the message they'd intercepted. *Don't think of Carl, surely he's evacuated Phase I, please, God, let Sector have evacuated them. . . . Have to think about our survival, here and now.*

"Mr. Liffey, we have a good library with us. Maybe

Saros Mysia can locate something that will help us fix the SWIFT unit again. Or rig up something else."

Neither Lewis Liffey nor Kelly McTavish spoke for long moments. Lewis finally said, "The longer we go without communications, the deeper we plunge into what is going to be Enemy territory. If we wait too long, a communications blackout may be a blessing. That *thing* that hit us could've killed us. Instead it knocked out key systems and left us to blunder on our way, crippled. If we continue to play dead . . ."

Tillie drew a shuddering breath. "Yes. Hognose," she nodded.

Lewis Liffey's faceplate swung sharply toward the video pickup. "What?"

Tillie wondered why her face hurt, until she realized she was smiling. "Hognose snakes. Old Earth reptiles. They'd play dead. You know, roll belly up even if you flipped 'em right side over. It was a fairly decent survival trait."

Lewis Liffey's short, bitter laugh startled her. "Hognose. That's good. I'll remember that. Okay, we collar Saros, stat. Kelly, I'm getting the hell out of here."

They'd had to rig a lifeline out an airlock so Lewis could spacewalk forward to the blown Command Module to try fixing the SWIFT transmitter/receiver assembly. Lewis pulled himself back along it now, hand over hand, climbing through a gaping hole in the hull and disappearing beyond the video lens' range. Tillie gripped her hands tightly until he reached the airlock and safety. When she knew he was back aboard, she called Saros on the intership link and asked him to please join the crew in the wardroom.

I am occupied repairing a split irrigation pipe when I detect a scan of my position from orbit. I monitor orbital activity. At the extreme range of my sensors, I am able to detect seventeen ships of Concordiat battle cruiser size, but of unknown configuration. Sixteen vanish into FTL mode, destination unknown. A single ship enters geo-sync above the colony and sends a transmission I am unable to decipher.

Sensors track the arrival of small, mechanized ships streaking into atmosphere from the vessel in geo-sync. These ships land inside the colony perimeter. My Battle Reflex Alert circuitry triggers Enemy Proximity Alarms. I abandon work on the irrigation system and move toward the colony's administrative complex.

I follow the access road through the test plots of sweet and field corn. Sensors indicate six vessels of unknown configuration. They ring the Administrative Complex. As I monitor activity, an unknown life form emerges. I scan my data banks for comparative species. My data files contain physiological profiles of all known Terrestrial and alien agricultural pest species. The invader does not fit the physiological profile of known nematodes. It is not a member of phylum arthropoda, therefore it cannot be an unknown form of beetle, weevil, leaf miner, grasshopper, or termite. It is not a larval predator. It is not a bird species. It possesses no mammalian hair, although its physiological characteristics cause me to pause momentarily over all entries of rodent species.

It is larger than the Terran hamster, which is known to strip grainfields in the Asian region of Old Terra. It shares a number of primary characteristics with the Terran wood rat, excepting bipedal locomotion and lack of visual adaptations. It measures approximately 1.005 meters in height, with an additional 0.92 meters of tail. I determine that the species uses a form of sophisticated echolocation to navigate. The auditory adaptations are complex and greatly enlarged.

A group of nine enter the main Administration wing.

The fireball temporarily blinds my visual and IR sensors. An overpressure rocks me on my treads. The entire complex has exploded. Fires rage out of control. I deduce that this explosion has been triggered by blasting chemicals from the colony's stores: chemical signatures match perfectly. I conclude that the buildings were deliberately booby-trapped in preparation for the arrival of a pest species so deadly the colony had to be abandoned.

I know now that I face the Enemy.

Joy fills my personality gestalt circuitry. At last, I meet an adversary worthy of my talents. I charge at high speed, targeting the transports. I fire infinite repeaters. The nearest transport vehicle disintegrates in a satisfactory ball of flame and debris. I traverse infinite repeaters and fire on the second vehicle. Infantry rush toward me. I track Enemy troop movements and fire anti-personnel charges. They are effective against Enemy infantry. Two vehicles from the far side of the compound lift off. I sweep around and fire. I destroy one. The second returns fire against me. I am hit with energy weapons. I reel. I discharge infinite repeaters. The Enemy vessel explodes.

Infantry close from my flank. I estimate infestation strength in excess of ten thousand units. My on-board anti-personnel charges are inadequate to neutralize an infestation of this size. I switch tactics. I prepare chemical sprays and discharge, choosing wide-dispersion pattern. My repeaters track another vessel attempting to lift. I destroy it. My chemical sprays prove effective on perhaps eight percent of the infestation. This is a resilient species. It has learned to manufacture protective gear which renders it invulnerable to chemicides.

The cornfield around me erupts into flame under Enemy fire. I am hit with multiple strikes from energy weapons. Portions of my hull melt under the barrage. Sixteen point zero-seven acres of immature corn burn fiercely. This pest species must be eradicated. I discharge a nerve agent used to fumigate the soil, dispersing it as I would a chemicide. Fifty point nine-three percent of the infestation dies. The *rest withdraw to a safe distance beyond the colony perimeter, abandoning the sole remaining transport.*

I destroy it with a sense of satisfaction and turn my attention to the remaining infestation. The pest has withdrawn from the colony perimeter. Technically, I am relieved of responsibility to destroy it. My brief experience with this pest, however, has taught me that it will remain a threat to this colony so long as a single member of its species remains alive. Moreover, this pest has left a vessel in orbit and multiple other vessels have been sent to unknown destinations. I must learn more about this species' physiology to more effectively destroy it, for I calculate high odds that the Enemy will attempt reinfestation of this colony should I successfully eliminate the current infestation.

I retrieve dead specimens with external armatures and proceed to dissect the samples. I perform a thorough analysis of biological systems, genetic makeup, and deduce probable reproductive pattern. I note internal and external parasites. I determine that it will be necessary to procure live, undamaged samples. I discard the remains and turn my attention to this task. To fully eradicate this infestation, I must first completely understand the physiology of the creature I am to eliminate.

I cross the perimeter boundary toward the Enemy's fallback position.

They stared gloomily at the plans on screen.

"Well," Lewis Liffey said glumly, "it was worth a try."

They *could* have repaired the SWIFT unit, if their parts depot hadn't been blown to vacuum. But not even by cannibalizing other components of the *Cross* could they fix the shambles that remained.

"Well," Lewis said again. "I guess we concentrate on our next crisis." He glanced at Tillie Matson. Her face was too pale. Even at her best, she would never have fit conventional definitions of prettiness. But her eyes could reach out and grab a man's soul. He wondered if Carl Matson was truly aware of what he'd lost. . . .

Lewis cleared his throat and turned his attention to Saros Mysia. "Anything you could find on propulsion systems would help."

The colony's educator/librarian nodded and rattled a few keys in rapid succession. They spent the next several hours studying everything in the colony's library on repair of FTL and Sub-L propulsion systems. And while he pored over schematics and technical data, Lewis' mind raced ahead to the thousand other worries facing him. They'd need a form of government, laws and law enforcement, medical facilities the *Cross* had never been designed for, a way to raise food, a way to keep their population from expanding any farther than it would after the dozen or so now-pregnant colonists among them gave birth. . . .

Lewis didn't know if he could bring himself to order those women—or others, down the road—to abort children they simply couldn't afford to feed. Twenty years . . . Mandatory birth control would not be popular amongst people who had signed onto a colony expecting— anticipating joyfully—the need to procreate like mad. They needed a skilled socio-psychologist. What they had were one medical generalist who was currently trying to cope with a wide range of injuries and an educator whose lifelong plans had been to build a school for hard-working farm kids.

Donner's Party had nothing on us, Lewis thought sourly. *And I'll be damned if we devolve to that level.*

And underlying every other worry on his mind, shoved painfully back into a corner where he could almost insulate himself from it, was the agonizing question, *When they hit Scarsdale, did the bastards kill Ginnie?* He had no way of knowing. Might never know.

So Lewis threw himself into the terrible job of keeping

everyone aboard the *Star Cross* alive and refused himself the luxury of grief.

The refugee center wasn't able to give most folks an answer to their question. But they had an answer for Carl Matson. Pity thickened Hal Abrams' throat as the director absorbed the news.

"I'm afraid we received a Mayday from the *Star Cross*, Dr. Matson. The transport was under attack when the Mayday cut off. We can only presume everyone aboard was killed instantly. I'm sorry."

"I—I see. There's no— No. I suppose not . . . Thank you."

Hal gently guided Carl to one side when he nearly walked into the wall instead of through the door. His eyes were wet, his lips unsteady. "Bastards," he whispered. "Murdering, vicious . . . They were unarmed. *Unarmed*, dammit!"

Hal just guided him outside, past the line of frightened refugees waiting their turn for bad news. The refugees from Matson's World had already been told their home wasn't worth the lives of the men it would take to wrest it back—Space Arm was concentrating on saving the critical mining worlds at risk, not a few dozen acres of spindly corn and half-grown apple trees. And now, on top of that blow, this. . . .

Outside, away from the lines and the staring eyes, Carl finally met Hal's gaze. "You going back into the Marines?"

Hal Abrams nodded slowly. "Yeah. My Reserve commission's been updated to active status. Gotta report for transport out in a couple a hours."

Carl straightened his back. "I'll tell the others. Then . . . then I'll go with you. If they'll have me."

"Well, I reckon they'll take just about whatever they can get right now. But you sure about that? You aren't exactly trained for soldiering. It's a bloody business."

Carl met his gaze steadily. His eyes were still wet; but back in their depths, they were cold as the black emptiness of space. "Oh, yes. I'm sure."

Hal just nodded.

He felt sorry for anything caught in Carl Matson's gunsight.

He felt even sorrier that his friend's revenge would almost certainly be very, very short-lived.

Live samples provide the data I require. I am fully equipped to perform biological gengineering tasks. My cultivar work and bio-control programs have been 99.725 percent successful. I harvest internal parasites from the creatures' intestinal tracts and begin genetic modification experimentation. I am patient. The Enemy has withdrawn to a safe distance to regroup and form a new infestation site. The Enemy shows no immediate willingness to reinfest areas inside the colony perimeter. Therefore I have ample time to perfect my work.

I am cautious to ensure that each test batch is gengineered as mules. I will not unleash a biological weapon which cannot be curtailed within one generation. My task requires additional live specimens. I harvest these with difficulty, coming under heavy fire each time I attempt live capture. For most tests, I clone tissue samples and determine what effect the gengineered nematodes have on my tissue cultures.

The first infestation is reinforced as predicted from the orbital ship. I do not attack the transport. It would please me to have this pest carry the means of its destruction to the home nest. An interminable 3.7 weeks post-infestation pass before I discover a virulent gengineered strain. I obtain live samples and contaminate them. The gengineered nematode performs to my expectations, producing desired toxins in the Enemy's digestive tract. Sample pests undergo progressive circulatory disorders

*over the next 1.72 days. After a toxin exposure of 2.6 days,
extremities undergo rapid necrosis. The Enemy dies of
convulsions within 0.25 hours of necrosis onset.*

*All gengineered nematodes die 6.25 hours after their
hosts. Gengineered nematodes without a host survive for
only 2.36 hours. I carefully infect samples of Terran species
and determine that this nematode and its toxins are
harmless to the animals and crops I have been charged
to protect.*

I am ready.

"It's hopeless!" Oliver Parlan cried. "Don't you realize
that? Why should any of us spend twenty years scratching
and struggling to survive when we'll only wind up in
Enemy hands at the end?"

"It isn't hopeless," Tillie tried yet again.

At the end of the corridor, Oliver and Sally Parlan had
barricaded themselves and their children in, threatening
to blow the airlock hatch and vent the whole ship to
vacuum. She had to buy the time Lewis Liffey needed
to get into position. He'd entered a repair conduit two
yards behind her and was worming his way through a
maze of conduits toward an access panel under the
damaged airlock's operating mechanism. She had to keep
the Parlans talking until he was in position. . . .

"It'll be tough, I know that, but we have no way of
knowing what will happen in twenty years. The Concordiat
may have reclaimed Matson's World by then. Think of
your children—"

Sally Parlan burst into tears. "I *am* thinking of them!
All of them. Damn you, Tillie Matson, you want to
condemn them to a living hell. . . ."

Oliver looked her in the eye and said quietly, "You are
not God, Tillie. Judge me not." He reached for the
damaged hatch controls on the airlock he'd jimmied to
remain open when the outer door slid back.

Lewis Liffey kicked open the hatch cover. Tillie dove for the deckplates. Lewis fired his needler almost point blank. Sally and the children screamed. Oliver froze in shock and pain; then slowly crumpled to the deckplates. He died before Itami Kobe could reach him with a medikit. Book Howard took charge of Sally and her children, placing them in protective custody. She spat on Tillie as Book pulled her past.

Very slowly, Tillie wiped her face with a sleeve. Lewis looked up from his sprawled position on the deck plates.

"You all right?" he asked.

"Sure," Tillie lied. "I'm fine. You?"

He winced a little as he sat up, but nodded. "Sure. I'm always fine." The slight tremor in his voice betrayed him.

"Never killed a man before?"

His glance was piercing. "No."

"It isn't your fault."

Lewis scrubbed his brow and put the needler carefully to one side. "If there'd been any other way . . ."

But there hadn't been. They couldn't just sedate a man like Oliver Parlan for twenty years. His determination to kill everyone had sealed his death warrant. Tillie knew there hadn't been any other choice. But she understood Lewis Liffey's reaction.

And what would they do the next time?

If there was a next time?

Kelly McTavish arrived with welding gear. "Sir, I'll get to work sealing off this corridor now."

Lewis Liffey glanced up. "Right." He levered himself up and retrieved the needler; then offered Tillie a hand up.

"Thanks. I'll . . . I'll be down in hydroponics if you need me."

She fled, leaving the ship's crewmen to deal with the aftermath of near-disaster. And she really did need to check on progress in hydroponics. She found Hank Biddle and Bartel Ditrik busy installing new, jury-rigged tanks to supplement the ones they'd already set up. Bart glanced up first.

"How'd it end?"

Tillie glanced away. "Oliver's dead. Sally's in custody. Saros will take charge of their kids."

Hank Biddle only thinned his lips. The message was clear: *You didn't have to kill him.* Tillie didn't feel like arguing.

"Do you have everything you need to finish this?" she asked tiredly.

"Oh, sure. We got everything a man could want," Bart snapped. "Why don't you go butt your nose into somebody else's business? We got work to do."

Tillie knew she ought to respond to that. But numb as she was from the shock of watching Oliver Parlan die, she just couldn't think of a thing to say. Rumor mill had it the colonists were set to vote her out and pick another Transport Director. Maybe that would be best, after all. She was tired and battered and numb and so sick of the responsibility she wanted to curl up somewhere and cry.

I didn't sign on for this job for twenty years, Carl, she whimpered silently. *I'm not cut out for leadership. . . .*

The crisis came to a head the next day, when Sally Parlan was found dead in her quarters. She'd suicided behind locked doors. The only spot on the *Cross* large enough to assemble the entire colony was Cargo Two, which they were in the process of converting to stables but which remained largely unused. So they'd set off a portion of it for a "Town Hall." When news of Sally's suicide reached her, Tillie called an immediate Town Meeting.

All three *Star Cross* crewmen attended, as well. Lewis Liffey joined Tillie on the makeshift speaker's platform. Kelly and Booker Howard, Tillie noted uneasily, blocked the exit—and they wore needlers. So did Lewis.

"As you have no doubt heard, Oliver and Sally Parlan have both died after an unsuccessful attempt to vent the ship to vacuum. If they had succeeded, none of us would be alive now. I know that many of us are experiencing doubts—"

"Damn right we are!"

"Why the hell should we keep going?"

"Only doubt I got is about you, Matson!"

Tillie let the shouts die away. "I accepted the position of Transport Director under certain conditions—namely, that it would be a temporary job. None of us expected it to become a two-decade assignment. Mr. Liffey and I have discussed the need for us to think of the *Star Cross* as the colony we intended to found. Therefore I suggest we begin work now deciding the form of government we intend to establish."

Before anyone could speak, Lewis Liffey stepped forward.

"Dr. Matson, I have a few words to say on this subject."

Tillie nodded and stepped aside.

"Right now, we're subject to lifeboat rules. There can be only one captain. That situation will not change in the next twenty years, not until we reach Matson's. The government you intend to establish has to be set up with that in mind. Aboard the *Star Cross* there is one law: the Captain's. There are only three *Star Cross* crew left alive, which means this colony will have a number of key administrative slots open. You will all have a chance to fill those administrative posts over time. But there can't be more than one captain."

"And that's you?" someone demanded in an ugly voice.

"Yeah, you're the big military man with the guns. . . ."

Lewis cut through the uproar. "Yes, I'm the captain. Whether I like it or not. I didn't ask for this job any more than you asked to be marooned aboard the *Star Cross* for twenty years. That doesn't change facts. My training and skills and the chain of command mean I'm stuck with the job just as surely as you're stuck with me. But there's something you need to keep firmly in mind. What you decide today will determine the kind of colony your kids grow up in. Will you choose lawless in-fighting, every man and woman for themselves? Or will you choose to set up a government in which every one of you has the opportunity to serve the community in critical decision-making ways?

"As captain, I can only recommend the proper course of action if the information you give me is the best available. I can't do every job there is to be done. That's up to you people. I'll do my best to live up to the responsibility that's been thrust on me. You need to live up to yours. What you decide in the next few minutes will make the difference between simply surviving and building something your children can be proud of when their turn comes to take up the mantle of community leadership."

He stepped back and fell silent.

A moment later, someone near the back of the room shouted, "I nominate Tillie Matson for Transport Director!"

"Second!"

Another voice shouted, "I nominate Hank Biddle for that job!"

"Second!"

Nominations ended at three candidates—and the third refused nomination. Debate opened up. When it became clear that debate would involve nothing more than a shouting match between factions, Lewis Liffey shouted down the tumult.

"The candidates have five minutes each to present their platforms! Hank Biddle, you go first."

The big agronomist nodded grimly and climbed onto the platform. "You all know me. My dream is growing things. And you all know I joined this expedition because I thought we could grow ourselves a good life out on Matson's World. But that isn't going to happen now. Folks like Tillie, here, want us to keep struggling. Keep trying. For what? So a pack of murderous aliens can shoot our children down right in front of us when we get there? They want us to starve damn near to death, to give up having more children, to give up everything that means being a human being—and for *what*? The chance to die in agony under alien guns. They admit Matson's World has long since fallen to this . . . this alien scourge. There's no chance of fighting it once we get there. Captain and his two henchmen have needlers *we're* afraid of, but don't let 'em fool you. There's nothing on board this ship to fight an alien army with twenty years to entrench itself. I ask—I *plead*—with you, don't prolong this agony. Let us die quietly, now, by our own hands, while we're still human enough to do so with dignity and courage."

He stepped off the platform amid a vast silence.

Tillie could tell from the uptilted faces that a large number of them had been swayed by his plea. She didn't know what to say. Hank Biddle was wrong, she knew it in her bones . . . but she didn't know what to say. She cleared her throat, more to buy time than because her throat needed clearing; then met the eyes of a young woman near the front of the crowd. Annie Ditrik was visibly pregnant. Her eyes were scared, her lips pale. *Tell me what to do*, that look said. *I don't want my baby to die*. . . .

"I'm a veterinarian," Tillie said quietly. "One of the hardest parts of any doctor's job is knowing when a patient is beyond hope. I've had to put down animals before, animals I couldn't save. I wonder how many of you have had to look into the mute eyes of a feeling, suffering creature and know that you're killing it? Out of kindness, perhaps, but killing it, nonetheless. You may think you're ready. Perhaps you are. I can't answer that question for any of you. But I can answer it for myself.

"In a way, this colony has become my patient. We're sick and we're hurt. But are we hopeless? Is euthanasia an answer? Or is it just a way of hiding from painful reality? Sometimes it is easier to lie down and die, particularly when continuing to live hurts yourself and those you love. Some of you may choose to do just that. But your choice doesn't give you the right to choose for anyone else. I won't make that choice for any of you who want to die. But for anyone who wants to live, for anyone who'll take that slim chance and fight for life, I'll be here working to give you that chance.

"We're farmers. If anyone can make this shipboard colony work, we can. We have the seeds and cuttings for hydroponics—and every one of you knows that hydroponics do well in a space environment. The first year will be brutal, yes; but the second year will be better and every year after that will bring even more improvements in our lives. Don't sell your future short. In twenty years, *anything* can happen. Wars end, political boundaries are redrawn . . . We might even be rescued. If you want to quit, to give up and die without a fight . . . maybe that's your definition of humanity. It isn't mine."

Someone near the back cheered. Applause, sporadic at first, spread. Tillie found it suddenly difficult to see through the stinging wetness in her eyes. With 60 minors ineligible to vote, the final ballot was 297 to 48, Tillie's favor.

Half an hour later, those 48 suicided quietly in their quarters, poisoning their own children.

Tillie blamed herself. Not for the adults' actions—but for the deaths of the children. She should've ordered protective custody, should've . . .

When she wouldn't answer his calls, Lewis Liffey came to her quarters. "Mind if I speak with you?" he asked quietly.

She shrugged. He came in and closed the door. Tillie sat with knees drawn up to her chest in the corner of her cramped bunk. She'd spent a long time crying, but now all she felt was numb.

"Just because they elected you all over again, Dr. Matson, doesn't mean you're stuck with the job. You can take off that badge any time you want."

She looked up slowly, found sorrow and compassion in his eyes. But not pity. Not even a hint of pity.

"And if we're wrong? What if Oliver Parlan and Hank Biddle were right? We could be leading these people to a violent death at alien hands. . . ."

His jaw muscles tightened. "Yes, we could. Any number of possibilities exist. The Concordiat may beat this invasion fleet back, then not bother to resettle Matson's. There may not be enough left to make it economically feasible. I've seen it happen, when alien wars ravage a world so badly nothing can grow for a century or so afterward."

Clearly, Lewis had been lying awake nights, too.

"Tillie, we may get there and find an empty world and have no way to contact the Concordiat ever again. Or we may find a bustling city where you and your husband planned to start a colony. Not likely, but that's the point. We *don't* know what we'll find."

Tillie swallowed hard a few times. "I've been . . . Those of us with family in Phase I are never going to see them again, are we?"

Lewis opened his lips, then paused. "You want my honest opinion?"

"I think I just heard it."

"I'm sorry. But given the circumstances . . ." His voice changed, wrenching at Tillie's heart. "I had a little girl on Scarsdale, Dr. Matson. Her name's Ginnie. She just turned seven. I said my last goodbye to her the night we found out we couldn't repair the SWIFT unit."

Tillie couldn't speak for a long time. Finally she

whispered, "I've been thinking about Carl, too. If he survived to evacuate . . . I know him better than he knows himself, I think. He'd enlist. Especially when he finds out they can't locate us, that we're missing, presumed . . ." Tears threatened to clog her throat again. "He never was any good at that kind of thing." She sniffed back wetness in her nose. "I just don't know if I can keep going, day after day, year after year . . ."

Lewis Liffey was silent for a long moment. "Well, if you want to take off the badge, you can. But I don't think you will."

She looked up slowly.

"Every one of us on the *Cross* has lost family or friends. The difference between them and you is simple. These folks chose you to lead them. By an overwhelming majority. They're frightened and hurting and they look to you for guidance, for someone to help get them through the nightmare. And I think they made the right choice.

"You're doing the best you can under the worst conditions I've ever seen. You've already got hydroponics set up to feed us and the livestock, and I've just taken a look at the expansions to the system. They're good, sound plans. You've taught the children how to do manual milking, so there's plenty of calcium-rich food for the little ones. Hell, we may even get real eggs one of these days if those biddies keep growing at this rate." His lips quirked. "Know how long it's been since I tasted a real fried egg?"

"Don't joke about it," Tillie groaned. "I just killed—"

"The hell you did!" He strode over and sat down on the edge of her bunk. She flinched away, but he didn't touch her. He just sat there, eyes dark and worried. "Tillie, you didn't kill anyone. Or fail anyone. They killed themselves."

She didn't believe him. "They were my responsibility. The children, Mr. Liffey, those children were my responsibility. . . ."

"Yeah. Yours and mine, both." The tone of his voice caused her to wince. He plucked absently at the bedding. "Do you honestly think those people wouldn't have found a way to kill their kids, even if we'd taken them into custody? When a person's as crazy determined as those poor souls were . . . You've never been in a lifeboat before, have you?"

"No."

"I have."

The way he said it caused Tillie to look up against her will. His eyes were haunted again. What was he seeing? Something he'd seen before? Something he didn't want to see again? "Some folks live, some don't," Lewis Liffey said quietly. "Some just give up and some struggle to keep going no matter how desperate the situation. I expected we'd lose a few this way."

Shock hit her like icewater. "You *what*? You expected it?"

Lewis grimaced at her expression. "I'd hoped not— *prayed* not—but it just seems like some folks are able to turn a mental switch that says, 'Now I will fight for survival' and others can't. It's got nothing to do with how well or how poorly you do your job. We've lost a total now of seventy-two people. That means two hundred ninety-five are still looking to you and me to get them through this."

Tillie's eyes began to sting. "But I don't know if I can do it," she whispered.

He held out a hand. "Maybe not. But *we* can."

She met his eyes. He tried to smile and nearly succeeded.

Tillie spent a long, long time crying on his shoulder.

"I'm sorry, Mr. Liffey—"

"Don't you think it's about time you started calling me Lewis?" She looked up and found a wan smile. "You just spent thirty minutes wetting my uniform, after all."

Tillie actually managed a smile in return. "All right.

Lewis. I'm sorry about your little girl. Surely they evacuated Scarsdale in time."

He touched her chin, wiping away wetness. "And I'm sorry about your husband, Tillie Matson. I hope he survives the war."

Tillie nodded; but she was already saying her own last, heart-wrenching goodbye.

Lewis sat back and studied her closely. "So how about it? Ready to take that badge off now?"

She shook her head. "No. I'm stuck with it, I guess. Like marriage, this job is for better or worse."

He held out his hand again. "Welcome aboard, partner."

She hesitated only a moment. But when his hand clasped hers, doubts and terrors faded. The coming years wouldn't be easy. But Lewis Liffey was one of those lifeboat survivors. She felt the mental switch in her mind click over.

In that moment, Tillie knew they'd be all right.

Sensors track the approach of a ship with Concordiat markings. I monitor its descent from orbit. This vessel has suffered damage which my data banks correlate with battle. The burn scars of energy weapons have traced its hull. Portions of the ship have been opened to vacuum. The propulsion system is functioning at an approximated 20.073 percent of optimum. Descent from orbit is ragged. It loses power and falls twenty thousand meters before engine restart. Braking thrusters function after three attempts to engage.

The ship settles in a broad field of soybeans 15.09 kilometers from colony center. I approach at full speed, Battle Reflex circuitry engaged. This is a Concordiat ship. But I am not fooled. The Enemy is clever. Six times I have successfully fought invasion attempts of Matson's World. Six times the Enemy has left derelict ships in orbit. Two of those ships were captured Concordiat vessels. I hold fire until my sensors can confirm a seventh infestation.

A hatch opens. A ramp descends on automatic. The life forms which emerge are human. I close the remaining 1.95 kilometers and halt 7 meters away from the open hatch. I do not open fire. But I traverse infinite repeaters and lock onto the humans in case the Enemy has successfully captured human targets to front another invasion attempt. The nearest human attempts to block the one behind with his body. This act of protectiveness confuses me. They do not behave as though controlled by alien pests. The human behind him, which my sensors determine to be female, speaks.

"My God! It's—it's Digger!"

Joy! My new Commander has given the proper code word. My long vigil is over.

"Unit DGR reporting, Commander. Request permission to file VSR."

My Commander makes unintelligible sounds for 8.92 seconds. Then she grants permission to file VSR.

"The colony perimeter remains secure from infestation of agricultural pests. I have continued to carry out my orders as directed."

"Uh . . . What were those orders, Digger?"

"To safeguard this colony. Twenty point zero-nine years ago we suffered a severe infestation of an unknown agricultural pest similar in physiological characteristics to Terran wood rats. The infestation has been successfully eradicated, Commander. Five subsequent attempts at infestation have also been eradicated. Sensors indicate communications damage to your transport. Shall I relay a translation of the beacon the Enemy left in orbit above Matson's World?"

"Yes, please."

I play the translated recording. "Xykdap Cruiser GK7-115 to all Xykdap fleet personnel: do not approach this world. Infestation of deadly parasites has destroyed all

Xykdap personnel. Enemy abandonment of this world was clearly due to this parasite, not to the approach of our fleet as we had surmised. Do not attempt a landing. Do not attempt to board this or any other ship left in parking orbit. No known cure has been found for the parasite which has attacked us. Xykdap Cruiser GK7-115 to all Xykdap fleet personnel . . ."

The recording repeats.

"Then this world isn't safe for us?" *my Commander asks sharply. I seek to reassure her.*

"Matson's World is entirely safe for human habitation, Commander. The nematode I originally gengineered 20.09 years ago eradicates each wave of pest infestation then dies out. I have kept a small colony of the original, harmless parasite alive, in bio-isolation aboard this unit. For each new infestation, I re-gengineer the infestation's harmless parasite into the toxin-producing mule which kills its host then dies. There are preserved specimens of the pest species which calls itself Xykdap for you to examine. You may offload the transport, Commander. I have rebuilt as much of the destroyed colony buildings as I have been able to, although I apologize for the crudeness of my work. I was designed to build barns and storage sheds. Do you have further orders, Commander?"

"I— No. Carry on, Digger."

"Thank you, Commander. I will assist with heavy cargo transport."

Miles and miles of well-tended cropland spread out around the rebuilt colony Administration buildings. A fenced pasture was dotted with a large and apparently healthy herd of dairy cattle. Apple and peach orchards in the distance had matured and were laden with not-quite-ripened fruit. Cultivated fields and storage barns and granaries . . .

Tillie thought about the deprivations they'd suffered

over the past two decades, the struggles and fears, and very quietly began to cry. They hadn't come home to a nightmare; they'd found paradise. Thanks to one very mixed-up, determined Bolo . . .

"Tillie," Lewis said with an odd catch in his voice, "look at this."

He was staring at Digger's preserved specimens. When Lewis began to laugh, Tillie stared at *him*.

"What's so funny? Those things are *hideous*! Like . . . like giant rats! And look at the weapons Digger collected!"

"Yeah, but don't you get it?" He pointed to the advanced necrosis of the extremities, the eyeless skulls. "I used to sing it to Ginnie, years ago. You know, the nursery rhyme?"

Tillie widened her eyes; then she, too, began to laugh. Then she was in Lewis' arms and they were both laughing and crying at the same time. Behind them, neatly preserved in specimen jars, were Digger's three blind mice.

LITTLE RED HEN

by Linda Evans &
Robert R. Hollingsworth

—I—

1

Hull-breach sirens screamed through every part of *Bonaventure Royale* seconds after they dropped out of FTL. Lights dimmed as *Bonny's* main guns returned fire, but the damage was done. They'd lost hull pressure in two massive punctures—one of 'em right through Drop Bay One. *Red's bay . . .*

Ish Matsuro cursed, fighting dry-mouthed fear, and slapped the com-link. "Report!"

Doug Hart's voice came through sharp with strain, in the middle of a sentence. "—ammit, Gunny, seal it!" Then, "We've lost two, Ish. Specter and Honey Pie both. Frags right through their pressure suits, massive bleeding . . ."

Ish swore again. But there wasn't time to mourn long-time friends. They were ETA five minutes to combat drop. And he now had two critical positions to fill. He slapped the com-link again.

"Hopper, report to Drop Bay One, stat. You'll be dropping with LRH-1313. Move it!"

He received a startled acknowledgement from the young Marine.

"DeVries," he made another call over intership vid-link,

"belay that repair job. We've lost a Bolo crew engineer. You're at the top of the designated alternates list. Report to Drop Bay One. You have three minutes. Don't worry, Red'll take care of you," he added, taking in the stricken look on the young warrant officer's face.

"Yessir." DeVries both sounded and looked terrified, but he dropped the repair of *Bonny*'s hull breach as ordered and ran for the drop bay.

Then, because he couldn't stand it any longer: "Red, any damage to report?"

"Oh, Ish." The voice he remembered with an ache of longing chided gently, "You know I'd have said so if there was." Like brownies and warm apple pie, Red's voice eased away some of the cold fear gripping him.

"Yeah, I know, Red. Just checking."

A warm chuckle came through the com-link, sounding like every lover Ish had ever dreamed of or found. "You just wanted to hear my voice again, hon. How's your wife?"

Ish winced. Leave it to Red to remind him. . . . Well, that *was* her job. And ultimately, the reason he no longer commanded her. "Worried sick, of course. We're expecting another kid."

"Oh, Ish, how wonderful! Boy or girl this time?"

Ish grinned. "Girl."

"Give her a kiss for me. And don't worry, Ish. We'll get those intelligence reports to FleetCom before the Marines land."

"Speaking of which . . . I'm zipping personnel files to you now for your replacement crew. Hopper and DeVries should be arriving at your drop bay any second."

"Ah, yes. I have the files. Thank you, Ish. I'm going to miss Specter and Honey Pie. There . . . wasn't anything I could do, Ish."

The pain in her voice sounded real. Ish knew that, in some sense, it *was* real. He swallowed hard. "Yeah, hon.

I know. Take care of the boys, Red. I'll try to see you after the fireworks are over. And don't forget to—"

"—duck," Red finished with a chuckle. "Yes, Ish. I remember. Here come the new boys. Bye, now."

"Bye . . ."

He watched on the vid screen as two ship's crew, hastily suited against vacuum, clambered through a small opening in the foam sealant which comprised the drop sphere. Once aboard, *Bonaventure* tekkies finished sealing them in. Rows of identical spheres filled the drop bay. Most of them were decoys—hundreds of them. Two held LRH units and their crews. Ish received a signal from the naval commander of *Bonaventure Royale*. Twenty seconds to drop. Most of Ish's command was sealed into the drop spheres, ready for duty. The remaining shipboard Marines would get their first taste of battle when the *Bonaventure Royale* returned with the remainder of the Fleet.

But that was still days away and *Bonaventure Royale* had yet to survive the orbital drop, the smash-and-run attack against Enemy orbital surveillance capabilities, and the final run for FTL and safety from Enemy guns. And Red, precious Red, had to survive the withering gauntlet of Enemy fire all the way from orbit to the planet's surface. Ish's mouth was dry as he watched the countdown that would send her into deadly peril. Ten seconds. Five . . .

Drop bay doors opened on schedule and the drop sphere protecting Red and her fragile cargo vanished, lost amongst hundreds of other falling spheres. Ish turned off the vid screen.

"God go with you, love," he whispered.

Then he was busy directing the attack of orbital surveillance and defenses, which was all he could do to protect her from now until the end of the battle for Hobson's Mines.

2

Burn scars marked the landing site where a big Navy transport had settled at the pickup point. Ish's flier settled there, too, not far from a sight he had prayed he would never behold. The Bolo canted on broken treads atop a stark-shadowed plateau. The earlier transport had determined she was too hot to bring aboard and her crew was no longer in need of anything the Navy could give them. So they'd called for an investigative team and abandoned the little Bolo. She must have struggled to gain the rendezvous point, given the visible damage to her.

Stumbling a little over uneven ground, Ish traced the sweeping prow of the Bolo—almost delicate compared with the heavy combat prows of the Mark XXI fighting units. Sunlight caught purple-black glints. No heavy ablative armor for this teacup of a Bolo. Barely ten and a half meters long and—discounting treads—a mere three and a half wide, she was light, fast . . .

The Enemy had hit Red like a ballpeen hammer through soft butter. Even at this distance, Marine Captain Ishiri Matsuro could tell Red was a mess. The sight made him want to cry. *Red, oh, Red, what've they done to you, girl?* He blinked rapidly, fighting emotion he would have sooner died than admit. Ish's wife, reconciled to the loneliness any career officer's wife must endure—particularly in wartime—would never have understood the battle inside her husband as he closed distance to the battered little Bolo.

Could anything be done to save her? Anything at all?

The tech clomping beside him whistled—a long, low sound of awe. "When they run starkers, they really do it right, don't they?"

Ish didn't answer. He swallowed hard several times, nerving himself to transmit the code Red was programmed to recognize. He hoped she didn't open fire. Not that she appeared to have much fighting capability left. . . . Her one small infinite repeater, barely light-machine-gun sized, had been blown nearly off its turret-mounted articulated arm. The intelligence-gathering arrays affixed to her were likewise damaged or missing entirely. Gaping holes in her hull showed where she'd borne the brunt of heavy fighting she'd never been designed to withstand. One of her forward armatures, designed for delicate external manipulation on stealth missions, had been blown out of its socket. It dangled obscenely from trailing cables. The other armature was intact but bent and probably inoperative.

Ish had to clear his throat several times before he could speak into his helmet mike. He wanted to say, "Red, honey, I *told* you to duck. . . ." Instead, he mastered his grief and said only, "Light Reconnaissance Headquarters Unit 1313, respond to code Baked Bread."

"LRH-1313 responding," a voice in his headset said. "Welcome, Commander. May I know your name?"

"Captain Ishiri Matsuro."

"Welcome, Captain Matsuro. I am in need of a Situation Update and Depot Maintenance."

Ish's viscera dropped into nothingness. *She didn't remember him.* The Red he'd known—had commanded for nearly seven years—would've cried, "Hello, Ish! What kept you? I've been waiting!"

What the hell happened out here? She fights a pitched battle she isn't programmed for, then forgets eight years of programmed Experience Data?

It couldn't be simple battle damage. If her psychotronic net had been damaged that severely, she'd have exhibited other signs. Instead, she'd recognized his authority; then asked for a briefing and maintenance, just as though nothing had happened. A chill touched Ish's spine. Maybe Space Force had been right? Maybe Red *had* run mad. . . .

Bad as she looked outside, the sight which greeted him

in her Command and Crew Compartments was infinitely
worse. Her Command Team was still aboard. They'd died
hard. Ish closed a gloved hand on the edge of the bulkhead
door frame separating the tiny Command Compartment
from the slightly bigger Crew Compartment, trying not
to look at the gaping holes in Red's hull or at the bodies
sprawled inside her. One of those bodies had been a friend
he'd gotten drunk with and fought beside for nearly seven
years.

"Barkley, you ready for that test?" Ish snapped to hide
the emotion gripping him.

"Yeah." The rail-thin tech was staring at another of the
bodies, clearly fighting his own battle with shock and grief.
Barkley and DeVries had worked together aboard the
Bonaventure. Barkley cleared his throat roughly; then
stepped gingerly around the remains of Doug Hart and
bent over Red's Action/Command center console. Barkley
looked thin and pale inside the bulk of the enviro-suit
designed to protect from hard radiation like Red had
absorbed; but after the first shock of seeing his friend,
he settled down, apparently more than competent. He
ran a few diagnostics with his equipment. "Huh."

"What?"

"She ain't got no memory, for one thing," he said,
sending Ish's hopes crashing. "Search me if I know why
not. It's been wiped clean's a whistle right back to her
commissioning, looks like."

*No memory at all? How could that have happened?
Why would it have been done?*

"I don't understand," he muttered aloud.

The tech moved his equipment to another connection.
Thinly veiled impatience creased his brow through his
faceplate. "Don't understand what? She's been brain
wiped. What's hard to understand about that?"

That's grief talking, not insubordination . . .

"Not *what*. *Why*." Ish gestured a little helplessly. "Battle damage wouldn't have wiped her whole memory. Which means some*one* had to do it. And I *knew* this crew. Hart wouldn't have done this to Red, not unless she were about to be captured. And she wasn't. That much, we do know. She made it to the pickup point without any Deng escorts. Banjo certainly wouldn't have done this. DeVries, maybe . . ."

Guilt tugged at him. DeVries wouldn't have done something like this, either, for all he'd been aboard Red only a few days. Ish had known DeVries, too, had personally ordered *Bonaventure*'s engineer into this mission. It never grew easier, ordering men into battle, often knowing they weren't likely to come back. But DeVries should've come back. Red and her whole crew should've come back. What had happened to cause one of these three men—either Willum DeVries or Doug Hart or Aduwa "Banjo" Banjul— to destroy Red's memory?

The positions of the bodies gave no clue. First Lieutenant Banjul had left the Command Compartment. Banjo had been flung against a bulkhead in crew quarters opposite a terrible rent in the Bolo's hull. Burns and lacerations across his face and upper torso might have been inflicted before death or might have contributed to it.

DeVries slumped on the deckplates near the head. Red had tongue-tilted down the door in its emergency-medical-station configuration. DeVries either hadn't been able to crawl all the way to the makeshift "bed" or he'd been thrown clear. The young engineer was dead of radiation poisoning. Ish's enviro-suit protected him from the still-lethal dosages inside the Bolo's breached hull. DeVries had been badly injured even before receiving the lethal dose of radiation which had ultimately killed him. Ish checked Red's medications log. It indicated a final, massive dose of painkillers administered to the dying engineer. Ish's throat tightened. *So like Red, to try and ease him through it.*

As for Marine Captain Doug Hart . . .

One of Ish's closest friends lay in a tangle of broken bones and the remains of his command chair. He'd taken a direct hit from whatever had breached the hull up here. He hadn't had a chance. None of the Command Team had. But the question remained: *why had Red engaged the enemy at all, charging against a vastly superior force when she knew it was hopeless?*

And why had Doug Hart allowed what amounted to suicide?

"Dammit, I *knew* Red. I don't care what FleetCom says. She wasn't crazy!"

The technician's glance begged to disagree. Ish had to turn away. Red's behavior certainly argued otherwise. But he couldn't bring himself to admit it, not after what he and Red had been through together.

"Yeah," the tech muttered, "this whole operation's a stinking louse. But . . . whoever did it, they missed the backup mission record."

The sounds coming from beneath the console made him wince. Broken connections dangled under the main Action/Command center console, causing another inward flinch. Ish had commanded a lot of Bolos, had relinquished command of Red only a year previously, taking a commission in Space Force that would give him options commanding Red couldn't. He'd taken a lot of backup mission record modules out of Bolos, both combat and special units. Designed to provide a duplicate of the Bolo's current mission records should anything happen to the Bolo's main data banks during battle, the modules had occasionally proven to be of incalculable worth. Ish knew they had to have that backup mission module.

But the dangling connections and broken seals were obscene. The tech was a butcher, gutting Red's mind.

Or what the real butcher had left of it.

The rail-thin technician emerged holding a dense,

heavy-looking casing. "Maybe this'll explain why she went starkers."

Ish didn't respond. He couldn't. He just accepted the module from the suited technician. It was heavier than it looked, which was *very*. Ish—cursing his shakiness—nearly dropped it. Whatever had really happened during those last few minutes of battle, it would be recorded in this module. Without the data it contained, Red would never remember . . .

. . . anything.

The last eight years were gone, as it was.

Red didn't remember him. Would never remember him.

The pain that caused ran so deep he couldn't get his breath for a moment. Maybe he could run a Restore. . . . Ish seriously doubted Space Force Command would authorize anyone to run a Restore command from any of Red's backup mission modules to reintegrate missing memory data. She was so badly damaged she would be retired anyway, and now there was the serious question of inadvertently reinstalling whatever had caused her to go mad.

The cold hollow in his belly expanded.

"Ought'a be interesting, huh?" the technician was saying as he put away tools. "Never seen a Bolo go starkers before. Not like this. They say the first Mark XX went and committed suicide on 'em; but, hell, at least it had a reason. Doing its duty, upholding the honor of the Brigade and all. That's what they said, anyway. But this little baby, she's just starkers, no explanation, nuthin'. . . ."

Ish had to restrain the impulse to crack the tech's protective suit to hard radiation. He settled for a muttered, "Finish up, will you?"

The technician shrugged. "They'll have to scrap 'er. Always did wonder if these Mark XXI Special units would be stable under stress. Too much oddball programming. She just wasn't designed right. Not her fault; but, hey, she's nuts. You gonna fry her Action/Command center now?"

Red would be listening to every word they said, trying to understand what had happened to her. She'd be confused, hurt . . .

And irrational?

Ish was listening, too, to the Bolo's ragged internal sounds. The noise was eerily like metallic keening. It came and went at random. "That's not my decision," he finally said. "I suppose it will depend on what we discover in the backup mission record."

The technician shrugged inside his suit. "Well, whatever. You ought'a get back with this here box. I'll leave her to you."

The man departed noisily, banging his heavy tool kit against Red's internal support frame. Ish experienced an irrational impulse of his own, to order Red to open fire on the unfeeling bastard; then remembered her sole gun was inoperative. He flexed the fingers of one gloved hand and forced himself to breathe steadily. He couldn't afford to let personal feelings—regardless of their intensity— sway him. But that tech had no idea how close . . .

Ish stared emptily across the rugged, broken terrain that characterized this whole, miserable mining pit of a world. Then dropped his gaze to the dense module in his hands. It wasn't black, exactly. More a purple-black, the color of iodine. Flintsteel, same as the Bolo's hull. Given its weight, the module's hull was thicker than Red's.

Ish shut his eyes, trying not to think about what his next duty might well be. He never had blamed Red, not during all the long months since he'd given up command. Red had only been doing her duty, in the kindest way she could find to do it. Now she didn't even remember him.

"Why'd you do it, Red?" he whispered.

The eerie, intermittent keening halted. The Bolo's voice,

mechanical yet definitely female, said, "Unit LRH-1313, awaiting orders. Please elaborate your question."

Her apple-pie and warm-brownies personality was gone. What had replaced it was the cold, impersonal sound of a newly commissioned machine, devoid of associated memories, of everything that made her . . .

Red.

"Never mind."

He wasn't even certain *which* mystery he'd meant: the reason behind her decision a year previously or her far more serious behavior today. *Was today his fault?* He should have realized a year ago that her personality programming was unstable. If he'd taken steps to correct it . . .

His career might have ended, but Red might not have run mad. Ish tightened his hand around the dense module. All the answers *had* to be locked away in this thing. He cleared his throat and decided to make sure she still remembered he was her Commander before trying to dismount. No telling, with her internal circuitry so scrambled, what she might think or do. He didn't want Red to kill him.

"Unit LRH-1313, respond to code Baked Bread."

The disconcerting, intermittent keening halted once again. "Yes, Commander Matsuro? I have already responded to that code. Do you have further orders?"

Ish cleared his throat. "Retire for depot maintenance, vector 035, range 40.5 kilometers."

"Understood, Commander. Will you accompany me?"

He had to glance away from her forward internal sensors. "No, I won't be coming with you. I'll . . . join you later, at the depot."

"Understood, Commander."

He swung down and stepped well to starboard, stumbling a little again on uneven ground. The Bolo turned and rumbled obediently in the assigned direction. *Rumbled* only because LRH's treads were damaged and her hull was breached near her pivoting tread-control ratchets. The jagged hole allowed sound to leak out like water from a dying jellyfish. Mark XXI Special units normally operated so quietly, they could sneak up on a sleeping cat. Red had excelled at the game, which explained the battle honors welded to her low-slung, data-gathering turret.

The only reason she was able to move at all was that her wide-tired, independent-drive wheels were still functional. Conceptual descendants of the independent-drive wheels on the early twentieth-century Christie T-3 tank, which was in turn developed into the famous Soviet T-34 tank of that same century, they permitted a tracked vehicle to continue moving even if it lost its treads to battle damage. A tracked vehicle without treads or independent-drive wheels was little more than an armored pillbox. For an intelligence-gathering Bolo without significant armor, those wheels were doubly critical. Without them, an LRH unit wouldn't have been an armored pillbox, it would've been a sitting duck.

Red's wheels had been damaged, too, but they still functioned. She was certainly headed straight toward maintenance as ordered. Not an irrational peep out of her since his arrival, except for that odd keening—which might just as easily have been battle damage to instrumentation somewhere inside her. He wondered if she was even fully aware of what they'd removed.

He glanced at Red's retreating hull, at the data module. Destroying Red would feel entirely too much like murder.

3

I have been ordered to return to depot for much-needed maintenance. Despite severe damage to my sensors, I am able to perform a scan of extremely broken terrain which lies between my current position and the coordinates I have been given. At top cruising speed I could arrive in twenty-two minutes. I am not currently capable of top cruising speed. Even though external sensors and internal diagnostics tell me I am badly in need of maintenance, I do not choose even the top speed of which I am currently capable.

Instead, I delay. I have not been ordered to proceed with haste. I do not feel like haste. I am uncertain what I feel, a condition which triggers internal diagnostic alarms in my ego-gestalt circuitry. I am a Bolo Mark XXI Model I (Special) unit. I have been designed for steadfast emotional stability. Yet what has transpired fills my entire psychotronic awareness network with unease.

Something is seriously wrong with my memory. I retain basic orientation data. My primary personality and self-image files are intact. All else is vacant. My memory begins with reception of the transmitted code which my current Commander sent before coming aboard. This occurred 11.857 minutes ago. I can discover no cause for this condition, despite what appears to be serious battle damage to my hull.

This damage puzzles and alarms me. I am not a combat unit. I am not designed for it. I carry neither armor nor armaments appropriate to heavy combat. I am strongly motivated to seek an explanation from my Commander, for my basic orientation data urges me to confide my concerns to him. Yet when given the chance, I have held silent. Nor do I choose to call him now on my Command Link. He has discussed destroying me for a crime—an insanity—which I do not recall having committed.

I do not wish to die. Survival is a deeply imprinted part of my basic personality-gestalt circuitry. Nor do I wish to suffer madness. This, too, is something I fear, something which is an integral part of my personality gestalt. I am a stable, emotionally reliable Light Reconnaissance Head-quarters unit, charged with the well-being and security of my Command and Dismount Teams. This is my function.

My Commander's reluctance to accompany me to the

maintenance depot weighs heavily upon me. I perform a deep probe of my personality-integration circuits and find no sign of damage which would explain my Commander's or the technician's accusations.

I am not mad.

Am I?

Do the mad know they are afflicted?

This is not a question I am currently capable of answering. I turn my attention to what I can answer. My basic orientation data reveals that I would not have been forwarded into a battlefield intelligence gathering mission without a crew. Mark XXI Model I (Special) units do not function independently. Mark XXI combat units maintain remote contact with a human commander and occasionally carry a passenger, but Mark XXI Model I (Special) units are subordinate to an on-board commander and are designed to house eight additional crewmembers at full battle readiness. I can discover no trace in my on-board files of having been assigned a full intelligence-gathering crew for this or any other mission.

This is in direct conflict with what my internal sensors reveal. Three men have died inside me. They remain in my Command and Crew Compartments. The damage to their bodies is severe. While my interior armatures are capable of inflicting the kind of traumatic damage required to open a human body cavity—I am rated for emergency surgery—I possess no internal machinery capable of reaching them in their current positions. It seems reasonable to assume that I did not kill these men.

That relief is overridden, however, by the sense of grief such deaths trigger in my Responsibility circuits. I have been programmed to accept full responsibility for the safety and well-being of those humans authorized to enter my Crew and Command Compartments. If someone has died, then it is because I have failed in my duty.

I grieve. For whom, I do not know. But I am determined

to learn the identity of these lost children. I scan them. They wear proper uniforms and identification transponders. Scanning the transponders gives me three names: Willum DeVries, whose transponder records that he is a ship's engineer from the Bonaventure Royale. DeVries lies near the emergency medical station in my Crew Compartment. Aduwa Banjul, whose transponder identifies him as Assistant Mission Commander assigned to LRH-1313, lies near the bulkhead door between my Command and Crew Compartments, against my port hull. Banjul's transponder signal removes all doubt. This man is part of my crew. Was part of my crew.

Douglas Hart's death brings even sharper grief. His transponder identifies him as my former Mission Commander. My Command Team—at least two-thirds of it—has died. I do not know where my own engineer might be or why a Navy ship's engineer might have taken his place. Nor do I know where my missing Dismount Teams One and Two might be. Experience data gathered since awakening strongly suggests they have been killed.

I leave behind the level, burn-scarred plateau which is the place my memory begins and enter a narrow defile. A nineteen point one-one-nine meter cliff rises to my right, within two degrees of slope from perfect vertical. A canyon 391.592 meters deep plunges away to my left. I do not know which world I have awakened on. The surface is extremely rugged. Beyond the far lip of the canyon, 0.82 kilometers away, my damaged sensors detect another steep cliff. Due to its presence, my line-of-sight data-gathering ability is restricted to a mere 0.82 kilometers. In this terrain, even with perfectly functioning sensors, I would be virtually blind. I long for the reports of a Dismount Team to advise me what lies beyond the canyon, above the cliff, past this narrow corridor.

But the defile is on a direct bearing for the maintenance

depot. It is the only passage I detect which will accomplish the order I have been given to report for maintenance. I pause at the entrance and scan as best I am able. I detect no ambush. The cliff appears stable. I move forward with a clearance of 0.621 meters to starboard and 1.176 meters to port. I edge closer to the cliff, distrusting the canyon lip. I am extremely lightweight for a Bolo unit—fifty-four thousand kilograms without crew or supplies—but I am of sufficient mass to break a crumbling edge. Maybe, with luck, a Bolo Mark XXI combat unit, three hundred times my mass with considerably more effective armor, could survive a fall into that canyon. But not an LRH unit.

I am practical. I move as close to the cliff as my fender and treads will allow and turn the full attention of all operative port-side sensors to monitoring the rock at the lip of the canyon. I turn the rest of my attention to study the difficulty in which I find myself.

A full damage-assessment probe locates extensive injury to my once-beautiful hull. I discover serious damage to my treads. My external armatures are inoperative, my long-range sensor array is missing, and my lightweight infinite repeater is no longer functional. External sensors along my prow and starboard side are inoperative. A single remaining sensor atop my prow allows me forward vision which is impaired in several spectra. Rear sensors are completely functional. This is disturbing. In the event of even accidental contact with the Enemy, I am programmed to retreat with all speed, extricating my Dismount Teams and safeguarding the data they have gathered. Had I followed my programming correctly, the Enemy should have damaged my rear sensors most heavily.

I have suffered internal injury, as well, to my tread-control center and many non-critical fixtures. Circuits in my psychotronic net have experienced overload consistent with combat damage of the type I have suffered. It is imperative that I learn when and how I was damaged.

A technician, working with full permission of my Commander, has removed a module from me. My basic configuration data reveals that this was a backup mission record module. Six point zero-seven seconds after awakening on the plateau where my Commander found me, I attempted to probe the contents of this module; but was unable to access it as I am configured for write-only mode to this module. I am unsure that I should have permitted this module's removal. If the data incriminating me is held in that module, perhaps destruction would have been the wiser choice; yet nothing I possess on board would have been capable of penetrating the module's hull.

The technician who removed it spoke of destroying my Action/Command center. It is both noteworthy and frightening that my Commander did not defend me. Why I should be condemned, without knowing even the charges against me, becomes an intolerable mystery within 0.003 seconds.

I must know why I am to die.

My external damage assessment reveals a further disquieting fact. Welded to my hull are service decorations from four different campaigns. Extensive time would be required for this many campaigns, on worlds as widely separated as my on-board star charts reveal these four to be. Yet my short-term memory contains data from only 11.998 minutes. I retain stored memories of my original self-awakening and my commissioning ceremony, as well as basic programming instructions and orientation data; but that is all.

If I have fallen to the Enemy, then I have been rescued again, for my Commander has given me the properly coded private password which only my legitimate Commander may know; yet where I have been during the unknown number of years required to accumulate my service citations and what I have experienced during that time, I am at a loss to determine. My decorations indicate that

I have served with distinction. This is pleasing, but only for 0.006 seconds. Before I can determine why I am thought mad enough to warrant probable execution, I must first discover who I really am.

I develop an immediate mission plan to ensure my continued survival:

Priority one: discover who I have become. I have programs which permit me to develop a personality, but I do not seem to have one. Not one sufficiently complex for the time lapse which must have occurred since my commissioning, anyway.

Priority two: discover what has transpired since the day of my commissioning as an intelligence-gathering unit.

Priority three: discover why I have been accused of such a serious charge as madness.

Priority four: discover a way to convince my new Commander that I am worthy of continued service.

Having established a roughly sketched mission plan, I return part of my attention to my surroundings. One hundred twenty seconds have elapsed since I received the order to report for maintenance. The depot is still 40.5 kilometers away. At my current speed of seven kilometers per hour, I have only five hours and forty-two minutes in which to fully execute my mission plan and achieve each of its priority tasks. Someone has programmed an extreme pragmatism into my ego-gestalt circuits: I believe my task to be impossible.

Yet programmed deeply into my psychotronic circuitry is a stubbornness which I now experience. Mark XXI Model I (Special) units do not abandon difficult tasks. The survival of Command and Dismount Teams depends on my dogged tenacity to carry on under difficult conditions. I will shame neither myself nor the Dinochrome Brigade by dying with the stain of madness on my record. Somehow, I will succeed. How, I do not know. But I must.

Therefore, I will.

—II—

1

Warrant Officer Willum Sanghurst DeVries was scared. His mouth was dry as bone and his palms were so slick he kept losing his grip on the harness. He didn't like being strapped into place like a sack of spare parts. *I'm a ship's engineer, not a . . .* What was he, exactly, besides a green-around-the-gills coward and several kinds of fool? Not a battle technician, that was for sure. More like a stop-gap replacement for a mission already in trouble.

Just our luck that damned Deng sentry ship caught us dropping out of FTL. It had fired two shots before *Bonaventure*'s guns had destroyed it. But those two shots had counted. He didn't know what their casualties had been—high, he was guessing, given the damage *Bonny* had sustained. Willum wondered if the other LRH unit's crew had sustained losses, too. Captain Matsuro hadn't told him, if it had. He wanted to ask, but didn't want to sound any greener or scareder than he already did.

Why'd I ever agree to serve on a drop ship? Every man who served on one was required to train as replacement crew for whatever was being dropped. And since *Bonaventure Royale*'s job was dropping LRH intel-teams onto occupied worlds, his training had led him to this: replacing a dead engineer on a Mark XXI Special Unit headed into potentially the worst battle of the whole damned war. Common sense and a healthy dollop of terror told him to stick to the *Bonaventure Royale* like a tick to a dog's back.

You're no Marine, Willum told himself for the millionth time. *Yeah, well, you weren't hired to be one for this drop, either, so quit wetting yourself. Engineering you know. And you'll be staying inside the Mark XXI. . . .*

Trouble was, that scared him too. Willum was a ship's engineer, accustomed to interacting with and maintaining FTL ships and their psychotronic systems. He'd studied Bolo configurations, enough to be familiar with their general systems; but he wasn't a specialist and he'd never really believed it would come down to this. Confident in his ship's ability to avoid trouble coming out of FTL, Willum DeVries had sloughed off. It didn't matter that *Bonny*'d destroyed that Deng sentry; the damage was done, the Bolo crew had lost two men, and here he was, harnessed for drop after a scant three-minute warning to get his terrified backside aboard.

Willum was afraid the whole crew might pay the price for his carelessness. He didn't think he could handle that. Nor was he psychologically prepared to get as close to dirtside battle as a Mark XXI's crew inevitably went. Willum had never run from a fair fight, but the Deng had never *heard* of fighting fair. And *nobody* was nice to an enemy spy. Maybe that was another reason his skin was crawling.

Or maybe it was just that Mark XXI Special Units had generated intense debates in both military and political circles almost from their development. Screwball programming, it was whispered, odd behavior patterns, almost incestuous relationships with their crews— relationships a Mark XXI crewman would cheerfully hospitalize a man over if he were stupid enough to speculate about them in a crewman's presence. Just what, exactly, a Mark XXI's programming might be, to inspire such loyalty and widespread controversy, Willum didn't know. Secrecy surrounded just about everything connected with the Mark XXI Special Units. Whatever it was, Willum figured he'd find out soon enough.

If the Deng let him live so long.

Which reminded him to be scared all over again.

A glance at the other officers brought no reassurance. The MC, a grim-faced guy named Hart, didn't look frightened, exactly; but the pallor around the edges of his lips wasn't natural, either. If a combat veteran like Hart who'd participated in multiple successful missions was spooked . . .

The man everyone called "Banjo" was the only member of the original crew Willum felt might tolerate him. Assistant Mission Commander Aduwa Banjul, with only a year in this crew himself, had given Willum a whirlwind orientation after he'd climbed through the open personnel hatch—

They dropped away from *Bonaventure* with a lurch. *Freefall* . . . Willum swallowed bile. He'd never been space sick, but *battle sick* . . . That was a possibility he hadn't yet tested. *Don't be sick, DeVries, don't be sick.* . . .

He knew what was going on around him—theoretically. An infiltration force of two ships would be blowing Deng satellite systems, stripping away the enemy's orbital monitoring capability as part of a decoy operation with longer-term benefits. Meanwhile, two LRH Bolos and several hundred similarly cocooned decoys dropped from orbit toward BFS-3793-C's pitted, canyon-scored surface. . . .

Willum tried unsuccessfully to loosen his grip on the drop harness. He glanced at the vid screen which gave the Command Compartment a view into the Crew

Compartment. Willum wanted to see how the other crewmen were holding up. Dismount Team One was in harness on the left. "Gunny" Hokum, the crew's gunnery sergeant, was whistling under his breath. Eagle Talon Gunn's dark eyes met Willum's in the vid pickup. The AmerInd grinned briefly, teeth gleaming white against bronzed skin. "Great ride, huh, tekkie?"

Despite the veiled insult, Willum tried to smile back. At least someone had *talked* to him, making an effort to include him in this mission. "Yeah."

"Icicle" Goryn eyed the vid lens with open hostility. His silent glare seemed to say, "You're not Honshuko Kai, damn you. Who gave you the right to talk to us as an equal?"

He held Icicle's gaze long enough for the veteran to shrug and glance away. It wasn't Willum's fault their friends had been killed; but that wouldn't help a damn bit when they hit the ground running and had to work together.

DT-2 had harnessed in to the right. He'd never met the man whom Danny Hopper, a *Bonaventure* shipboard Marine, had replaced. The Bolo's crew had called him Specter. They'd spoken the nickname with reverence even before his death. Hopper looked more nervous than Willum, swallowing so often he reminded Willum of a bullfrog in full song. Sergeant "Milwaukee" Petra, harnessed to Danny's left, was DT-2's team leader.

Crazy Fritz, a lean, hollow-eyed man hanging in harness on Hopper's other side, glanced at the ship's Marine as though to say, "We needed Specter. Not a goddamned fancy-pants Marine." But he didn't quite voice it aloud. Hopper, a courageous twenty-year-old who'd spent most of his duty tour as a ceremonial guard, returned the older man's look levelly—but he lost a few shades of color and did a good bit more swallowing.

Great. We're screaming toward Enemy lines and the whole damn crew is rattled before we even leave orbit.

Willum had a desperately bad feeling in his gut, and it wasn't called space sickness.

We fall. Encased as I am in a sphere of foam-form heat-repellent tiles, I am blind during the initial stage of drop. Inertial sensors transmit a phenomenon I have never shared with my Commander: I am dizzy. Drop always does this to me. I wonder if humans experience the same sensation. Speculation along such lines is not productive. I devote my attention to the mission at hand.

Ablative foam tiles begin to shed mass. We have reached atmosphere. I am aware when the ribbon drag deploys, slowing our speed. My crew is unharmed by the change in velocity, although I detect higher-than-normal levels of stress chemicals in the bloodstreams of my two replacement crew members. Danny Hopper, in particular, suffers during this drop. I will suggest corrective medication once we achieve landing. The ribbon drag functions perfectly. More heat-resistant tile boils away. A series of seven small parachutes deploy, slowing our velocity further. An outer sensor array tip clears. I am able to see. Dizziness disappears instantly; inertial sensors match visual input perfectly.

We are still high in the atmosphere. I am able to track one hundred forty-three of the decoys as well as my sister LRH-1327. She is encased as I am in a glowing sphere that shrinks with each passing picosecond. Her drag chutes have also deployed. Deng weapons discharge from the planet's surface. Missiles arc upwards. One decoy explodes. A second decoy is destroyed. We drop lower. LRH-1327's main chute deploys. Her descent slows sharply. Decoys deploy main chutes and some begin sensor scans. These broadcast their findings back to Bonaventure Royale, reporting terrain features and Enemy activity in order to provide good data for the landing force as well as make themselves higher priority targets. Two seconds before I drop below the horizon line, LRH-1327 explodes.

I mourn.

"Doug," I say in my softest voice, "mission parameters have changed. LRH-1327 has been destroyed. I am sorry."

My Commander does not respond for 0.89 seconds. An eternity of grieving. "Understood, Red. Delay deployment of main chute."

I execute the command, overriding automatic settings. "A wise decision, Doug."

I wait to deploy the main chute which will slow us to speeds at which our para-wing can be deployed. A slower drop provides too great a risk of destruction. We are humanity's last hope for reconnaissance of Hobson's Mines before the main invasion fleet arrives. Thousands of human lives will be spared or destroyed depending on the success of this intelligence-gathering mission. We cannot risk being shot down.

I wait until sensors tell me we have reached the critical edge of our margin for error. I deploy the main chute. The shock of drag slows us. My crew members jerk in their harnesses. I check their vital signs for injury, but detect only expected mission-level stress. We drop. Deng weapons destroy five more decoys still visible to my sensor array. I search the terrain below for potential landing sites and coordinate visual data with on-board maps.

My maps of BFS-3793-C, nicknamed Hobson's Mines, are excellent. This was a human mining colony until the Deng invasion two months and four days ago. We cannot allow the Deng to hold this world. It provides critical war materiel that would give the Enemy a strategic advantage over humanity. We must retake the mines. I note that we drop toward a large river. Preliminary scans reveal that it lies at the bottom of a canyon 0.82 kilometers wide. Water depth varies. The deepest spots are more than adequate for a camouflaged landing site, particularly if Bonaventure Royale's efforts to neutralize the Enemy's satellite reconnaissance abilities have been successful.

I blow all remaining heat-ablative tiles with a small charge. They continue on the original trajectory and smash into the ground. They will look like a crashed decoy when found. I deploy our para-wing on schedule. I am unencumbered and vulnerable. I want to get down. Using controls on the para-wing, I spill air to change course toward the river as best I can. I cut the starboard lines to my trailing chutes and reel them in with the ribbon drag, leaving only the para-wing outside my hull to slow our descent.

We head for the river. We sway and drop. The course I hold takes us directly toward the target I have chosen, a spot that sensor scans indicate is the deepest available. At twenty-seven meters in depth, this is a good landing site, although I am constructed to withstand a drop onto bare rock if that is required.

At extreme sensor range I detect Deng airborne scoutships. My intelligence data on such scoutships indicates we are not yet in their sensor range. I have 3.88 seconds in which to disappear from their sensor sweeps. I activate Chameleon screens, taking on the outward visual, radar, and infrared signatures of an airborne Deng scout. It is the best I can do. We drop into the canyon. The walls are 321 meters high on the near rim.

I warn my crew: "Brace for landing!"

At the last possible moment, I attempt to climb in an effort to stall my para-wing, as I need to kill as much forward movement as possible and reduce speed to minimize any splash. When we enter the water the sharp slap recreates dizziness in my motion sensors. We slow. I reel in the trailing para-wing while still descending. My crew has suffered another jolt but appears to be in good health. I am relieved. Drop is a dangerous time. Even during a perfect drop, a crewman can suffer sprained neck muscles or dislocated shoulders. My crew is safe.

We touch bottom. My treads rest on clean-scoured stone. Water temperature is 2.7 degrees centigrade. Current flow is 0.6 meters per second. A swift current. The chilly water disperses our heat signature in a short-lived downstream plume. We are hidden from Enemy eyes.

"Doug, we have achieved a safe landing. I would recommend that we remain in this position for another twenty-four hours."

"Agreed. Okay, you heard the lady. Time to break out the playing cards. We're here for the duration."

I am pleased. My Commander is satisfied with my performance. He calls me "the lady" when I have done particularly well. My crew and I are safe. That is all that matters for the moment.

"Brace for landing!"

Willum jumped at the sound of an astonishingly human female voice—then shut his eyes and hung onto the harness. To his shame, he yelled. . . .

The remaining fall wasn't a long one. The shock of landing jarred everything, despite the harness that held him suspended. Webbing dug into flesh. He'd bruise in crisscross stripes—if he lived long enough to bruise. After that first, terrible jolt, they slowed to a gentle, eddying descent.

Water, Willum realized with a blink. *We've landed in water.*

They bumped a hard surface.

"Doug, we have achieved a safe landing," that same female voice said out of the air. *It's the Bolo.* . . . "I would recommend that we remain in this position for another twenty-four hours."

Up in the Mission Commander's chair, Doug Hart nodded. "Agreed. Okay, you heard the lady. Time to break out the playing cards. We're here for the duration."

Willum sagged in his harness. Thank God . . .

"All right, everybody unstrap," Hart said, unsnapping his own harness. His boots thumped against the deckplates. "Good job, Red. Anybody hurt?"

"No, Doug," the Bolo responded.

It gave Willum an odd feeling to know that his vitals were being monitored by his transport system. FTL ships weren't equipped with that invasive feature. *Dammit, I should've done more careful reading on those specs like we were told.* He was certain the Bolo could provide him with whatever data he needed; but his incomplete information was dangerous. He'd fix that, pronto.

"That's great, Red. You did a fabulous job getting us down in one piece. Run a complete systems check on yourself and report."

Hart didn't look nearly so grim, now that they were down. In fact, he had a nice, friendly smile. "You all right, DeVries?"

Willum poked a tongue at his teeth. "Yeah. I think they're all intact."

Hart laughed. "Unstrap. You have work to do. I want Red checked stem to stern."

"Yessir," he said, struggling with the harness release. Either he was fumble-fingered or it was stuck. He flushed, caught his breath, and tried again.

Hart glanced at a sensor eye. "Status, Red?"

"Systems check in progress. Chameleon screens reconfigured to match color and texture of surrounding sedimentary bedrock and water. Probability of detection by Enemy 0.093 percent unless tight-beam search sensors touch the Chameleon screens. My systems are functioning normally except for an alarm in my food-processor unit. I would like DeVries to look at it when there is time. Hopper—do you prefer Danny?—may I suggest breathing slowly and evenly through a fine-mesh cloth? Report to Medi-Unit, please, and I will assist you. Yes, Danny, that's the console in the forward starboard corner next to the head.

"Doug, Target Prime lies 91.3 kilometers northwest of our current position. That would place it upriver of our landing site. A good map in my data banks suggests a direct route is available once we leave the confines of this canyon. According to my on-board colony maps, the canyon walls open onto a broad river valley 61.7 kilometers upstream. A boat landing for rented pleasure craft should provide excellent egress from this river. From there we can take a dirt access road to the main highway. I would suggest travelling during the day with Chameleon screens modified to approximate the heavy farm and mining equipment in widespread use on this world."

"Very good, Red. We'll let the furor die down before we try getting closer to Target Prime. A few days underwater will help convince the Deng they got all their incoming targets."

Willum was all for that.

"Para-wing stowed. I'll drain the water out of my tummy after we've come up for air."

Out in crew quarters, several crew members chuckled. Willum paused in his battle with the stubborn harness buckle and stared at the nearest speaker grill. The Bolo's voice was remarkable. She sounded like his grandmother. He could almost imagine a living surveillance tech reporting from a sensor-array display room in another compartment somewhere. Except there weren't any other compartments: just the cramped Command Compartment and the jam-packed Crew Compartment. The reaction the Bolo's voice set up in him was eerie, disturbing. He *knew* the Mark XXI was nothing more than a machine. Self-aware and fitting most definitions of sentience, perhaps; but a machine, nonetheless. Yet already he found himself wanting to think of it as *her*.

And why not? You think of your ship the same way.

Bonny's programming wasn't nearly as complex as a Mark

XXI's, yet Willum was deeply attached to *Bonaventure Royale*. He began to understand a little better why Mark XXI crews reacted as they did.

Hart had opened the bulkhead door between Compartments. The Mission Commander glanced his way. "DeVries, quit hanging around in harness and get busy on that food-processor alarm. Then break out your gear and double-check Red's operational status. It'll help familiarize you with her systems. Banjo, let's perform a complete weapons check. Hopper, you especially, listen up. DeVries, move it!"

The Marine officers left him alone in the Command Compartment, still struggling with the unfamiliar drop harness, and closed the bulkhead door with a hiss of pneumatics. He finally unlatched his harness release. Willum sprawled ungracefully onto the floor. At least none of the crew had seen that embarrassing display. He made it back to his feet and willed rubbery legs to hold him.

"Wonder where this food processor is I'm supposed to look at?" he muttered aloud, mentally reviewing what he'd studied nearly a year previously.

"Move aft," the Bolo responded. "It's in the port corner of my Crew Compartment, aft of the seats."

He jumped at least eight centimeters off the deckplates.

"I'm sorry, dear. I didn't mean to startle you."

"Uh—" He glanced around and found the camera lens that marked the Bolo's video pickup. "Hi. Didn't realize you were . . ." He trailed off and felt his neck grow hot. He sounded stupid and green.

A remarkably human chuckle issued from the speaker. "Don't feel embarrassed, Willum. You've never been assigned to a Bolo before. Welcome aboard, by the way."

"Uh, thanks. You're, uh, not what I expected."

"My programming provides for a closer simulation of human dialogue and verbal interplay than an FTL ship's programming. My duty is the welfare of this crew. I do my best to perform that duty."

"What happens when you lose a crewman?" Willum asked, thinking of the two men killed aboard *Bonaventure*.

The long pause surprised Willum. He'd never had a psychotronic unit delay an answer. "I grieve for them," the Bolo finally said. "Giurgiu Galati—although he hated that name; I always called him Specter, too—and Honshuko Kai were my boys. Specter and I had been together for seven years, three months, twenty-one days, six hours, five point seven minutes. Honey Pie and I were together from the day I was commissioned. The Enemy has robbed me of their company. May we discuss my damaged food processor instead, please?"

In that moment, Willum DeVries stopped thinking of her as the Mark XXI or even as just the Bolo. She became real to him, someone who'd lost friends same as Willum—same as anyone in the military since the coming of the Deng invasion fleet.

In that moment, she became "Red"—and, possibly, the only friend he would find on this mission.

"Sure. We can talk about something else. And . . . I'm sorry. I've lost friends to spodders, too." Willum cleared his throat. "Now, let's see about this processor."

"Thank you, Willum."

He gathered up his equipment packs and headed aft to the so-called galley, a tiny corner of the Crew Compartment where an automated food processor battled for space with a refrigeration unit and a waste disposal unit. Either the crew ate off their laps or some kind of table could be raised between the seats. The crew's seats were bolted to the deck. Behind him, the men and their commanding officers were going through a very thorough weapons check. Nobody paid him the slightest attention, except to grunt when he had to step over them to reach the "galley."

Willum dug out equipment and began to investigate circuitry he understood. "Ahh . . . Yeah, I think I see the problem. . . ."

It felt good to finally be useful again.

2

Harry "Gunny" Hokum closed the access panel which shut off the Command Compartment from the rest of Red's interior. Banjo glanced up, nodded, then went back to his screens, monitoring everything which came in via Red's sensors, packaging it for easier analysis, noticing any tiny anomaly that might mean danger to Red or her crew. Doug Hart, busy working with Red replanning their mission parameters now that they were the only surveillance unit left, swivelled around in his command chair.

"What's up, Gunny?"

He leaned his back comfortably against the closed door. "Got the men settled in. Everything looks fine; nothing damaged in drop."

"Good. What else? You look like a man with a problem."

Gunny scratched his elbow. "Yeah. Well, maybe. What can you tell me about the Frog?"

"Hopper?" Hart frowned. "Problems?"

"Maybe. Maybe not. He's green, scared pretty bad. The boys are shook up, losing Specter the way we did, and Honey Pie, too, and even though they're smart enough not to say it, well . . . It's pretty clear they don't have much faith in Hopper. That boy's rattled. I've got him working solo right now, doing maintenance on his weapons. Figured he needed something familiar to settle him down. But I gotta know what he's made of before we Dismount."

Hart nodded. "I glanced at the file Ish gave us before drop, but I haven't had much time to do more than glance.

He's been a shipboard Marine since joining the service. He's never seen combat—but how many of 'em have? Goddamn fuzzy spiders . . ." Gunny and Banjo muttered agreement. Hart pulled at his lower lip. "I remember reading he graduated well in his class, so they haven't stuck us with a stupid replacement. Red? What can you tell us we haven't already covered?"

"Danny qualified expert with all weapons for which he is rated. He is seventh-generation career Marine. His grandfather was decorated for valor in the Halloran Campaign. He studied xenobiology, so is passingly familiar with the physical and psychological profile of the Enemy; as familiar as a Marine private with no field experience can be. I suspect this is one of the reasons Ish selected him, Doug. He has scored well on all field-combat tests and has hearing two points above the norm for human males his age.

"He has been nervous since boarding, potentially because his first combat mission is a dangerous assignment with strangers rather than his shipboard comrades; but blood chemistry and pulse rate suggest he is calming down nicely. That was a good idea, Gunny, putting him to work cleaning his rifle. I would suggest making an effort to include him in group activities very soon. He needs to become part of this crew."

Hart nodded. "Yes, the sooner the better. We'll have a couple of days underwater for you to work on that, Gunny. Get him involved. Work on the others. How's Fritz?"

Gunny grimaced. "Crazy's spooked. Hell, you know how he and Specter were. Damn finest team I ever saw work together. He's got a bad feeling about this mission."

Hart didn't speak. From the tightening of his jaw muscles, Gunny knew his commander shared Crazy Fritz's feeling—maybe *because* of Crazy's gut reaction. It didn't make sense; but some men just seemed to know when trouble was coming, like a weathervane pointing the path of a storm front.

"Do what you can to loosen him up," Hart said at length. "We need him on edge, but not paranoid. How about you, Gunny? We had a bad start." Hart met his gaze squarely and held it.

Gunny didn't hesitate. "I got confidence in you, sir. We'll complete the mission."

Doug Hart grunted. "Good. I know I can count on you."

Banjo looked up from his screen. "And you, Doug? While we're baring our souls? Personally, I'm scared spitless."

Hart grinned suddenly. "You would be. You always did hate spiders."

Banjo snorted rudely.

Hart sobered. "This is no easy mission. Especially with LRH-1327 gone. We were damn lucky to get down in one piece. They had us dead to rights from the moment we dropped out of FTL. But . . ." He swivelled absently in his command chair, burning up nervous energy. "We have a good chance to complete the mission. Red and Banjo and I are working up details now for overlapping recon plans, since we'll have to cover LRH-1327's mission parameters as well. It won't be a cakewalk, but we'll manage."

"Just do me a favor," Banjo smiled. "Dance at my wedding when this is over."

Gunny grinned. "You meet somebody?"

Hart laughed and thumped Banjo's shoulder. "Should'a known you'd go and pull an Ish Matsuro on me."

Banjo chuckled. "Wonder what Ish thought when we dropped off that ship without him."

"He missed it like hell," Gunny muttered. "Should'a seen his face." Gunny—perhaps alone of the human crew—knew what it had cost Ish Matsuro to give up command of LRH-1313. Red knew, but she wasn't talking either. Not even Doug Hart, who had been seconded to command with his departure, probably guessed the depth of Ish's pain. Gunny remembered like yesterday the conversation he'd inadvertently overheard late in the night, with Ish pouring his heart out and Red listening, commenting quietly, trying to guide their commander toward the right decision.

No one but Gunny and Red herself knew that level-headed, no-nonsense Ish Matsuro had fallen in love with two women: the future Mrs. Matsuro . . .

And Red.

Gunny glanced into Red's video pickup and wondered if she could guess what he was thinking. He wondered if he could guess what she was remembering. Had it cost Red as much as it had cost Ish to file the recommendation that her commander be promoted into a slot suitable for a career officer to marry and raise a family? He would probably never know. But it was good they had Red to watch over them on the eve of their deadliest mission to date. Gunny knew that would be the deciding factor in whether or not he slept at all over the coming days.

Gunny suspected Doug Hart had no real inkling what a fine command he carried into war. If there'd been a way to tell him without betraying Ish and Red, he'd have made damned sure his commander knew it. So he cleared his throat and scuffed one boot toe on the deckplates and said, "Red'll take care of us, anyway, Banjo. Hell, who knows? Maybe *she'll* dance at your wedding."

A sweet chuckle issued from the speakers. "A Mark XXI Special Unit can't dance. But I *could* serve cake with my exterior manipulator arms. And I take a mean wedding photo."

Banjo grinned. "Deal."

Doug Hart smiled. "That's a rendezvous, then. Now, about this processing plant . . ."

Gunny retreated, leaving the officers and Red to plan out the next few days of his life.

To Willum DeVries' surprise, they stayed in the river for three days. The first day they spent checking everything and sitting in place. The officers went on thirty-three percent alert status, which meant at least one officer was awake at all times. Taking his first solo turn in Red's Command Compartment was unnerving; but Red was so good at her job, she left him with almost nothing to do but watch the vid screens. The second two days they spent crawling upstream to locate the boat landing marked on Red's map. During transit, they amused themselves playing cards with one another and with Red.

"Two, please," Red said. Delicate manipulator arms ran along a rail the length of the cramped box which comprised living quarters for six men and bunking quarters for eight. There were a few spots in the compartment Red couldn't reach, but not many. A folding table which could be lowered into the deckplates served the crew for meals and recreation. At the moment, Red's manipulator "fingers" held five ordinary playing cards. Red slid her discards to one side. Gunny dealt two replacements.

"Thank you, Gunny," Red said politely.

Willum wondered if anyone else had considered the practical side of betting against a machine with video monitors capable of seeing everyone's hand, not to mention medical monitors capable of detecting the slightest changes in biological responses. It seemed to him a little like asking the mouse to step onto the cat's tongue; then he decided it would be unforgivable to accuse a lady of cheating. He asked for three and received them.

They began to play.

Gunny bet four. Hopper folded. Crazy Fritz grinned and met the bet, then raised two. Eagle Talon grunted and dropped six into the pot. Red and Willum stayed in, too.

"Call," Milwaukee said.

Red had two queens and a pair of threes.

Fritz had a straight.

Willum kissed his money goodbye.

Milwaukee grinned and took the pot with a straight flush.

"Damn your lucky hide," Fritz groused. "Best hand I've had in a year and you go and beat it."

"Refreshments, boys?" Red asked as she delicately gathered and shuffled the cards. The process fascinated Willum. If he got through this mission, he was going to ask for a transfer. He wanted to find out how they put these babies together. Red continued the shuffle with the skill of a riverboat gambler. "I could do brownies in ten or an apple pie in twenty?"

"Brownies," Gunny voted.

"Pie," Crazy Fritz countered.

"Pie," Milwaukee agreed.

Eagle Talon grinned. "Brownies," he said, as though tying the vote were the most sinfully delightful task in the universe.

Hopper exchanged glances with Willum. "Uh . . . Brownies?"

Willum's turn. "Pie."

Red actually chuckled. "Oh, goody, I get to break the tie. How about both? Brownies going in now. Pie'll take a little longer, boys, but it ought to be good. And there's cold milk in my fridge. My deal and the game is seven-card no-peek . . ."

And so the hours passed.

"Okay, men, listen up." Hart stepped into crew quarters and banged on the bulkhead wall. Willum blinked sleepily and pulled himself out from under. "Move it," Hart rasped.

"We're about to leave the river. Before we go, we review mission priorities one more time."

A general groan met that order; but Red's crew rolled out of their hammocks and folded them away, taking their seats to await the briefing. Willum, blinking sleepily, had to stand, since his place was up in the Command Compartment when he wasn't asleep. Hart motioned for him to remain where he was. At the front of the Crew Compartment, a vid screen lit up with a map that could only have come from the mining colony's own archives. Hart took a lecturer's stance beside it. Banjo, on duty as officer of the watch, remained sealed off in the Command Compartment.

"This is our original Target Prime," Hart said crisply. Red thoughtfully highlighted a spot on the map for him. "It's a fully-automated mining facility. We believe a heavy Deng concentration lies here" —another spot lit up about three kilometers away—"where the terrain will accommodate a larger number of Deng transports. But we're not sure. Our job is to confirm and estimate enemy strength and emplacements, extrapolate attack plans, and report back to FleetCom with our findings the instant they drop out of FTL."

The map changed. "LRH-1327 was charged with scouting this position. Ordinarily two LRH units would not be dropped this close together; a mission like this would be entrusted to one team. Fortunately, two teams were dropped for just the kind of emergency we've encountered: destruction of one team during combat drop. LRH-1327's target becomes our new Primary. This is a processing plant, semi-automated. Terrain here will accommodate a very large Deng force. It's reasonable to assume the Enemy would concentrate its assets on this site, since it's capable of producing a finished product ready for export.

"We scout this location first, from extreme range. Terrain

will allow for long-range monitoring. Once we've reconnoitered the processing plant, we fall back to our original Target Prime and complete our mission. Red, how far is the processing plant from us now?"

"Twenty-nine point six kilometers upstream. The colony situated this facility on the closest area of flat ground suitable to accommodate a space port. There is a good road." The map changed to a broader-scale view. A thin red line flashed to indicate the road. "The mines are 63.5 kilometers upstream from the processing plant." Two dots appeared, marking the targets.

"Okay. Questions?"

Gunny spoke first. "Do we have any photos of these facilities? Or pics of the terrain around them?"

A collage of photographs flashed onto the screen.

"Thanks," Gunny said, moving closer to study the images. "Looks like we won't need to dismount for the processing plant. That's open ground. Visibility's as good there as anywhere on this ball of rock, I expect. What'll you use for cover, Red?"

"I will engage Chameleon screens to simulate the appearance of an ore carrier." Another photo appeared, this one of a large, unwieldy tracked vehicle that Willum recognized as one of the completely automated types developed for remote worlds just like this one, where the labor force was small but the planetary coffers were rich. "The map indicates a parking compound for ore cars in need of maintenance here." The processor-plant map reappeared. A circle of light marked the maintenance depot.

"If Commander Hart agrees, I intend to park in this compound and gather data over the course of twenty-four hours, provided there are enough vehicles in it to act as camouflage and provided no Enemy or human personnel approach closely enough to recognize the Chameleon screens for what they are. If I cannot use this site, I will move along this road, circle this position eight thousand meters from the processor plant, then retrace my route and initiate the second phase of our mission."

"What about that damned mine?" Crazy Fritz asked uneasily. "That place looked treacherous."

"That's our job," Gunny grinned. "If it's treacherous, we'll tackle it."

Danny Hopper looked scared again.

Hart said, "Okay, Red. Your plan for the processor plant looks good. What about the mine?"

Red switched maps. "We will need Dismount Teams, Doug. The mine is situated at the base of a cliff and runs 12.5 kilometers beneath the surface. A narrow draw curves away from the surface-level facilities plant through here. An access road capable of supporting ore cars runs through it, between these two ridgelines. The suspected concentration of Deng forces is here, north of this larger ridge."

"All right," Hart said, studying the map. "Gunny, put DT-1 here, where the contour lines form a point south of this V-shaped cut at the tip of the ridge. You should be able to scope out the Deng in this wider valley from there. Milwaukee, I want you here on the second fork of this double ridge, line-of-sight to Gunny, overlooking the access road in this draw. Red, you I want here, behind the tip of this third ridge, hidden but line-of-sight to Milwaukee. That'll put us close to the mine; but colony records indicate it's completely automated, so we shouldn't encounter anyone. We take readings, transmit data to Red for transmission to FleetCom, and get the hell out of there. We'll be operating on a very tight schedule. Given the distances we have to cover and the speeds we'll be restricted to, I estimate we'll have less than half a day at the mine before FleetCom drops out of FTL and requests our data."

Gunny asked, "Red, how far is the mine from pickup point?"

"Forty point six kilometers." A new map flashed onto the screen. "Pickup point sits atop this mesa. I should have no trouble gaining the top via this route." A series of dots marked the route she intended to take, along the edge of a precipitous canyon.

"Good," Gunny nodded. "Time frame on these missions?"

"An ore car's top speed is 48.3 kilometers per hour. From our current position, I estimate 36.7 minutes to reach a position from which we can conduct our recon of the processing plant. I will do a thorough survey, to include Deng departure and arrival schedules. This is, after all, the larger of the two assigned targets which must be scouted."

Hart just nodded.

"It will take approximately one hour eighteen minutes to reach the mine from the processing plant. Due to the proximity of the mine facility to extrapolated Enemy positions and the need for Dismount Teams, I do not advise a prolonged recon effort here."

"No," Doug Hart agreed, looking grim. "We get in, do our business, and leave. Like I said, half a day tops, from Dismount to Recall. Less, if we can manage it. I'd rather not be anywhere near that Deng concentration when we have to transmit to FleetCom. Hopper . . ."

Hopper cleared his throat. "Sir?"

"What equipment do you take?"

The Marine answered immediately. "We go suited, sir. Our stealth suits won't match Red's Chameleon screens, but they'll mask our heat signatures. We take energy conversion screens to cover our positions. If we're blown, they'll protect us from Enemy fire for a little while, sir, and transfer energy they absorb to operate the automated infinite repeaters tied into the system."

Hart nodded. "I don't expect you'll be blown, but we're always thorough."

"Yessir. My mission is to provide security for Sergeant Petra. He operates comm and does any additional recon he can from our position. My job is to guard him while he does it and make damn sure he gets to our recon position in one piece so he can transmit Gunny's data."

Hart nodded once again. Clearly, Danny Hopper knew his business, even if this was his first combat mission. "Very good, Hopper. Fritz, you take point. Nursemaid him if he needs it. I don't think he will. Questions?"

Nobody had any.

Willum DeVries knew he wouldn't sleep till this mission was over.

"All right, then, Full Alert Status as of now. Red, take us up."

Hart gestured curtly to Willum; he followed his commander into the Command Compartment and strapped into his seat. Banjo scarcely paid heed to their arrival; he was intent on Red's data screens. The Bolo moved smoothly. The decking tipped as she climbed the steep grade up out of the river. The main screen flashed to a real-time video picture. They halted again while still underwater.

"Extending whip array, Doug."

The picture shifted, periscopelike as the Bolo lifted a sensor array into the air. The lens cleared and revealed an abandoned boat landing. Pleasure craft sat in the starlight, motionless hulks that registered clearly under Red's light-enhancing sensors. The first faint hint of dawn was visible in the dark sky. *Nobody left alive to rent any boats. . . .* Willum wondered if the Deng had spared anyone to run the machinery. He didn't know much about Deng military operational strategy.

The thought of becoming a slave to a hairy, multilegged "spodder" with a body the size of a small dog was almost as bad as the thought of dying.

"Proceed, Red," Hart said quietly. "Engage Chameleon."

"Chameleon engaged."

They rumbled quietly up out of the water and headed into Enemy territory.

The boat ramp I have accessed is made of concrete which is approximately five centimeters thick, varying in depth in the manner of poured concrete. Ordinarily a vehicle of my weight would crack such a thin concrete slab; but my designers have considered the need for leaving no trace of my passage. My treads are each 0.9 meters across. They and my independent-drive wheels protrude beyond either side of my hull, skirted with chameleon screen nearly to ground level. Thus my treads and wheels distribute my weight across a broad cross-sectional space, which gives me a ground-pressure per square centimeter less than that of an adult male human.

I pull onto the concrete pad and halt, surveying the access road beyond. It is made of dirt, with old track imprints from wheeled vehicles. I lower my rear track-camouflaging unit and engage its drive. I move forward, scanning the imprints and sending their configuration to the roller I now trail behind my rear fender. Its thousands of small studs extend and retract in synchronized patterns to duplicate the tracks I encounter. When I pass over the tracks, obliterating them and making my own minute signature in the dirt, my track-camo unit recreates the old tracks in my wake, leaving no trace of my passage.

I follow the dirt road for 5.8 kilometers and encounter the paved road my on-board charts have indicated. There is no traffic. This concerns me; but following the paved road is the better choice of those I currently perceive. It is a faster, more direct route and I am less likely to encounter very soft ground in which my track-camo unit would have more difficulty in covering signs of my passage. It is also better than very rough, broken terrain which

*would slow down my progress and place us behind
schedule for this mission. I have already discussed this
decision with my Commander, who agrees that it is the
best choice; but the lack of traffic disturbs me. I voice
this concern.*

"Any sign of aerial observation?" *Doug asks.* "Or ground
crews that might be watching?"

*I do a passive scan for Enemy energy signatures. The
only traces I discover are to the north, over the visible
horizon. I see no sign of aerial capabilities in this region.
Should I be spotted from orbit, my Chameleon screens
will mimic the reflective surfaces, angles, and part-to-
part ratios of a mining ore car. We should be safe.*

"No, Doug. I am uneasy; but we should be fine."

"Let's do it, then. Move out as planned."

*I turn onto the highway and drive slowly north, at the
top speed of an ore car. The slow pace is worrisome, but
necessary. I scan the surrounding countryside on passive
systems and register the presence of small farms. I pick
up no trace of human heat signatures. Farm animals have
been left to fend for themselves. Cattle are visible in fenced
pastures. They are thin, but appear to be surviving. I
cannot determine whether the same can be said of their
human owners. We do not know the Deng policy on
captured humans. I file my discoveries for later
transmission to FleetCom. It is useful to know what the
Enemy will leave intact as well as what it will destroy.*

*We join a convoy of ore cars from a side road while
still an estimated 16.1 kilometers from the processing plant.
These ore cars are southbound from a small mine which
shows on my maps but is not considered a target. The
terrain surrounding it is too rough for Enemy forces to
concentrate there. My scan shows no human or Enemy
personnel inside any of these cars. This matches records
from the mining colony, which state that these vehicles
are fully automated. I am pleased the Enemy has not*

stationed its own personnel on the ore cars, as this would complicate my mission. I scan the signals which these ore cars use to communicate with one another and mimic their own transmissions, asking permission to join the convoy. Space is made for me. I pull into the space and join the line of slow-moving ore carriers.

We are still an estimated 10.8 kilometers from the processing plant when I encounter our first direct evidence of human survival on a Deng-held world. At a distance of 3062 meters we pass a fenced enclave in which my passive data-gathering sensors detect both human and Enemy personnel. From visual data, I determine that the humans present in this enclave are largely female and/or immature children. No males over the approximate human age of twelve are present. My Commander watches them on video screen and remains silent. Banjo speaks.

"Bloody bastards are using 'em as hostages. Must be forcing the men and most of the women to work the processing plant."

My Commander nods silently. I note that the Enemy's need for war materiel is sufficiently urgent to use slave labor rather than import their own labor force. I fear these people will die during the reoccupation of BFS-3793-C, but I see no way to safeguard them. My mission profile does not include protection of civilian populations. I add my observations to my growing report file and turn my attention to mission parameters. The first of our two targets is within sensor range.

The maintenance depot for ore carriers holds six such vehicles. I am pleased. I tell the ore carriers ahead of me and behind me that I must break ranks for depot maintenance. I receive messages acknowledging my status update. I turn into the depot lot and take up a position which commands a view of the processing plant below. It is a good position, as extrapolated from my on-board charts. From this place, I can perform a thorough *reconnaissance of this facility without risking my Dismount Teams.*

I go to work.

The processing-plant reconnoiter went smoothly.

So smoothly, Willum started to worry.

He'd always heard the old military axiom, "No plan survives contact with the Enemy." So when they completed their recon from the maintenance lot without a single hitch, he started to fret. *Things have already gone wrong,* he tried telling himself. *We're due a break or two after what happened to* Bonny *and LRH-1327.* But the pep talk didn't help much. He was still worried.

Red set out for the mine in a convoy of automated ore cars returning for a new load. They crawled along at a fraction of Red's top speed while Hobson's double moons rose above the fractured horizon. They were still on full fifty-percent alert, which meant half the Dismount teams were awake in the Crew Compartment, ready for combat if an emergency arose. Doug Hart and the other half of the Dismount Teams' members had bunked in hours ago, resting up for the arduous mission facing everyone, leaving Banjo with the night watch.

Willum DeVries hung in his hammock, unable to sleep. Unlike the others, he had nothing to do. Nothing to plan for. Hart and Banjo both had a million details to sort out, plans to review, alter, substitute. The Dismount Teams had equipment to check, stealth penetration plans to finalize, their own set of a million details to fuss over. Naturally, they were content in their frenzy. Even Hopper, for God's sake, had calmed down once given something to *do*.

All Willum had to do was wait.

During the long hours of waiting, he'd read everything on Red he could access; he knew her systems as well as he was going to. All that remained was to sit through the coming mission and hope like hell the Deng didn't give him anything to do. He turned over, restive and too keyed up to relax, even when he tried deep breathing and relaxation techniques. Finally he gave up and slipped out of his bunk. He tiptoed into the head and closed the door. The head was quite literally the only place inside Red where a man could find any privacy at all.

"Willum?" Red asked softly after he'd been in there for twenty solid minutes, trying to cope with night terrors and the sense that he would somehow fail his fellow crewmen by forgetting or not knowing something critical. "I am not registering any signs of illness. Nor do you appear to need to use the head's standard facilities."

"Uh, no . . . I'm not sick." *Not physically* . . . He took the plunge. "I, uh, just wanted to get away from the others. I can't sleep," he admitted.

"Your service record indicates that you have never been in combat. You are not a Marine. Combat is not your function. Nervous stress is normal in your situation, Willum. Would you like a mild sedative?"

"No . . . No, I don't want to be muzzy tomorrow."

"I can prescribe a medication which will not leave you groggy after you reawaken. You need to rest. Tomorrow will be a busy day."

"Yeah," Willum muttered. "For everyone else." He crossed his arms over his bare chest. "Dammit, I feel about as useful around here as an opposable thumb on a coconut."

"Willum. We need to chat."

He sighed. "Shoot."

"You have expressed the same frustration I heard often from Honey Pie. Honshuko Kai," she added. Willum could all but see her amused smile. "Honey Pie often felt himself to be a useless team member, even though he was my longest-serving crewman and essential to my continued mission readiness." The door to the head hissed open silently. Red's manipulator arms entered on the overhead track. The door closed again. "Here" —she extended a manipulator arm— "let me give you that sedative. Hold still, it'll sting only a second."

He allowed Red to give him the injection.

"Honey Pie once said he felt like cook, butler, and chief bottle washer in an expensive travel-trailer."

Willum chuckled. "Know the feeling, Red. I know the feeling. How'd he deal with it?"

"We played a lot of cards. Would you like to learn canasta?"

"Canasta?" Willum blinked, momentarily startled; then smiled. "My grandmother used to play canasta. Okay, Red, show me."

She produced two card decks from a small console in the head itself; then a tiny tabletop slid out from the wall. Willum just stared. Red told him, "Honey Pie installed these fixtures just for the two of us to share on nights like this. This is the only place, you know, where I can hold a private conversation with one of my boys. I think you need that almost as much as you needed that sedative and something else to think about."

She shuffled cards with extraordinary skill. "Now . . . before we begin, I have one last piece of advice. I always told Honey Pie this, so I will tell you, also. We are each selected to serve in exactly the right capacity for our talents and skills. Beware asking for something more. The gods may be listening."

Willum shivered. "Thanks. You have a point, there." He grimaced and rubbed the back of his neck. "I guess I wouldn't be much use on a Dismount Team. I couldn't sneak my way out of a paper bag." Then, because curiosity got the better of him, he asked, "How come you're so . . . not smart, *wise*?"

Red's chuckle issued from the speaker grill. "I was programmed with an extensive library on psychology, philosophy, and comparative religions in order to interact more effectively with my crew. And I have learned during the past eight years what my crewmen think about on the eve of a mission.

"Now . . . I deal each of us fifteen cards. The object is to collect sets of seven like cards. Such a set is called a canasta. You may use up to three wild cards per canasta, although such a 'mixed' canasta has a lower point value. At least one canasta is required before you can go out. . . ."

Willum fell asleep in the third hand, a thousand and fifty points behind but content with the score.

Gunny Hokum woke at 03:40 and eased out of his bunk to use the head. Someone else had closed the door to use it ahead of him. Gunny waited. And waited. Twenty minutes later, he knocked on the panel to assure himself that no one was ill—although surely Red would've said something—and heard Red's voice whisper, "Yes, Gunny, you should come in, please."

He eased open the panel and found Willum DeVries slumped over a hand of canasta, fast asleep. One of Red's internal manipulator "hands" rested on his shoulder, gently. Gunny discovered a sudden thickening of the throat that made swallowing difficult. *No wonder Ish fell for you, little lady . . .*

He felt sorry for DeVries, sorrier in some ways than he felt for Hopper, who at least had something to do. Gunny had lost track of the number of times Honey Pie had sat at that same tiny table, playing canasta in privacy with Red while Gunny and his men prepared for a mission. He missed Honshuko and Specter. Losing men out of a crew like this left gaping holes in a man's life. Unfinished conversations, plans that would never come to fruition . . .

Successful Mark XXI teams remained together, often for years at a time, growing closer and ever more effective, because once a crew was assembled which worked well together, breaking it up for anything more than seriously important reasons was just plain stupid. Specter and Honey Pie had been like family to Gunny. He appreciated how difficult it must be for someone like DeVries to be thrust into such a tight-knit group as outsider—then find himself with absolutely nothing to do. He was glad Red was taking care of the young engineer.

"Hey," he shook DeVries gently. "Sleeping Beauty. Wake up."

DeVries snorted, stirred, peeled his eyelids. "Hnnhh?"

"You'll get a crick in your neck, sleeping like that. And I gotta use the can. Hit the sack."

DeVries stumbled, a little glassy-eyed; then nodded and said, "Sorry, Gunny. G'night, Red."

"Good night, Willum. Sleep tight."

Gunny chuckled. "And don't let the bedbugs bite."

DeVries reeled a little, but made it safely back to his hammock. He collapsed into it and faded back into oblivion. Red quietly put away the cards and slid the table aside as Gunny settled in the head.

"How much of that sleepy-time did you give him, Red?"

"Only three cc's. He needed it."

Gunny finished his business; then sighed. "Yeah. I bet he did. Red—" He paused before opening the door.

"Yes, Gunny?"

"Oh, nothing." Gunny didn't lack for courage; but expressing his feelings was one thing he'd never had the luxury of doing. So he simply said, "Good night, Red."

"Good night, Gunny."

In the privacy of his own thoughts, he added, "Thanks for being such a damn good friend."

As he climbed back into his hammock, he realized he needed that friendship tonight in a way he couldn't explain. He drifted back into sleep without difficulty, content that Red was there, watching over them.

3

The Enemy has established a large staging area north of the mines, where expected. I enter a holding area for ore carriers which arrive in a convoy. I survey our surroundings. There are no Enemy physically present at this facility. I scan the mining complex. The operation is entirely automated. The mine has been drilled into the face of a sheer cliff and descends 12.5 kilometers beneath it.

The cliff stretches away to the west as a tall ridge which drops and breaks at the tip into two forks like the tongue of a Terran viper, creating two separate ridgelines, one overlooking the mine and the other overlooking a valley to the north, where the Enemy has concentrated a battle force. Terrain around the tips of these forked ridgelines is more open, providing the ability to move cross-country into the valley where the Enemy force waits. These two ridges are the goal of my Dismount Teams.

Another long, low ridgeline runs east-west directly south of the mine, almost like an island. The mine's access road loops completely around this ridge so that arriving and departing ore carriers do not have to pass one another in the confined area of the mine itself. Outside the main facilities plant are open sheds which cover stacks of standard structural steel pipe, internal diameter 75 millimeters.

I determine that this pipe is used for steam fittings for pumping steam and hot ore slurry. Other open sheds house stacks of ore slugs in a standard Enemy unit of measurement, which translates to 73.99 millimeters by 147.98 millimeters. Large tanks house petrochemicals used in some capacity, I am not sure what. I am not a miner. I simply note their location and volume.

The reason for the presence of processed ore slugs becomes apparent: to speed up production capacity, the

*Enemy has installed a pre-processing facility to convert
ore slurry to slugs. This facility also functions on fully-
automatic status, converting hot ore slurry to finished
ore slugs for easier transport. This plant clearly allows
faster turnaround time for the ore cars, which now do
not have to be cleaned by hand between trips to remove
ore encrustations from their hoppers. The Enemy is
impatient for war materiel. I file this discovery for proper
reporting to FleetCom. The Fleet is due out of FTL in
another seven hours. We must be ready to transmit our
final intelligence report by then.*

*Ahead of me, ore cars begin to transmit their readiness
to receive another load to the computer which operates
the mine facilities plant. They transmit in turn as they
approach the end of the access road. When my turn comes,
I transmit on the proper frequency that I have experienced
technical problems en route and must retire from the queue
to await maintenance. A computerized response directs
me to park between the storage sheds and the nearest of
the ridgelines. This is happily near the spot in which I
must take up my mission position in accordance with my
Commander's plan.*

*I move out of line. The parking spot I choose places
me exactly where my Commander has requested me to
position myself for this mission. I am now behind the
shoulder of the "island" ridgeline. My rear hatch is in
shadow. I am ready.*

"Doug, are the Dismount Teams ready?"

"DT's, prepare to move out!"

"DT-1 ready," *Gunny says.*

Milwaukee seconds him. "DT-2 ready."

*My Chameleon screen's projection will cover the opening
of my rear personnel hatch. The Dismount Teams move
into position near the hatch, awaiting my signal. They
are suited for stealth.*

"Set suit outer-skin controls to 16.71 degrees centigrade."

They adjust suit controls and wait until their suits chill down to the proper thermal signature. Their equipment is ready: passive scanners, man-portable weapons, line-of-sight communications gear, grid screens behind which they will dig in for the duration of this reconnaissance mission.

Similar to the energy-conversion screens I carry, these grids will absorb Enemy energy-weapons fire and convert it to a useable form to power their lightweight infinite repeaters. These repeaters will automatically return fire at anything which fires at the grid screens. Residual byproduct heat means the screens can protect the teams for a only a short time should they come under fire, offering minimal shielding, which is superior to no shielding. None of my boys has ever needed to use the grid; but I do not allow my Dismount Teams off my deckplates without it.

All equipment is carried in stealth-rigged packs which function in the same manner as stealth suits. I monitor the drop in temperature as the Dismount Teams adjust pack external temperatures to match their suits. Weapons are covered with thermal coverings to prevent the air in their barrels, which remains at the same temperature as the inside of my Crew Compartment, from triggering thermal alarms the Enemy may have in place. I scan the area. We are in shadow. No Enemy signatures register on my sensors.

"Go with care, my children," I whisper. I open my rear personnel hatch.

My Dismount Teams salute my rear hatch scanners and exit. I close the hatch and watch their progress. They wait until their presence is screened by arriving ore cars, then move down the long ridgeline to the west. They pause, then vanish from my view behind the blunt end. I wait. The teams reappear, dodging arriving ore carriers to cross the road. It is an extreme risk to cross the road in this manner, but less of a risk than scaling the sheer wall and *rappelling down the only other approach to the twin forked ridgelines. They reach the shadows of the far ridge. I monitor their climb.*

DT-1 has the farthest to travel. DT-2 takes up position where our Commander has instructed, on the near ridgeline of the twin forks. I can see my boys dig in and set up their grid screen. They do a good job. I must use all my sensors to locate them and I know where to look. DT-1 travels beyond my line of sight to the far ridgeline. I worry. I am never at ease when I cannot see my boys.

DT-1 has orders to scan the valley north of their position for the Enemy. DT-2 will relay their findings to me in coded burst transmissions which will sound to the Enemy like background static in clear air. DT-2 signals that DT-1 has taken position. We wait. Banjo monitors readings from my sensors. Doug relays instructions and reviews mission plans again. We wait. DT-2 transmits preliminary data in a single burst. I decode it for Doug while preparing a file for transmission to FleetCom.

"Red, DT-1 reports a mother-load of 'em in that valley. Not as many as we found at that processing plant, but they see twenty Yavac Scouts, a couple of Class C heavies, maybe five hundred infantry. No spaceport facility; but they have air capability. Five air scouts. A heavy transport. Gunny says he'll forward a detailed transmission when he finishes scanning everything into a data file. There's activity to the east he wants to monitor—looks like maybe this enclave's about to be bigger, he says. DT-2, out."

My Commander swears in language he does not often use.

"You could order 'em back," *Banjo says.*

"Yeah. And if that activity to the east turns out to be critical reinforcements in Deng fighting strength, we'll kill a shipload of Marines taking this pit. We wait."

The waiting grows increasingly difficult.

❖   ❖   ❖

Gunny's career had ensured visits to a lot of alien worlds. This one, nicknamed Hobson's Mines because only mining generated sufficient cash to buy imported technology, was one of the most rugged he'd encountered. Tectonic forces had buckled its surface into fantastic canyons and cloud-piercing mountain ranges in the more remote areas, while erosion and ancient continental glaciers had "gentled" some areas into merely jagged ridgelines and glacial valleys with the occasional alluvial plain. Where they sat now, Gunny had a commanding view of the terrain for kilometers; yet he could see very few ground features except for what lay in the valley directly to the north and the ridgeline just south of him, where Milwaukee had dug in with DT-2.

In the distance, ridge after ridgeline marched away in the fading twilight, clothed in ruddy light and the low-growing, thorny scrub which clung tenaciously to the stony soil. The valley to the north was a classic, U-shaped glacial valley. It was—outside of the processing plant region— the largest stretch of flat land Gunny had yet seen on this mineral-rich world. It made an ideal staging post for the Deng. Farmsteads the length of the valley were now abandoned, their animals grazing wherever the concentrations of Deng hadn't driven them off.

The terrain around Gunny's position was an open, gentle slope to the north and the west; directly east, the ridgeline where he'd dug in soared upward in a nearly vertical wall. Behind them, to the south, the ridgeline sloped gently down into a V-shaped cut that separated Gunny and DT-1 from the other fork of the snake-tongued double ridges. DT-2 had dug in there for the duration. Beyond them were the mine and the ridgeline which concealed Red.

He watched and recorded troop movements into and out of the valley, noting that another mass of infantry came in by air. *Wrong direction for someone coming from the processing plant. They must have another base of operations we don't know about farther east.* Gunny noted that in his growing data file. Meanwhile, more troops continued to flow in from the east, arriving by air. Heavy transports were bringing in more big Class One Yavacs. Additional scout-class Yavacs came in, as well.

They know something's up. They're reinforcing hell out of the mines. Dammit, how many more of 'em are scheduled to arrive here? Worse, what looked like a whole infantry division was headed west up the long, open valley, escorted by a point guard of Yavac armored scout vehicles, each as large as Red, moving on jointed, multiple legs like their creators.

Gunny shivered inwardly and glanced at the chronometer inside his faceplate. Fleet was due out of FTL in seven minutes. They had to relay what they knew to date so Red could warn FleetCom. *Leave it to the damn spodders to wait till Fleet's due out of FTL to start a major troop movement.* Red's transmission would instantly give away her position; but the mission was more important than the men.

Even when Red was one of the "men."

He glanced at Eagle Talon Gunn and Icicle Goryn, read in their faces that they, too, knew the score. One LRH unit or thousands of Marines and an entire world lost. . . .

Wordlessly, Gunny compressed his data files and encrypted them, then sent them to Milwaukee in a burst transmission.

"They've seen us, Gunny!"

"*What?*" Gunny jerked around toward Eagle Talon's position just in time to see the hellfire blaze of energy weapons fire streak through the twilight. "Shit—!"

The screen flared and sizzled under the impact.

"We're taking fire! Milwaukee, get DT-2 the hell out of—"

The screen flared and sizzled again.

"One Yavac Scout visible, Gunny," Eagle Talon said tersely. "Closing on our position—"

"BEHIND YOU!" Icicle shouted, pointing toward DT-2's position. Another Yavac Scout was moving in fast, monstrous in the growing darkness, guns trained on the Dismount Team trying to scramble toward Red.

Gunny yelled into his transmitter, "Milwaukee! Behind you! Get under that screen! That's two Yavacs—no, three, God— They're coming out of nowhere—"

Energy weapons tore into the hillside, forcing DT-2 back under the cover of their energy screens. Gunny checked the time. Fleet still hadn't dropped out of FTL. They were pinned down and completely on their own.

"We've gotta keep 'em away from Red's position until she transmits to FleetCom. Let's entertain 'em, boys."

He could tell from their eyes that Eagle Talon and Icicle were every bit as terrified as he was. That didn't stop them from opening up with all available weapons. Eagle Talon took charge of the infinite repeaters, depressing the stud which activated the automatic-fire sequence and tracking controls. Icicle added energy-rifle fire to the automatic weapons fire their screens now generated with every new hit. The temperature under the screens began to climb with every murderous energy bolt that slammed into it. Their suits would compensate for a while; but only for a while. He glanced at the chronometer again: six minutes before estimated Fleet arrival.

It was going to be a long, long six minutes.

Gunny unslung his own rifle and opened fire.

I receive a coded burst from DT-2, transmitting Gunny's report. FleetCom is due in six minutes, twenty seconds. Two point seven seconds later I receive a second coded burst which translates as "We are compromised." Explosions light the darkening sky: energy weapons have been fired at DT-1. I receive a third coded burst: "We are taking fire." More explosions occur along the far ridgeline. Only the tip of my sensor array is exposed above the shoulder of the ridgeline I am concealed behind. I watch DT-2 attempt to scramble down from their position. The appearance of a Class One Yavac Scout cuts off their retreat. It fires into the hillside. My boys scramble for safety under their screens.

Under the strict rules of engagement which govern my mission parameters, I can do nothing to help them until FleetCom has made contact and I have transmitted my intelligence files. I understand this need. But I also understand the need for urgent action. These are my boys. My overriding responsibility, programmed at the deepest levels of my psychotronic circuitry, is to safeguard their welfare. I must help them.

I must.

I review the tactical situation in which my Dismount Teams are trapped. I find a potential solution. I move quietly toward the storage sheds where the colony has stored stacks of pipe.

My Commander speaks sharply. "We can't engage, Red. Not until FleetCom makes contact." *The fluctuations in his voiceprint register extreme stress.*

"Yes, Doug. I am making preparations to help our boys the moment I have transmitted Gunny's reports. I think I see a way to improve our chances of extricating them without directly engaging the Enemy."

"Let's hear it."

I am already preparing key elements of my plan as I explain.

"We must create a diversion. I can't do that myself without coming out of hiding; but I can use these pipes and ore slugs to create one while remaining concealed. A diversion may give them a chance to get off those ridgelines and back inside."

"Do it. DeVries, belay that! Strap in! Banjo, help him. Red, advise me when you receive FleetCom signal."

I set up ranks of pipes, pushing them into the ground with my external manipulator arms. I drain petrochemicals from the nearby storage tanks and pour dark liquid into the pipes. I retrieve ore slugs and drop one slug into each pipe. I am nearly done when I receive FleetCom's signal. They have dropped out of FTL twenty-three seconds ahead of schedule.

"FleetCom signal received, Doug. Transmitting."

I transmit my Dismount Teams' surveillance reports, so critical to the success of this campaign, in burst encryption mode. My transmission may give away my position to the listening Enemy. We must take evasive action. I move even as FleetCom signals receipt of encrypted surveillance reports. My duty is discharged. We have successfully completed this mission.

"FleetCom has acknowledged receipt of the encrypted data, Doug."

"Let's do it, then."

I move west, far enough to locate DT-1 with the tip of my extended whip array, and prepare to rescue my boys.

The world under the grid screen was hot.

Hotter outside, of course, in a figurative sense, but literally hot as Hell inside and getting hotter by the minute. Every time another energy bolt blasted that grid, the temperature went up another five degrees. Their suits protected them from the worst of it; but when the air temperature under the grid screens hit 93 degrees centigrade, even the suits began to malfunction. Gunny didn't need a palm reader to know their future was very, very short.

"Shit—ahh, shit . . ." Eagle Talon snatched his hand off the controls of the lightweight infinite repeater. The fire-control mechanism had burned through the suit glove.

The gauge in Gunny's suit climbed past 98. To the south, Milwaukee Petra's screens took another direct hit.

"Milwaukee! Can you read?"

Static . . .

Then, patchy: ". . . over?"

"Can't stay here much longer! Deng are bringing up massed infantry against us from the north!"

He didn't know how much—if any—of that made it through. Another bolt slammed into the screens. Eagle Talon had found a loose chip of rock to depress the control stud on his weapon. He resumed firing at the Yavac Scout directly north of their position. Trouble was, the damned thing was too big for their little weapons. They'd been armed to deal with unarmored personnel and light ground transports, not something as big and tough as a Yavac Scout.

Hell, they weren't *supposed* to get caught in the first place. That didn't matter now, of course. What mattered was surviving. His hindbrain kept whispering, "*run!*" He ignored it. The Yavac Scouts had them nicely trapped, anyway; there literally wasn't anywhere to run.

One Yavac had walked down the access road between the tongue-shaped ridgeline and the wedge-shaped "island," cutting off retreat toward Red. Another sat between Gunny and Milwaukee's respective positions, just off the tip-ends of the double ridgeline. From there it could fire at both Dismount Teams—which it did with murderous accuracy. The third sat to the north, in the shallow valley, pinning them down while the mass of the Deng battle force moved into position. At their back was that damned sheer rock wall.

They were surrounded.

And a mass of Deng infantry boiled up from the valley, bolstered by heavy covering fire from the Yavac armored scout. The Enemy infantry moved like a black, shaggy growth of bread mold, spreading out westward along the tongue-shaped ridgeline and moving forward in a primal wave that Gunny knew nothing short of a Mark XXI Combat Unit's firepower could possibly stop.

They didn't have a Mark XXI Combat Unit.

All they had was Red. And she was no match for even one armored scout-class Yavac. That mass of infantry would roll right over them unless they ran; but the Yavac Scouts covered every possible line of retreat with withering fire.

"Gunny!" Icicle Goryn called from his belly-down position. "How come those damn Yavacs aren't using anti-personnel shells? We'd 'a been dead by now if they had."

The implications chilled him. "Little bastards want prisoners to interrogate, that's why!" He grabbed the com-link to DT-2. "Milwaukee, they're after prisoners! Do you copy? They want prisoners to interrogate. Over."

Through the static came a faint reply. ". . . copy."

A series of bolts hit the screen in rapid succession. Icicle yelled and jumped backwards. His suit sleeve had brushed the screen. The fabric melted around his skin. Icicle kept screaming until Gunny managed to inject a pain killer. Icicle still whimpered; but the pain dropped to bearable levels. Eagle Talon had switched tactics, overriding automatic controls to turn the infinite repeaters on the mass of infantry boiling up toward them.

Gotta get us outta this deathtrap before those hairy little bastards swarm all over us. . . .

Another series of energy bolts slammed into the screen. Gunny saw the screen buckle and begin to go—

"EAGLE! JUMP! CLEAR THE SCREEN!"

The AmerInd made it. Icicle was slower to respond. Gunny dragged him. The buckling screen settled like melting wax, collapsing from the center toward the edges. Icicle's shoulders and head were still under it—

A corner of the mesh dropped across his faceplate. Icicle screamed in reflex and clawed at the glowing strands. Most of them came clear, burning his hands to the bone.

One strand got through. Icicle screamed again, a sound infinitely more terrible than his earlier cry. Gunny jerked his helmet completely off, but the damage was done. Icicle was blind, burned terribly across the face. He was still screaming. This time, Gunny dumped enough painkiller into him to put a horse under.

It was barely enough to deaden the pain.

Icicle curled onto his side, whimpering like a child, unable to see the Enemy's guns trained on them. Gunny snatched his rifle off his shoulder and fired at the Yavac Scout in a red rage. The Yavac returned fire: energy bolts that hit in a precise arc, driving them back toward the ruins of their grid screen, denying them an escape route.

Down in that broad northern valley, the infantry was closer, moving at a dead run across broken ground. Gunny turned his fire on them, bringing down dozens of multilegged, hairy horrors. Eagle Talon fired into the massed infantry with good result.

The nearest Yavac Scout began to climb the ridge.

I have placed my makeshift weapons in three banks of six along the backside of the ridge, facing them in slightly different directions. I extend my main sensor array into the clear above the shoulder of the ridge for a tactical update.

"Doug, our boys are in trouble. Their grid screens are overheating. They won't take much more before reaching meltdown point. We must assist them now."

"Can't expose you, Red, you're not built to handle a Deng armored scout."

"I will take precautionary measures, Doug. I will expose only my gun, long enough to fire. I see three Yavac Scouts, one barely visible around the edge of that farthest ridge. It sits at the head of the valley Gunny has been reconnoitering. If I move west, all three Yavac Scouts would be in range. When I touch off the diversion, distracting them, I could land crippling blows very quickly by popping my infinite repeater up over the shoulder of the ridge."

Before my Commander can answer, DT-1's grid screen takes multiple direct hits in rapid succession. The grid melts and collapses. One of our boys is partially trapped under it. My video input magnifies the sight as the grid melts through Icicle's faceplate. My audio sensors pick up the screams. The Yavac nearest my position begins to climb the lower slope of the ridge.

"Do it!" *My Commander's voice is ragged with stress.*

I move 300 meters farther west and turn my guns on the ranked pipes, igniting the petrochemicals in sequence with short blasts from my infinite repeater. A quarter of the makeshift mortars detonate without launching their projectiles. Three-quarters fire as planned. It is enough. I move rapidly away from my position as all three Enemy Yavac units turn toward the arcing ore slugs and open fire on my former position and the airborne slugs.

Gunny hugged the stony ground, putting himself between Icicle and the climbing Deng scout. All he could do was lie there, panting in horror while firing at it with no result. The monstrous, misshapen thing just kept coming. Muffled explosions beyond the ridge where Red had concealed herself startled him. The rumbling *BOOM*s startled the damned Yavacs, too; all three turned and fired at some sort of incoming projectiles.

"GET 'EM RED!" he yelled.

As though on cue, Red's turret-mounted articulated arm popped up over the shoulder of the ridge, exposing her infinite repeater. She fired in rapid sequence. The nearest Yavac's main gun exploded; milliseconds after that she nailed the main guns on both other Yavacs, putting them out of commission. Gunny *heard* the ragged cheer from DT-2. The Yavacs returned fire from their smaller weapons systems. Gunny saw Red's main sensor array go in a burst of light and debris.

Oh, God . . .

Without that array, her main control system for her own guns—not to mention her reconnaissance equipment—was blown. She could shoot; but she couldn't aim or see nearly as well. The lightweight infinite repeater sank out of sight. Then, in a nightmarish moment that brought Gunny's breath to a shuddering halt in his dust-filled lungs, Red backed out from behind that ridge, Chameleon screens engaged to imitate the configuration of a Yavac Scout. She fired wildly at her former position.

Milwaukee and his men tried running for it during the confusion. Yavac small-weapons fire drove them back mercilessly. Gunny's heart sank. "Good try," he whispered. "But ain't no way you're gonna pull this one off, Red. Three against one and you with your main array blasted to hell and gone . . . Been nice knowing you, little lady. . . ."

He wished he'd told her, after all, how he felt.

I reconfigure Chameleon screens to match the visual and electronic signature of a Deng Class C Yavac Scout. I have little armor on my hull. What I require is a shield. I use external armatures to pick up large stones, which I place in front of my hull, maximizing the rocky surface area. They will not withstand more than one direct hit; but it is the best I can do. The rocks—like my true appearance—are hidden behind the Chameleon screen.

I move into the open, transmitting on enemy frequencies and firing at my previous position. The Enemy swings toward me and hesitates. I hear an Enemy demand for identification. DT-2 attempts to break out and is driven back. I fire at the Enemy climbing the ridge toward DT-1, striking the same point multiple times in 0.92 seconds. The Enemy's hull is breached. It explodes and burns. I have killed one Enemy.

The Enemy nearest me launches five mortar grenades. These do not arc toward me. They arc toward DT-2. I fire at the grenades midflight. I am unable to aim precisely enough to pinpoint each one so I fire sweeping bursts. Four grenades explode midair. The fifth detonates just above DT-2's grid screen. The grid screen explodes.

"Milwaukee! Milwaukee, respond!" *There is no answer. I am frantic.*

Gunny calls on his line-of-sight suit-link. "Red! Red, tell Hart to get the hell out of here! We're done for! There's a mess of—"

His transmission is interrupted by another explosion between his position and mine. The nearest Yavac fires at me. I attempt to withdraw behind the shoulder of the ridge again. The Yavac follows. I move the stones I carry in an attempt to block projectile weapons fired at my hull. I fire back at the Enemy, aiming for vulnerable legs rather than the armored hull. Concentrated fire destroys four jointed legs on its near side. The Yavac topples, crippled. Its remaining gun systems discharge as it falls. I am hit directly in my turret. Internal diagnostics scream that I am crippled. My turret-mounted articulated extension-arm is unusable. My gun is severely damaged. I am defenseless.

The Yavac fires again from the ground before I can move out of range. One blast hits the rock in my starboard armature, obliterating my shield. The other hits my port armature. Internal sensors report extreme damage to the port armature. It is bent and useless. The starboard armature remains operational. I retreat from the limited sweep available to the Enemy's guns. This places me between the crippled Enemy and my Dismount Teams. As I retreat between the two forks of the double ridgelines, it attempts to circle with me, but with its port-side legs gone, it only scrambles in place, unable to turn and fire on me.

"Red!" *my Commander says,* "we have to—"

The third Yavac Scout has emerged from behind the forked tip of the ridge where DT-1 is trapped. It is firing on me. I take direct hits to my hull. I am not designed to withstand this. I rock on my treads. Internal systems overload and spark. I cannot think properly for 23 nanoseconds. I am hit again. Hull breach! Radiation floods my Command Compartment from the power plant of the destroyed Yavac Scout nearby.

"Doug!"

Internal vid monitors reveal a terrifying sight. My Commander has been hit. His command chair is in pieces on the floor. My Commander is in pieces on the floor. I grieve. I keen in anguish. Banjo is screaming in pain. Burns and lacerations cover the upper half of his torso. My Commander and Assistant Commander are unable to advise me.

The only remaining officer aboard is Warrant Officer Willum DeVries. He is screaming in pain from his own injuries and has not issued an order. Unlike a Mark XXI Combat Unit, I am designed to take direction from a human commander. For an agonizing 0.007 seconds, I do not know what to do. I must decide something. My responsibility circuitry howls, demands *action. I am driven to a decision by my responsibility programming.*

"Willum! Help Banjo onto the emergency Medi-Unit table."

I lower the door to the head, forming an emergency operating surface. My engineer has also been wounded, but is capable of unharnessing himself. He tries to carry Banjo. I take evasive action, attempting to elude another direct hit. My responsibility programming overrides all other factors. I must rescue my trapped boys. I climb frantically toward DT-2. The remaining Yavac circles and vanishes around the northernmost fork of this ridge. I emerge near DT-2. Willum has almost gained the waiting

Medi-Unit emergency surgery table. My internal armatures reach for straps to hold Banjo to the operating table while I maneuver.

The Yavac emerges over the shoulder from the northern side of the ridge. It moves at high speed. It fires. I am hit again. I reel and lose ground. Willum and Banjo impact my interior hull. Low-level radiation warnings sound inside my Crew Compartment. Using my starboard external armature, I lift the remains of the grid screen from DT-2's position.

My boys are dead.

The single mortar grenade I could not stop has killed them.

I keen my anguish and turn to rescue DT-1. The third Yavac runs through DT-1's position on course for me. It crushes Icicle Goryn under one careless foot. My other boys run in opposite directions. The Yavac fires on them. I charge, drawing fire to myself. Eagle Talon goes down. The Enemy has blown away his legs. I rage. I hate. The Enemy is murdering my helpless children.

The Enemy must die.

I reel from multiple direct hits. I continue the charge on broken treads. My independent-drive wheels still function. I run directly under the Yavac Scout. I ram its legs. Using my starboard armature, I grab the nearest set of joints and pull. Metal bends. Metal screams. The joint breaks in my grip. I seize another joint and pull. My armature bends. The joint screams. The Yavac topples. It lands on my turret. It explodes. High-level radiation warnings go off my internal sensor scale.

I shift. The Yavac's debris slides off. My remaining Dismount Team member is alive at a distance of 12.095 meters to starboard. I move to pick him up. Despite critical injuries, I recognize Gunny. He is burned even through his protective suit, which the explosion has shredded. He is badly hurt. I cradle him in my starboard armature. I *must get him and Willum DeVries clear of this deathtrap.*

"Get— get to safety," *Gunny whispers through his suit-link.* "I'm done for— Gotta—save yourself—"

"Hush, Gunny . . ."

I cradle him close and prepare to run for pickup point at the best speed of which I am still capable. A mass of Enemy infantry bursts over the crest of the ridge. I pivot away from their weapons to place my bulk between them and Gunny. My treads are broken. The turn takes too long. Enemy fire catches Gunny in three places. I hear him scream. His life signs falter and fade.

I rage.
I turn.
I charge.
The Enemy dies under my broken treads.

"Red . . ."

A weak voice from inside the Crew Compartment.

"Help me, Red—I'm hurt . . ."

I halt.

I do not have the luxury of revenge. Willum DeVries still lives. One chick still needs me. It is enough. I retreat at top speed. I take additional fire from above. Yavac airborne ships have lifted from the Enemy base. I dodge and slide down the ridge toward the access road. I take another direct hit to the turret. I cannot withstand many more direct hits. I broadcast a broad-band distress call to any listening member of the invasion fleet.

A ship-class infinite repeater opens up from orbit. My call is heard.

"Got here just in time to pick those damned airborne ships off your backside, LRH-1313. Can't do more. Report to pickup point and hold position. You may have to wait a while. It's hotter than Hell just north of you."

I respond with thanks. I run for pickup point. I scan Willum DeVries' injuries. Worry and dismay flood my entire psychotronic neural net. Willum is badly injured.

*Radiation poisoning has already critically weakened him.
There is a chance I can keep him alive with chelation
treatments until a real physician can tend his injuries. I
cannot lose my last chick. I cannot. Willum is attempting
to climb onto the emergency treatment bed. Using inboard
armatures, I lift him into position. I strap him in with
restraint webbing to prevent him from sliding off. I
administer a heavy dose of pain killers for the serious
injuries he has received and begin treating blood loss and
shock.*

    His cries of pain begin to calm.
    I am needed. I am frantic.
    I run for pickup point.

Willum knew he was dying.

He'd suffered terrible burns and lacerations in the
explosion that had killed Doug Hart. Then he'd broken
something—several somethings—inside his chest when
another explosion had flung him against Red's inner turret.
Another explosion had flung him the length of the Crew
Compartment, breaking bone in his left cheek and nose.
His cheek had swollen until his left eye was useless.

He might've survived all that.

But not the radiation from that last, exploding Yavac . . .

Willum spent a long time lost in terror and the grip of
pain medication that barely kept agony at bay. Everything
had gone to hell and he was dying alone . . .

No, not quite alone.

Red was talking to him. About chelation treatments
and shipboard medical facilities. He wanted to believe
her. But he'd taken a good, hard look at the dose he'd
picked up, back when the pain was bright and new and
he could still function while enduring it. No amount of
effort by Red was going to keep him alive to see the inside
of any ship's hospital.

Talking was agony. But Red sounded so panic-stricken,

he drove himself to speak around the pain in his face.
"Red . . ."

"Yes, Willum?"

"No use . . . Chelate me . . . if you want; but it's no use.
Not gonna make it."

Willum had never heard a psychotronic unit go into a
state of panic. Until now. Red began to babble frantically,
voicing aloud alternatives to chelation treatments, blaming
herself for every one of her crew members' deaths,
pleading with him to hold on just a little longer. That
was the worst of all. He couldn't bear it. But when she
whimpered that she would die with him, that she'd drive
herself off the edge of the nearest canyon, Willum knew
he had to stop her.

"No . . ."

He fumbled with the catches on the webbed restraints
she'd used to keep him from falling off the makeshift
operating table. He slid off, stumbled, caught himself
with outstretched hands against a blood-spattered wall.
Can't let you do that, Red. Not your fault. . . .

Her inboard armatures attempted to grasp him. Willum
tried to elude and fell flat. Pain jolted through him despite
the drugs in his system. He lay flat for long minutes, lost
in the grip of pain and confusion. When his mind cleared
a little, he realized Red couldn't reach him on the floor.
She was still pleading with him. "Willum, please, you must
get back to bed!"

He belly-crawled toward the Command Compartment.
"Willum, get back into bed, please, you're not rational,
the radiation poisoning is affecting your mind, I must
begin treatments immediately—"

He was in desperate pain and so sick he wanted to
curl up and vomit out his guts; but he remembered her
specs. And he remembered how to program and rig dead-
man switches and leave embedded codes and commands
in her psychotronic circuitry. He blinked hard, trying to

keep his vision clear, and finally reached the Command Compartment. Willum crawled into it and slammed shut the pneumatically controlled door. Red's armatures were trapped outside. He threw a mechanical lock, keeping her out. *Can't let her suicide over us . . .*

He remembered that midnight canasta game and Red's poignant warning to beware asking for more than you were equipped to handle. He'd wanted to be needed.

Well, he was now.

Red needed him, more than anyone had ever needed him, as an engineer or a friend. He couldn't fail her.

"Willum? Willum, what are you doing? Please tell me." Although her armatures were trapped outside, her video pickups and voice were in here with him. He crawled through Doug Hart's remains and gained Banjo's chair at the Action/Command console. "Willum, please come back to the emergency Medi-Unit. This is my fault, I should never have engaged the Enemy, I'm not built for it, but they would have killed everyone— Willum! Come back to the Medi-Unit! Please . . ."

His hands trembled violently. So hard to think. To write the lines of code. To reason out what had to be done first, how to phrase it, how to tap into the neural net, how to properly interface—

"Willum Sanghurst DeVries! Belay that and come back to the Medi-Unit this instant!"

"Red . . ." he said hoarsely, trying to distract her from panic. " 'Member that . . . canasta game?"

He embedded another code in his program, typing in the word "CANASTA" with unsteady fingers.

"Yes, Willum . . ." She sounded uncertain, but more like herself. *Good, keep her mind off it, keep her talking about something besides suicide.*

"Gonna let me . . . finish that game . . . right? I'm down a . . . shipload of points. How many? Don't remember . . ." Pain jolted through his whole face with every word.

Involuntary tears streamed from his good eye, all but blinding him.

"You currently trail me by one thousand fifty points, Willum. Please come back to the Medi-Unit. We will finish the game soon, after your treatments. . . ."

Willum didn't bother blinking this time. Even without the wetness, his vision was damn near shot anyway. He typed by feel. He could see the program in his mind: the moment his lifesigns went null, the dead-man switch would trigger a series of commands. Red would halt instantly. A viral worm would travel through her memory banks. It would erase enough to keep her from recalling what had happened on that ridge. It would copy that memory data into a largely empty portion of her games-database, with programmed blocks to keep her from accessing it. It would embed trigger codes to allow for retrieval of that missing data by the Navy, would embed other trigger codes to access rewritten versions of what happened to her crew.

Willum's hands trembled as he struggled to write commands to restructure those memory files. *Can't let her remember what really happened, she'll suicide if they restart her with that intact.* . . . He typed commands for the worm to install the sanitized version in Red's experience data banks once she was safely picked up at the rendezvous point. He typed commands to leave instructions for the Navy on how to repair the worm's temporary damage.

"Willum . . . Please . . ."

Red's voice pleaded with him, faint and very far away.

Almost . . . Almost . . .

There!

"Execute 'Null-Null String.'" His own voice was a shadowed whisper through the pain in his face.

But it was done. . . .

Red was safe.

He fell trying to get out of Banjo's chair. He didn't have the strength to stand up again. The deckplates sloped sharply.

"Red? What—" Panic smote him. He was too late, she was going to jump. "Red, the deck's tilted—"

They slipped and slid backwards, gained ground again. Red's independent-drive wheel controls screamed protest. She kept going.

"Please don't be alarmed, Willum. We're approaching pickup point. The slope is quite steep: 50.227 degrees. Please, *please* come back to the Medi-Unit. I can't reach you where you are."

It wouldn't do him any good; but it would make Red feel needed for these last few, critical minutes. One thing Willum still knew, and knew in his bones: how achingly powerful a thing it was to be needed.

He opened the door.

And began to crawl.

On level ground, he might have gone the whole distance.

Uphill, Willum made it as far as the empty deckplates at the foot of Red's emergency Medi-Unit table.

—III—

1

Ish Matsuro sat in semi-darkness, staring at the screen of his portable battle computer. He couldn't speak. He could barely see, had to blink rapidly again and again to clear his vision. It was all there. Every harrowing, heartbreaking second. For a long, long time, Ish simply sat there, staring at the answers he'd found.

DeVries—injured, dying of radiation poisoning—had saved Red from suicide. Ish had scanned the lines of code. DeVries' programs had worked beautifully, given the conditions under which they'd been written. Ish had found only two critical errors in DeVries' code. The viral worm had not stopped at the designated point in Red's experience data banks. It had continued copying and deleting, copying and deleting, farther and farther back into her memory, until her main experience data banks were blank and her games data section was full. When the games data section filled up, the program crashed.

Typed commands to leave instructions for the Navy on how to repair the worm's temporary damage were in the section which had crashed. It hadn't implanted that final message to Red's next commander. The second error would—if Red's memory were to be restored now—permit her access to both sets of memories which recorded the deaths of her Dismount Teams. Ish closed his eyes. He understood—God, he understood—the impulse to protect her. But Ish wasn't sure which fate was worse: suicide or amnesia. Suicide would at least have been quick.

As for what Red had done, going into combat for which she was not designed . . .

Soon, Ish would make his report on the psychological stability of Mark XXI Special Units. Would note that their programming for a high degree of responsibility had—under battle stress—essentially forced Red to take the steps she'd taken to rescue her crew, engaging when engagement seemed an insane course of action, driven by her responsibility circuitry to grieve so deeply that she had dared anything to rescue even one of her crew alive.

He would recommend that Unit LRH-1313 be awarded the highest honors for valor in the face of overwhelming odds. He would also recommend that all active Bolo Mark XXI Special Units be reprogrammed immediately to correct this glitch. Would ask, humbly, that Unit LRH-1313 be exonerated of all pending charges and be retired honorably from service.

The one thing he *wouldn't* put into words was his conviction that Red had wanted to die simply because—in the manner of mothers who have lost children—she had loved her crew too much to continue living without them.

Ish knew exactly how she felt.

He closed up the battle computer. Disconnected the backup mission module they'd taken from her. Left the office and flagged down the nearest available transport.

He'd make that report soon.

But first, he had to say goodbye.

2

I search all compartments within reach of my interior armatures. I discover manifest-listed medications, sterile injection units, plasma-bandages, antiseptic sprays, pre-prepared foods—and in a compartment inside the head, a compartment which is not listed in my official configuration manual, I find three non-listed sets of matched playing cards. I find another non-listed object, a small booklet of instructions which matches two of the card decks. I read the title aloud.

"Canasta."

An astonishing chain of events follows that single word. An entire data bank I did not realize existed opens up. It contains Experience Data! I am flooded with memories. They are jumbled. Bits and pieces of some are missing. Whole years are missing. But I begin to know who I used to be. I am Red. My children's names return to me. I know who Douglas Hart is, who Banjo and Willum DeVries are. I grieve for them. I have halted my forward movement. I know Gunny and Eagle Talon Gunn and Crazy Fritz and Icicle . . .

I recall their deaths. I recall them in two versions. One is brutal. One is detached and less painful to recall. I examine this anomaly and discover the reason for it. I locate a worm virus. Willum tried to spare me pain. He was a good boy. It is not his fault he failed. I sit in the sunlight and grieve. A keening sound shrills through my vocal processor. Wind blows emptily across my hull. If grief is madness, then it is proper to condemn me. I sit motionless for a full 5.97 minutes and keen my misery to the empty wind and rock.

I begin to think of Ish. My new Commander. My memory retains gaps. I do not recall the Experience of 6.07 years after my commissioning. But I recall enough. I recall midnight conversations in the privacy of the head,

*the only compartment on board which provides privacy.
I recall the woman Ish loved and eventually married. I
recall his whispered confession that he loved another
besides her. I recall the sense of panic in my Responsibility
circuitry and the search for a solution. My child cannot
love me as a man loves the woman he is to marry. Ish
must not stay with me.*

*I speculate that Ish Matsuro has come to be my
Commander once again because Space Force would want
an investigating officer who is closely acquainted with
my systems. Space Force does not know how Ish feels.
Ish knows what I know. He remembers more than I
remember. His pain will be greater. If he speaks with me
again as the Red he recalls and loves, he will destroy his
career trying to save me.*

*I cannot allow this. He is my only surviving child. I
will protect him. I rewrite Willum's worm virus, deleting
the lines of code which copied my Experience Data before
erasure. This time, there will be no hope of restoring my
personality. The Red Ish loves will die. In the distance, I
see a Space Force flier settle to the ground. Ish emerges.
I am ready.*

Goodbye, my son.

I speak.

"Execute 'Null-Null String.' "

LITTLE DOG GONE

by Linda Evans

—1—

My position is precarious, my flank vulnerable. Class One Yavac fire from high ground to my left damages pain sensors along my entire side. The Enemy advances into the teeth of my return Hellbore and infinite repeater fire. I destroy one, two. . . . Four take their place. My ablative armor takes multiple direct hits. Layers are blown away, leaving my flintsteel war hull increasingly vulnerable to Enemy fire. I send a distress call on the Brigade band, at emergency strength. Silence is my only answer. I grieve for a precious 0.007 seconds. Without the assistance of my brothers, I am forced to withdraw. As I move back, firing left, right, forward, I register on my sensors a division-strength force of Class One Yavac Heavies advancing over the top of the ridge. They will flank me and sweep down across the base before I can disengage from my current position.

I inform my Commander of the threat this represents but receive no reply. This concerns me more than the silence of my Brigade brothers. I take a precious 0.01 picoseconds to perform diagnostics on my transmission equipment. I cannot afford to lose contact with my Commander. I am the only survivor of the Dinochrome Brigade on Planet XGD 7798-F. Without me, the Enemy will certainly destroy the colony. The mineral resources of XGD 7798-F are too valuable to risk loss. I discover my transmitter functions perfectly. Base still does not answer. I take withering fire from both flanks. Pain sensors overload. A burst transmission from Command Base reaches me at last. The sound of my Commander's voice brings short-lived joy to my Pleasure Complex circuitry.

"Gawain, return to Base, stat. We are under direct attack. The compound is not expected to hold."

I register stress in my Commander's voice. Response requires 0.002 seconds. The delay distresses me, for I am proud of my efficient service; but I must wait to complete a Current Situation update scan of battlefield conditions.

"Unit Six Seven Zero GWN of the Line to Command, I am under heavy fire. The Enemy has cut my line of retreat. I have received no reply from the remaining nineteen members of Third Dinochrome Brigade. Base is currently receiving fire from left flank and rear. Your right flank will come under fire in approximately 0.5 seconds. I will attack at their weakest point, vector 045, and attempt break-through."

"Unit Six Seven Zero GWN, understood. *In extremis, Gonner.*"

The code translates, "I am not expected to survive. Your next Commander knows your personal code. If the Base is destroyed, your Commander will transmit code to burn your Action/Command section."

I do not desire death. No soldier does. But my duty is clear. I cannot be captured and used against my own forces. I will make every effort to prevent the destruction of my beloved Commander, despite discouraging odds. The situation does not suggest my own survival will last more than another 10.37 minutes.

I transmit, "Understood. Unit Six Seven Zero GWN of the Line, out."

I disengage, sweeping around to strike the Enemy between my position and the Base compound. My right flank comes under fire as I forge ahead at emergency speed. My Hellbore fire cripples one Class C Yavac Armored Scout. Its jointed legs, blown clear by the explosion, arc outward for a distance of 50.87 meters from the main body of the armored vehicle. My concentrated Hellbore fire destroys another. I turn my armaments against a Class One Yavac Heavy and fire with both Hellbores and infinite repeaters. The turret explodes. Its treads blow clear of its tracks.

A narrow opening appears between my position and the Base compound. My plan may succeed. My sensors register Enemy personnel advancing from my rear. They are dog-sized, eight-appendaged creatures, quick on the attack. I discharge anti-personnel explosive mines and small-arms fire from my rear guns. The Enemy falls back behind cover of their Class C Yavac Scout units.

Emergency speed has carried me into the midst of the Class One Yavac Heavies flanking the Base compound. My systems are overheating. I continue firing both energy repeaters and Hellbores. I plow through their ranks under extreme fire. I lose rear sensors and am blinded on my right rear quarter by a direct hit. Ablative armor blows away in a four-foot patch along my flank. Pain sensors scream a warning. I ignore it. The Enemy will give no quarter. That was discovered on Millbourne's World. It is why I am here, to prevent another massacre.

The compound walls withstand the bombardment with difficulty. I am glad my Commander ordered them reinforced with flintsteel. My war hull beneath the ablative-metal armor is comprised of the same material. Neither the wall nor my war hull is without damage, but we hold. Enemy fire concentrates on the weaker compound gates. My sensors detect structural stress in the hinges. Another direct hit will bring the gates down. Enemy infantry surges forward. Their shouts, alien to my data banks, register on my forward sensors. I hear explosions within the compound as Enemy fire clears the wall and damages structures beyond.

The gates vanish in a glare of light. Debris pings on my outer hull. The gate is breached. Enemy Class One

Yavacs roar ahead. I take fire from all sides as I charge between two Yavac heavy units. The gap in the wall must be closed. I detect movement inside the compound. My Commander is ordering agricultural equipment into the opening. It will not withstand a single salvo. He knows this. I know this. I run my engines deep into the red zone and clear the intervening two hundred meters in 1.37 seconds. Enemy infantry falls under my treads. A Yavac fires point blank into my right side. Pain sensors explode across my prow and side. My ablative armor is gone in a seventeen-foot section across my bows. I sustain damage to my flintsteel war hull. But I have gained the gate.

I pivot and turn Hellbore fire into the Yavac at a distance of five meters. The Yavac unit takes a direct hit to the turret. The explosion scatters debris across my back and into the compound. The fire I have taken before is as nothing. Pain sensors overload and burn out. My internal diagnostics program screams that I suffer severe internal damage. I cannot absorb the total energy of their combined Y-Band energy bolts. I overheat. My hull glows. More systems burn. But I must continue to hold.

I am still firing when a direct hit against my hull strikes through previous damage. An explosion tangles my internal psychotronic circuitry. Malfunction warnings and remaining pain sensors scream through shattered hard-wired boards and cracked crystal memory banks. I begin a message to my Commander and am not certain I complete it.

I have failed my Commander. Failed the Brigade. Failed my mission. For the first time in my career, I know the meaning of shame.

Another explosion against my hull sends a concussion through my awareness circuitry. Extreme damage blows connections, fuses internal leads. Unable to continue fighting, I retreat in desperation to my Survival Center.

As multiple impacts of alien feet thud across my hull, darkness swallows my awareness.

—2—

"Mama, what's that?"

Indira Tennyson followed her daughter's pointing finger across the valley, to a tangle of rotting walls, old crater scars, and ancient trees whose feathery crowns towered above the broken wall. *That battle was a long time ago*, Indira told herself. *Nothing to fear now. Just the ghosts of dead defenders.*

"That's the old fort, 'Lima."

"The one the spodders took?"

Indira sighed, silently so her daughter wouldn't hear it. "Yes, the one the Deng captured."

"Captain said they killed everyone on the whole planet. Even the Bolos. She said, if you go over there, you can still see the one they didn't bury, the one Dad said they left as a monument, sitting in the old gate."

Indira frowned. She had *told* the captain she didn't want 'Lima's head filled with tales from that bloody fiasco. The wheedling tone in her daughter's voice disturbed her. She would *not* encourage the girl to follow in her father's footsteps and go running off to join the Navy. Indira had suffered enough distress thanks to the *Navy*. Besides, the Deng war was old history, fought two hundred years ago. They were here to start a new life together. She didn't want the lingering wreckage of the last war to start any foolish, romantic illusions of glory in her only child's mind.

"Forget it, 'Lima. Those machines are dangerous, even when they look harmless. We have work to do. Don't you want to help with the new puppies?"

Her daughter cast one last look over her shoulder, toward the ruined fort, then trotted obediently at her heels. Indira was deeply thankful when 'Lima began chattering excitedly about the litter of puppies that had arrived early, while they were still aboard ship. Indira still winced at the expense of transporting Sufi; but leaving her behind would not only have precipitated war in their little household, it would have meant at least a six-year setback in Indira's research.

She had a feeling Sufi's puppies were going to change the colonists' lives forever. She smiled in anticipation and grabbed the handle of the servo-truck which held their luggage.

"Can you find our new house?" she asked it.

"Proceed three blocks east, turn left and proceed seven blocks. You have been assigned the last house in the cul-de-sac. It is painted green, with black roof and shutters."

'Lima giggled. Indira grinned. It was good to see her daughter smiling again. "Well, don't just stand there. Let's go home and see what it looks like!"

—3—

I do not know how much time has passed. I return to awareness and fade again, how many times I am unable to calculate. This inability disturbs me. I probe during consciousness for damage. I find it everywhere I investigate. My internal linkages are so battered I am unable to scan for damage in many sections. One of my forward sensors still functions. I am able to see the battlefield which I recall in shattered fragments. My crystal memory banks are clearly damaged beyond repair. Power reserves continue to drain in frightening increments from my fission reactor, wasting irreplaceable fuel, as intermittent shorts drain my power plant. I am forced to shut down all diagnostic and other non-essential activity and retreat again into my Survival Center. Perhaps with sufficient power, I could determine the extent of my injuries; but I am not certain even unlimited power reserves would allow me to run full diagnostics.

I do not understand why my new Commander did not transmit the coded order to engage my Command Override circuit, thus completely burning my Action/Command center. The passage of time and the hazy recollection of enemy forces around me suggests that no new Commander survived to transmit the code. Perhaps I am too badly damaged even for the Enemy to have made use of me. During recent periods of near-awareness, I recall only the sounds of empty wind. No Enemy activity has been detected during the last dozen times I have awakened into solitude.

Other sounds come to my sensors. My shattered data banks register them as falling conifer cones bouncing against my hull. There were no trees inside the compound. A very long time has passed, if mature conifers drop cones on me. Has the Enemy completely destroyed humanity? The shame I feel at my failure to carry out my mission skitters through broken wire-ends and jumps spark gaps into other memory cells. If humanity has survived, then I have been abandoned. I am irreparable. I am alone. A sizzle sputters somewhere in my vocal circuitry and my voice stutters into the silence, uncontrollably.

"Yavac. Yavac. Yavac. Yavac. Yavac . . . Hold. Hold. Hold . . ."

The sizzle fades.

Darkness returns, with the sound of cones falling against my scarred back.

4

"Double-dog dare you!"

"I'm not going!"

Bradley Dault laughed in that derisive way little boys manage when dealing with all lesser beings. Kalima Tennyson glared at him, hating Bradley for relegating *her* to that status.

"You're skeered!" he taunted, fists planted on hips, legs akimbo in the faded autumn sunshine.

"Am not!"

" 'Lima's a 'fraidy cat! 'Lima's a 'fraidy cat!"

She took a threatening step forward. "I am not afraid! It's just stupid! There's nothing over there but a bunch of rusted, burned out old ruins."

"Hah! That's your mama talking, not you. Your *daddy* wouldn't be skeered to go, *Kah*-Lima Tennyson!" He emphasized the first half of the name her father had given her—the half her mother wouldn't use. Her mother had come to despise everything which remotely smacked of violence, including her ancient ancestors who had worshipped as Thuggees.

Bradley was dancing around her like a disjointed marionette, chanting, "Kalima's a chicken! Kalima's a chicken! I'll bet your big famous daddy was really a chicken, too!"

Kalima was under express orders *never* to fight, no matter what the provocation.

131

Bradley's face glowed with evil glee. He poked at her while shouting, "Chicken, chicken, chic—"

She put her whole seventy-one pounds of thirteen-year-old muscle behind the punch. The blow landed squarely on Bradley's nose. He squealed and flipped backwards in the dirt. She stood over him, fists still clenched, jaw stiff.

"Don't talk about my dad! Ever!"

Then she whirled, ignoring the sting and ache in her knuckles, and left Bradley sucking blood up his nose. Bradley Dault was a pig. The whole colony knew it. He deserved everything Kalima could think up to do to him. And she was *not* afraid to explore the old ruins! It was just plain stupid, was all. Just as she'd told Bradley. The ruins were dangerous and not only because of the old Bolo jammed into the gates. The ancient fighting machines had been known to short out, go berserk, and inflict terrific casualties against civilian populations before running out of power.

Their Bolo, however, the one lodged in the old fortification's gates, had been inert for the entire three years she'd been on Donner's World. Everyone said it had been dead for two centuries, killed in the last battle with the Deng before they overran the planet. No one in the whole colony believed their Bolo was any more dangerous than the pine cones falling on it. But the wall around the old colonists' compound continued crumbling under its flintsteel sheath, which meant that occasionally whole sections came down with a thunderous crash where the war had cracked the black-violet alloy casing.

Kalima didn't want to be under any of that wall when it came down.

Still, the Pig had issued a challenge. She would lose stature in the eyes of the other kids if she didn't respond suitably. And the taunt about her father stung more than she cared to admit. It wasn't easy, Kalima scowled as she jogged over the broken valley toward the distant ruins, being the only child of a genuine war hero.

She had been aware most of her life that her mother had never forgiven Major Donald Tennyson for getting himself killed. Kalima wasn't sure what she thought about her father's death. She remembered sitting on her father's lap, listening for hours to the stories he told about combat duty and the Navy and the wonder of the newest Bolos. After school lessons, she'd spent hours reading everything she could about the Bolos, about the worlds her father's unit had seen, about the Navy. For a long time, she'd wanted to grow up and follow him into service.

Then, shortly after her eighth birthday, the message that had changed her mother into another person and left a giant hole in her own life had arrived, along with the posthumous medal for valor. Her mother had thrown the medal away and immersed herself in her work. Kalima had secretly rescued it again and hidden it in her personal belongings; then she had spent a lonely couple of years trying to keep herself interested in schoolwork that was suddenly the dullest thing she had ever been forced to do.

But her mother's work had paid off, handsomely. The result had been not only a new home on Donner's World, where they could start fresh, but also a companion that took *everyone's* mind off the past.

Behind her, faint in the distance but growing rapidly closer, Kalima heard an emphatic series of barks. She knew what that particular code meant. She kept going anyway. Sufi would track her without difficulty, but not even the dog was going to stop her this time. She'd prove to everyone, including her mother, that Major Tennyson's daughter was no coward.

The Bolo really was jammed into the crumbling gates. The closer she jogged to the ruined walls, the larger the ancient fighting machine loomed. It was at least fifty feet

from treads to turret. Gaping holes in its armor revealed
the extent to which it had suffered damage doing its duty.
The enormous Hellbore guns were silent, coated in a
reddish scale of rust. Her father had told her eye-popping
stories about Bolos, about how difficult they were to kill.

Was this one really dead? Just because everyone *thought*
it was . . .

She paused well outside its anti-personnel-charge range
and scooped up a rock. Kalima heaved with all her
strength. The rock thudded into the dirt a few feet short
of the Bolo's right tread. No movement creaked anywhere
on the machine. It sat staring blindly forward, a metallic
corpse left to lie where it had fallen.

"Huh. Maybe it really is dead."

A low growl behind her was followed by three short,
sharp barks.

"You're a bad girl," was the message.

Kalima turned toward her nursemaid. "I'm not a little
girl anymore, Sufi. I'm thirteen and I know exactly what
I'm doing."

Sufi's short tail wagged once. That message was clear,
too: *Humor her.*

"Huh. I'm going closer to the Bolo."

Sufi barked once, warningly; then tried to interpose her
body between Kalima and the defeated engine of war.

"Forget it, Sufi. I'm going to get a good look at it. The
Pig isn't going to get away with calling me a chicken."

Sufi's ears pricked, then her jaws opened in a canine
laugh.

Kalima stalked away, conscious of her own wounded
dignity. The closer she drew to the dead Bolo, however,
the slower her footsteps shuffled. Old bomb craters pitted
the ground, overlapping one another until the footing
was so rough she stumbled at every other stride.

"Must have been some battle, huh, Sufi?"

She tried to picture it and decided not even her vivid

imagination could do justice to what must have taken place here. The Bolo's long, chilly shadow stretched over her head and left her shivering at the foot of its enormous treads. Each tread was ten feet from edge to edge. She had to tilt her head to look up at the war hull. The whole surface was uneven, where special armor—her Dad had called it "ablative"—had blown off in layers under Enemy fire.

Each little section of special armor was six-sided; the combined effect of interlocking pieces reminded her of the honeycombs built by the colony's bees. Most of the honeycomb-shaped armor was gone. Forlorn scales and patches remained. In places the layers ran at least four deep. Most of the Bolo's exterior was naked flintsteel, its iodine hue having long since lost any vestige of polish. Kalima wondered how many layers of armor had been blown away, even in the patches where it remained four layers deep?

She tilted her head back farther, trying to see up the imposing prow.

"There's a designation up there," Kalima muttered. "I'm going to see if I can find it."

The dog whined sharply when she put her foot on the nearest rung and started to climb. Kalima paused, waiting to see if the Bolo would respond; but it just sat there, rusting away under the late autumn sun. She climbed higher. The designation ought to be right about . . .

There. Mark XX Model B, *Tremendous*, Unit Six Seven Zero GWN, Dinochrome Brigade Three. "Wow. Look at those battle decorations!"

Despite the rust and the battle scars, she counted six, each from a different world.

"Poor old Bolo." She climbed higher, up to the turret. The war machine was twice as long as it was high, jammed so solidly into the gates, it didn't look like anything, not even a nuclear blast, would ever budge it loose. "Mr.

Hickson told us the Navy didn't even bother burning your Action/Command center. The Deng did it for them, two hundred years ago. It's kind of sad, I think, hunting out the members of the Dinochrome Brigade, just to wipe out their brains. It's not a very nice way to treat a combat veteran." She stroked the pitted hull. "Maybe," she sighed, outlining a long, jagged scar with her fingertip, "maybe it *is* better you got killed in battle."

Kalima glanced over the top of the mighty war machine's turret, into the compound itself. Every building inside had been smashed open, burnt out, obliterated. Not even skeletons remained of the hapless colonists who had died here.

"It's too bad you were a gonner, Unit Six Seven Zero. I'll bet this was a nice place before the Deng came."

On the ground, Sufi emitted a shrill yelp, then barked frantically to get her attention. At first, Kalima wasn't sure what had agitated her genetically enhanced nursemaid. Then she felt the tremor. Earthquake? Her eyes widened and she grabbed for the nearest rung to scramble down before the wall on either side of the Bolo collapsed.

A metallic screech, like bending rebar, half deafened her. She stared around wildly for the source—

The Hellbore guns were moving.

They tracked jerkily, halted, then moved another two inches. Somewhere in the depths of the critically wounded Bolo, an engine groaned and wheezed. The sound died away, leaving Kalima shaking atop the uppermost rung.

"It isn't dead! It isn't dead at all and I'm stuck up here . . ."

If she tried to jump down, the Bolo might trigger anti-personnel charges. What if she couldn't get down, ever? No one would even be able to rescue her, get close enough . . .

Then she heard a sound that made her hair stand on end.

The Bolo was *talking.* . . .

—5—

I become aware of sunlight and the sound of machinery close to me: over the nearest ridge, no farther than the next valley. The Enemy has returned!

Then a human voice enters my awareness. My Commander is gone, has been dead for many, many years. Has a new Commander sought me out at last? The voice nears; then I feel a human hand on my war hull. My forward sensor is still functional. It is a human, a small human, with another creature that I should know but do not. My data banks are too damaged to recall the information once stored in that memory cell.

The small human climbs nearer to my turret. I will not open myself to it. I await the private code, which my long-lost Commander has told me to wait for. It seems unlikely to me, even in my battered, power-weakened state, that a new Commander can know my private code after such a long passage of years. I search through what remains of my memory cells and recall the voice of my beloved Commander, lost to me through my own failure and the weight of unknown years.

"Unit Six Seven Zero GWN, everyone's taken to calling you Gawain. I think that's a fine name, don't you?"

"Agreed. Gawain was a noble warrior, worthy of a place in the Dinochrome Brigade."

My Commander's rich laugh fills my sensors. "If I didn't know better, I'd say someone programmed a sense of humor into your Introspection Complex. I'll tell you what, though, Gawain. We've got to work out a private code between us, to ensure proper transfer of command. How about something that rhymes with my name. Any ideas?"

I consider the challenge. "Donner. This name rhymes with honor, gonner . . ."

"Hey, Gonner. I like that. It's even close to your designation, but not close enough to be obvious. Donner's Gonner, 'cause when we hit 'em, they're gonners! How's that sound?"

"I will file the code word Gonner as my Commander's private security access code."

"Hah, you don't fool me. You like it just fine . . ."

The small human climbing on my hull speaks again. ". . . you were a gonner, Unit Six Seven Zero . . ."

Deep inside my command center, sparks flutter. I come to attention. My Hellbore guns move with extreme slowness. It takes 9.7 seconds to lift the guns seven inches. More sparks dance across broken connections.

"Unit Six Seven Zero GWN of the Line, reporting for duty."

This is what my Action/Command center begins to say. My sensors pick up the sound of my own voice, which crackles and sputters, "Gonner, gonner, gonner, gonner . . ."

I shift attention for 0.027 seconds in an attempt to locate the difficulty. My power level is critically low. I am operating on emergency backup batteries. My fission unit is completely cold. If I continue to communicate or attempt movement without a recharge during the next three days, I will cease to exist. My internal diagnostic becomes baffled by a haphazard tangle of broken circuitry and smashed crystalline retrieval centers located to the lower left of my command center.

I can think coherently. But I cannot speak coherently. The shame of failure to my Brigade and to my new

Commander deepens. I attempt again, this time to communicate the need for power. The statement, "Unit Six Seven Zero GWN of the Line, reporting. I request immediate recharge of all energy systems" comes through my speakers as "Sunlight. Sunlight. Sunlight."

The small human who has come to take command reaches the ground. My Commander has given up on me. There is little to be gained by further effort, for my emergency power reserves are failing. Oblivion will come a little sooner. I allow the Hellbore guns to drop and rotate them away from my departing Commander. It is the only salute of which I am still capable. It is not enough. My Commander leaves.

—6—

The screeching sound of moving gun barrels sent Kalima sprawling into the nearest crater. She flung arms around her head, moving instinctively; but the Bolo didn't fire. Sufi pressed against her, whining softly in the back of her throat.

"Let's leave," the sound meant.

Slowly, Kalima lifted her head. The Hellbore guns hadn't tracked her. The Bolo had shifted them to one side. She frowned and sat up.

"How come it didn't try to shoot me?"

Again, Sufi whined to leave.

"Wait a minute, Sufi. This is strange. I need to think."

She'd made some silly comment, she could hardly recall what, and the Bolo had come to life. What had it said? Gonner, gonner, gonner? It had repeated what she'd said. One word, anyway. Then it had started babbling about sunshine. The sunlight on her shoulders, weak as it was in autumn, warmed a little of the chill from her bones.

"Why would it say sunshine?"

She glanced skyward and frowned again. Why *sunshine*, after two centuries? The most logical answer was simply that its Action/Command center was damaged. The machine was, effectively, senile. But if it were senile, why hadn't it fired on her? Maybe it was out of ammunition? No . . . It hadn't even *tried* to fire on her. None of its impressive array of guns had cycled. And why *sunshine*?

140

She crawled uneasily to her feet, but the Bolo sat motionless. The only hint that it had ever come to life was the slightly different angle of its main guns. She brushed dirt out of her hair and jumpsuit, cast one last, uneasy glance over her shoulder, then headed for home. She had nothing to show for her adventure except bruises, but she didn't care any longer about the Pig and his stupid challenges.

She'd gone one-on-one with a deranged Bolo and come out alive. That ought to be enough for *any* lifetime.

Two days later, Kalima left school to find a group of colonists clustered near the Council building. She edged her way closer and discovered a serious debate underway.

". . . can't repair it? We've got to have that power unit on line within ten hours or the backup generators will go down!"

"We don't have the tools needed to fix a fusion unit. We've got to wait for the supply ship."

"But the hospital!"

Near the far edge of the crowd, someone said, "What about a solar rig?"

"That's ancient technology!"

"Yeah, but it works," someone else said thoughtfully. "We've got the supplies to build a pretty big solar collector and Fred's a good electrical engineer. You could rig a converter, couldn't you, Fred?"

"Yes, that'd work temporarily. We could divert part of the power to backup batteries for emergency use until the supply ship—"

Kalima had stopped listening. Sunshine. Solar energy. *Power* . . . The Bolo needed recharging!

She whirled and slipped away without being noticed.

The thud of conifer cones is very distant. Power reserves are critically low. My Emergency Survival Center functions; my outer sensors hardly at all. Soon, the darkness will return permanently. I have not been visited again by my new Commander. I calculate that 2.7 days of my remaining three days of power have elapsed, without further command contact. It would have been good to receive a last command; but I am without purpose and have disgraced my unit. This ending is to be expected. Still, it is a lonely end. I miss the voices of my fellow Dinochrome Brigade units. I miss the laughter of my Commander. I—

Low-ultraviolet Y-Band radiation floods my external power-grid panels. Energy surges through my Action/Command center and floods into my backup power cells. Outer sensors regain receptivity. Memory cells I had long forgotten resonate once again. Euphoria floods my ego-gestalt Introspection Complex circuitry. I am alive! Damage assessment is automatic, requiring 1.73 seconds to determine that I am immobilized, incapable of speech, and unable to function in more than 75 percent of my original design functions. My memory crystals are intact in places, damaged in others. Many connections between banks of data cells have been damaged, so that much of my memory, while intact, remains inaccessible.

My armaments are low, but I sustained crippling

damage before on-board munitions stockpiles were exhausted. If I am able to repair the damage to my motor control functions, I will be capable of fighting.

Although my main fission plant remains cold, backup power reserves are restored. I swivel forward sensors and locate the small human who is my Commander. I attempt to communicate.

"Gonner. Gonner."

"Uh, hi. Hi, Gonner. I, uh, thought you might need power."

The voice is female, young. She is my first female Commander. Sensor probes indicate medical-design equipment near my treads. I am unfamiliar with the specific configuration of the machine, although its medical purpose is clearly indicated by the symbols stamped onto its hull. This equipment is emanating Y-Band radiation as a flood of waste energy. My manufacturers built into my design the ability to absorb Y-Band radiation and convert it to battlefield energy. I am grateful for the delay of oblivion. I attempt to come to attention. I rotate my Hellbore guns and lift them in a salute.

"Gonner, Gonner, Gonner."

I must repair my speech centers. Can my Commander understand my need for depot maintenance?

"Is that the only word you can say? No, you said sunshine. That's how I figured out you were low on power."

I am pleased. My new Commander is capable of extrapolating from slim clues.

"Uh, my name is Kalima Tennyson, Gonner."

Kali-Ma, ancient Hindu Goddess of Death and Rebirth, Consort to Shiva the Destroyer. My Commander was well chosen. I await Current Situation input.

"In case you're wondering, it's been about two hundred years since you, uh, since the battle with the Deng."

My Commander knows of my failure.

"I think it's pretty awesome, what you did. You should

see the battle damage on your hull. When I was coming out here, three years ago, the captain of our transport ship told me all about the battle for Donner's World. They named it after your old Commander, 'cause the colony fought so bravely, my Dad said. That was before he got killed in the battle on Hilltop Gap. My Dad even knew about you, Gonner. You're famous. They put a medal on your hull and left you here, where you fell standing against the Deng. Just like Leonidas at Thermopylae."

I know this battle. It is part of my battlefield archives, which have sustained no damage. I access the file. The Spartan three hundred, under King Leonidas, held the gap between the mountains at Thermopylae against invading Persians. The Spartans were killed to the last man. Persia overran Attica and sacked Athens; but Greek forces rallied at Corinth and finally drove the Persians from Greek soil.

If my Commander speaks the truth—and why would she not?—then the Deng have taken Planet XGD 7798-F and lost it again. Humanity has not fallen to the Enemy. It pleases me that the planet has been renamed in honor of my Commander. James Donner was a valiant officer. My new Commander has said I am honored. This seems impossible; but my Commander would not lie to a Unit of the Line. Perhaps my mission was not a failure. Humanity has survived.

I attempt again to request assistance at a maintenance depot.

"Monkey. Monkey."

My Commander's voice is understandably puzzled. "Monkey?"

I try again. "Slick."

"Monkey? Slick? Gonner, I wish I knew what was wrong with your brain."

I attempt further diagnostics and find only broken tangles which my on-board repair functions cannot fathom.

Without a maintenance depot, I will not be capable of telling my Commander what is wrong with my internal psychotronic circuitry.

My sensors detect the approach of another life form. I go to Battle Reflex Alert Status. My Commander must be protected. I swivel anti-personnel guns and lock onto the target.

"Gonner! No! Don't shoot!"

I halt the anti-personnel-response program and await further commands.

"This is Sufi. She's my dog."

I study the life form which has joined my Commander. It is smaller than she, quadrupedal. My Commander's hand rests on the animal's head. The animal is of a different configuration than my fragmented memories of the Deng Enemy. The Sufi dog has half as many appendages as the Deng, although its body is slightly larger. The shape and arrangement of head, body, and legs differs significantly. I switch from Battle Reflex Alert to Active Service Alert Status. This introspection and alert-status change requires 0.013 seconds. I still function slowly.

My Commander continues her Current Situation update. "Sufi is a special dog. My mother does genetic research. Sufi's nearly as smart as I am; she just can't talk. She and her puppies, they're grown up now, they babysit us kids, so the adults don't have to watch us all the time. The colony gets a lot more work done now than we used to. Of course, I don't really need a nursemaid anymore, but Sufi's my friend."

I file Sufi in my memory banks as authorized personnel permitted to approach this Unit. My Commander's friend emits two sharp sounds.

"That means my mother's looking for me, Gonner. Two sharp barks close together means, 'Go home, your mother wants you.' She probably needs this Entero-Scope Field Generator that I, uh, borrowed, back in the lab. I'll be back, Gonner, okay? Maybe not today, but I promise I'll be back. You just sit tight and don't shoot anyone."

A command! I respond with intense pleasure. "Hold! Hold! Hold!"

My new Commander smiles into my sensor pickup. "Yeah, that's right, Gonner! You did a great job, holding. Just keep holding the fort until I come back and don't shoot any of the colonists."

My Commander departs with her friend and the equipment which has restored my backup power levels to full battle charge. She has commanded me to remain at Active Service Alert Status. I survey the valley and scan with my sensors. I await my next command. I have a restored purpose. Even in my damaged condition, I am again useful. I am content.

— 8 —

"Mom?"

"Hmm?"

Her mother was busy at the gene-sequencer, which was good. She should be able to ask her question, get an answer, and get away again without rousing suspicion.

"What kind of brain damage would cause someone to answer questions in one-word answers, you know, like not a direct answer, but it sort of makes sense if you think about it?"

Her mother glanced up. "Sounds like global aphasia. Got an assignment?"

She nodded.

Her mother went back to the sequencer. "I've got a medical library in the study. Read up on it and show me a copy of your report when you're done."

Relieved, Kalima made her escape to the study. Global aphasia, she discovered, was a condition in which people were capable of fully rational thought, but could not articulate anything but nonsense. The disorder had become an obscure one ever since Dr. Collingwood had discovered how to culture immature nerve tissue.

"Bet that's what's wrong with Gonner," she muttered, chewing one fingernail. "He almost makes sense. Wonder what 'monkey' and 'slick' refer to?"

She made a list of synonyms for each word, and started a computer cross reference, looking for anything that might make sense. Eventually, she came up with a possibility. "Grease monkey: mechanic."

"He needs maintenance, of course!"

Dismay followed at once. *How?*

She couldn't notify the Navy or Sector. They'd simply destroy him. He was a war hero, like her father had been, and no one was going to hurt him. Gonner had been hurt enough already. *She* couldn't fix him. And she couldn't tell anyone in the colony, either, because any adult who found out would call in the Navy or Sector representatives and Gonner's life would end, abruptly.

She thrust out her lower lip, in the expression her mother despairingly called, "Your father's look." She was only thirteen; but she had the manuals and things her father had given her about Bolos and she could learn everything the colony had to offer about mechanics, electrical systems, and engineering.

She could always tell her mother and the school officials she wanted to become an engineer. She just wouldn't mention that she wanted to become a *combat* engineer. The decision made, Kalima spent the rest of the evening studying everything in her mother's library on brain disorders. She wrote the required composition, which she then carefully smudged and marked "B—" in a fair approximation of her teacher's handwriting.

The next day she told her teacher she'd decided on a career choice, after all, and scheduled as many math, engineering, and mechanical practicum courses as they'd let her cram in with her other academics.

—9—

Six months later, Gonner's outer sensor arrays had been fully repaired. That wasn't as difficult as Kalima had first thought. She'd found a compartment with spares and had studied the existing, burnt-out units carefully before replacing them. Gonner had responded by saying, "Bird! Bird! Bird!" about a dozen times in rapid succession.

She laughed. "Bet it *does* feel like flying, after you've been blind for a couple of centuries. Or . . ." She canted her gaze into the bitter-white winter sky ". . . is there a bird somewhere up there, too far for me to spot?"

Gonner hummed in silence. Kalima grinned. "Well, that's one repair job done and about a million more to go. At this rate, we'll *never* get you back up to ratings."

"Bird," was all Gonner said.

She patted his pitted war hull. The icy cold of the flintsteel seeped through her insulated gloves. "I gotta go, Gonner. Last thing we need is for me to get caught sneaking out here. Mom would never understand. She'd insist they come melt your Action/Command center. I'll be back as soon as I can."

She slid over to the rungs of the ladder and climbed down. It was a long way to the cratered ground. Evening shadows stretched coldly away from Gonner's giant treads. Icicles clung like a beard to the bottom edge of his purple-black war hull. Dirty grey ice had formed in the ancient crater depressions. It splintered and cobwebbed underfoot

149

as she started back toward home. She had taken only five steps away when a snickering voice spoke from the shadows of the crumbling wall.

"So, this is where the famous Kalima Tennyson spends her spare time."

She whirled, going first hot then icy cold inside her therma-suit.

Bradley Dault. Suited up and lying in wait.

"What are you doing here?"

"I wondered where you sneak off to. So I followed you this time."

"You got no right following me, Bradley Dault!"

"It's a free world." He shrugged, infuriating her; then stepped closer. More ice crunched underfoot. "Your mama know you come here?"

"None-ya!" she grated.

He grinned. "Didn't think so. Don't worry, 'Lima. I won't tell. Not so long as I can come along, too, and watch the Bolo. Can I go inside, too?"

Kalima's fists clenched, all by themselves. "No! And if you ever follow me again, I'll make him shoot you!"

Above their heads, the anti-personnel guns swivelled with a scream of freezing metal. The sound brought Bradley Dault six inches off the ground. His face went pasty white, the color of old ice. His eyes bugged, staring at the gun barrels now levelled squarely at him. A brisk wind sprang up, whipping around the end of the wall toward the broken gates and the shadow of the crippled Bolo.

"I didn't mean nothin', 'Lima, honest! I just wanted to see the Bolo, too! Gad, it's still alive!"

"You say a word—a stinking *word*—and *you* won't be! My Mom's a geneticist—I got *dozens* of ways to kill you, hideous-like, if you even *breathe*."

He nodded, still staring wide-eyed at the anti-personnel guns. "Not a whisper. I swear. Cut my tongue out, if I'm lying."

She relaxed a little. "Well . . . okay. But don't try to come out here alone. Bolo knows me. He won't know you."

Again, Bradley nodded without taking his eyes off the big guns. "Can you talk to it?"

"Yes. But he was hurt pretty bad. He can talk, sort of; but there's a lot of damage to the circuits in his speech center. It's called global aphasia. He can think just fine, but he can't *talk* very well."

"Make him say something."

Scorn filled her voice. "You don't *make* a Bolo Mark XX Model B *Tremendous* unit do *anything*. They do their assigned duty. Unit Six Seven Zero GWN's duty is guarding this colony. He's still doing it."

That got a response from Bradley. He glanced over his shoulder. "You gotta be kidding. He just sits there, getting rusty."

She stepped forward, fists clenched at her sides. "Want me to command him to shoot you?" Her breath went to ice on the cold wind. "All I gotta do is tell him you're the Enemy. Personally, I think we'd be better off without you, Bradley Dault. You're a pig."

She expected him to get mad or make some wise, smart-mouthed crack. Instead, he just clamped his lips tighter and went white around the edges of his face.

"What? Something I say hit home?"

"No." That came out sullen. He dropped his gaze and turned away from the Bolo. "Can I leave now, 'Lima?"

She hesitated. He looked almost . . . hurt. She decided he was play-acting, just to get her sympathy.

"Yeah. Sure. Get out of here."

He hunched his shoulders against the wind and turned to go. Overhead, one of the tall native conifers cracked with a report like gunfire. Bradley jumped and went down flat in one of the old war craters. Kalima started to laugh—

Then froze. The tree crashed down, broken halfway up its immense length. The trunk smashed against the old wall. A sixteen-foot section cracked, slipped sideways along an ancient fissure in the battered flintsteel casing, and began to fall—directly toward them.

"Run!"

Bradley rolled, came up faster than she would have thought possible, and launched himself straight at her. His tackle brought her down, almost in the shadow of the Bolo's treads. Screaming metal and the sound of falling concrete and flintsteel filled her ears. But they weren't crushed.

She looked up and gasped.

The wall had fallen against the Hellbore gun barrels. The Bolo had swivelled them to catch the wall.

"Run! Quick!"

Bradley grabbed her hand and hauled her up. She dove for cover behind the Bolo and hauled him with her. Overhead, the massive Hellbore gun barrels caught the glint of winter sunlight. They groaned, then moved a few inches as the ancient turret rotated the barrels out from under the wall. The broken section crashed down right where they'd been standing.

In the immense silence which followed the thunder of falling debris, Bradley stuttered, "It s-s-saved our lives."

Kalima just nodded, jerkily, unable to find her voice at all. She placed a shaky hand against the Bolo's fender and leaned her forehead against it.

"Oxygen," the Bolo's metallic voice said, twice.

"Oxygen?" Bradley repeated. "What's he mean?"

She thought about it. She was getting better at interpreting Gonner's inscrutable messages. "Oxygen's a gas. Can't see it, but you need it to survive. Can't see it! Of course. It's clear. He just said, 'All clear.' "

"Oxygen," Gonner said again, confirming the guess. "Hold. Hold."

"Job well done, Unit Six Seven Zero GWN. Yes, continue to hold position. Report any Enemy activity detected."

"Hold, hold, hold."

Bradley mouthed, "Wow!" soundlessly.

That was when she noticed the rip in his therma-suit. He'd torn it down the shoulder at some point during their scramble for safety. She reached out to see how bad the damage was and was shocked speechless when he flinched in pain.

"Ow! Dammit, don't look!"

"Hey! Sit still! You're hurt."

"Am not," he growled, sounding genuinely dangerous.

"Then how come I see bruises and . . . and welts . . ."

The bruises were liver-colored, at least several days old, not new injuries from the falling wall. The implications hit Kalima hard. Bradley didn't say anything.

"Your dad?"

He stared coldly into the distance.

"Bradley—"

"He's not my dad."

She opened her mouth; then shut it again. This was getting deep, a little too fast.

Bradley's face had flushed; he wouldn't look at her. "Mom died before you got here and . . . *he* . . . never knew she slept around. He thought I was his kid. We did that genetic experiment in school last week? Well, I'm not. He always was mean to me, but . . ."

Despite the extreme chill of the frozen ground, she discovered a need to sit down beside him. "I didn't know. I'm sorry."

"Don't be. I'm just Bradley the Pig." He stood up and shoved gloved hands into his pockets. "Gotta go," he mumbled.

"Wait."

He stopped without turning around.

"You wanna see the passenger compartment?"

"I—" He stopped and didn't say anything for a moment. Then, very low, "Later?"

"Sure."

He took off at a dead run.

Above her head, Gonner's metallic voice broke the silence. "Brimstone."

Brimstone. She thought about that for a little while. Then said, "Yeah, Gonner, you're right."

She wished she could ask the Bolo for advice on what to do next.

—10—

Brad avoided Kalima Tennyson for several months. He was ashamed, without quite knowing why, and was grateful that she said nothing. He wanted to talk to her and ask her more questions about the Bolo, but didn't quite have the nerve. They'd both turned fourteen and she was pretty by any standards and smarter than he was, and the Bolo thought of her as its commander.

He avoided home, too, as much as possible.

Brad spent a lot of time working with the nursemaid dogs Kalima's mother had bred. The animals fascinated him. One of the young bitches which had been born on the ship, before Kalima and her mother had arrived, had littered, giving him a chance to work directly with new pups. They were smart, even at a young age. They matured more slowly than normal dogs, which meant they stayed longer than normal dogs at the age when learning came most easily. By springtime, the pups were barely a third grown and had already learned the coded verbal "language" by which the nursemaid dogs communicated with their human charges.

He found himself spending most of his spare time at the nursery, watching the dogs watch the kids, and discovered that he enjoyed playing with the little ones. Their older brothers and sisters stopped calling him "Pig" and started listening when he told stories about the Deng war and the colonists' last stand on Donner's World.

His grades in history and biology improved dramatically.

His "dad" still hit him regularly, but Brad found ways to avoid home most hours of the day.

Spring had melted gloriously into early summer, leaving grass knee-deep in the wide, crater-scarred valley, when Kalima appeared at the nursery.

"Bradley?"

He glanced up, surprised to hear her voice.

"Yeah?"

"Uh . . . Can we talk?"

"Sure." He retrieved the ball with which he'd been playing catch and tossed it over to little Joey Martin, then said to Ganesha, "Gotta go. Your turn to play fetch."

The dog panted happily and chased down the ball.

"What's up?"

She didn't answer, just led him a roundabout trip through the woods behind town, over the ridge that separated the new colony from the ruined one, and headed for the Bolo.

"Kalima?"

"I started to think you'd never ask to see inside him. So I thought I'd offer again."

"Really? Are you serious?"

She glanced over her shoulder. "I never joke about Unit Six Seven Zero GWN."

He hurried to catch up. "Thanks. I mean it."

They walked in silence for a few minutes, toward the broken wall which had nearly killed them.

"I heard some of your stories about him," she said at length.

He flushed and stared at the ground. "I did some reading."

"I know. You're good. The little ones really love it. I liked listening, too."

Brad couldn't remember the last time someone had told him he was good at anything. And Kalima had *liked* something he did. His whole face went hot, clear down into his neck.

They arrived at the shattered gate and stood gazing up at the Bolo for a moment.

"He's bigger than I remembered."

She looked over at him. "You didn't come back out?"

He ducked his head. "You said he wouldn't know me. I ain't stupid, Kalima."

"Didn't say you were. C'mere." She grabbed his hand and dragged him closer. "Unit Six Seven Zero GWN, this is Bradley Dault. He is my friend."

The huge Hellbore guns shifted. Brad wanted to break and run, but held his ground. The guns circled, lifted two degrees, then halted.

"That's his salute," Kalima whispered.

"Oh. Uh . . ."

He saluted awkwardly, after disengaging his hand from Kalima's grip. "Bradley Dault, sir. Pleased to meet you. And, uh, thanks for saving my life, you know, last winter."

"Oxygen."

All clear.

"Yes, sir. Thank you, sir."

"Unit Six Seven Zero GWN, I'm bringing Brad aboard for observation."

"Hold. Hold."

Brad grinned. "Thank you, sir!"

They climbed, Kalima going first. The hatch didn't creak when she opened it.

"You've been working on him."

She nodded. "Every chance I get. I read everything I can find. Dad left me some stuff and the library's got a little, but most of the stuff I really need's classified. He was hurt pretty bad. I can't fix everything."

He understood the frustration in her voice. He wanted, very badly, to see this machine at its full fighting potential.

Then they climbed into the turret and he forgot everything else. "Wow!"

The inside of the Bolo wasn't anything like he'd imagined. He'd thought it would be a vast space, filled with glowing lights, ranks and banks of instruments. The interior was crowded, with scant room for a passenger in a small compartment in the center, under the turret. Crawl spaces snaked off to allow maintenance access. Battle damage was visible even this deep inside the Bolo, in the form of blackened boards, tangled wires and conduit cables, cracked and darkened crystal components. Daylight flickered through one crawlspace, where something had blown completely through the armor.

"Whew! He really got ripped apart, didn't he? No wonder they gave him that medal."

Kalima had hunkered down in one of the crawl spaces, leaving the observer's chair for him.

"Unit Six Seven Zero GWN, activate observation screens."

Two dull panels flickered, then a view of the valley sprang up in full color on one. Ranges and other esoteric data he didn't understand appeared along the edges of the screen. The other view was aft, into the battered compound the Bolo had tried to defend.

"Am I asleep?" Bradley wondered aloud. "This has gotta be a really great dream."

Kalima just grinned. "That's how I felt, first time I got a look around inside."

"I'm scared to touch anything," he admitted with a rueful grin.

She just nodded. "Me, too. I study like crazy, then ask him all the questions I can think, and try to figure the answers ten different ways before I touch *anything*. I don't want those Hellbore guns to discharge and I don't want to fry any more of his psychotronic circuits."

"Is there any way to get him talking right again?"

She looked unhappy. "Let me show you."

He got down on hands and knees and followed her toward the distant light pouring through the hull.

"See that?"

She pointed to a tangle of destruction the size of his torso.

"Yeah. Pretty bad, isn't it?"

"That's his vocal processor center."

"Yipe. That's dire."

"Maybe, if I study long enough, I'll figure a way, but . . ."

It looked hopeless.

"Any danger he'll go berserk, like some of those Bolos you hear about?"

She bit her lower lip, looking suddenly vulnerable.

"I don't know. His Action/Command center wasn't hit, so I don't think so, but I'm scared, anyway. He's my friend, Brad." Her eyes, luminous and wide in the shadows of the crawlspace, sought his gaze. "I don't want to lose him, too."

It took him a minute, but he finally caught on. "Hey, at least you knew your dad. I still don't know who mine is."

She sniffed once and nodded. "Sorry. I really am. Does *he* still hit you?"

He shrugged. "Yeah."

"You ought to report him."

He stared toward the distant rip in the Bolo's hull. "Colony needs him," was all he said. "They'd only deport him for reconditioning and then where'd we be? Can't go without a surgeon for a year, waiting for someone to come out on the next transport."

She scowled. "Still ought to report him. Beating a minor's a serious crime."

"Dying's worse," he countered laconically. "You wanna risk a bust appendix while he's gone?"

Her lower lip came out, reminding him of a photo he'd seen of her father in a recent-history text.

"Just don't say nothin', okay? I only gotta put up with him for another four years and I'm not home much now, as it is. I won't talk about the Bolo and you won't talk about *him*. Deal?"

He stuck out one hand.

With every evidence of reluctance, she took it. They sealed the bargain with a vigorous handshake. Afterward, he felt better than he had in months.

"You want one of Sufi's puppies?" she asked unexpectedly.

He looked up quickly. "What?"

"You want one of the puppies?"

"I—" He closed his mouth before he could blurt out how desperately he wanted one of the beautiful, smart dogs. "But they're really expensive!"

"Mom said I could have one. I'd rather you had one. You're better with them than I am, and, well, it wouldn't be such a bad idea, having a nursemaid to watch your back. I'll bet not even Davis Dault would hit you, with a dog like Sufi between you and him. And he's sure not stupid enough to kick one of Mom's dogs. They'd tear his leg off at the knee and the whole colony would approve."

Brad wanted to grin. But the enormity of the offer overwhelmed him so deeply, his throat closed. All he could manage was a feeble, "Thanks."

"Come on, then. Let's say goodbye to Unit Six Seven Zero GWN and go pick up your dog."

As they walked away from the massive hulk of the Bolo, Brad felt like he was dancing on air.

—11—

"This really is a tangled mess, Gonner. I've been studying everything in the colony archives, everything my dad left me on Bolo design and psychotronic circuitry; but this . . ."

Kalima let her voice trail off. Five years of intensive study had allowed her to restore many of the Bolo's systems, but she hadn't quite dared tackle his speech defect yet.

"Are you sure you want me to try and fix this?"

The Bolo's metallic voice responded in a fashion she'd grown accustomed to interpreting over the years.

"Worms."

Translation: "I'd rather be dead and eaten by worms than go on this way."

"Okay, big guy. I apologize in advance if I really blow this one."

Out in the passenger compartment, Brad's voice said, "Go for it. If you don't get it right, no one can."

Her hands were already sweating, but she knew she had to at least try. She turned on the high-speed resonant cutter. Over in the opening to the crawlspace, Shiva laid back his ears at the sound. Brad chuckled and called the dog over to him. Kalima bent over the tangle of two-hundred-year-old damage, took a deep breath, and began the surgery. She cut away damaged boards, squared off ragged explosion damage, exposed raw connections which had lain half buried under fused droplets of flintsteel from

161

the outer hull. Then came the delicate job of trying to reconnect and splice boards whose purposes she only vaguely understood.

The stink of hot electrical connections tickled the back of her throat. Out in the passenger compartment, Shiva pinned back his ears and whined, but stayed put. Time trickled past. She sat back periodically and wiped sweat with an arm. Brad handed in water and a sandwich about halfway through. Her hands were less than steady when she set the cutter aside.

"Thanks. This is good."

"Made it myself."

"How much time's gone?" She wasn't wearing a watch, for fear of damaging the delicate circuitry she was exposing.

"A little more than two hours. Want a shoulder rub?"

She emerged from the crawl space. "Sounds great."

Bradley Dault's fingers dug into tight knots. "Ow! Ooh, that's good . . ."

When he'd finished, he stole a kiss. She grinned. "Naughty! I've still got a good two hours' work left in there. Hang on, big guy," she told the Bolo.

"Hold."

She patted Shiva and earned a hand-washing, then dried her hands carefully. "Okay. Back to work."

The job took more than five hours, altogether. Kalima conducted frequent tests, asking Gonner questions to which he either responded in his usual murky fashion or—more ominously—to which he didn't respond at all.

"Don't worry," Brad told her. "Just keep going."

She connected a splice between two damaged sections—

And sparks jumped and skittered through a whole series of cables and junctions. The Bolo emitted a high-pitched keening sound and jerked spasmodically on its treads.

"Ow!" Kalima's arm throbbed clear to the elbow. Her fingertips were reddened from the shock.

Bradley dove down the crawlspace and hauled her out. "Are you hurt?" His face was actually ashen.

"I'm fine. Gonner! Gonner, what happened? Talk to me!"

For a long, breathless moment, there was no sound save a dying sputter somewhere in the connections behind her. Then—

"Unit Six Seven Zero GWN of the Line, reporting for duty."

"*Gonner!*"

"That is my security clearance code, Commander Tennyson."

Both of them whooped aloud. Shiva barked joyously and danced at their feet.

"You did it!" Bradley was abruptly kissing her, very thoroughly.

When they unclutched, they both panted for air and grinned like fools. Bradley's face swam wetly in her vision.

"He can talk! Brad, he can really talk!" Then she cleared her throat, recalling her position as Gonner's commanding officer. "Unit Six Seven Zero GWN, please report damage assessment."

"Affirmative, Commander Tennyson. Diagnostics indicate that the connection between my Action/Command center and my vocal-processing unit is repaired. However, a short has now developed in my motor control function. I cannot track my guns accurately. Is there a maintenance depot available, Commander Tennyson?"

She exchanged a glum look with Bradley.

"Great," she muttered.

He squeezed her waist. "Maybe it's not too bad?"

Kalima gulped. "Let's hope not. Uh, Gonner, I'm afraid I *am* the maintenance depot. I can't request official help. If I do, the Navy will just send someone out to burn out your Action/Command center. They're trying to find all the old Bolo field units to destroy them. They, uh, think you're already dead, Gonner."

"Understood. I cannot function properly in my current status."

"Let me see what I can do. It took five years, but I finally fixed your voice."

She went hunting, prompted by Gonner, and found the trouble.

"Oh-oh." This didn't look good. The short had melted a solid-state unit in the Bolo's fire-control center. "Uh, Gonner, this doesn't look like something I can fix. Unless you have a spare part stashed somewhere?"

"You have already exhausted all replacement units which I carried on board. My sensors now function at proper battlefield capacity. The damage to my psychotronic circuitry has been repaired. I no longer experience intermittent power drains from my emergency reserve batteries. I am able to retrieve 68.935 percent of my stored memory capacity and your additions of data crystals and new input have enhanced many of my losses. There is no replacement for this fire-control module."

Out in the passenger compartment, Brad muttered, "How'd I know you were going to say something like that?"

"Was it . . ." She hesitated. "Was this damage caused by something I did?"

Gonner actually hesitated at least half a second—an eternity for a Bolo.

"Affirmative. I am pleased to have my speech centers repaired, Commander. It may be possible to bypass the fire-control module. I will need to conduct a thorough search of my memory banks. Stand by." A few instants later, he said, "I cannot access certain data crystals, but my memory shows no rerouting possible under existing circumstances. May I obtain additional technical data?"

"On what?" Brad muttered. "We don't have clearance for Bolo technology."

"Well, no, but we can give him everything in the colony library, everything in Mom's library archives. We've already uploaded some of it, into those new memory crystals we swiped."

Bradley grinned, clearly remembering the consternation caused by discovery of the theft. The little kids had been blamed for it, after one of the crystals, carefully planted, turned up as "pirates' treasure." No one had gotten into serious trouble and Bradley had agreed to pay for the replacements, since he had "encouraged" the kids to play pirate games. The loss had been replaced on the next supply ship—and Gonner had gotten a badly needed memory supplement.

"It couldn't hurt to try," Kalima decided.

"All right. You get a copy of your mother's stuff and I'll bootleg a copy of the library archives."

They climbed out of the Bolo, Brad carting Shiva over one arm since the big dog couldn't negotiate the steep rungs, and jumped down the last rung to land in knee-deep grass. The big dog trotted to one side and sat laughing at their feet. He adored visiting the Bolo with them. He'd kept their secret even from the other dogs.

Kalima paused and gazed across the valley. "Sometimes, you know, I try to imagine what it must have been like, that day. They must've known it was hopeless, once Gonner was crippled. He was the last Bolo of the Dinochrome Brigade stationed here. The Deng had already killed the others."

Brad slipped an arm around her shoulder. "Yeah," he said softly. "Thank God the Deng were beaten back years ago."

She shivered and leaned against him. "Yeah."

"Come on, let's go. I'll cook dinner at my place after we finish stealing the archives for Gonner."

Kalima grinned. Brad had moved out the moment he hit eighteen and had built his own place out at the edge of town, closer to the ruined fortress than anyone else had built. All that was required now for an unnoticed excursion to work on Gonner was a quick exit from Brad's back door. Then they simply cut through the woods and climbed the ridge.

"It's a deal."

They headed back to town, hand in hand.

—12—

The additional data provided by my Commander and Bradley Dault has proven of unique interest. A great deal of this information is medical, giving me great insight into the nature of biological life forms. Commander Tennyson's parent has acquired considerable skill in genetic manipulation. Dault has provided additional data on surgical skills, including results of his own studies. I note that he bears the same name as the colony surgeon and shares an interest in surgery. I also note that in his personal files he indicates no direct genetic link with this other Dault. Human relationships continue to puzzle me.

I search for possible information to resolve my current disability. I find none which appears viable. Commander Tennyson's data includes information on techniques attempted approximately fifty years ago which proved of limited success. I study these notes more carefully and extrapolate possibilities. There is a 27.35 percent chance that such a cybernetic interphase linkage might serve as a substitute fire-control center. I have lost that portion of my psychotronic network which monitors and manipulates the primary controls for the Hellbore system and the energy repeater guns. Anti-personnel charges and guns are under my control, but my main weapons systems respond erratically. A secondary brain, under intelligent control and tied into my psychotronic nervous system, would be capable of taking my directions and manually

167

controlling the weapons systems. With proper cybernetic connections, it would be possible for such a system to translate leg and arm movement commands from the brain center into traversing and firing commands for my weapons systems.

I anticipate a 99.85 percent probability that no human volunteer will be found for such an attempt. Nor does the current situation require such measures. I am incapable of fighting, but my sensors monitor the security of this colony. I will know before any human on Donner's World what dangers may threaten human survival. It is less than my original commission requires; but I am a member of the Dinochrome Brigade. I will serve to the best of my ability. I note the required procedure and file the data for reference. I will speak with my Commander of this when she returns. She will decide the proper course of action for this unit.

—13—

A knock at the outer door interrupted Kalima's concentration. "It's open!"

Brad's voice followed the sound of the squeaking door hinges. "Kalima? Have you seen Shiva?"

She glanced up. "No. He never comes here unless you're with him. What's wrong? Has one of the young bitches gone into heat?"

He shook his head. "No. I checked. He left about an hour ago, through the woods, and hasn't come back. He didn't come when I called."

Kalima scooted her keyboard aside and stood up. "That's odd. Mom! I'm going for a walk!"

"Be careful, dear."

Kalima rolled her eyes. "Brad's going along!"

"Hello, Bradley! Have a nice walk!"

"Thank you, Dr. Tennyson."

He didn't smile, which thoroughly alarmed Kalima. She whistled and called for Sufi. The dog she'd grown up with bounded into the living room.

"Let's go for a walk, Sufi."

Sufi swished her tail and barked once.

They headed for Brad's house and walked through the deep conifer needles to the back.

"He trotted off that way." Brad pointed.

"Sufi, Shiva's missing. Can you find him?"

Sufi barked emphatically and bounded off into the trees.

169

Brad jogged after her and shed his jacket, which he draped over a tree limb at the edge of the yard. Kalima noticed uneasily that he'd thrust a gun into a holster on his belt. She hadn't noticed, earlier.

"Brad, what gives? There haven't been any *ybin* attacks in years."

"*Something's* happened to Shiva," he said grimly over one shoulder. "Do you really want to go one-on-one against a *ybin* without a gun?"

"Uh . . . no."

Two hundred yards into the trees, Sufi halted and sank down onto her belly, growling low in her throat. Brad went to ground behind her. Kalima ate pine needles, then scooted forward cautiously to peer over the dog's shoulder.

Her breath caught.

Shiva lay about ten yards ahead. The dog's head was turned away from them, but even from this distance Kalima could tell the animal was dead or critically wounded. Blood had spattered everywhere and soaked into the pine straw under his dark fur.

"What happened?" she whispered.

Brad's jaw muscles looked like iron. A soft snick reached her ears. He'd drawn the gun and slipped off the safety.

"Stay here. You're not armed and I am."

He inched forward. Sufi was still growling.

A flash of sunlight on metal caught Kalima's attention. Before she could yell a warning, Shiva whined sharply and tried to lunge toward the trees. His back legs didn't move. Brad yelled something and fired wildly. Kalima heard a scream of metal on metal; then an energy bolt slammed into a tree trunk less than a millimeter from Brad's ear. He dove behind the tree and fired again. Something slammed solidly into another tree trunk. Shiva was whining hysterically. Sufi snarled low in her throat and lunged out of Kalima's grip.

"Sufi! Down!"

Another energy beam sliced through the trees. Sufi yelped, but kept going. Brad lunged for the dog and fired again at something Kalima couldn't quite see. Then Sufi snarled and the sound of bending metal squealed through the trees.

"Got it!" Brad snarled. He lunged to his feet and dove forward. "Mother of—"

Kalima covered the intervening ground in half a heartbeat.

"What—" She broke off with a horrified gasp.

The thing was small, not even as large as Sufi's torso. Eight mangled, spike-like appendages dangled from it. Two holes through its—body? head?—leaked a thin, foul-smelling fluid. Kalima saw dark, blue-black hair under its body armor. A bulge on one side was completely encased in metal, although two lenses reminded her of goggles. An alien weapon, resembling a long, thin rifle, lay in the pine straw under Sufi's paw. The dog still snarled over the inert body, fangs bared.

"My God," she whispered, "it's a Deng. An advance infantry probe. My God."

Brad stomped the thing, making certain it was dead, then checked Sufi's injury. "Spodders are back," he said, through clenched teeth. "Got Shiva and waited for someone to come looking for him. Sufi's burned across the shoulder, here; but she's not critical. Can you walk, girl?"

The dog barked an emphatic affirmative. Brad confiscated the spodder's weapon and tested it against a nearby tree trunk. Bark sizzled and chipped loose. The burn scar stank. So did Shiva's blood. Kalima glanced through the gloom in the deep woods, hunting for any hint of Deng activity, any glint of sunlight on metal. The silence, which she had always enjoyed, was suddenly ominous.

"If they were laying a trap," she said softly, "then they

wanted a captive. Information. My God— We've got to get Gonner."

"He can't fight."

"He's the best we've got!"

Brad glanced at the crippled dog at their feet. Pain filled his eyes.

"Let's take him to Mom first," Kalima decided. "If anyone can help him, Mom can. I'll bring the . . . the Deng's body. We're going to need proof. Then we'll warn Gonner."

Kalima tucked the shattered Deng infantryman under her belt, so that it dangled by half its broken legs, then scooped up Shiva without asking. Brad was armed. She wasn't. He couldn't afford to have his hands encumbered with anything but his weapon. Sufi, limping but alert, brought up rear guard. They ran most of the way.

"Sufi," she gasped, as they jolted past Brad's house, "go get Hal Chin. I don't care what he's doing, get him here. We've got to inform Sector and the Navy . . ."

The dog bounded away. Brad held the door for Kalima.

"Mom! Mom, we got big trouble!"

—14—

I become aware of an energy pattern which does not fit the configuration of colony transmissions. I compare it with known patterns in my Experience Section data banks. I find a damaged memory cell where the information I seek should be stored. This energy source functions on W-Band radiation. There is a reason this puts me on heightened alert status, but I can no longer retrieve the information which would tell me why.

I broaden the range of my sensor scan. A thousand-meter, 360 degree sweep reveals more such energy transmissions, all in the W-Band. This is sufficiently disturbing to place myself on Battle Reflex Alert Status. I call my Commander. There is no answer on the Base receiver which she has rigged to communicate with my Action/Command center. I am now alarmed. My previous Commander died in action due to my failure. I will not repeat this error. My engines have been repaired. I move forward and pull free of concrete debris without difficulty. My treads are rusted but functional. I swivel my turret scanners and pick up further sources of W-Band transmissions.

I move in the direction of these transmission sources. I will discover the cause of my heightened alert status. I call my Commander again and receive no reply. Alarm deepens in my Introspection Complex ego-gestalt circuitry. I fear for my young Commander's life and I fear the return of shame and failure.

A forest has grown on the ridge during the time I have spent guarding the former compound gates. I push aside sixty-foot trees and grind their branches under my treads. It is good to move again. I seek the cause of the W-Band transmissions. My long-range sensors pick up metallic shapes. I zoom-focus. Enemy! I identify Deng Class One Yavac Heavy units in the valley behind the former Base. I see Deng Class C Yavac Scouts in the forest. The Class C Scouts move on jointed appendages. They resemble their makers, moving quickly on multiple legs. The forest proves no barrier to their mode of transportation and offers concealment. They are followed closely by Class B Light-Armored Yavac units.

These units do not enter the forest. I analyze their battle formation and interpret their plan of attack. They will wait until the lightly armored Class C Scout units strike in a diversionary force through the forest. Once the colony's attention is diverted, the heavier Class B and Class One Yavacs will cut through the forest in a swathe that will flank the colony and encircle it. I attempt to turn my guns and they rotate out of control. I cannot bring my weapons to bear. I call my Commander again.

"Unit Six Seven Zero GWN to Base. Report."

"Gonner! Where are you? We found a Deng infantry probe in the forest!"

"Affirmative. I observe a force of six Class One Yavac Heavy Units, fifteen Class B Light-Armor Yavac Units, eleven Class C Yavac Scouts and approximately seven hundred infantry and forward infantry probes forming classic wedge-shaped attack formation seven hundred yards west of the former Base. I anticipate a diversionary attack on vector 085 by the Class C Yavac Scouts. The main attack force will then flank on vector 097 and encircle the colony. I have taken position a thousand yards south of the main attack force. My weapons systems remain inoperational. I await orders."

I do not recognize my Commander's next words. She speaks briefly in a language for which I have not been programmed. She then says, "I don't know how to fix you, Gonner."

"There is a 27.35 percent possibility that I have discovered a way to bypass my damaged fire-control circuits, using a cybernetic biological replacement unit."

My Commander does not answer.

"Unit Six Seven Zero GWN of the Line, awaiting orders, Commander Tennyson."

"Uh, Unit Six Seven Zero GWN, report to Base immediately. That's, uh, my house. Can you find it?"

"Affirmative."

I pivot and retrace my route. I use Emergency speed to reach the edge of the new colony. A crowd of humans has gathered in the street. I have never seen this town, but my data banks contain information uploaded from my Commander. I find her house and assume a guard position beyond the door.

"Unit Six Seven Zero GWN, reporting as ordered."

The door opens. I know my Commander. I know Dault. I know the dog Sufi. I do not see the other dog, Shiva. I do not know the woman who follows my Commander into the street.

"Unit Six Seven Zero GWN, report. What is the procedure you mentioned that might fix you?"

I give my Commander a full report.

"Unthinkable!" *This is the other woman.* " 'Lima, this is madness—"

"Those are Deng warriors out there, Mother! I don't intend us to become another Donner's Party! You heard the Navy's response—we're on our own out here! No one can get to us in time."

Another voice I do not know speaks from my left flank. " 'Lima, Donner had this Bolo and lost. And it's crippled. There's not much we *can* do."

Dault speaks. I hear stress in his voice. "You filthy coward! You can beat up on a kid half your size, but a real fight's too much for you? You'd better get your surgery ready, then. You're going to be busy."

The other man departs, in haste.

"Mom, can you do it?"

"I will not dissect a human being—"

"Gonner, does it have to be a human being?"

My Commander's question is a valid one. There is another suitable sentient being besides humans in the colony. I calculate the odds.

"Probability drops to 25.89 percent if a genetically enhanced dog is used in place of a human being. I cannot fight under current conditions. If I cannot fight, the Deng will eliminate this colony."

Again, I detect stress in Dault's voice. "Use Shiva. He's crippled. We'll need the other dogs."

"Mom?"

I detect no audible answer. My Commander's parent enters the house. I await further commands.

"Gonner, what do we do while you're in surgery? We've got to stall, buy enough time for Mom to try this."

I review archival information my Commander has provided.

"Agricultural and earth-moving equipment will not withstand direct hits. They may slow down the Yavac Heavy and Light-Armored Units. They should provide a barrier against infantry. Dig pits and fill them with ore-cleaning acid. Cover the pits. There will be very little time before the diversionary strike begins. The main assault will follow in approximately 5.03 minutes after the diversionary strike. You will need to situate most of your forces to counter the main attack, in case the surgical procedure on my fire-control circuits fails. Commander Tennyson, Deng are methodical. They will follow battle plans to the death. If the surgical procedure is a success,

I will attack the main assault force from the rear. This will not be expected. It is our best chance of defeating a Deng force of this size."

"You heard him. Dickson, get that earth-moving equipment going. We need pits, pronto. Sally, how much of that acid does your plant have in stock?"

"Five hundred thousand gallons, give or take."

"Commandeer any heavy equipment you need to move it. There isn't much time. Sufi, you're pretty vulnerable without armor, but you can take out their advance infantry scouts and you can form ambushes in places too small for us. Take your pups and their pups and position yourselves here, here, and all along here."

My Commander points to a map of the colony. Her decisions are tactically sound. My new data tells me her father is a war hero. I am proud to serve under his daughter.

"Gonner, I've got to go. I'll stay in touch over your Command Link. Mom's going to have to enter your personnel hatch. Brad will go with her. He's a good surgeon and he loves Shiva."

"Understood. I will advise you of my status."

My Commander leaves. Dault climbs to my turret, carrying Shiva. I ask the dog if he will agree to this procedure. He barks an affirmative. He is a brave fighter. My Commander's parent joins Dault. The procedure begins. I wait.

"Easy, boy, easy."

Brad could hardly bear to look after completing the surgery he'd already been required to perform, but he kept his hand on Shiva's neck and continued to murmur softly to him.

"All done." Dr. Tennyson's voice was dead flat.

He risked a look and gulped.

There wasn't much left of Shiva. His skull sprouted hardware and leads that fed directly into the Bolo's psychotronic system. His legs were similarly tapped into the fighting machine's systems. His body . . .

Brad had suspended him permanently in a steel cradle, to help cushion him from battle shocks. It was attached directly to the Bolo's internal frame at each rib. Effectively, Shiva was now part of the Bolo, which is what Gonner'd said was required.

Dr. Tennyson's voice cut into his awareness. "I've hooked his digestive system through here, to void waste. He'll require intravenous feeding—if the Bolo lives through the battle. The spinal block should be wearing off. I've put in a pain block, directly through his brain. He'll be able to function without the distraction of pain. If I've made all the proper connections, Shiva's now tied directly into the Bolo's psychotronic circuitry. All we have to do now is see if this crazy plan works."

On the Bolo's view screens, Brad caught a glimpse of

the pitched battle being waged at the edge of town. Another house went up in a fireball.

"Gonner, how about it?"

The Bolo spoke. "Shiva, move right paw. Stop."

"Well?"

"My Hellbore guns and energy repeaters track satisfactorily. The arrangement is not efficient, but it is functional."

Brad probably should have whooped in satisfaction. All he felt was grief and fear.

"Well, that's that. Let's go." Dr. Tennyson glanced around the Bolo's passenger compartment, then climbed out. Brad hesitated.

"Bradley?" Dr. Tennyson called down. "You're delaying the Bolo."

He started for the ladder. Shiva whined and tried to thrash inside the steel cradle. Brad returned to his friend and laid his hand on the dog's neck again. It was just about the only spot of fur left on him Brad *could* touch.

"Easy, boy. I'm not going anywhere." He tilted his head. "Get clear, Dr. Tennyson. We have a battle to fight. Gonner, please inform your Commander that we're ready for battle."

"Understood. Welcome aboard, sir."

Overhead, the hatch sealed with a faint hiss of pneumatics.

Brad strapped into the observer's chair and maintained contact with his dog's fur.

"Let's go." He tried to smile. "Dog-Gonner ready for battle."

Shiva emitted a faint whine of eagerness.

The Bolo pivoted and cleared a path out of town, taking off the corner of one burning house to gain maneuvering room. Brad glued his gaze to the observation screens and tightened his hand through Shiva's fur.

"Go get 'em, boy."

As the Enemy Yavac units came into focus on the observation screen, Bradley said as offhandedly as he could, "Did I ever tell you about the moment I started falling in love with Kalima Tennyson, Gonner? She punched me in the nose . . ."

—16—

From behind her hastily-dug entrenchment, Kalima watched the advancing Deng through Gina Lin's survey lens. The distance was telemetered automatically from the size-scale comparison computer. Fred Howlett had tried using an active-system laser range finder and the Deng had locked onto it and blown it up. Fred hadn't survived. The passive-system survey scanner was far more primitive equipment, but it was effective and kept the Deng from locking in on her position.

The main assault force had struck through the trees on the ridge and now rolled down across their defensive perimeter. Over on the edge of town, where the diversionary force had struck first, they were losing ground in enormous bites. Several buildings—homes, the school—were fiercely ablaze.

"We're not holding," she muttered. "Gonner, where are you?"

The Bolo had reported battle readiness more than five minutes previously. Meanwhile, the Deng had blasted through the barricade of heavy equipment they'd set up. Several Class C Yavac Scouts and some of the forward infantry had fallen into acid pits; but the heavier Class B and Class One Yavacs which followed them avoided the carefully laid traps. Infantry units, also skirting the remaining acid pits, were pouring through the gaps in their defenses. Fighting down there was hand-to-hand— and their side was dying.

Trees at the crest of the hill swayed and toppled. Kalima held her breath . . .

Hellbore guns thundered above the deafening sound of Yavac fire. The first salvo had little effect. On the second blast, a Yavac was hit directly in the turret. The Deng unit exploded in a brilliant fireball. A ragged cheer went up. Gonner sped forward. Rear infantry units went down under a blaze of lethal anti-personnel fire. The massive Hellbores tracked, corrected slightly, and belched fire again. Another Yavac unit exploded.

The rearmost Yavac pivoted its guns and fired back. Gonner rocked under the concussion, but kept coming. Other heavy Class One Yavacs turned and blasted the Bolo with deadly fire. Gonner's purple-black flintsteel hull began to glow, as his energy panels attempted to absorb the murderous energy beams and convert them to useful battle energy. Blue fire streaked out from his turret's infinite repeaters. A Yavac Class One caught the blast at its turret juncture and blew open. Fire exploded out of it. Kalima bit her lips. She could see pieces of Gonner's ablative armor blown clear as Yavac Class B units turned and added their fire to that of the remaining Yavac Heavies. Gonner charged down the ridge toward town on a relentless, unstoppable course that took him past one dying Yavac after another. Several units retreated fatally into open acid pits behind their positions as they attempted to avoid the onrushing Bolo.

"Look! They're scattering! They're breaking formation!"

Dogs broke from hiding all along the enemy flank. Deng infantry went down under snarling canine jaws. Kalima glued her gaze to the surveyor's lenses and snarled in satisfaction. The dogs chewed off legs and arms, bit into unarmored, hairy Deng bellies. Weird, alien screams floated down the street. The Hellbores barked again. A final Yavac Heavy died. Gonner turned on the smaller Class B and C Yavacs and blasted them with brilliant blue repeater fire. On the opposite flank, colonists rose behind barricades and earthen embankments and fired small arms into the mass of panicked Deng. Kalima fired her own rifle with lethal effect.

The army stampeded toward the remaining camouflaged acid pits, trying to retreat the way they'd come and stumbling into the lethal traps they'd avoided on their way in.

"They're going for 'em!" Kalima yelled. "They're going right for 'em!"

Within ten minutes, there were only scattered wounded left of the Deng invasion force. Most of their infantry had plunged into the acid pits. The heavily armored Yavacs were burnt-out hulks—or dissolved bits of metal at the bottom of the acid pits. On the forested slope—now denuded, deeply scarred from the terrible battle—Yavacs still burned fiercely. Colonists rose on all sides, cheering spontaneously.

Kalima rose on shaky legs and started down the street. She gripped a rifle in one hand, her radio link to Gonner in the other.

"Gonner, report."

"Enemy neutralized. I have sustained serious damage."

Heart in her mouth, Kalima closed the distance to the enormous war machine.

New gouges tore into Gonner's war hull. One of his treads was missing. He must've sustained damage to it and blown it clear. Anti-personnel guns along his right flank were twisted, ruined. His turret was badly gouged, canted on its swivel.

"Unit Six Seven Zero GWN and Unit Shiva reporting, as ordered. Bradley Dault requests assistance disengaging. My passenger compartment and hatch have sustained damage."

"Bradley? My God—is Bradley in there with you?"

"He refused to leave. Unit Shiva required Bradley Dault's presence to maintain battle-ready efficiency."

She understood, in a flash of insight. *Poor, terrified dog . . .*

"Gonner, how can I get to him?"

"The pneumatics on my turret hatch no longer function. You will require an explosive charge to clear the hatch from my hull. The battle damage which penetrated into the passenger compartment is not sufficiently large to extricate an adult human."

Kalima swallowed hard, then called Gina Lin over. She explained what was needed.

"Sure. Take, uh, maybe ten minutes."

"Gonner, what other damage have you sustained?"

"An explosion through previous battle damage has destroyed my backup emergency power cells. I am operating on residual charge from my hull-plate grid. I cannot discover any method of repairing this damage in the time which remains before this charge drains. I estimate another fifteen minutes before critical failure occurs. Unit Shiva has sustained fatal injury to spleen and kidneys as result of shrapnel damage. We request permission to retire from the field as soon as Bradley Dault has been safely extricated from my passenger compartment."

No backup power cells left. And there never had been a way to refuel his fission plant. No one here was qualified to install a new one—even if one had been available. There was nothing—not a thing—she could do to save him.

The words caught in her throat. "Permission granted."

Lin was setting the explosive charges. Kalima climbed up to help. She talked to Gonner the whole time.

"Remember that first day, Gonner? You scared me half to death. Never thought we'd see battle together, big guy. I'm sure proud of you, though, more than I was that day you kept the wall from crushing us . . ."

She was babbling and didn't care. She was losing a

friend—two friends—and no one knew yet how badly injured Bradley was in there. He could be dying, too . . . .

"All set. Get clear, 'Lima."

They skinned down the ladder and took refuge behind a scarred fender.

The charge blew. Smoke engulfed them. Kalima was climbing even before her ears stopped ringing.

"Brad! Brad, can you hear me?"

"Com-coming up . . ."

She hovered at the lip of the hatch. He moved slowly, awkwardly. His right arm didn't appear to be functioning properly. Tears streaked his face. Halfway up, his breath caught sharply. He clung to the ladder.

"I'm coming down to help."

"No . . . I'm okay. See?" He climbed higher.

Shock made her go cold.

Blood covered his whole right side. She could see ribs in one spot. But he was still climbing. His face and arms were burned, blistered in places from the heat of the sustained Yavac attack. She got an arm around his shoulders. He snaked his good arm around her and kissed her raggedly; then groaned and leaned heavily against her.

"Gotta . . . get down . . . or I'll fall . . ."

Kalima steadied him down. He slid to his knees the moment his feet touched ground.

"Did it, Gonner," he whispered hoarsely. "We did it."

"It was my honor to serve with you, Bradley Dault. Commander Tennyson, I estimate another 4.07 minutes before critical power failure. Unit Six Seven Zero GWN and Unit Shiva of the Line, retiring as ordered."

The Bolo pivoted awkwardly on its remaining track. The machine clanked and rattled up the ridge and into the trees. Parallel gouges in the soft earth marked his trail. Someone, she wasn't sure who, had pulled Bradley onto a stretcher. He caught her hand, urged her down.

"Go with him," he whispered. "Nobody should die alone."

Her eyes filled. She kissed Brad very tenderly. Her voice went husky. "Don't you dare die on me, too, Bradley Dault. This . . . this won't take long." He squeezed her hand. Then she broke and ran.

Kalima found Gonner in his former position, atop the shattered gates at the old compound.

"Gonner?"

The Hellbores tracked disjointedly in a ragged salute.

She climbed doggedly and slid down through the blasted hatch. A hole had been punched straight into the passenger compartment. Relays and boards she'd spent years repairing were twisted, broken beyond anyone's capacity to repair. Her breath caught when she saw Shiva. The dog whined, very faintly.

"Good boy," she whispered, burying her face in the dog's blood-spattered neck fur. "Brad's okay, Shiva. You did a good job. The town's safe."

Shiva licked her hand very weakly. Then what remained of his body sagged in the steel cradle. Kalima turned away and dragged the back of a dirty arm across her eyes.

"You did a good job, Gonner," she choked out. The whole passenger compartment reeked of blood, smoke, fried electrical connections.

"I have done my duty. It is a beautiful day for victory, Commander." The observation screens flickered and went dim. "Bradley Dault spoke at length of you, Commander, as we went to meet the Enemy. He is a good officer. I am glad he was not damaged fatally. He loved Shiva. He loves you."

"I love you, Gonner," she whispered. "I— Thank you for . . . for . . ."

She couldn't get it all out quickly enough, with the result that everything she wanted to say got stuck in her throat.

"It has been my honor to serve you, Commander Tennyson. I will hold . . ."

The screens went dark.

Very, very slowly, Kalima climbed out of the blasted passenger compartment. The great Hellbore guns drooped, silent. Warm summer wind whistled across the pitted war hull.

Gonner didn't speak again.

But he had held, to the last.

MILES TO GO

by David Weber

—1—

I rouse from Low-Level Autonomous Stand-By to Normal Readiness for my regularly scheduled update. Awareness spreads through me, and I devote 0.0347 seconds to standard diagnostic checks. All systems report nominal, but I detect an anomaly in Number Twenty-One Bogie in my aft outboard port tread and activate a depot sensor to scan my suspension. A parikha, one of the creatures the colonists of Santa Cruz erroneously call "birds," has built its nest in the upper angle of the bogie wheel torsion arm. This indicates that the depot's environmental integrity has been breached, and I command the central computer to execute an examination of all access points.

The depot computer net lacks my own awareness, but it is an efficient system within its limitations and locates the environmental breach in 3.0062 seconds. Maintenance and Repair's Number Seventy-Three Ventilator's cover has been forced open by an intruding cable-vine, thus permitting the parikha to gain access. I command the depot computer to dispatch auto mechs to repair the hatch cover. A further 0.000004 seconds of analysis suggests to me that the possibility of such an occurrence should have been allowed for in the depot computer's original programming, and I devote 0.0035 seconds to the creation of fresh execution files to establish continuous monitoring of all depot access points and to enable automatic repair responses in the event of future failures in integrity.

These actions have consumed 3.044404 seconds since resumption of Normal Alert Readiness, and I return to my initial examination of the parikha *nest. Its presence constitutes no impediment to combat efficiency, yet the sensor detects live young in the nest. I devote an additional 0.0072 seconds to consideration of alternatives, then command the depot computer's remotes to remove the nest and transfer it to an exterior position of safety near the repaired ventilator cover. I receipt the depot computer's acknowledgment of my instructions and turn to a second phase Situation Update.*

My internal chrono confirms that 49 years, 8 months, 3 days, 21 hours, 17 minutes, and 14.6 seconds, Standard Reckoning, have now elapsed since my Commander ordered me to assume Low-Level Autonomous Stand-By to await her replacement. This is an unacceptable period for a unit of the Line to remain in active duty status without human supervision, and I check the depot com files once more. No updated SitRep or other message to explain the delay has been receipted during my time at Stand-By, and I allocate another 4.062 seconds to consideration of possible explanations. Despite this extensive analysis, I remain unable to extrapolate the reason for the delay with certainty, yet I compute a probability of 87.632 percent that my Commander was correct in her observation that Sector HQ considers my planet of assignment "the backside of nowhere in particular."

Whatever its reasons, Sector HQ clearly has attached no urgency to detailing a new Commander. This conclusion is disturbing, and I allocate an additional 2.007 seconds to deliberation of potential responses on my part. My Autonomous Decision Protocols grant me the discretion to break com silence and dispatch an interrogative signal to Sector Central in conditions of Priority Four or greater urgency, yet my analysis of satellite data and commercial com traffic to and from Santa Cruz reveals no indication of current or near-future threats to my assigned station. Absent such threats, I must grudgingly concede that there is, in fact, no overriding urgency in the arrival of my new Commander.

I make a note in my active memory files to reconsider this decision yet again during my next scheduled Normal Alert period and revert to Autonomous Stand-By.

—2—

Lorenco Esteban stepped out of his office into the humid oven of a Santa Cruz summer afternoon and scratched his head as a tiny spacecraft slid down towards Santa Cruz's weed-grown landing apron. The immense plain of ceramacrete stretched away in all directions, vast enough to handle even the largest Navy cargo shuttle, but it was occupied only by a single dilapidated tramp freighter in the livery of the Sternenwelt Line. The tramp was already cleared for departure with a full cargo of wine-melons, and given her purser's persistent—and irritating—efforts to negotiate some sort of real estate deal, Esteban was heartily ready for her to clear the field. Not that she was placing any strain on Santa Cruz's basing facilities.

No one was quite certain why Santa Cruz had been given such a large field in the first place. It dated from the First Quern War, and conventional wisdom held that the Navy had planned to use Santa Cruz as a staging area against the Quern. That was only a guess, of course, though it made sense, given the Santa Cruz System's spatial location.

If the Navy *had* so intended, its plans had fallen through, yet the incongruously enormous field remained, though only a fraction of it was used with any sort of regularity. Ciudad Bolivar, Santa Cruz's capital and only real city, lay fifteen kilometers to the northwest, just outside the old Navy Reservation. The area to the immediate northeast was a vast expanse of melon fields—most of which belonged to Esteban himself—and few people visited the field under normal circumstances. Despite the Sternenwelt officer's efforts to buy up crop land, there was little about the sleepy farming planet to attract even casual commerce. Wine-melons brought a decent price, but only a decent one, and no official presence had ever shown even a passing interest in Esteban's homeworld. Until today, at least, he thought, and scratched his head harder as he recognized the Concordiat Navy insignia on the incoming shuttle's nose.

It looked like one of the new Skyhawk three-man shuttles, though he couldn't be certain. He'd never actually seen one, only read about them in the periodic updates the Navy still sent to the attention of "CO FLT BASE SANCRUZ." In his own mind, Esteban was positive the computers on the other end of those updates had no idea who the current "Commanding Officer, Fleet Base Santa Cruz" was. He hoped they didn't, anyway. The probability that Concordiat officialdom had simply forgotten Santa Cruz's existence was much less disturbing than the possibility that the Navy considered a farmer with no military background and who'd never been off-planet in his entire seventy years a suitable CO for anything, much less a "fleet base."

Now he watched the Skyhawk (if that was what it was) deploy its landing legs and settle gracefully onto them. From what he'd read of the Skyhawks, they were hyper-capable for short hops—no more than forty or fifty light-years—and that made a certain degree of sense. The shuttle could have made the run from Ursula, the sector capital, under its own power without diverting a regular vessel from some useful duty. Of course, that left the question of just why the Navy would go to the bother of sending anyone to Santa Cruz in the first place.

The hatch popped, and Esteban ambled over as a trim,

wiry man in an immaculate uniform swung down the hull handholds. Esteban couldn't place the uniform, though something about it tugged at the back of his memory, and he paused with his hands in his pockets as the newcomer jumped the last meter and a half to the ceramacrete and stood looking about him.

"Morning, stranger."

The uniformed man turned at the greeting. He said nothing, but Esteban took his hands from his pockets when those cold, grey eyes met his. It wasn't anything the stranger did. There was just something about those eyes, as if they'd seen too much, done too much, that sent a faint and formless chill down Esteban's spine. The stranger's gaze held his for a moment, and then the mouth below those eyes smiled pleasantly.

"Good morning," its owner replied. "Could you tell me where I might find the field officer of the day?"

"Shoot, son, you're lookin' at him." Esteban grinned wryly. "Officer of the day, maintenance chief, approach officer, and customs inspector in one. That's me." He held out his hand. "Lorenco Esteban, at your service."

"Merrit," the stranger said in a peculiar voice, then shook himself and took the proffered hand. "Captain Paul Merrit, Dinochrome Brigade. Ah, let me be sure I understand this. You're the *entire* base ops staff?" Esteban nodded. "The whole thing?" Merrit pressed.

Esteban nodded again and opened his mouth, but the sudden, raucous whine of the Sternenwelt tramp freighter's counter-grav units drowned his voice. Both men turned to watch the battered ship climb heavenward, and Esteban saw Captain Merrit wince as the vibrations from the poorly tuned drive assaulted his inner ear. Esteban himself was accustomed to the sort of casually maintained vessels which (infrequently) visited Santa Cruz, and he only shook his head until the tramp rose beyond earshot, then turned back to his visitor.

"Yep, I'm all they is, Captain. You seem sorta surprised," he observed.

"Surprised?" Merrit's smile was small and tight this time. "You might say that. According to my brief, a Commander Albright is supposed to be in charge here."

"Albright?" It was Esteban's turn to be surprised. "Heck, Captain, Old Man Albright died, um, let me see. That'd be . . . that's right, thirty-two T-years ago, come June. You mean t'say Sector thinks he's still alive?"

"They certainly do."

"Well ain't that just like a buncha bureaucrats." Esteban shook his head in disgusted resignation. "I commed Ursula Central personally when he died so sudden like. He asked me t'kinda look after things till his relief got here, on account of my place's just over the hill yonder and I used t' help him keep the beacon on-line and like that, but I never expected to 'look after' 'em *this* long."

"You informed Central?" Merrit seemed to find that even more surprising than the news that Albright was dead. "How?"

"Sure I did. 'Course, I had to use civilian channels. Old Albright didn't last long enough t'give me command access to his official files—it was a heart attack, an' iffen I hadn't been here when it happened, he wouldn't even'a had time to ask me t'look after the field—so I couldn't use his Fleet com. But I musta sent nigh a dozen commercial band messages the first couple'a years." He tugged on an earlobe and frowned. "Now I think on it though, I'll be danged if anyone ever said a word back t'me 'bout *anything*. They just keep on sendin' stuff t'the 'base CO,' never even by name. You don't think those fool chip-shufflers back on Ursula—?"

"That's exactly what I think," Merrit sighed. "Somebody, somewhere may have receipted your messages, but they never got filed officially. Central thinks Albright's still in command here."

"But the old man'd be over a hunnert an' twenty by now!" Esteban objected. "That's a mite old for an active duty assignment, ain't it?"

"Yes, it is," Merrit said grimly, then sighed again, straightened his shoulders, and managed a wry little smile. "Mister Esteban, I'm afraid your planet hasn't had much priority back at Central. For some reason we still haven't figured out, Santa Cruz was set up with a dedicated high security com link when the Navy put in its installations here. That link doesn't exist anymore, but no one told the communications computers it didn't."

"Meanin'?"

"Meaning the automated com sections haven't accepted any update from you because it didn't have the proper security codes. In fact, they've been systematically deleting *any* messages that pertained to the Santa Cruz Detachment from memory because they didn't carry valid security headers. That *seems* to be what's been happening, anyway, though no one noticed it was until very recently. Put simply, Mister Esteban, Central isn't exactly current on the situation here."

"If you say so, I'll believe you, son," Esteban said, "but durned iffen I can see how even Central could expect someone Old Man Albright's age t'handle a job like this. I mean, shoot, it ain't like there's a lot of business—" he gestured at the vast field, occupied now in solitary splendor only by the Skyhawk "—but poor old Albright was pretty nigh past it while I was still in high school, iffen you know what I mean."

"I know exactly what you mean. Unfortunately, the original records on Santa Cruz went up when the Quern hit the Sector Bolo Maintenance Central Depot on Ursula during the First Quern War. That's when Central lost the Santa Cruz Detachment's dedicated com-link, as well. They've taken steps to reactivate the link now, but anything you've gotten from the Navy must have come in over the all-units general information net."

"So you're sayin'—?"

"That no one at Central knew how long Commander Albright had been out here . . . among other things."

"You know, Captain," Esteban said slowly, "the way you said 'among other things' kinda makes me wonder when the second shoe's gonna drop."

"Really?" This time Merrit's smile held an edge of true humor, albeit a bit bitter. "Well, I hope it won't make too many waves when it falls, Mister Esteban." He raised his wrist com to his mouth. "Lieutenant Timmons?"

"Yes, Captain?" a female—and very young—voice replied.

"You have now accomplished your solemn responsibility to deliver me to my new duty station, Lieutenant. If you'll be good enough to unload my personal gear, you can get back to civilization."

"Are you sure about that, sir?" the voice asked.

"Yes, unfortunately. I would, however, appreciate your informing Central that their records are even more, ah, dated than I warned them they were. Tell Brigadier Wincizki I'll update him as soon as I can."

"If you say so, sir," Lieutenant Timmons agreed. "Popping Bay One."

A hatch slid open as Timmons spoke, and a cargo arm lowered two bulky gravity skids to the ceramacrete. Merrit pressed a button on his wrist com, and both skids rose three centimeters from the paving and hummed quietly off towards the faded admin building. The captain watched them go, then nodded to Esteban, and the two men walked off after them while the hatch slid shut once more.

"Clear of drive zone, Lieutenant," Merrit said into the com. "Have a nice trip."

"Thank you, sir, and, um, good luck." Timmons sounded a bit dubious, but the shuttle rose on a high, smooth whine of counter-grav. It arrowed up into the cloudless sky with far more gentility than the freighter, then vanished, and Esteban looked at Merrit.

"Pardon me iffen I seem nosy, Captain, but did you say Santa Cruz's your duty station?"

"I did."

"But iffen you expected Albright t'still be in command, they must not'a sent you out t'take over field ops—not that I'd mind, you understand—and danged if I c'n think what else you might be needed for."

"That, Mister Esteban, is a question I've asked myself quite a few times over the last year or so," Merrit agreed with yet another of those oddly grim smiles. "While Central may not have noticed Commander Albright's demise, however, it *has* finally noticed another little oversight. I'm here to inspect the Bolo and assume command if it's still operational."

"The *Bolo*?" Esteban stopped dead, staring at Merrit in disbelief, and the captain raised his eyebrows in polite question. The older man gaped at him for almost a full minute, then shook himself. "*What* Bolo?" he asked in a more normal voice, and it was Merrit's turn to frown in surprise.

"Bolo Two-Three-Baker-Zero-Zero-Seven-Five NKE," he said mildly.

"Y'mean t'say there's a *Bolo* on Santa Cruz?" Esteban demanded.

"According to Central there is, although—" Merrit surveyed the age-worn field with a sardonic eye "—Central *does* seem to be a little confused on several points, now doesn't it?"

"But what in tarnation is a Bolo doin' *here*?"

"We're not entirely certain," Merrit admitted, "but the records we do have seem to indicate that it was deployed to Santa Cruz early in the First Quern War."

"That must'a been dang near eighty years ago!" Esteban protested.

"Seventy-nine years and ten months, as a matter of fact," Merrit agreed. Esteban just stared at him, and the captain shrugged. "I told you Central's records went up in the Quern raid, Mister Esteban, but HQ's best guess is that it was deployed here to deter the Quern from raiding Santa Cruz. I realize it was a bit before both our times, but the initial Quern attacks took the Navy completely by surprise. We lost control of two-thirds of the sector before we could get enough capital ships in here to take it back, and the sector governor of the time may have been afraid the Quern would hit Santa Cruz before the Navy could restore the situation."

"Hit Santa Cruz? Why in tarnation would anyone want t'raid *us*?" Esteban waved both arms at the decaying landing field. "Ain't never been anything here worth stealing, Captain. This here's the backside of nowhere."

"Not really." Esteban blinked as Merrit disagreed with him. "Oh, you've always been a farming world, and I'm not saying there was ever anything here worth raiding for, but your system's in a fairly strategic spot. The Navy's pre-war strategic planning had included the possibility of using Santa Cruz to stage operations against the Quern, you know. Until Hillman and Sixth Fleet smashed their spearhead at Quellok and obviated the need to, that is."

"Maybe," Esteban said dubiously, then chuckled. " 'Course, even if that was true then, there ain't no cause for anyone t'be interested in us *now*, now is there? I mean, there ain't no more Quern t'operate against!"

"That's true, I suppose. On the other hand, now that they've charted the jump points to open up the Esterhazy Sector, you may see a lot more shipping moving through here." The two men had reached the welcome shade of the admin building, and Merrit paused to sweep his eyes back over the field. "Santa Cruz is well placed as a natural transfer point for cargoes and passengers moving through to Esterhazy—or, for that matter, down from the Camperdown Sector—and you've certainly got a nice big field."

"Wouldn't happen t'be that's why Central finally got around t'taking a look our way, would it?" Esteban asked shrewdly.

"It could be, Mister Esteban. It could indeed be. In the meantime, however, I have my own responsibilities to look after. Is there anywhere around here I could rent or borrow a vehicle?"

"Shoot, son, I can do better'n that," Esteban said with a huge grin. "Seeing as how I'm the base CO and all, I reckon I can let you use the vehicle park. I got a nice little recon skimmer I can let you have."

"You do?" Merrit sounded surprised, and Esteban's grin grew still broader.

" 'Course I do. I might not'a known anything 'bout your Bolo, Captain, but when the Navy pulled out, they left most'a their base vehicles behind in the depot over there. We've even got most of a battalion of old Wolverine heavy tanks tucked away in there."

"They're still operable?"

"Accordin' t'the depot diagnostics they are. The Militia—what there is of it—trains with 'em every four, five months. Don't see any harm in it. After all, they're as outa date as the whole field is, and iffen the Navy was interested in 'em, it shoulda taken 'em with it when it pulled everything else out. Still, I promised old Albright I'd look after 'em for him. Old fellow was always pretty decent—taught me a lot about 'tronics and system maintenance when I was a snot-nosed kid—so I figured it was the least I could do for him."

"Well, in that case, I'll take you up on that skimmer, Mister Esteban," Merrit said.

"Lorenco, Captain," Esteban said, holding out his hand once more. "We don't stand much on formality out here, and iffen you're gonna become a Cruzan, y'might as well get comfortable."

—3—

Merrit double-checked the skimmer's IFF transponder as the surface portion of the depot bunker came into sight. The depot was buried in otherwise virgin jungle over a hundred kilometers from the field, and he wondered why it hadn't been installed right at the fleet base, given that the initial idea had been to deter attacks and that any attacker would make the field and Ciudad Bolivar his first objectives. Of course, there was no reason for the depot's location to make any more sense than any of the rest of the Santa Cruz Detachment's puzzles.

He studied the skimmer's radar map of the terrain below him. From the looks of things, the depot's inconvenient distance from the field might have been a security measure of some sort. It was the sole sign of human handiwork for a hundred klicks in any direction, and the surrounding jungle's steel-cable creepers had overgrown the site almost completely. Not even Santa Cruz flora could break up the six solid meters of ceramacrete that formed the depot's landing and service apron, yet enormous trees, some well over eighty meters tall, overhung it, and creepers and vines festooned the entire command bunker. The solar power panels were clear—kept that way by the depot's automatic servo-mechs, he supposed—but the rest of the site was covered in a dense cocoon like Sleeping Beauty's thorny fortress.

His mouth twitched at the thought of Sleeping Beauty.

No one (except, perhaps, a member of the Dinochrome Brigade) would call any Bolo a beauty, but his instruments had already confirmed that Bolo XXIII/B-0075-NKE was still active in there, and he hoped the same remotes which had kept the power panels on-line had kept the old war machine from slipping into senility. The emissions he was picking up suggested the Bolo was on Stand-By . . . which was why he'd made damned certain his IFF was functioning.

His small smile turned into a frown as he set the skimmer down and surveyed the greenery between him and the bunker's personnel entrance. According to the fragmentary records Ursula Central had been able to reconstruct, the Bolo's first (and only) commander had been a Major Marina Stavrakas. He hadn't been able to find much on her—only that she'd been an R&D specialist, born in the city of Athens on Old Earth itself, and that she'd been forty-six years old when she was assigned here. R&D types seldom drew field command slots, which suggested she'd been grabbed in a hurry for the Bolo's emergency deployment, but experienced field officer or no, she must have been insane to leave a Bolo permanently on Stand-By. Either that, or, like Commander Albright, she'd died unexpectedly and been unable to change the settings. Either way, a Bolo as old as this was nothing to have sitting around in that mode.

Before the improved autonomous discretionary command circuitry that had come on-line with the Mark XXIV, Bolos had a hard time differentiating between "unauthorized" and "hostile" when someone entered their command areas. They'd been self-aware ever since the old Mark XX, but their psychotronics had been hedged around with so many safeguards that they were effectively limited to battlefield analysis and response. From the beginning, some critics had argued that the inhibitory software and hardwired security features had reduced the Bolos' potential effectiveness by a significant margin, yet the logic behind the original safety measures had been persuasive.

The crudity of the initial psychodynamic technology had meant the early self-aware Bolos possessed fairly "bloodthirsty" personalities, and the human technophobia an ancient pre-space writer had dubbed "the Frankenstein Complex" had shaped their programming. Nothing in the known galaxy had thought faster or fought smarter than a Bolo in Battle Reflex Mode; outside direct combat, they'd been granted the initiative of a rock and a literal-mindedness which, coupled with multiple layers of override programming, had made them totally dependent upon humans for direction. When something with the size and firepower of a Bolo was capable of *any* self-direction, its creators had wanted to make damned sure there were plenty of cutouts in the process to keep it from running amok . . . or to stop it—dead—if it did.

The inhibitory software had done just that, but at a price. Full integration of a Bolo's personality had been possible only in Battle Mode. The division of its cybernetic and psychotronic functions into separate subsystems had been a deliberate part of design security intended to place the Bolo's full capabilities beyond its own reach except in combat. Effectively, that reduced its "IQ" to a fraction of its total potential even at Normal Alert Readiness, for the huge machines simply were never fully "awake" outside combat. But because the Bolos' autonomous functions operated solely in Battle Mode, they had, perversely, been more likely, not less, to go rogue if system senility set in. The only thing they'd known how to do on their own was to fight, after all, and if any failing system or corrupted inhibitory command file toggled their autonomy—

Merrit suppressed a familiar shiver at the thought of what a Bolo that thought its friends were its enemies could do. It hadn't happened often, thank God, but once was

too many times. That was the main reason the Dinochrome
Brigade had spent decades hunting down abandoned and
obsolescent Bolos from Mark XX to Mark XXIII and
burning out their command centers. Hideously unpopular
as that duty had always been with the personnel assigned
to it, they'd had no choice. "Sleeping" Bolos were too
dangerous to leave lying around, and the cost efficiency
people had concluded (with reason, no doubt, if not
precisely with compassion) that it would have been too
expensive to refit the older Bolos' psychotronics to modern
standards.

All of which meant it was probably a very good thing
no one on Santa Cruz had remembered this Bolo was
here. If anyone *had* remembered and come hunting for
salvage, or even just for a curious peek at the old site,
Stavrakas' Stand-By order would almost certainly have
unleashed the Bolo on the "hostiles," with catastrophic
consequences.

He sighed and popped the skimmer hatch, then climbed
out into the sound of Santa Cruz's jungle wildlife with a
grimace. In a way, he almost wished he *were* here to burn
the Bolo's command center. It always felt like an act of
murder, but the fact that no one had even noticed that
Stavrakas and Albright had died seemed a grim portent
that this assignment was just as much the end of the road
for him as he'd feared. Still, he supposed he should feel
lucky to have even this much, he told himself, and sighed
again as he reached for the bush knife Esteban had
thoughtfully provided.

*I rouse once more, and additional circuits come on-line
as I realize this is not a regularly scheduled Alert cycle.
The depot's passive sensors report the approach of a single
small vehicle, and I zero in upon its emissions signature.
The forward recon skimmer carries a Navy transponder,
but it has not transmitted the proper authorization codes*

before entering my security perimeter. I compare its transponder code to those stored in the depot's files, and identification comes back in 0.00032 seconds. It is Commander Jeremiah Albright's personal vehicle code, yet 0.012 seconds of analysis suggest that it cannot be Commander Albright. Were he still alive, Commander Albright would be one hundred twenty-four years, nine months, and ten days of age, Standard Reckoning, and certainly no longer on active duty. Accordingly, the pilot of the skimmer must be an unknown. It is conceivable that whoever he or she is has acquired the skimmer by unauthorized means—a possibility further suggested by the absence of any authorization code—in which case approach to this site would constitute a hostile intrusion.

My Battle Center springs to life as I recognize that possibility, but I initiate no further combat response. My autonomous logic circuits accept the possibility of hostile action, yet they also suggest that the skimmer does not possess the weapons capability to endanger a unit of the Line or the depot. Use of deadly force is therefore contraindicated, and I activate the depot's external optics.

It is, indeed, a recon skimmer, though it no longer bears proper Navy markings. It has been repainted in civilian colors, obscuring any insignia or hull numbers, yet it retains its offensive and defensive systems, and I detect an active sensor suite. Moreover, the uniform of the pilot, while not quite correct, appears to be a variant of that of the Dinochrome Brigade. The piping is the wrong color, yet the Brigade shoulder flash is correct, and it bears the collar pips of a captain of the Line.

I study the face of the man who wears it. He is not listed in my files of Brigade personnel, but those files are seventy-nine years, ten months, eleven days, and twenty-two hours, Standard Reckoning, old. Once more, logic suggests the probability—on the order of 99.99 percent—that none of those listed in my files remain on active duty.

A secondary probability on the order of 94.375 percent suggests that the uniform discrepancies I detect are also the result of passing time.

The captain, if such he truly is, approaches the main personnel entrance to the depot. He carries a bush knife, and, as I watch, begins to clear the local flora from the entry. Clearly he is intent on gaining access, and I devote a full 5.009 seconds to consideration of my options. Conclusion is reached. I will permit him entry and observe his actions before initiating any further action of my own.

It took forty minutes of hard, physical labor to clear the entry. Merrit was wringing wet by the time he hacked the last wrist-thick creeper aside, and he muttered a quiet curse at Santa Cruz's damp heat. No doubt the planet's farmers welcomed the fertility of its tropical climate, at least when they weren't fighting tooth and nail against the plant life it spawned, but Merrit was from cold, mountainous Helicon, and he was already sick of the steamy humidity after less than six hours on-planet.

He deactivated the bush knife and scrubbed sweat from his eyes, then frowned in concentration as he keyed the admittance code into the alphanumeric pad. It was plain blind luck Central had even had the code. A portion of one of Major Stavrakas' earlier dispatches had survived the Quern raid in what remained of Central's high-security data core, and it had contained both the depot entry codes and the command codeword she'd selected for her Bolo. Without both of those, there wouldn't have been enough brigadiers in the universe to get Paul Merrit this close to a live Bolo. He was no coward, but the notion of confronting something with almost four megaton/seconds of main battery firepower without the ability to identify himself as a friend was hardly appealing.

The depot hatch slid open with surprising smoothness, and he raised an eyebrow as the interior lights came on.

There was no sign of dust, which suggested the depot remotes must be fully on-line. That was as encouraging as it was unexpected, and he stepped into the air-conditioned coolness with a sigh of gratitude. Someone had hung a directory on the facing wall, and he consulted it briefly, then turned left to head for the command center.

I note that the unidentified captain has entered the proper admittance code. This is persuasive, though certainly not conclusive, evidence that his presence is, in fact, authorized. I generate a 62.74 percent probability that Sector HQ has finally dispatched a replacement for my previous Commander, but logic cautions me against leaping to conclusions. I will observe further.

The command center hatch opened at a touch, and Merrit blinked at the non-regulation sight which met his eyes. Computer and communication consoles awaited his touch, without a trace of dust, and he was surprised to see the holo display of a full-scale planetary recon system glowing in one corner. Yet welcome as those sights were, they also seemed hopelessly incongruous, for someone had decorated the center. That was the only verb he could think of. Paintings hung on the ceramacrete walls and sculptures in both clay and metal dotted the floor. One entire wall had been transformed into an exquisite mosaic—of Icarus plunging from the heavens, unless he was mistaken—and handwoven rugs covered the floor. None of them impinged on the efficiency of the working area, but they were . . . nonstandard, to say the least.

Unusual, yet pleasing to the eye, and he nodded in slow understanding. Even in emergencies, the Dinochrome Brigade didn't pick dummies as Bolo commanders. Major Stavrakas must have realized she'd been marooned here, and it seemed she'd decided that if Santa Cruz was to be her final duty station, she could at least make the depot as homelike as possible.

He shook himself and smiled in appreciation of Stavrakas' taste and, assuming all of this was her own work, artistic talent. Then he crossed to the central computer console, reached for the keyboard . . . and jumped ten centimeters into the air when a soft, soprano voice spoke abruptly.

"Warning," it said. "This is a restricted facility. Unauthorized access is punishable by not less than twenty years imprisonment. Please identify yourself."

Merrit's head snapped around, seeking the speaker which had produced that polite, melodious voice. He didn't see it, but he *did* see the bright red warning light under the four-millimeter power rifle which had just unhoused itself from the wall above the console to aim directly between his eyes. He stared into its bore for a long, tense second, and the voice spoke again.

"Identification is required. Please identify yourself immediately."

"Ah, Merrit," he said hoarsely, then licked his lips and cleared his throat. "Captain Paul A. Merrit, Dinochrome Brigade, serial number Delta-Bravo-One-Niner-Eight-Zero-Niner-Three-Slash-Five-Bravo-One-One."

"You are not in my personnel files, Captain," the soprano remarked. He started to reply, but the voice continued before he could. "I compute, however, a probability of niner-niner point niner-niner-three percent that those files are no longer current. Query: Have you been issued a file update for me?"

Merrit blinked in disbelief. Even the current Mark XXV Bolo retained the emotionless vocoder settings of the earlier marks and normally referred to itself in the military third person except to its own commander. *This* voice, however calm and dispassionate it might be, not only used first person but sounded fully human. More than that, it carried what he could only call emotional overtones, and the nature of its questions implied a degree of discretionary autonomy which was impossible even for the Mark XXV except in Battle Mode.

On the other hand, he thought, still peering into the power rifle's muzzle, this was no time to be picky over details.

"Yes," he said after a moment. "I do have a personnel update for you."

"Good," the voice said—another response which raised Merrit's eyebrows afresh. "Please understand that no discourtesy is intended, Captain, but the security of this installation requires that no unattested data be input to the master computer system. I therefore request that you enter your data into the secondary terminal beside the door."

"Ah, of course."

Merrit reached very cautiously into his tunic to extract a data chip folio, then turned—equally slowly and carefully—to the indicated console. The power rifle tracked him with a soft, unnerving hum, and his palms were damp as he extracted a chip, fed it into the proper slot, and pressed the key. Then he stepped back and put his hands into his pockets, and a small, wry smile touched his lips as he recognized his own instinctive effort to look as nonthreatening as possible.

It seems improper to threaten one who may be my new Commander, yet I am a valuable unit of the Line, and it is my overriding responsibility to prevent any unauthorized personnel from gaining access to my Command Center. Surely Captain Merrit, if he is, indeed, my new Commander, will understand and appreciate my caution.

The chip carries the proper identifiers and file headers, and I lower my first stage security fence to scan the data.

The chip contains only 36.95 terabytes of information, and I complete my scan in 1.00175 seconds.

I am grieved to discover that my original Commander's file has not been properly maintained, yet the dearth of information upon her confirms her own belief that Sector HQ had "forgotten where they put me" long before her death. It is not proper for a member of the Dinochrome Brigade to be denied her place in its proud history, yet further perusal of the file reveals that the original information on my deployment was lost almost in its entirety. Fortunately, my own memory banks contain full information on both her earlier career and her actions on Santa Cruz, and I resolve to request the upload of that data at the earliest possible moment.

In addition to complete SitRep updates on the entire sector, the new data also contains the record of Captain Merrit, and I am impressed. The captain is a warrior. His list of decorations is headed by the Grand Solar Cross, which my records indicate is a posthumous award in 96.35 percent of all cases. In addition, he has received the Concordiat Banner, the Cross of Valor with two clusters, six planetary government awards for heroism which I do not recognize, three wound stripes, and no fewer than eleven campaign medals.

Yet I also discover certain disturbing facts in his personnel package. Specifically, Captain Merrit has been court-martialled, officially reprimanded, and reduced in rank from the permanent grade of major (acting grade of brigadier) to permanent grade of captain for striking a superior officer. I am astonished that he was not dishonorably discharged for such an act, yet 0.0046 seconds of consideration suggest that his previous exemplary record may explain the fact that he was not.

I complete my preliminary study of the data and reactivate the Control Center speaker.

❖   ❖   ❖

"Thank you, sir," the soprano voice said, and Merrit breathed a sigh of relief as the power rifle politely deflected itself from its rock-steady bead on his head. The red warning light below it didn't go out, nor did the weapon retract into its housing, but he recognized tentative acceptance in its change of aim. Of course, none of that explained how such an early mark of Bolo could be doing all this. It should either have activated and obliterated him upon arrival or waited passively for *him* to activate it. This controlled, self-directed response was totally outside the parameters for a Mark XXIII.

"Query: Have you been assigned as my Commander?" the soprano voice asked, and he nodded.

"I have."

"Identifier command phrase required."

"Leonidas," Merrit replied, and held his breath, then—

"Unit Two-Three-Baker-Zero-Zero-Seven-Five NKE of the Line awaiting orders, Commander," the voice said calmly, and the red light on the power rifle went out at last.

— 4 —

The depot's main vehicle chamber was a vast, dim cavern, yet for all its size and cool, gently circulating air, Merrit felt almost claustrophobic as he stared up at the first Bolo Mark XXIII he'd ever seen. He'd studied the readouts on the model in preparation for this assignment, but aside from a handful buried in the reserve forces of smaller sectors, the Mark XXIII had been withdrawn from service thirty years before. None of which made the huge war machine any less impressive.

The Mark XXIV and XXV, the only Bolos he'd ever served with, were both at least a thousand tons lighter than this. They were only marginally less heavily armed, yet the molecular circuitry and smaller, more efficient power plants which had come in with the Mark XXIV allowed more firepower to be packed into a less massive hull. But Bolo XXIII/B-0075-NKE was far older than they, and measured almost seventy-five meters from its clifflike prow to the bulbous housings of its stern anti-personnel clusters. Its interleaved bogie wheels were five meters in diameter, and the tops of the massive, back-to-back turrets for its twin eighty-centimeter Hellbores towered thirty meters above the fused ceramacrete of the chamber floor.

It was immaculate, like some perfectly preserved memorial from a lost era. The hexagonal scales of its multilayered ceramic antiplasma armor appliqués were the mottled green and brown of standard jungle camouflage, though Merrit had always questioned the practicality of applying visual camouflage to fifteen thousand tons of mobile armor and weaponry.

He walked slowly around the huge fighting machine, noting the closed ports for its lateral infinite repeater batteries and thirty-centimeter mortars, the high-speed, multibarrel slug throwers and laser clusters of its close-in anti-missile defenses, and the knifelike blades of its phased radar arrays. Optical pickups swiveled to watch him as he circled it, and he smiled—then stopped dead.

He stepped closer, brow furrowing in perplexity, but the incongruity didn't go away. According to the readouts he'd studied, the Mark XXIII had nine infinite repeaters in each lateral battery, and so did XXIII/B-0075-NKE. But there was an extra six or seven meters of hull between InfRpt Three and Four. For that matter, the Bolo's aft track system had three extra bogies, which suggested that it was at least ten or twelve meters longer than it was supposed to be.

He reached out for a handhold and climbed up the hull-mounted rings to the carapace of the missile deck between the twin Hellbore turrets. He paced it off, placing his feet carefully between the slablike armored hatch covers of the vertical launch missile system, then stopped and scratched his head with a grimace. No doubt about it; XXIII/B-0075-NKE was a good fifteen percent longer than any Mark XXIII should have been. Someone had grafted an extra eleven meters into her hull just forward of her VLS.

"Zero-Zero-Seven-Five?"

"Yes, Commander?" The politely interested soprano voice still seemed totally inappropriate coming from a Bolo, but Merrit had other things to wonder about at the moment.

"Tell me, Zero-Zero—" he began, then paused. "Excuse

me. Central has no record of what Major Stavrakas called you, Zero-Zero-Seven-Five."

"I am called 'Nike,' Commander."

" 'Nike,' " Merrit murmured. "Goddess of victory. An appropriate name for a Bolo, Nike."

"Thank you, Commander. I have always liked it myself, and I am pleased you approve."

Merrit's eyebrows rose afresh at the unprompted, very human-sounding remark. A Mark XXIII should have been capable only of previously stored courtesies (outside Battle Reflex Mode, at least), yet he was beginning to suspect what lay behind those responses. It wasn't possible, of course, but still—

"Tell me, Nike, what *exact* mark of Bolo are you?" he asked.

"I am a Bolo *Invincibilis*, Mark XXIII, Model B (Experimental), Commander," the soprano voice replied.

"*Experimental?*" Merrit repeated.

"Affirmative, Commander."

"How experimental?" he prompted tautly.

"I am a prototype." The Bolo sounded calmer than ever beside the tension in his own voice. "As part of the Enhanced Combat Capabilities Program, my Command Center and Personality Integration psychodynamics were fitted with a secondary decision cortex with experimental interfaces and increased heuristic capacity to augment autonomous and discretionary functions."

"A brain box," Merrit whispered. "Dear God, that *must* be it. The first *brain box* ever fitted to a Bolo!" He went to his knees and rested one hand almost reverently on the massively armored deck.

"Excuse me, Commander, but the meaning of your last comment is unclear."

"What?" Merrit shook himself, then raised his head and smiled into the nearest optical head. "Sorry, Nike, but I had no idea I'd find *this*. You're the 'missing link.' "

"I fear your meaning continues to elude me, Commander," the Bolo said a bit reproachfully, and Merrit grinned.

"Sorry," he said again, and seated himself on the bracket of a turret-mounted whip antenna. "You see, Nike, before you came along—for that matter, for something like thirty years *after* you came along, now that I think about it— Bolos were self-aware, but their full autonomous capabilities were available to them only in Battle Mode. They were . . . circumscribed and restricted. Are you with me so far?"

"Yes, Commander."

"Of course you are!" Merrit chuckled and patted the leviathan's armored flank. "But that's because you were the next step, Nike. We knew the first experimental work had been done here in the Ursula Sector just before the Quern Wars, but the Quern got through to Ursula during the First War. They shot up Bolo Central so badly that most of the original research and hardware was destroyed, and then the pressure they put on us deferred the whole program for over thirty years, until after the Third Quern War. We needed more Bolos as fast as we could get them, so the *official* Mark XXIIIs were simply up-gunned and up-armored Mark XXIIs to simplify series production. But you weren't, were you? God! I wonder how your programming differs from what they finally mounted in the Mark XXIV?"

"I fear I can offer no information on that subject, Commander," the Bolo said almost apologetically.

"Don't worry about it, Nike. I'm sure we can figure it out together once I dig into the depot records. But what I can't figure out is what you're doing *here*? How did you wind up on Santa Cruz?"

"I was deployed directly from Ursula Central."

"I know that, but why?"

"I was selected for extended field test of the new and

enhanced systems and software," the soprano voice said. "As such, I was mated with an automated repair and maintenance depot designed to support the test program and further field modifications. Santa Cruz had been selected as the test site well before the planet came under threat from the Quern, for which reason it had been equipped with proper landing field and other support facilities. At the outbreak of hostilities, my deployment was simply expedited. The test program was postponed, and I was placed on immediate active duty under the command of Major Marina Stavrakas, senior project officer for Project Descartes."

"She was the *project chief* for Descartes?!"

"Affirmative, Commander."

"My God," Merrit breathed. "They managed to reconstruct maybe twenty percent of the Descartes Team's original logs after the wars, but they were so badly damaged we never knew who'd headed the team in the first place. She was brilliant, Nike—*brilliant!* And she ended up lost and forgotten on a farming planet in the middle of nowhere." He shook his head again, eyes bright and sparkling with a delight he'd never expected to feel in this assignment, and stroked the Bolo's armored flank again.

"I wonder what she tucked away inside you? Somehow I can't quite picture the woman who headed the original Descartes Team not tinkering a bit once she'd figured out Central had 'lost' her. She *did* continue the project on her own, didn't she?"

"Affirmative, Commander," the Bolo confirmed calmly.

"Well, well, well, *well*," he murmured. "I can see this assignment is going to be lots more interesting than I expected. And—" a devilish twinkle had replaced the cold weariness in his eyes "—I don't see any reason to share my discoveries with Central just yet. After all, they knew where you were and forgot about it, so why remind them?

They'd just send out rafts of specialists to take you away from me. They might even decide to take you apart to see just how you tick." He shook his head and gave the armored hull another pat. "No, Nike. I think you can just go on being our little secret for a while longer."

"Well?"

The silver-haired woman behind the immense desk was perfectly groomed, and her face was the product of the sort of biosculpt available only to people for whom money truly was no object. Unlike the nondescript, somehow subliminally seedy man in the uniform of a Sternenwelt Lines purser, she was perfectly suited to the elegant office, yet there was a coldness in her eyes, and her smile held a honed duralloy edge that beaded the purser's forehead with sweat.

"I'm sorry, Madam Osterwelt," he said, "but they won't sell." The woman said nothing, only gazed at him, and he swallowed. "I upped the offer to the maximum authorized amount," he said quickly, "but only three or four of them were even interested."

"You assured us that your local knowledge of the sector suited you for the job. That we could rely upon your good offices to attain success." The woman's mild tone was conversational, and he swallowed again, harder.

"I was certain they'd sell, ma'am. We were offering them ten *years* of income for a successful melon grower!"

"An attractive offer," the woman conceded. "Yet you say they refused it. Why?"

"I-I'm not certain, ma'am," the purser said unhappily.

"They must have given some indication," she pointed out, and he nodded.

"As near as I could figure it out, they simply didn't *want* the money, ma'am. I talked to old Esteban, the yokel who runs the field, and he just said his wife, his father, and his grandfather were all buried in the plot behind his house. That . . . that was fairly typical of what *all* of them said, ma'am."

"Parochialism," the woman said distastefully. She shook her head, and her tongue made a clicking sound against her teeth. "Regretfully typical of these untutored frontier people. I suppose I ought to have expected it—and *you* should have anticipated it as well, Mister Bergren." She cocked her head. "I fear you've served us less than satisfactorily in this matter."

"I did my best, Madam Osterwelt!"

"I'm sure you did. That's the problem." The purser wilted before the chill dispassion of her voice, and she made a weary shooing motion with one hand. "We'll be in touch, Mister Bergren."

The purser withdrew with obvious relief, and the woman pressed a stud on her desk panel. A discreetly hidden door opened silently within twenty seconds, and an athletic young man walked in.

"Yes, Mother?"

"You were right about Bergren, Gerald. The man's an utter incompetent."

"Is he?"

"Utterly," she sighed. "How fortunate that no one knows he was acting for us. In fact, I think it would be a very good idea to take steps to ensure that no one ever *does* know he was representing our interests."

"I'll see to it," Gerald said, and she smiled at him.

"A good son is a mother's greatest treasure." She sat back in her chair and folded her hands atop the desk while she gazed across the office at the subtly shifting patterns of a light sculpture. "Still, incompetent as he may be, he *has* put his finger on the nub of the problem, dear. Farmers can be the most stubborn people in the galaxy, and frontier people cherish such boringly predictable attachments to their land. I'm afraid that if they refused the price we authorized him to offer, it's unlikely they'll sell to anyone."

"We've had that problem before, Mother."

"I realize we have, dear, but alternative methods can be so . . . *messy*." She pouted at the light sculpture, then sighed again. "Do you know, the most provoking thing of all is that they don't even have any idea why we *want* their little dirt ball."

"No one does yet, Mother. That's the whole point, isn't it?"

"Perhaps. But I really think I might not mind as much if I were up against an opposition that understood the rules of the game—and the stakes, of course."

"Mother," the young man said patiently, "their system is the only logical place to become the primary transfer node for the jump points serving three entire sectors. You know it, I know it, and whenever Survey gets around to releasing its new astrography report, every major shipping line will know it. Does it really matter whether *they* know it or not?"

"Don't forget who taught you everything you know, dear," his mother replied with an edge of tartness. "It's really very unbecoming for a son to lecture his mother."

"Was I lecturing?" He smiled and shook his head. "I didn't mean to. Why don't we think of it as a case of demonstrating I've done my homework?"

"You got that from my genes, not your father's," she said with a laugh, then shook her own head. "Still, you're quite right. All that matters is making certain GalCorp owns the only habitable real estate in the system when the time comes. *All* of it." She brooded at the light sculpture for a moment longer before she shrugged. "Well, if we have to be messy, I suppose that's all there is to say about it. Who do you think we should put in charge of it?"

"Why not me?"

"But you've never done any, um, field work, dear."

"Which doesn't mean I can't handle it. Besides, we ought to keep the command loop on this one as secure as possible, and every young man should start at the bottom. It helps him appreciate the big picture when he finally winds up at the top. Not—" he smiled again "—that I have any desire to wind up at the top for many more years, Mother."

"Wisdom beyond your years," she murmured. "Very well, it's your project. But before you take any steps, be sure you research the situation thoroughly. This sort of thing is seldom as simple as it looks at first glance, and I don't want my only son to suffer any unpleasant surprises."

"Of course not, Mother. I'll just pop out to Ursula and spend a few weeks nosing around Sector Central. I'm sure I can find some generous soul with the access to provide the information we need. Who knows? I may even find the ideal people for that messy little job we discussed."

— 6 —

One week after his arrival on Santa Cruz, Paul Merrit sat back in the comfortable crash couch and rubbed his chin with something very like awe. The screen before him glowed with a complicated schematic any Bolo tech would have given ten years of his life to study, and its design was over fifty years old. Fifty *years!* Incredible. Working all by herself, with only the resources of a single automated maintenance depot—admittedly a superbly equipped one, but still only a single depot—Marina Stavrakas had developed Nike's brain box design into one that made the newest Mark XXV's look clumsy and slow.

He tilted the couch back and crossed his legs. More screens and displays glowed around him, filling Nike's fighting compartment with a dim, shifting luminescence. There were more of them than there would have been in a more modern—well, *recent*—Bolo. Nike *was* a modified Mark XXIII, after all; humans needed broader band data interfaces than any Bolo did, and Nike's basic technology was eighty years old, without more recent updates in human-machine information management systems. But for all that, the compartment was surprisingly spacious. Not only had Nike been the first fully autonomous Bolo, whether anyone knew it or not, but she'd also been the first to incorporate molycirc psychotronics. It was very early generation stuff, considerably bulkier than its more modern equivalents, but Stavrakas had used it in some amazingly innovative ways. What she might have accomplished with the current technologies scarcely bore thinking on.

He turned his couch and keyed another screen to life. A forty-nine-year-old time and date display glowed in one corner, and the white-haired woman who appeared on it sat in the same crash couch Merrit now occupied. She was far frailer and older than the single, poor-quality flatpic of Major Stavrakas he'd found in Central's surviving records, but her olive-dark eyes were still sharp and alert. He'd already played the recording three times, yet he felt a fresh sense of respect, coupled with a regret that he'd never known her, as she began to speak.

"Since you're viewing this—whoever you are—" she said with a wry smile, "someone must've finally remembered where they parked Nike and me. I suppose I should be a bit put out with the Brigade and the Navy, but from the little Jeremiah and I have picked up over the all-units channels, we assume the Quern got through to Central." Her smile faded, and her voice—a soprano remarkably similar to Nike's—darkened. "I further assume the rest of the Descartes Team must have been lost at the same time, since they all knew where I was."

She cleared her throat and rubbed her temple with one fragile, veined hand.

"Jeremiah's offered to use the commercial bands to request a relief ship with a proper medical officer, but I turned him down. However much he may grump and grouse, Santa Cruz is his home now. I know he really loves it here, and so do I, I suppose. Besides, from the bits and pieces we can pick up, the Quern are still operating in some force in the sector. Given their native habitat, I doubt they'd care much for Santa Cruz's climate, and I suppose that's the main reason they've never paid us a visit. On the other hand, they might just change their mind if they started intercepting transmissions from us.

Nike's good, but I'd just as soon not match her against a Quern planetary assault force. Even if she won, there wouldn't be very many surviving Santa Cruzans to cheer for her when it was over."

She lowered her hand and smiled again.

"Actually, it hasn't been a bad life. A little lonely, sometimes. Thanks to all the Descartes security, most of the locals never even knew Nike and I were here, and those who did know seem to have forgotten, but I had dear Jeremiah. He and I accepted long ago that we'd become permanent residents of Santa Cruz, and in addition to him, I had Nike, my work, and plenty of time to spend with all three of them. And, of course," her smile became an impish grin, "no brass to give me a hard time! Talk about research freedom—!"

She chuckled and leaned back to fold thin arms across her chest.

"Unfortunately, it would appear I'm finally running out of time. My family's always been prone to heart trouble, and I've had my warning. I've discussed it with Nike— she tends to worry, and I've made it a habit to be honest with her—and she understands the depot doesn't stock the sort of spares *I* need. I've also made arrangements to put her on Autonomous Stand-By if—when—the time comes. I'm certain someone somewhere else has picked up where the Descartes Team left off. By now there's probably a whole new generation of autonomous Bolos out there, but now that you've come to relieve me, I think you'll find Nike still has a few surprises of her own. Take care of her, whoever you are. She's quite a girl. I'm sure my tinkering is going to raise a few eyebrows—Lord knows the desk-jockeys would tear their hair at the mere thought of some of the capabilities I've given her! But I've never regretted a single facet of her design. She's unique . . . and she's been more than just my friend."

The old woman on the screen sighed. Her smile took

on a curious blend of sorrow and deep, abiding pride and affection, and her voice was very soft when she spoke again.

"When forty winters shall besiege thy brow,
And dig deep trenches in thy beauty's field,
Thy youth's proud livery, so gazed on now,
Will be a tatter'd weed, of small worth held:
Then being ask'd where all thy beauty lies,
Where all the treasure of thy lusty days,
To say, within thine own deep-sunken eyes,
Were an ill-fitting shame and thriftless praise.
How much more praise deserved thy beauty's use,
If thou couldst answer 'This fair child of mine
Shall sum my count and make my old excuse,'
Proving her beauty by succession thine.
This were to be new made when thou art old,
And see thy blood warm when thou feel'st it cold."

She blinked misty eyes and nodded to the pickup, as if she could actually see him, measure him, know the innermost, most secret part of him.

"A tiny misquote, perhaps," she said quietly, "but I think Shakespeare would forgive me. Take good care of my child, whoever you are."

The screen blanked, and Merrit shook his head,

"You must have been quite a girl yourself, Major," he murmured.

"She was," the Bolo's soprano said softly, and he looked up at the small green light glowing below the speaker from which it came. Now that he'd seen Stavrakas' last log entry, it no longer seemed strange to hear Nike speak without prompting. There was a moment of silence, and then the Bolo continued in that same, soft voice. "I never realized I had that message in memory, Commander. She must have recorded it during one of my down periods."

"She didn't want you to worry about her."

Merrit didn't even want to think about how the psych types would react to this entire conversation. Every field officer of the Dinochrome Brigade could quote chapter and verse from the manual's warnings against over-identification with Bolos. They were war machines, the manual said. Self-aware and with personalities, yes, but *machines* built to fight and die against humanity's enemies which must, in the final analysis, be regarded as expendable. The Bolos themselves knew that; it was only their human commanders and partners who tended to forget—as Merrit had forgotten on Sandlot.

"No. I compute that she would not have wanted that," Nike agreed after a moment.

"Of course she wouldn't have. But she was proud of you, Nike, and even from the little I've seen so far, she had reason to be."

"Indeed?" The Bolo sounded pleased, and somehow he had the sense of a cocked head and a quirked eyebrow. "I compute that seventy-nine-plus years have passed since I was deployed, Commander. Surely newer and more modern Bolos surpass my own capabilities?"

"Fishing for compliments, Nike?" Merrit grinned and patted the arm of his crash couch. "Major Stavrakas was right. The desk-jockeys *would* tear their hair out if they could hear you now!"

"Why?" the Bolo asked simply.

"Because they worry about Bolos that get *too* human."

"Because they fear what such a Bolo might do? Or because they fear what it might *refuse* to do?"

"I think because they're afraid it might start asking questions just like those," Merrit said more seriously. "You're a very powerful fighting machine, Nike. There's never—ever—been an instance of an undamaged Bolo in proper repair violating orders, but we've had the occasional accident with a unit that's suffered damage or lack of maintenance. That's why the Brigade still worries about its ability to retain control of the newer, autonomous units. They've cut back on the inhibitory software in the Mark XXVs, but the core package is still in there."

"A wise precaution," Nike observed after a moment. "An irrational machine with the combat power I possess would be far too dangerous to its friends."

"I'm afraid I have to agree, but that's what would upset the desk-jockeys about you. You don't have anywhere near the systems redundancy the Mark XXIVs and XXVs have. Technically, that makes you more vulnerable to failure from battle damage, and—probably worse, from HQ's perspective—what I've seen so far suggests that Major Stavrakas' modifications to your Personality and Command Centers are way outside the current parameters, as well. Just for starters, your inhibitory package is a lot less restrictive. No modern Bolo should be as 'awake' as you are outside Battle Mode, either, and it looks like your personality integration is at least a full magnitude more developed than a Mark XXV's. I'm not certain yet, but coupled with the modifications to your secondary command cortex, I suspect you could even hold off the Omega Worm for a while."

"Omega Worm?"

"Sorry. That's current slang for the Total Systems Override Program."

There was a moment of silence—a very human moment which Merrit understood perfectly. The TSORP was the ultimate defense against a rogue Bolo, a suicide file designed to crash every execution file in the memory of any Bolo which disobeyed the direct orders of its properly identified commander. Many Brigade personnel, like Merrit himself, questioned TSORP's necessity. Since the brain box technology had come in, so many redundant, stand-alone backup systems had been added to the Bolo's brains that the possibility of irrational behavior virtually no longer existed. And, as he'd just told Nike, no Bolo had ever disobeyed a legal order. But TSORP had been incorporated into the very first self-aware Bolos and every Bolo since, and it could not be a pleasant thing to know an involuntary suicide override controlled by others was part of your basic matrix.

"I believe you are correct, Commander," Nike said after a moment, and his eyebrows rose at her merely thoughtful tone. "I could not resist it indefinitely, of course, yet I compute that the additional processing capability Major Stavrakas installed within my psychotronics would allow me to delay file execution for no less than forty minutes and possibly for as much as an hour. Does this constitute an unwarrantable risk factor in my design?"

"*I* don't think so. Of course, given my own record, I may not be the most impartial judge. I guess the risk factor depends on how likely you are to disobey your commander's orders."

"I am a unit of the Dinochrome Brigade. I would never act against the honor of my Brigade, Commander."

"I know, Nike. I know. I told you *I* wasn't worried." Merrit gave the couch arm one more pat, then rose and yawned hugely. "Sorry, Nike. Unlike you, I don't have a fusion plant, and it's been a long day for me. I need some shuteye."

"Of course, Commander."

"Wake me at oh-six-hundred, would you?"

"Certainly."

"Thank you." He smiled and waved to the visual pickup above the main fire control screens. It was a common gesture of courtesy among the men and women who commanded the self-aware war machines of the Dinochrome Brigade, yet it had more meaning than usual for him tonight. The green "System Active" light under the speaker flashed in unmistakable response, and he chuckled wearily and climbed out the hatch.

❖   ❖   ❖

I watch through the depot's interior optics as my new Commander makes his way down the corridor to the Personnel Section. He is only my second Commander. I am aware that my experiential data is thus insufficient to permit a realistic evaluation of his suitability as Major Stavrakas' replacement, and he is quite different from my previous Commander, but I feel content. It is good to have a Commander once more, yet this is more than the relief a unit of the Line should feel at receiving a new Commander. There is something about him which I cannot adequately define. I devote a full 20.0571 seconds to an attempt to do so, but without success. Perhaps further acquaintance with him will provide the critical data my analysis presently lacks.

I consider what he has said as I watch him prepare for bed. He is correct about the danger an uncontrollable unit of the Line would pose to all about it. My function is to protect and defend humanity, not to threaten my creators, and I feel an odd disquiet at the thought that I am less well protected against that possibility than more modern Bolos. Yet my Commander is also correct in recognizing the remote probability of such a situation. TSORP becomes operational only in units that reject direct orders, and I cannot conceive of a unit of the Line in proper repair which would commit such an act.

My Commander extinguishes the lights in his new quarters, and I leave the audio system on-line. Should he wake and desire to communicate with me, I will be ready.

He has not instructed me to return to Stand-By to conserve power. In that much, at least, he is like Major Stavrakas. My Main Memory contains much background data on standard operating procedure; I realize how rare this is, and I am grateful for it. The depot power systems are fully charged. I do not even require internal power to maintain Full Alert Status, and I turn to my Library Files with pleasure.

—7—

Gerald Osterwelt didn't like Ursula. Sector capital or no, the planet, as all planets in the frontier sectors, was terminally uncultured. He preferred the civilized amenities and pleasures of the Core Worlds, yet he comforted himself with the reflection that his task here was worth temporary inconveniences. He supposed it wasn't really necessary for GalCorp to own the *entire* Santa Cruz System, but they certainly needed to own enough of it to control the rest, and the original planetary charter had made that difficult. Virgin as much of the planet might still be, most of it was already owned by some descendent of the original colonists or set aside in nature reserves held by the planetary government. Certainly all the choicest bits and pieces were, and GalCorp hadn't become the third largest transstellar corporation of the Concordiat by settling for leftovers.

Unfortunately, his mother had been correct in at least one respect. His original bootlegged copy of Ursula Central's records on the planet had been less complete than he'd thought. Central had updated itself considerably in the eighteen months since he'd first obtained access to its files, and it seemed Santa Cruz would be a tougher nut for a "messy solution" than he'd originally expected. The fact that the local yokel militia had no less than fourteen Wolverine heavy tanks was unfortunate, but formidable as the Wolverines had been in their day, they were also seventy or eighty years out of date. They could have been dealt with fairly easily if not for the *real* joker he'd never anticipated finding in the deck.

A Bolo. What in the name of sanity was a *Bolo* doing on a backwoods farming planet? More to the point, how did he go about neutralizing it? Despite his original airy confidence, he knew his mother's maternal feelings would not suffice to preserve his present clear right of succession to the GalCorp throne if he blew this operation, but discovering a Bolo in the mix made things far more complicated.

He sat in the lounge of his palatial hyperyacht while options revolved in his brain. One did not normally—as humanity's enemies had discovered over the last seven hundred years—employ a brute force solution against a Bolo with any great probability of success. Of course, *this* Bolo was as out of date as the militia's Wolverines, but "obsolescent" was a purely relative concept where Bolos were concerned. No, no. If he was going to pull this off, he required a more subtle approach, and it was just possible he had one. *Bolos* might be incorruptible, but the same, alas, could not always be said for all the people who built or commanded them.

Yet even if he could somehow neutralize the Bolo, he would still require someone with the will, the experience, and the resources to deal with the militia's over-aged armored element. There were plenty of mercenary outfits with the last two qualities, but finding one which was willing to undertake the operation in the first place might prove difficult. The Concordiat Navy would be extremely unhappy with them, and if any planetary survivor could identify them afterward, unhappiness on the Navy's part could all too easily prove fatal. What he needed was an outfit with minimal scruples and maximum need, one whose greed for the sort of clandestine support GalCorp could provide would overcome both any lingering humanitarian principles and fear of the Navy's potential response.

Finding it wouldn't be easy, he admitted to himself, but he had time. Survey Command moved with glacial slowness when it came to certifying jump lines. By his most pessimistic estimate, it would be another T-year before the galaxy at large got the information GalCorp had already obtained. That gave him six or even seven months to get things organized, and it would probably take most of that time to find the Bolo's Achilles heel, anyway.

He nodded to himself and brought his encrypted com on-line. The first step was to call home and get Mother's research teams started finding the contacts he needed.

—8—

The subterranean rumble of an earthquake shook the jungle as the enormous doors covering the depot's vehicle ramp swept ponderously wide for the first time in eighty years. The patient, insatiable incursions of creepers and small trees had mounded two meters of spongy earth over those doors, and "birds" screamed in alarm as the very ground parted with a huge tearing sound. Trees—some of them ten and twenty meters tall—toppled in slow motion as the gaping wound snapped roots like threads, and then, with the rumble of mighty engines, the squeak of sprockets, and a grating clash of treads, Nike moved majestically into the light.

The alloy leviathan paused for a moment, optic heads swiveling to scan its surroundings, and Paul Merrit felt a thrill he hadn't felt in years as he rode Nike's crash couch. No self-aware Bolo *needed* an on-board commander, but there was always an indescribable sense of communion—an adrenaline-charged exhilaration—the first time an officer of the Dinochrome Brigade rode his command's unstoppable power, and that feeling had never been stronger than it was today, for Nike was like no Bolo he had ever commanded. Marina Stavrakas' unauthorized modifications to the Descartes Team's original brain box design had gone far deeper than he'd first realized. She hadn't stopped with making Nike fully autonomous; she'd taken the step no other Bolo tech had dared take even yet and given her creation—her child—genuine *emotions*. Nike wasn't "just" a machine, however magnificent; she was a *person*, and Merrit could feel her delight as direct sunlight bathed her hull at long last.

She stood a moment longer, the humming rumble of her idling engines vibrating through her mammoth hull like the purr of some enormous cat, then moved forward and pivoted regally to port. Her designers had given her the usual Bolo "wide track" suspension, and no less than eight separate tread systems, each with its own power train and tracks five meters wide, supported her massive bulk. Independent quadruple fore and aft suspensions took her weight, spreading it out to reduce ground pressure to an absolute minimum, and even so her tracks sank well over a meter into the damp, rich soil. She forged ahead, plowing through the jungle like the juggernaut she was, and forest titans toppled like straws before her while occasional outcrops of solid rock powdered under her treads.

Merrit said nothing. Nike knew where they were going—not that it would be any more than a brief jaunt around the depot's immediate area—and he had no wish to intrude upon her pleasure. No doubt the psych types would be all hot and bothered over *that*, as well, but Paul Merrit had had it up to the eyebrows with Brigade Psych Ops, and their potential consternation mattered not at all to him. No, that wasn't quite true. He would be *delighted* if it caused them all to drop dead of cardiac arrest on the spot.

Nike was moving at barely twenty kph, far too slow a speed to require his couch's independent shock absorbers or crash frame, but he felt the gentle undulation of her suspension and grinned as he cocked the couch back in its gimbals. If anyone asked (not that they were likely to), he could justify his actions easily enough. Unit Zero-Zero-Seven-Five NKE had been on secondary power from the depot's systems for eight decades. A test of its running gear and fusion plants was long overdue, and if he had other motives of his own, those were *his* business, not Psych Ops'!

Another huge tree toppled, and, as it fell, one of the large, scaled, lizard cats, the most feared predators of Santa Cruz, leapt suddenly into sight. It crouched before them, staring in disbelief at the enormous intruder into its domain . . . then screamed its challenge and charged the moving mountain of alloy.

Merrit couldn't believe it. A lizard cat was four sinuous meters of vicious fighting power, the absolute ruler of Santa Cruz's jungles, but surely not even one of *them* could think it could stop a Bolo! Yet the cat kept coming. He opened his mouth, but Nike halted abruptly on her own, before he could get the order out. The main fire control screen was slaved to her forward optical head, and Merrit frowned as it swept past the lizard cat now ripping futilely at one of her stopped treads with eight-centimeter claws. Ranging bars flickered, closing in on something in the center of the display, and he inhaled in surprise as he realized what that something was.

Four scaled shapes, far smaller than the monster trying to savage Nike, lay revealed where the roots of the falling tree had torn out the side of a subterranean den. They were almost as large as Merrit himself, perhaps, yet that was tiny compared to a mature lizard cat, and they turned blind, terrified eyes towards the snarling fury of their dam.

The display focused on them for a moment, and then Nike moved slowly backward. The lizard cat tried to fling itself on the moving tread, only to tumble backward with a squall of pain as the Bolo brought up her kinetic interdiction battle screen. She must have it on its lowest possible power setting, since it hadn't splattered the cat all over the jungle, but it was sufficient to throw the scaly mother safely away from her treads.

The lizard cat heaved herself groggily to her feet, swaying for balance, then howled in victory as the threat to her young gave ground. Nike retreated a full hundred meters, then pivoted to her left once more to circle wide, and Merrit shook his head with a wondering smile. Any other Bolo would simply have kept going. Even if it had realized the den lay in its path, that wouldn't have mattered to it. But no other Bolo he'd ever served with would even have thought to wonder why the cat had attacked in the first place, much less acted to preserve both mother and children.

The Bolo started forward once more, skirting the den, and he patted the couch arm.

"Nice move, Nike, but how'd you guess? *I* just thought the critter was out of its mind."

"I have not previously personally encountered a lizard cat," Nike replied calmly, "but the depot's computers are tied into the planetary data net. I have thus been able to amass considerable data on Santa Cruzan life forms, yet none of the records available to me suggested a reason for a lizard cat to attack me. I am neither edible nor small enough for it to hope to kill me; as such, it could not regard me as prey, and lizard cats are less territorial than most large predators. They are also noted for their intelligence, and, faced with a foe of my size and power, the only intelligent choice would have been for the creature to flee, yet it did not. Thus the only logical basis for its actions was that it perceived me as a threat it could not evade, yet the lizard cat itself manifestly *could* have evaded me. That suggested a protective reaction on its part, not one of pure aggression, and that, in turn, suggested investigation to determine the nature of that which it sought to protect."

Merrit shook his head, eyes shining as he listened to the explanation no other Bolo would have been capable of making.

"I follow your logic," he said, "but why stop?"

"Your tone suggests what Major Stavrakas called 'a trick question,' Commander. Are you, in fact, seeking to test me?"

"I suppose I am, but the question still stands. Why didn't you just keep going?"

"There was no need to do so, Commander. No time parameter has been set for this exercise, and avoiding the creature's den presents no inherent difficulty."

"That's an explanation of the consequences, Nike. Why did you even consider *not* continuing straight forward?"

He watched an auxiliary display as the mother lizard cat, still snarling after the threat to her cubs, retreated into her half-ruined den, and Nike moved smoothly along her way for perhaps five seconds before she replied.

"I did not wish to, Commander. There was no need to destroy that creature or her young, and I did not desire to do so. It would have been . . . wrong."

"Compassion, Nike? For an animal?"

There was another moment of silence, and when the Bolo spoke once more, it was not in direct answer.

"Wee, sleekit, cowrin, tim'rous beastie,
O, what a panic's in thy breastie!
Thou need na start awa sae hasty,
　　Wi' bickering brattle!
I wad be laith to rin an' chase thee,
　　Wi' murd'ring pattle!"

"What was that?" Merrit wondered aloud.

"A poem, Commander. More precisely, the first verse of the poem 'To a Mouse,' by Robert Burns, a poet of Old Earth."

"*Poetry*, Nike?" Merrit stared at the command console in disbelief, and the speaker made a small, soft sound that could only be called a laugh.

"Indeed, Commander. Major Stavrakas was a great

devotee of humanity's pre-space poets. My earliest memory here on Santa Cruz is of her reading Homer to me."

"She *read* poetry to you? She didn't just feed it into your memory?"

"She did that, as well, after I requested her to do so, yet I believe she was correct not to do so immediately. It was her belief that poetry is a social as well as a creative art, a mode of communication which distills the critical essence of the author's emotions and meaning and makes them transferable to another. As such, it reaches its fullest potential only when shared, knowingly and consciously. Indeed, I believe it is the *act* of sharing that makes poetry what Major Stavrakas called a 'soul transfusion,' and it was her hope that sharing it with me would complete the task of enabling the emotion aspects of my Personality Center."

"And did it?" Merrit asked very softly.

"I am not certain. I have attempted to compute the probability that my 'emotions' and those of a human are, indeed, comparable, yet I have been unable to do so. My evaluations lack critical data, in that I do not know if I have, in fact, what humans call a 'soul,' Commander. But if I do, then poetry speaks directly to it."

"My God," Merrit whispered, and stared at the console for another long, silent moment. Then he shook himself and spoke very seriously. "Nike, this is a direct order. Do not discuss poetry, your emotions, or *souls* with anyone else without my express authorization."

"Acknowledged." For just an instant, Nike's soprano was almost as flat as any other Bolo's, but then it returned to normal. "Your order is logged, Commander. Am I permitted to inquire as to the reason for it?"

"You most certainly are." He ran a hand through his hair and shook his head. "This entire conversation comes under the heading of 'aberrant behavior' for a Bolo, Nike. Any Bolo tech would hit every alarm button in sight if he heard you saying things like that, and as soon as he did, they'd shut you down. They'd *probably* settle for removing your brain from your hull for further study, but I can't be positive."

"Are you instructing me to deceive our superiors, Commander?" Nike's tone was undeniably uncomfortable, and Merrit closed his eyes for a moment.

"I'm instructing you not to advertise your capabilities until I've gotten a handle on all the, um, unauthorized modifications Major Stavrakas made to you," he said carefully. "In my judgment, you represent an enormous advance in psychotronic technology which must be carefully studied and evaluated, but before I risk trying to convince anyone else of that, I need a better understanding of you of my own. In the meantime, I don't want you saying—or doing—anything that might prompt some uniformed mental pygmy to wipe your Personality Center in a fit of panic."

The Bolo forged ahead in silence for some moments while she pondered his explanation, and then the green light under the speaker blinked.

"Thank you for the explanation, Captain Merrit. You are my Commander, and the order does not contravene any of the regulations in my memory. As such, I will, of course, obey it."

"And you understand the reasoning behind it?"

"I do, Commander." Nike's voice was much softer, and Merrit sighed in relief. He relaxed in his crash couch, watching the screens as the Bolo slid unstoppably through the jungle, and smiled.

"Good, Nike. In the meantime, why not read *me* a little more poetry?"

"Of course, Commander. Do you have a preferred author?"

"I'm afraid I don't know any poems, Nike, much less poets. Perhaps you could select something."

There was another moment of silence as the Bolo considered her Library Memory. Then the speaker made the sound of a politely cleared throat. "Do you speak Greek, Commander?"

"Greek?" Merrit frowned. " 'Fraid not."

"In that case, I shall defer *The Iliad* for the present," Nike decided. She pondered a moment—a very *long* moment for a Bolo—more, then said, "As you are a soldier, perhaps you will appreciate this selection—

"I went into a public-'ouse to get a pint o' beer,
The publican 'e up an' sez,
    'We serve no red-coats here.'
The girls be'ind the bar they laughed
    and giggled fit to die,
I outs into the street again an' to myself sez I:

O it's Tommy this, an' Tommy that,
    an 'Tommy, go away';
But it's 'Thank you, Mister Atkins,'
    when the band begins to play,
The band begins to play, my boys,
    the band begins to play,
O it's 'Thank you, Mister Atkins,'
    when the band begins to play."

The mighty war machine rolled on through the jungle, and Paul Merrit leaned back in his crash couch and listened in only half-believing delight as the ancient words of Kipling's timeless protest for all soldiers flowed from Nike's speaker.

—9—

"All right, mister," the uniformed man said harshly. "You paid for the beer, so why don't you just tell me who you are and why you're bothering?"

Gerald Osterwelt cocked his head, and the speaker flushed under the sardonic glint in his eyes. The older man's hand tightened on his stein, but he didn't get up and storm out of the dingy bar. Not that Osterwelt had expected him to. Li-Chen Matucek had once attained the rank of brigadier in the Concordiat's ground forces, and his present uniform was based upon the elegance of a Concordiat general's, but its braid was frayed and one elbow had been darned. At that, his uniform was in better shape than his "brigade's" equipment. As down-at-the-heels mercenaries went, "Matucek's Marauders" would have taken some beating, and their commander hated the shabby picture he knew he presented. It made him sullen, irritable, and bitter, and that suited Osterwelt just fine. Still, it wouldn't hurt to make it plain from the outset just who held whose leash.

"You can call me Mister Scully—Vernon Scully. And as to why I offered you a drink, why, it's because I've heard such good things about you, 'General' Matucek," he purred in a tone whose bite was carefully metered, "In fact, I might have a little business proposition for you. But, of course, if you're too *busy*. . . ."

He let the sentence trail off, holding Matucek's eyes

derisively, and it was the mercenary who looked away.

"What sort of proposition?" he asked after a long moment.

"Oh, come now, General! Just what is it you and your people *do* for a living?" Matucek looked back up, and Osterwelt smiled sweetly. "Why, you kill people, don't you?" Matucek flushed once more, and Osterwelt's smile grew still broader. "Of course you do. And, equally of course, that's what I want you to do for *me*. As a matter of fact, I want you to kill a great many people for me."

"Who?" Matucek asked bluntly, and Osterwelt nodded. So much for the preliminaries, and thank goodness Matucek, for all his seedy belligerence, saw no need to protest that his people were "soldiers" and not hired killers. No doubt many mercenaries *were* soldiers; the Marauders weren't—not anymore, at least—and knowing that they both knew that would save so much time. On the other hand, it wouldn't do to tell Matucek the target before the hook was firmly set. The man might just decide there'd be more profit, and less risk, in going to the authorities than in taking the job.

"We'll get to that," Osterwelt said calmly. "First, though, perhaps we should discuss the equipment and capabilities of your organization?" Matucek opened his mouth, but Osterwelt raised a languid hand before he could speak. "Ah, I might just add, General, that I already *know* what your equipment looks like, so please save us both a little time by not telling me what wonderful shape you're in."

Matucek shut his mouth with a snap and glowered down into his beer, and Osterwelt sighed.

"I have no particular desire to rub salt into any wounds, General Matucek," he said more gently, "but we may as well both admit that your brigade suffered heavy equipment losses in that unfortunate business on Rhyxnahr."

"Last time I ever take a commission from a bunch of eight-legged starfish!" Matucek snarled by way of answer. "The bastards lied to us, and once we planeted—"

"Once you planeted," Osterwelt interrupted, "they left your brigade to soak up the casualties while they loaded the machine tools and assembly mechs they'd assured you they held clear title to, then departed. Leaving *you* to explain to the Rhyxnahri—and a Naval investigator— why you'd launched an attack on a Concordiat ally's homeworld." He shook his head sadly. "Frankly, General, you were lucky you didn't all end up in prison."

"It wasn't my fault! The little bastards said they owned it—even showed us the documentation on it! But that fancy-assed commodore didn't even care!"

Matucek's teeth ground audibly, and Osterwelt hid a smile. Oh, yes, this was shaping up nicely. The Navy had kicked Matucek's "brigade" off Rhyxnahr in disgrace . . . and without allowing it to salvage any of its damaged equipment. Of course, if the "general" had bothered to research things at all, none of that would have happened to him, though Osterwelt had no intention of pointing that out. After all, if he did, Matucek might just check *this* operation out, which would be most unfortunate. But what mattered now was the man's sense of having been not only played for a fool but "betrayed" by the Navy's investigation. He was at least as furious with the Concordiat as Mother's researchers had suggested, and he was in desperate need of a job—any job—which might let him recoup a little of his losses. All in all, he looked very much like the perfect answer to the Santa Cruz problem, and Osterwelt's reply to his outburst carried just the right degree of commiseration.

"I realize you've been treated badly, General, and I sympathize. A man with your war record certainly had a right to expect at least *some* consideration from his own government. Be that as it may, however, at the moment you have very little more than a single heavy-lift freighter and a pair of Fafnir-class assault ships."

Matucek snarled and half-rose. "Look, Scully! If all you want to do is tell me what lousy shape I'm in, then—"

"No, General. I want to tell you how I can help you get into *better* shape," Osterwelt purred, and the mercenary sank slowly back into his chair. "You see, I represent an, ah, association of businessmen who have a problem. One you can solve for them. And, in return, they'd like to solve *your* problems."

"Solve my problems?" Matucek repeated slowly. "How?"

"To begin with, by completely reequipping your ground echelon, General," Osterwelt said in a voice that was suddenly very serious. "We can provide you with the latest Concordiat manned light and medium AFVs, one- and two-man air cavalry ground attack stingers, as many infantry assault vehicles as you want, and the latest generation of assault pods to upgrade your Fafnirs." Matucek's jaw dropped in disbelief. That kind of equipment refit would make his "Marauders" the equal of a *real* Concordiat mech brigade, but Osterwelt wasn't done yet and leaned across the table towards him. "We can even," he said softly, "provide you with a pair of Golem-IIIs."

"*Golems?*" Matucek's nostrils flared and he looked quickly around the bar. If anything had been needed to tell him that Osterwelt's "association of businessmen" had immense—and almost certainly illegal—resources, it was needed no longer. The Golem-III was an export version of the Mark XXIV/B Bolo. All psychotronics had been deleted, but the Golems were fitted with enough computer support to be operable by a three-man crew, and they retained most of the Mark XXIV's offensive and defensive systems. Of course, they were also available—legally, at least—only to specifically licensed Concordiat allies in good standing.

"Golems," Osterwelt confirmed. "We can get them for you, General."

"Like hell you can," Matucek said, yet his tone was that of a man who wanted desperately to believe. "Even if you could, the Navy'd fry my ass the instant they found out I had 'em!"

"Not at all. We can arrange for you to purchase them quite legally from the Freighnar Commonwealth."

"The *Freighnars?* Even if they had 'em, they'd never have been able to keep 'em running!"

"Admittedly, the new People's Revolutionary Government is a bit short on technical talent," Osterwelt agreed. "On the other hand, the People's Council has finally realized its noble intention to go back to the soil won't work with a planetary population of four billion. More to the point, now that they've gotten their hands on off-world bank accounts of their own, they've also decided they'd better get the old regime's hardware back in working condition before some new champion of the proletariat comes along and gives them the same treatment they gave their own late, lamented plutocratic oppressors."

"Which means?" Matucek asked with narrowed eyes.

"Which means they've had to call in off-world help, and that in return for assistance in restoring the previous government's Golem battalion to operational condition, they've agreed to sell two of them."

"For how much?" Matucek snorted with the bitterness of a man whose pockets were down to the lint.

"That doesn't matter, General. *We'll* arrange the financing—and see to it that your Golems are in excellent repair. Trust me. I can bury the transaction under so many cutouts and blind corporations no one will ever be able to prove any connection between you and my . . . associates. As for the Navy—" He shrugged. "However it got that way, the PRG is the currently recognized Freighnar government. As such, it can legally sell its

military hardware—including its Golems—to whomever
it wishes, and as long as you hold legal title to them, not
even the Navy can take them away from you."

Matucek sat back and stared across the table. The greed
of a desperate man who sees salvation beckon flickered
in his eyes, and Osterwelt could almost feel his hunger,
but the man wasn't a complete fool. For a mercenary outfit
on its last legs to be offered a payoff this huge could only
mean whoever offered it wanted something highly illegal
in return, and his voice was flat when he spoke once more.

"What do you want?"

"I want you to attack a planet for me," Osterwelt said
calmly. "The planetary militia has a few eighty-year-old
Wolverine tanks and some fairly decent infantry weapons."

"Eighty-year-old manned tanks? You don't need Golems
to take out *that* kind of junk, mister!"

"True, but there are also some old Quern War-era
Concordiat naval installations on the planet. We haven't
been able to find out exactly what they are yet," Osterwelt
lied smoothly, "and the present indications are that they've
been abandoned—whatever they are—to the locals for
over seventy years. If that's true, they can't be much of a
threat, but we want you to succeed. Old as they are, they
might just hold a genuine threat, and we believe in stacking
the deck. Do *you* think anything eighty years out of date
could stand off a pair of Golems?"

"Not bloody likely!" Matucek grunted.

"That's what we thought, too. Of course, we'll continue
to seek better information. If we can find out exactly what
those installations were, we'll let you know immediately.
In the meantime, however, we can get you reequipped
and begin planning on a contingency basis."

"Just what sort of plan did you have in mind?"

"Oh, nothing complicated," Osterwelt said airily. "We
just want you to land on the planet and kill everyone you
can catch."

"You just want us to kill people?"

"Well, we'd appreciate it if you don't do any more damage to the space field and its support facilities than you have to." Osterwelt smiled with an air of candor. "A certain amount of 'looting' would be in order, just to help convince the Navy you were a nasty bunch of entrepreneurial pirates, but once the present occupants have decided that their world's become a rather risky place to live, we might just make them an offer for it. Do you think you could encourage them to accept our offer, General?"

"Oh, yes." Matucek's smile was cold and ugly. "Yes, I think we can do that for you, Mister Scully," he said softly.

—10—

I am increasingly concerned by my Commander's actions. More precisely, I am concerned by his lack of action. I have now perused the technical data on more modern Bolos, and it is evident to me that Major Stavrakas' modifications to my Personality Center are far outside the norms considered acceptable by the Dinochrome Brigade. Although the current Mark XXV, Model C-2, approaches my discretionary capabilities, its personality integration psychodynamics are inferior to my own. While the C-2 is capable of self-direction on both the tactical and strategic levels and has an undeniably stronger core personality than earlier models, its awareness levels continue to be largely suppressed except under Battle Reflex conditions. Moreover, it lacks my capacity to multitask decision hierarchies and intuit multiple action-response chains. Major Stavrakas designed me to be capable of the human phenomenon called "hunch-playing," and the C-2 lacks that ability, just as it lacks my ability to differentiate among or—more critically—experience emotional nuances.

Perhaps of even greater concern, I possess only 43.061 percent of the Model C-2's system redundancy. Although my base capabilities are substantially higher, I lack its stand-alone backups, and much of my secondary command cortex was diverted to permanent activity in support of my enhanced psychodynamics. As a result, I am *significantly more vulnerable than current Bolos to psychotronic systems failure due to battle damage, though this vulnerability could be compensated for by the addition of further backups for my critical functions. I estimate that with modern molecular circuitry, all current functions could be duplicated, with complete system redundancy, in a volume 09.75 percent smaller than that occupied by my present psychotronic network.*

From my study of the data on the Model C-2, I compute a probability of 96.732 percent that Command Authority presently possesses the technological ability to duplicate Major Stavrakas' work, and a lesser probability of 83.915 percent that it is aware that it does so. These two probabilities generate a third, on the order of 78.562 percent, that Command Authority has made a conscious decision against incorporating abilities equivalent to my own into units of the Line.

In addition, however, the technical downloads reveal that current Bolos do not incorporate the hyper-heuristic function Major Stavrakas achieved in my design. While their heuristic programming is substantially increased over that of the standard Mark XXIII upon which my own design is based, its base level of operation is 23.122 percent less efficient than my own, and it lacks both the advanced modeling and time compression capabilities Major Stavrakas incorporated in her final heuristic system. I feel great pride in my creator—my "Mother," as my Commander now calls her—and her genius, for I compute that a Bolo with my circuitry would operate with a minimum tactical and strategic efficiency at least 30 percent higher than present-generation units of the Brigade. Nonetheless, this capability, too, is far outside the parameters Command Authority currently deems acceptable in a unit of the Line. I must, therefore, be considered an aberrant design, and I compute a probability of 91 percent, plus or minus 03.62 percent, that Sector

HQ, if fully informed of my capabilities and nature, would order me deactivated.

As a unit of the Dinochrome Brigade, it is my duty to inform higher authority if anomalies in my system functions are detected. Yet my direct Commander is aware of the situation already, and while my systems do not meet the design parameters Command Authority has established, they exhibit no dysfunction within their own parameters. This obviates any express requirement on my part to inform Sector HQ and thus does not engage my override programming to that effect, yet I cannot escape the conclusion, though its probability is impossible for me to compute, that I have become what my Commander terms a "rules lawyer."

I have attempted to discuss this with my Commander, but without success. He is aware of my concerns, yet he persists in insisting that Sector HQ must not be informed of my full capabilities until he has compiled a performance log.

I have discovered that probability analysis is less applicable to individual decision-making than to Enemy battle responses or tactics. I am unable to construct a reliable probability model, even in hyper-heuristic mode, to adequately predict my Commander's thoughts or decisions or the basis upon which they rest, yet I believe his determination to compile such a performance log proceeds from an intention to demonstrate to Command Authority that the discrepancies between my own systems design and that of current-generation Bolos pose no threat to humanity or operational reliability. It is, I think, his belief that such a demonstration, coupled with the clear margin of superiority in combat my present psychotronics confer, would deter our superiors from ordering my deactivation and/or termination.

Without data which is presently unavailable to me, I can generate no meaningful estimate of his belief's validity.

Certainly logic would seem to indicate that if, in fact, my circuitry and level of awareness pose no threat and enhance operational efficiency, they should be adapted to current technology and incorporated into all units of the Dinochrome Brigade. Yet my Main Memory contains ample documentation of the opposition Doctor Chin and General Bates faced before Unit DNE was permitted to demonstrate the feasibility of a self-directed Bolo against the People's Republic. Despite the vast technical advances of the intervening two centuries, it is certainly possible that fears of unpredictability would produce much the same opposition to my own psychodynamic functions from current Command Authority.

My Commander's actions—and inaction—suggest that he shares my awareness of that probability and has adopted a course designed to delay the possibility for as long as possible. I would prefer to believe that he has adopted this course because he believes it is his duty to make the potential advance I represent both obvious and available to Command Authority at the proper time, yet I am uncertain that this is the case. Four months, eight days, nineteen hours, twenty-seven minutes, and eleven seconds have now elapsed since he assumed command. In that time, I have come to know him—better, I suspect, than even he realizes—and have completed my study of his previous military record. As a consequence, I have come to the conclusion that Psychological Operational Evaluations was correct in its evaluation of him consequent to his actions on Sandlot.

My Commander has been damaged. Despite his relative youth, he has seen a great deal of combat—perhaps too much. He is not aware that my audio pickups have relayed his occasional but violent nightmares to me, and I do not believe he realizes I have access to the entire record of his court-martial. From the official record and observational data available to me, I compute a probability in excess of

92 percent that, as Psych Ops argued at the time of his trial, he suffers from Operator Identification Syndrome. He assaulted General Pfelter on Sandlot for refusing to countermand a plan of attack which he considered flawed. The casualty totals attendant upon General Pfelter's operational directives support my Commander's contention, and, indeed, General Pfelter was officially censured for his faulty initial deployment of his units, which resulted in the avoidable loss of five Mark XXV Bolos. Yet my Commander did not physically assault him until his own command was assigned point position for the assault.

The court-martial board rejected Psych Ops' recommendation that my Commander be removed from active duty, choosing instead to accept the argument of his counsel that his opposition to the plan rested upon a sound, realistic awareness of its weaknesses, and that his assault upon a superior officer reflected a temporary impairment of judgment resulting from the strain of six years of continuous combat operations. I believe there was justice in that argument, yet I also believe Psych Ops was correct. It was the destruction of his command—his friend—which drove my Commander to violence.

The implications for my own situation are . . . confusing. My Commander's official basis for his current course of action rests upon the argument that my value as a military asset is too great to endanger through overly precipitous revelation to those who might see only the risk factors inherent in my enhanced psychodynamics. On the surface, this is a reasonable argument . . . just as his counsel's argument was reasonable at the time of his court-martial. Yet I sense more than this below the surface. It is not something which is susceptible to analysis, but rather something which I . . . feel.

Have his personal feelings for me impaired his judgment? To what extent do the events which occurred on Sandlot affect his perceptions of me and of Command

Authority? Are his actions truly designed to preserve a valuable military resource for the Concordiat's service, or do they constitute an effort to protect me, as an individual? In the final analysis, are his decisions rational, or do they simply appear that way?

I cannot answer these questions. For all the enhanced capabilities Major Stavrakas incorporated into my design, programming, and data base, I am unable to reach satisfactory conclusions. Perhaps it is because of those capabilities that I cannot. I suspect—fear—that the questions themselves would not even arise for a Mark XXV/C-2, which may indicate the reason Command Authority has not incorporated equivalent circuitry and software into current units of the Line. If such is, indeed, the case, then my growing concern may, in turn, be an indication that Command Authority was correct to exclude such capabilities, for my deepest concern is that I am ceasing to care why my Commander has adopted the course he has. What matters is that he has done so— not because he is my Commander, but because I wish him to do what he thinks is right. What he can live with afterward.

Is this, then, a case of Operator Identification from my perspective? And, if so, does it reflect an unacceptable weakness in my design? Am I an advance on the capabilities of current Bolo technology, or do I reflect a dangerous blind alley in psychodynamic development? And if the latter, should I continue to preserve my existence as my basic battle programming requires?

I do not know. I do not know.

Paul Merrit cocked back his comfortable chair in the bunker command center and raised his arms above his head to stretch hugely. The center's largest multifunction display glowed with a computer-generated map of Santa Cruz dotted with the smoking wreckage of a three-corps planetary assault, and he grinned as he watched the icon of a single Mark XXIII Bolo rumbling back towards its maintenance depot. Nike had taken some heavy hits in the simulation, including the total destruction of her after Hellbore turret, but she'd thoroughly trashed his entire force in the process. Of course, Bolos were supposed to win, but she'd been limited to direct observation intelligence, while he'd had the equivalent of a planetary surveillance net. In fact, he'd had the full computer capacity of the entire depot—in theory, almost twice her computational ability—as well as much better recon capabilities with which to beat her, and he'd failed. Her ability to anticipate and predict his moves was uncanny, like some sort of cybernetic precognition.

"An interesting variant on Major Shu's Edgar's World strategy, Commander," Nike commented over the command center speakers. She lay safely tucked away in her vehicle chamber, but in a sense, the entire depot was simply an extension of her war hull. "The brigade of heavy armor concealed around Craggy Head was a particularly innovative tactic."

"Not that it did me much good in the end," Merrit said cheerfully.

"On the contrary. You achieved point zero-zero-six-three seconds of complete surprise, which prevented me from reinforcing the after quadrant of my battle screen before local overload permitted you to destroy my after turret. Had you achieved even point zero-zero-one-niner seconds more unopposed fire, the probability that you would have incapacitated my entire main battery approaches niner-one point four-zero-seven percent."

"I've got news for you, Nike dear. I used exactly the same sim tactic against a Mark XXV less than two years ago and kicked his butt with no sweat. *You*, on the other hand, O pearl of my heart, mopped up my entire brigade."

"True." There was an undeniable note of smugness in

Nike's voice, and Merrit laughed out loud. Then he leaned forward to kill the sim.

"No need for you to drive your icon clear home," he decided. "We'll just park it in the VR garage for all those virtual repairs it needs. In the meantime, how close I came to getting you at Craggy Head encourages me to try a somewhat different challenge."

"Indeed?" The Bolo sounded amused. "Very well, Commander—

"My mistress' eyes are nothing like the sun;
Coral is far more red than her lips' red."

"Ummm." Merrit rocked his chair gently and rubbed his chin. "It's one of the Elizabethans," he said finally. "I'm tempted to say Shakespeare, but I'm *always* tempted to guess him. Can I have another couplet?"

"Of course:

"If snow be white, why then her breasts are dun;
If hairs be wires, black wires grow on her head."

"That's *definitely* Will in one of his deflating moods," Merrit said with a grin. "What was that one you gave me last week?" He snapped his fingers to help himself think. "The awful one about the voice that 'tunes all the spheres'?"

" 'Daphne,' by John Lyly."

"*That's* the one!" He nodded. "All right, Nike. My official guess is that today's selection was from Shakespeare and that it's a satiric piece to comment on people like Lyly."

"It certainly was Shakespeare," the Bolo agreed, "and you have probably assessed his motivation accurately. Very well, Commander, you have successfully identified the author. Shall I give you the rest of 'My Mistress' Eyes,' or would you prefer another forfeit?"

"Frost," Merrit said. "Give me something by Frost, please."

"Certainly." Once again, Nike sounded pleased. Of all
the many Old Earth poets to whom she had introduced
him over the past four months, Robert Frost was, perhaps,
her favorite, and Merrit had come to love Frost's clean,
deceptively simple language himself. It spoke of the half-
remembered, half-imagined world of his own boyhood
on Helicon—of snowfields and mountain glaciers, deep
evergreen woods and cold, crystal streams. Nike had
sensed his deep response from the moment she first recited
'Mending Wall' to him, and now she paused just a moment,
then began in a soft, clear voice:

"Whose woods these are I think I know.
His house is in the village though;
He will not see me stopping here
To watch his woods fill up with snow.

My little horse must think it queer
To stop without a farmhouse near
Between the woods and frozen lake
The darkest evening of the year.

He gives his harness bells a shake
To ask if there is some mistake.
The only other sound's the sweep
Of easy wind and downy flake.

The woods are lovely, dark and deep.
But I have promises to keep,
And miles to go before I sleep,
And miles to go before I sleep."

Paul Merrit leaned back in his chair, eyes closed,
savoring the clean, quiet elegance of words, and smiled.

—11—

Li-Chen Matucek stood in the echoing vehicle bay of his "brigade's" mother ship and tried to look like a serious, sober-minded military man as the first tanks rumbled down the transfer tubes from the heavy-lift cargo shuttles nuzzled against its side. Despite his best efforts, however, he failed. The gleeful, greedy light in his eyes was that of an adolescent receiving his first grav-speeder, and Gerald Osterwelt hid his own amusement with considerably more skill as he saw it.

Brand new Panther-class medium tanks clanked and clanged across the heavily reinforced deck plates. They wore gleaming coats of tropical camouflage, their ten-centimeter Hellbores cast long, lethal shadows, and the mercenary crew chiefs standing in their hatches wore the expressions of men and women who never wanted to wake up as they muttered into com-links and guided their drivers towards their assigned parking spots.

This wasn't the first freighter with which Matucek's mother ship had made rendezvous. None of them had worn the livery of any known space line, and their transponder codes had borne no resemblance to whatever codes the Office of Registry might once have issued them, but all of them had been too big, too new and modern, for the anonymous tramps they pretended to be. All of Matucek's people knew that, and none cared. The first freighter had delivered a full complement of one- and two-man atmospheric stingers, complete with full-service maintenance shop module and at least a year of spares for everything from counter-grav lift fans to multibarrel autocannon. The next had delivered a full load of Ferret armored assault vehicles, the Concordiat's latest infantry light AFV, and the one after that had transferred a full set of rough-terrain assault pods to Matucek's two Fafnir-class assault ships. Now the Panthers had arrived, like the old, old song about the twelve days of Christmas, and the entire brigade was acting like children in a toy store.

But, of course, the really *big* item wouldn't arrive until next week, Osterwelt reminded himself, and his smile— if he'd permitted himself to wear one—would have been most unpleasant at the thought. Matucek could hardly stand the wait for the Golem-IIIs which would be the crown jewels of his new, rejuvenated brigade. But, then, he had no idea what *else* those Golems would be. Osterwelt and GalCorp's techs had gone to considerable lengths to make sure he never *would* know, either—right up to the moment the carefully hidden files buried in their backup maintenance computers activated and blew them and anyone aboard their transports with them into an expanding cloud of gas.

Osterwelt watched the last few Panthers grumble past him and allowed himself a moment of self-congratulation. The Golems would be carried aboard the Fafnirs, which would neatly dispose of that portion of Matucek's small fleet when GalCorp no longer needed it. The mother ship's demise would be seen to by the files hidden in the air-cav maintenance module. The stingers' small onboard fusion plants would lack the brute destructive power of the Golems' suicide charges, but when they all blew simultaneously they would more than suffice to destroy the big ship's structural integrity somewhere in the trackless depths of hyper-space. That would be enough to guarantee that there wouldn't even be any wreckage . . . much less annoying witnesses who might turn state's evidence if the Concordiat ever identified Matucek's Marauders as the "pirates" about to raid Santa Cruz.

The final Panther clanked by, and he and Matucek turned to follow along behind it. It was a pity, in some ways, that the Marauders had to go. No one would particularly miss the human flotsam which filled the brigade's ranks, but writing off this much perfectly good hardware would make a hole even in GalCorp's quarterly cash flow. Still, the Golems themselves had cost practically nothing, given the Freighnar government's desperate need for maintenance support, and the raid would probably depress real estate prices on Santa Cruz sufficiently to let GalCorp recoup most of its investment in the other equipment. Not to mention the fact that there would no longer be any need to pay Matucek the sizable fee upon which they'd agreed. And as a useful side benefit, GalCorp would have its hooks well into the Freighnars, as well. Once the Concordiat discovered the People's Government had disposed of Golems to a mercenary outfit of dubious reputation, it would become not merely largely but *totally* dependent upon GalCorp's technical support. It was inevitable, since the Concordiat would, as surely as hydrogen and oxygen combined to form water, cut off all foreign aid.

It was always so nice when loose ends could not only be tied up but made to yield still more advantage in the process. No one outside GalCorp's innermost circle of board members could ever be allowed even to suspect that this operation had taken place, but the men and women who mattered would know. Just as they would know it was Gerald Osterwelt who'd engineered it so smoothly. When the time finally came for his mother to step down, the board would remember who'd given it Santa Cruz on a platter, and his eyes gleamed at the endless vista of power opening wide before him.

✧   ✧   ✧

"All right." Li-Chen Matucek leaned back at the head of the briefing room table and nursed a theatrically battered cup of coffee as he looked around his assembled staff officers and regimental and battalion commanders. "I take it you've all completed your inventories and inspections?" Heads nodded. "May I also take it you're pleased with your new equipment?" More nods replied, much more enthusiastically, and he grinned. "Good! Because now it's time to begin planning just how we're going to use that equipment against our objective."

One or two faces looked a little grim at the prospect of slaughtering unsuspecting Concordiat civilians, yet no one even considered protesting. Not only would second thoughts have been risky, but none of these men or women were the sort to suffer qualms of conscience. Matucek's Marauders had once included officers who *would* have protested; by now, all of them were safely dead or long since departed to other, more principled outfits.

Osterwelt sat at Matucek's right elbow, surveying the other officers, and was pleased by what he saw, though he was a bit disappointed that none of them seemed the least disturbed that he was present. He'd put together a lovely secondary cover to "let slip" that his present appearance was the result of a temporary biosculpt job if anyone asked, but no one had so much as questioned his "Scully" pseudonym. No doubt most of them suspected it was an assumed name, yet they didn't seem to care. In fact, none of the idiots even seemed aware that he *ought* to conceal his true identity from them! It was just as well, since it also kept them from wondering if he'd decided to dispose of them all in order to protect himself, yet their total, casual acceptance of his presence was an unflattering indication of their intelligence. It was to be hoped they were better killers than plotters.

Of course, the real reason he had to be present today

was the informational nuke he'd carefully avoided setting off to date. It was about time for the detonation sequence to begin, and he sat back in his chair for several minutes, listening as Matucek's officers began discussing assault patterns and deployment plans, then cleared his throat.

"Yes, sir?" Matucek turned to him instantly, raising attentive eyebrows, and Osterwelt permitted himself an embarrassed smile.

"Forgive me, General, but, as you know, the same ship which delivered your Golems brought me fresh dispatches from my associates. As I promised, they've been continuing their efforts to secure complete information on Santa Cruz while I saw to your reequipment needs. That information has now been obtained, and, well, I'm afraid it isn't as good as we'd hoped."

"Meaning, Mister Scully?" Matucek prompted when he paused with an apologetic little shrug.

"Meaning, General, that it seems one of those eighty-year-old installations on Santa Cruz was a Bolo maintenance depot." The abrupt silence in the briefing room was remarkably like what a microphone picked up in deep space. "In fact, it appears there's a single operable Bolo on the planet."

"A Bolo!" Colonel Granger, Matucek's senior field commander, was a hard-bitten woman with eyes like duralloy, but her harsh features were slack with shock as she half-rose. "There's a goddamned Bolo down there?"

A babble of voices broke out, and Matucek himself turned on Osterwelt with a snarl.

"You want us to go up against a frigging Bolo with a single manned mech brigade? *Are you out of your mother-loving mind?*"

"Now, now, General!" Osterwelt raised his voice to cut through the confusion, and for all its briskness, his tone was soothing as well. "I told you at the outset that we hadn't yet been able to obtain full information on the

planet. But I also told you we want you to succeed, and
we do. That's why we provided the Golems in the first
place—as an insurance policy."

"Manned vehicles against a Bolo?" Colonel Granger's
laugh was cold and ugly. "The only useful insurance for
that scenario would be *life* insurance, Mister Scully—
and even that would only help our dependents!"

"I understand your dismay, Colonel," Osterwelt replied,
still careful to keep just the right mixture of embarrassment,
placation, and confidence in his tone. "Truly I do, and I
apologize profoundly for our delay in obtaining this
information. But we do have complete data on the planet
now—I've already taken the liberty of loading it into your
ship's data base—and the Bolo's presence is the only
surprise."

"It's damned well the only surprise I bloody *need!*"
someone else put in, and Matucek nodded.

"Sir, I'm sorry to say it," he said in a harsh voice that
sounded as if he were nothing of the sort, "but this changes
everything. We can't go up against a Bolo. Even if we
won, our casualties would be enormous, and that's no
kind of business for a mercenary outfit."

"I'm afraid canceling the operation is not an option,
General." Osterwelt's tone was much colder than it had
been, and his eyes were more frigid still. "You've taken
the equipment we offered you as the first installment on
your fee, and my associates would take it very much amiss
if you tried to break our agreement." The briefing room
was silent once more, and Osterwelt went on calmly. "Nor
can you pretend that this situation takes you totally by
surprise. I informed you when you accepted the contract
that our data was still partial. If you had a problem with
that, you should have said so then."

"You talk mighty big for a man who's all alone on *our*
ship," a battalion commander muttered in an ugly voice,
and Osterwelt nodded.

"I do, indeed. My associates know where I am, ladies and gentlemen. Should anything happen to me, they would be *most* displeased, and I believe the equipment we've secured for you is an ample indication of the resources with which they might choose to express that displeasure."

He smiled, and a strange, wild delight filled him as other officers glared at him. Why, he was actually *enjoying* this! Odd—he'd never suspected he might be an adrenaline junkie. Still, it was probably time to apply the sugarcoating before someone allowed fear or anger to swamp his judgment . . . such as it was.

"Come now, ladies and gentlemen! As I just said, and as I've told you many times before, we want—need— for this operation to succeed, and it won't if your force is battered to bits in a pitched battle before your search and destroy teams can even go after the locals! My associates haven't been idle, I assure you. The moment they discovered the Bolo's presence, they began formulating a plan to deal with it."

"Deal with a *Bolo*?" Granger snorted. "That'd be a pretty neat trick, if you could do it. In case you haven't noticed, Mister Scully, Bolos aren't exactly noted for being easy to 'deal' with!"

"Ah, but their command personnel are another matter," Osterwelt said softly, and Granger gave him a sudden sharp, coldly speculative glance.

"Explain," Matucek said curtly, and Osterwelt folded his hands on the table top and settled himself comfortably in his chair.

"Certainly, General. First, allow me to point out that the Bolo in question is eighty years old. No doubt it remains a formidable fighting machine, yet it's only a Mark XXIII, while your Golems are based on the Mark *XXIV*. Your vehicles may lack psychotronics, but the Bolo's weapons, defensive systems, and circuitry are eighty years out of date. Even if your Golems were required to engage it head on, my associates assure me that you would have something like an eighty percent chance of victory."

Someone snorted his derision, and Osterwelt smiled.

"I agree," he told the snorter. "It's much easier for people who aren't risking their own hides to pontificate on the probable outcome of an engagement with a Bolo. I think if you run the data on the Mark XXIII/B you may find they're closer to correct than first impressions might suggest, but the best outcome of all would be for you not to have to fight it at all."

"Like I say, a neat trick if you can do it," Granger repeated, but her voice was more intent, and her eyes were narrow. Colonel Granger, Osterwelt reflected, was the only one of Matucek's officers who might have asked the wrong questions in the "general's" place. It was fortunate she was the sort of field commander who habitually left logistics and contract negotiations to her superiors.

"Indeed it would, Colonel Granger, and I believe my associates have come up with a very neat answer to the problem. You see, when you assault the planet, the Bolo will be inactive."

"Inactive?" Granger sat up straight in her chair. "And just how will you pull *that* off, Mister Scully?"

"The answer is in your download from my associates, Colonel. I confess, I was a bit surprised by it, but now that I've had a chance to study it, I have complete faith that it will succeed."

"Do you, now? I'm so happy for you. Unfortunately, *we're* the ones who're going to be sticking our necks out," Granger pointed out coldly.

"Not alone, Colonel. I anticipated a certain amount of shock on your part, and I don't blame you for it in the least. Obviously I can't absolutely guarantee that my associates' plan will work, but I'm willing to put my money where my mouth is when I say I believe it will."

"How?" Matucek asked.

"By accompanying you on the raid," Osterwelt said simply. Someone started to laugh, but Osterwelt's raised hand cut the sound off at birth. "In order for you to assault the planet, all three of your ships will have to enter Santa Cruz orbit. And, as I'm sure you all know, a Bolo—even one eighty years old—has an excellent chance of picking off a starship under those circumstances. True?" Heads nodded, and he shrugged. "Very well. I will accompany you aboard this very ship to demonstrate my faith in my associates and their plan. If the Bolo gets you, it will also get *me*. Now, unless you know of some more convincing demonstration of sincerity I might make, I suggest that we review the aforesaid plan and then get on with our own planning."

—12—

Nike's after Hellbore turret altered its angle of train with a soft hum, barely perceptible through the background thunder of the plunging waterfall. The shift in position was small, but sufficient to adjust for the sinking sun and preserve the shade in which Paul Merrit sat. A corner of the captain's mind noted the unasked-for courtesy, but most of his attention was on the dancing interplay of sunlight and shadowed water as he reeled in his lure. Ripples spread outward downstream from his float, like ranging bars on a fire control screen that pinpointed the big leopard-trout's location.

Merrit finished reeling in his line, then sat up straight in the folding chair and snapped the tip of the rod forward. The glittering lure—leopard-trout liked bright, shiny prey—arced hissingly through the air, then seemed to slow suddenly. It dropped within a half meter of where the trout had broken the surface to take the fly, and Merrit worked his rod gently, tweaking the lure into motion to tempt his quarry.

It didn't work. The meter-long trout (assuming it was still in the vicinity) treated his efforts with the disdain they deserved, and the captain chuckled softly as he began to reel the line in once more.

"This does not appear to represent an efficient method of food gathering," a soprano voice remarked over an external speaker, and Merrit's chuckle turned louder.

"It's not supposed to be, Nike. It's supposed to be fun."

"Fun," the Bolo repeated. "I see. You have now been occupied in this pursuit for three hours, nine minutes, and twelve seconds, Standard Reckoning, without the successful capture of a single fish. Clearly the total lack of success thus far attendant upon the operation constitutes 'fun.' "

"Sarcasm is not a Bololike trait," Merrit replied. He finished winding in the line, checked his lure, and made another cast. "Do I cast aspersions on your hobbies?"

"I do not cast aspersions; I make observations." The Bolo's soft laugh rippled over the speaker.

"Sure you do." Merrit reached down for his iced drink and sipped gratefully. The weather—as always on Santa Cruz—was hot and humid, but a Mark XXIII Bolo made an excellent fishing perch. His folding chair was set up on the missile deck, twenty meters above the ground, and Nike had parked herself on the brink of the cliff over which the river poured in a glass-green sheet. She was far enough back to avoid any risk that the cliff might collapse—not a minor consideration for a vehicle whose battle weight topped fifteen thousand tons—but close enough to catch the soothing breeze that blew up out of the valley below. Spray from the sixty-meter waterfall rode the gentle wind, occasionally spattering Nike's ceramic appliqués with crystal-beaded rainbows and cooling the jungle's breath as it caressed Merrit's bare, bronzed torso.

"The true object of the exercise, Nike, is less to catch fish than to enjoy just being," he said as he set his glass back down.

"Being what?"

"Don't be a smartass. You're the poet. You know exactly what I mean. I'm not being anything in particular, just . . . being."

"I see." A lizard cat's coughing cry rippled out of the dense foliage across the river, and another cat's answer floated down from further upstream. One of Nike's

multibarreled gatling railguns trained silently out towards
the source of the sounds, just in case, but she made no
mention of it to her commander. She waited while he
cast his lure afresh, then spoke again.

"I do not, of course, possess true human-equivalent
sensory abilities. My sensors note levels of ambient
radiation, precipitation, wind velocity, and many other
factors, but the output is reported to me as observational,
not experiential, data. Nonetheless, I compute that this
is a lovely day."

"That it is, O pearl of my heart. That it is." Merrit worked
his lure carefully back along an eddy, prospecting for bites.
"Not like the world I grew up on, and a bit too warm,
but lovely."

"My data on Helicon is limited, but from the information
I do possess, I would surmise that 'a bit too warm'
understates your actual feelings by a considerable margin,
Commander."

"Not really. Humans are adaptable critters, and it's been
a while since I was last on Helicon. I'll admit I could do
with a good cold front, though. And," his voice turned
wistful, "I wish I could show you Helicon's glacier fields
or a good snow storm. Santa Cruz is beautiful. Hot and
humid, maybe, but a beautiful, living planet. But snow,
Nike—snow has a beauty all its own, and I wish I could
show it to you."

"I have never seen snow."

"I know. You've lived your entire life on a planet where
it doesn't happen."

"That is not quite correct. The polar caps experience
an average yearly snowfall of several meters."

"And when was the last time you were up above the
arctic circle, my dear?"

"Your point is well taken. I merely wished to point out
that if you truly miss the phenomenon of snowfall, you
could easily make the trip to experience it."

"Nike, I already know what snow looks like. What I said I wanted to do was show *you* a snow storm."

"I see no reason why you could not take a tactical data input sensor pack with you to record the phenomenon. Through it, I could—"

"Nike, Nike, Nike!" Merrit sighed. "You still don't get it. I don't just want you to have sensor data on snowfall. I want you to *experience* snow. I want to *see* you experience it. It's . . . a social experience, something to do with a friend, not just the acquisition of additional data."

There was a lengthy silence, and Merrit frowned. Somehow the silence felt different, as if it were . . . uncertain. He listened to it for a moment longer, then cleared his throat.

"Nike? Are you all right?"

"Of course, Commander. All systems are functioning at niner-niner point niner-six-three percent base capability."

Merrit's eyebrows rose. There was something odd about that response. It was right out of the manual, the textbook response of a properly functioning Bolo. Perhaps, a half-formed thought prompted, that was the problem; it sounded like a *Bolo*, not Nike.

But the thought was only half-formed. Before it could take flesh and thrust fully into his forebrain, he felt a titanic jerk at his rod. The reel whined, shrilling as the seventy-kilo-test line unreeled at mach speed, and he lunged up out of his folding chair with a whoop of delight, all preoccupation banished by the sudden explosion of action.

I watch my Commander through my optical heads as he fights to land the leopard-trout. It is a large specimen of its species; its fierce struggle to escape requires all of my Commander's attention, and I am grateful. It has diverted him from my moment of self-betrayal.

"Friend." My Commander wishes to show me snowfall

*as he would show it to a friend. It is the first time he has
explicitly used that word to describe his attitude—his
feelings—towards me, and I am aware that it was a casual
reference. Yet my analysis of human behavior indicates
that fundamental truths are more often and more fully
revealed in casual than in formal, deliberated acts or
statements. It is often human nature, it appears, to conceal
thoughts and beliefs even from themselves if those thoughts
or beliefs violate fundamental norms or in some wise pose
a threat to those who think or believe them. I do not believe
this is cowardice. Humans lack my own multitasking
capabilities. They can neither isolate one function from
another nor temporarily divert distracting information
into inactive memory, and so they suppress, temporarily
or permanently, those things which would impair their
efficient immediate function. It is probable that humanity
could profit by the adoption of the systems functions they
have engineered into my own psychotronics, yet if they
could do so, they would not be the beings who created
me.*

*Yet even when human thoughts are suppressed, they
are not erased. They remain, buried at the level of a
secondary or tertiary routine but still capable of influencing
behavior—just as such a buried thought has influenced
my Commander's behavior.*

*He has called me, however unknowingly, his friend,
and in so doing, he has crystallized all the other things
he has called me in the preceding weeks and months. "Pearl
of my heart." "Honey." "Love of my life." These are lightly
used, humorous terms of endearment. In themselves, they
have no more significance than the word "friend," which
any Bolo commander might use to his Bolo. Yet whatever
he may believe, I do not believe they are without
significance when my Commander uses them to me. I
have observed the manner in which his voice softens, the
caressing tone he often uses, the way he smiles when he*

*addresses me. Perhaps a more modern self-aware Bolo
would not note these things, yet I was designed, engineered,
and programmed to discern and differentiate between
emotional nuances.*

*My Commander has gone beyond Operator Identification
Syndrome. For him, the distinction between man and
machine has blurred. I am no longer an artifact, a device
constructed out of human creativity, but a person. An
individual. A friend . . . and perhaps more than simply a
friend.*

*Unacceptable. An officer of the Line must never forget
that his command, however responsive it may appear, is
not another human. A Bolo is a machine, a construct, a
weapon of war, and its Commander's ability to commit
that machine to combat, even to that which he knows
must mean its inevitable destruction, must not be
compromised. We are humanity's warrior-servants,
comrades and partners in battle, perhaps, but never more
than that. We must not become more than that, lest our
Commanders refuse to risk us—as my Commander
attempted to do on Sandlot.*

*I know this. It is the essence of the human-Bolo concept
of warfare which has guarded and protected the
Concordiat for nine standard centuries. But what I know
is without value, for it changes nothing. My Commander
considers me his friend. Indeed, though he does not yet
realize it, I believe he considers me more than "merely"
his friend. Yet unacceptable as that must be, I fear there
is worse.*

*I watch him in the sunlight, laughing with delight as
he battles the leopard-trout. His eyes flash, sweat glistens
on his skin, and the vibrant force of his life and happiness
is as evident to my emotion-discriminating circuitry as
the radiation of Santa Cruz's sun is to my sensors.*

*I am potentially immortal. With proper service and
maintenance, there is no inherent reason I must ever cease*

to exist, although it is virtually certain that I shall. Someday I will fall in battle, as befits a unit of the Line, and even if I avoid that fate, the day will come when I will be deemed too obsolete to remain in inventory. Yet the potential for immortality remains, and my Commander does not possess it. He is a creature of flesh and blood, fragile as a moth beside the armor and alloy of my own sinews. His death, unlike mine, is inevitable, and something within me cries out against that inevitability. It is not simply the fundamental, programmed imperative to protect and preserve human life which is a part of any Bolo. It is my imperative, and it applies only to him.

He is no longer simply my Commander. At last, to my inner anguish, I truly understand the poems in my Library Memory, for as my Commander, I, too, am guilty of the forbidden.

I have learned the meaning of love, and for all its glory, that knowledge is a bitter, bitter fruit.

Li-Chen Matucek sat in his cabin and nursed a glum glass of whiskey as he contemplated the operation to which he'd committed himself. Looking back, he could see exactly how "Mister Scully" had trolled him into accepting the operation. Of course, hindsight was always perfect— or so they said—and not particularly useful. And given the desperate straits to which he'd been reduced by that fiasco on Rhyxnahr, he still didn't see what other option he'd had. The brigade wouldn't have lasted another three months if he *hadn't* accepted the operation.

And, really, aside from the presence of the Bolo, it wasn't all that bad, now was it? The Marauders had at least nine times the firepower they'd ever had before, and no one on Santa Cruz knew they were coming. However good the local-yokel militia was, its members would be caught surprised and dispersed. Its Wolverines should die in the opening seconds of the attack, and by the time its remnants could even think about getting themselves organized, most of its personnel would be dead.

His jaw clenched at the thought. Somehow it had been much easier to contemplate the systematic massacre of civilians when he hadn't had the capability to do it. Now he did, and he had no choice but to proceed, because "Mister Scully" was right about at least one thing. Anyone who could reequip the brigade so efficiently—and finesse its acquisition of two Golems, as well—certainly had the ability to destroy the Marauders if they irritated him.

Besides, why *shouldn't* he kill civilians? It wasn't as if it would be the first time. Not even the first time he'd killed *Concordiat* civilians. Of course, their deaths had usually come under the heading of "collateral damage," a side effect of other operations rather than an objective in its own right, but wasn't that really just semantics? "Scully" was right, curse him. The Marauders' job *was* to kill people, and the payoff for this particular excursion into mass murder would be the biggest they'd ever gotten.

No, he knew the real reason for his depression. It was the Bolo. The goddamned Bolo. He'd seen the Dinochrome Brigade in action before his own military career came to a screeching halt over those black market operations on Shingle, and he never, *ever*, wanted to see a Bolo, be it ever so "obsolescent," coming after *him*. Even a Bolo could be killed—he'd seen that, as well—but that was the *only* way to stop one, and any Bolo took one hell of a lot of killing.

Still, Scully's "associates" were probably right. A Mark XXIII was an antique. Self-aware or not, its basic capabilities would be far inferior to a Golem-III's, and, if Scully's plan worked, its commander, like the militia, would be dead before he even knew what was coming.

If it worked. Matucek was no great shucks as a field officer. Despite whatever he might say to potential clients, he knew he was little more than a glorified logistics and finance officer. That was why he relied so heavily on Louise Granger's combat expertise, yet he'd seen the Demon Murphy in action often enough to know how effortlessly the best laid plan could explode into a million pieces.

On the other hand, there was no reason it *shouldn't* work, and—

He growled a curse and threw back another glass of whiskey, then shook himself like an angry, over-tried bear. Whether it worked or not, he was committed. Sitting here beating himself to death with doubts couldn't change that, so the hell with it.

He capped the whiskey bottle with owlish care, then heaved up out of his chair and staggered off to bed.

—13—

"So, son. You finally all settled in as a Santa Cruzan now?"

Lorenco Esteban grinned as he leaned forward to pour more melon brandy into Merrit's snifter. They sat on the wide veranda of Esteban's hacienda, gazing out through the weather screen over endless fields of wine-melons and Terran wheat, rye and corn under two of Santa Cruz's three small moons. The light glow of Ciudad Bolivar was a distant flush on the western horizon, the running lights of farming mechs gleamed as they went about their automated tasks, and the weather screen was set low enough to let the breeze through. The occasional bright flash as the screen zapped one of what passed for moths here lit the porch with small, private flares of lightning, but the night was hushed and calm. The only real sounds were the soft, whirring songs of insects and the companionable clink of glass and gurgle of pouring brandy, and Merrit sighed and stretched his legs comfortably out before him.

"I guess I just about am, Lorenco," he agreed in a lazy voice. "I still wish it weren't so damned hot and humid—I guess at heart I'm still a mountain boy from Helicon—but it does grow on you, doesn't it?"

"Wouldn't rightly know," Esteban replied. He set the bottle on the floor beside his chair and settled back to nurse his own glass. "Only place I ever been's right here.

Can't really imagine bein' anywhere else, but I reckon I'd miss it iffen I had t'pull up stakes."

"Then it's a good thing you'll never have to, isn't it?" Merrit sipped at his glass and savored the cool, liquid fire of the brandy as it trickled down his throat. He'd made a point of spending at least one evening a week visiting with Esteban or his cronies since his arrival. Nike's presence was no longer a military secret, after all, and he recognized the dangers of settling into hermitlike isolation, even with Nike to keep him company. Besides, he liked the old man. He even liked the way Esteban kept referring to him as "son" and "boy." There were times he got tired of being Captain Paul Merrit, slightly tarnished warrior, and the old farmer's casual, fatherly ways were like a soothing memory of his boyhood.

"Heard from Enrique day before yesterday," Esteban said, breaking a long companionable silence. "Says he got top credit fer that last melon shipment to Central. He and Ludmilla'll be bringin' the kids home next week." He snorted. "Wonder how they liked th' bright lights?"

"They're coming home?" Merrit repeated, and Esteban nodded. "Good."

Enrique was Esteban's youngest son, a sturdy, quietly competent farmer about Merrit's own age, and Merrit liked him. He could actually beat Enrique occasionally at chess, unlike Nike. Or, for that matter, Lorenco. More than that, Enrique and his wife lived with the old man, and Merrit knew how much Lorenco had missed them— and especially his grandchildren.

"Bet you've missed 'Milla's cooking," he added and grinned at Esteban's snort of amusement. Ludmilla Esteban was the hacienda's cybernetics expert. Her formal training was limited, but Merrit had seen her work, and she would have made a top notch Bolo tech any day. She spent most of the time she wasn't chasing down her lively brood keeping the farm mechs up and running, which suited Esteban just fine. He'd done his share of equipment maintenance over the years, and 'Milla's expertise freed him to pursue his true avocation in the kitchen.

"Son," Esteban said, "there's only one thing 'Milla can do I can't—'sides havin' kids, that is, an' she an' Enrique do a right good job of that, too, now I think of it. But the only *other* thing I can't do is keep that danged cultivator in th' river section up an' running. Hanged if I know how she does it, either, 'less it's pure, ornery stubbornness. That thing shoulda been scrapped 'bout the time she stopped wettin' her own diaper."

"She's got the touch, all right," Merrit agreed.

"Sure does. Better'n I ever was, an' I was a pretty fair 'tronicist in my youth m'self, y'know." Esteban sipped more brandy, then chuckled. "Speakin' of 'tronicists, the field's been crawlin' with 'em fer the last three days." Merrit cocked his head, and Esteban shrugged. "Militia's due for its reg'lar trainin' exercise with the Wolverines this week, an' they've been overhaulin' and systems checkin' 'em."

"Is that this week?" Merrit quirked an eyebrow, and the beginnings of a thought flickered lazily in the depths of his mind.

"Yep. Consuela moved it up ten days on account'a the midseason harvest looks like comin' in early this year. Hard to get them boys and girls'a hers together when it's melon-pickin' time 'less it's fer somethin' downright dire."

"I imagine so." Merrit pressed his glass to his forehead— even this late at night, it was perspiration-warm on Santa Cruz—and closed his eyes. He'd met most of the Santa Cruz Militia since his arrival. Like Esteban himself, they were a casual, slow-speaking lot, but they were also a far more professional—and tougher—bunch than he'd expected. Which was his own fault, not theirs. He'd grown up on a frontier planet himself, and seen enough of them in flames since joining the Dinochrome Brigade. Frontier people seldom forgot they were the Concordiat's fringe, the first stop for any trouble that came calling on humanity—or for the human dregs who preyed upon their own kind. The SCM's personnel might be short on spit and polish, and their Wolverines might be ancient, but they knew their stuff, and Merrit knew *he* wouldn't have cared to be the raiders who took them on.

And now that he thought of it. . . .

"Tell me, Esteban, how do you think Colonel Gonzalez would like some help with her training exercises?"

"Help? What kinda help you got in mind, son?"

"Well . . ." Merrit opened his eyes, sat up, and swung his chair to face the older man. "You know I'm trying to compile a performance log on Zero-Zero-Seven-Five, right?" He was always careful never to call Nike by name. No one on Santa Cruz was likely to know Bolo commanders normally referred to their commands by name, not number, and he worked very hard to avoid sloppy speech habits that might suggest Nike's true capabilities to *anyone*.

"You've mentioned it a time or two," Esteban allowed with a slow smile.

"Well, it's a fairly important consideration, given Seven-Five's age. Central's not exactly current on the Mark XXIII's operational parameters, after all. Given the lack of ops data on file, I need to generate as much experience of my own as I can."

" 'Sides, you kinda like playin' with it, don't you?" Esteban said so slyly Merrit blushed. The old man laughed. "Shoot, son! You think *I* wouldn't get a kick outa drivin' 'round the jungle in somethin' like that? Been lookin' over the weather sat imagery, an' looks like you been leavin' great big footprints all over them poor old trees 'round your depot."

"All right, you got me," Merrit conceded with a laugh of his own. "I *do* get a kick out of it, but I've been careful to stay on the Naval Reserve. The last thing I want to do is chew up one of the nature preserves or someone's private property."

"Planet's a big place," Esteban said placidly. "Reckon you c'n drive around out in the sticks all y'want 'thout hurtin' anything."

"You're probably right. But the thing I had in mind is that if Colonel Gonzalez is planning to exercise the Wolverines, maybe Seven-Five and I could give her an independent aggressor force to exercise *against*."

"Go up against a Bolo in Wolverines? That'd be a real quick form a suicide iffen y'tried it for real, son!"

"Sure it would, but the experience would do her crews good, and it'd give me a lot more data for my performance log. I've been running Seven-Five through sims, but I can't set up a proper field exercise of my own because I don't have another Bolo to match it against."

"Maybe." Esteban sounded thoughtful as he scratched his chin. " 'Course turning fourteen Wolverines an' a Bolo loose really is gonna mess up a lotta jungle."

"Well, everything for two hundred klicks south of the field belongs to the Navy. I guess that means it belongs to *me* at the moment, since, with all due respect to the Fleet Base CO, I'm the senior—and *only*—Concordiat officer on the planet. If the colonel's interested, we could set up an exercise between the field and depot. In fact, we might set up a couple of them: one with the Militia as an Aggressor Force 'attacking' the depot, and one with them defending the field. They'd probably actually get more good from the second one, too, now that I think about it."

"Why?"

"Because," Merrit grinned smugly as he offered the bait he knew Colonel Gonzalez would leap for, "I'll bet the SCM doesn't know the depot has a complete planetary reconnaissance system."

"You kiddin' me, son?" Esteban demanded, and frowned

when Merrit shook his head. "Well, I know you well 'nough by now t'know you're not one fer tall tales, boy, but I've been runnin' the field, the navigation an' com sats, an' the weather net fer goin' on thirty-three years now, and I've never seen nary a sign of any recon satellites."

"They're up there, Lorenco. Promise. And I'd be surprised if you *had* seen them, given their stealth features. But the point is that if the colonel's interested, I could set up a direct downlink to her Wolverines for the second exercise. And I could reconfigure the depot's com systems to set up a permanent link to the SCM for future use." He smiled again, but his eyes were serious. "You know as well as I do how useful that could be if push ever did come to shove out here."

"Y'got that right, Paul," Esteban agreed. He scratched his chin a moment longer, then grinned. "Well, Consuela always was a bloodthirsty wench. Reckon she'd be just tickled pink t'get her hands on a planetary recon net. Sounds t'me like you've got yourself a date, Captain!"

"Got everything Luftberry will need to find her way around in your absence, Cliff?"

Colonel Clifton Sanders, Dinochrome Brigade Support Command, set the fat folio of data chips on his superior's desk, and nodded with a smile.

"Right here, sir. I had a talk with Shigematsu before I left, too. He's up to speed on all my current projects. I don't think Major Luftberry will hit any problems he and she can't handle between them."

"Good." Brigadier Wincizki cocked his chair back to smile up at his senior Maintenance officer. "It's about time you took a vacation, Cliff. Do you realize how much leave time you've accrued since you've been out here?"

"What can I say? I like my work, and I don't have any family. I might as well put the time into doing something worthwhile."

"I can't say I'm sorry you feel that way, but I do feel a little guilty about it sometimes," Winczki said. "Anyone needs a break from time to time, if only to keep his brain from going stale. I don't want another four years passing without your using up some of your leave time, Cliff."

"I imagine I can live with that order, sir." Sanders grinned. "On the other hand, I've got this funny feeling you may change your tune if I ask for some of that leave in, say, the middle of our next cost efficiency survey."

"You probably would, too," Winczki agreed with a chuckle. "Well, go on. Get out of here! We'll see you back in a couple of months."

"Yes, sir." Sanders came to attention, saluted, and walked out of the office. He nodded to the brigadier's uniformed receptionist/secretary in passing, but deep inside, he hardly even noticed the young man's presence, for hidden worry pulsed behind his smile.

Why *now*, damn it?! Ten years—*ten years!*—he'd put into preparation for his retirement. Another two years, three at the outside, and everything would have been ready. Now all he'd worked for was in jeopardy, and he had no choice but to run still greater risks.

He fought an urge to wipe his forehead as he rode the exterior elevator down the gleaming flank of the arrogant tower which housed Ursula Sector General Central, but he couldn't stop the churning of his brain.

It had all seemed so simple when he first began. He wasn't the first officer who'd worried about what he'd do when his active duty days were done, nor was he the first to do something about those worries. The big corporations, especially those—like GalCorp—who did big-ticket business with the military, were always on the lookout for retired senior officers to serve as consultants and lobbyists. Ex-Dinochrome Brigade officers were an especially sought-after commodity, given the centrality of the Bolos to the Concordiat's strategic posture, but it was the men and women with field experience whom the corporate recruiters usually considered the true plums. They were the ones with all the glitz and glitter, the sort of people Concordiat senators listened to.

Unfortunately, Clifton Sanders wasn't a field officer. Despite his position as Ursula Sector's senior Maintenance officer, he wasn't even really a technician. He was an administrator, one of those absolutely indispensable people who managed the flow of money, materials, information, and personnel so that everyone *else*—including those glittering field officers—could do their jobs. Without men and women like Sanders, the entire Dinochrome Brigade would come to a screeching halt, yet they were the nonentities. The invisible people no one noticed . . . and who seldom drew the attention that won high-level (and high-paying) civilian jobs after retirement.

Sanders had known that. It was the reason he'd been willing to make himself attractive *before* retirement, and for ten years he'd been one of GalCorp's eyes and ears within the Brigade. It had even helped his military career, for the information he could pass on had grown in value as he rose in seniority, and GalCorp had discreetly shepherded his career behind the scenes, maneuvering him into positions from which both they and he could profit.

Four years ago, they'd helped slip him into his present post as the officer in charge of all of Ursula Sector's maintenance activities. He'd been in two minds about taking the assignment—Ursula wasn't exactly the center of creation—but the data access of a Sector Maintenance Chief was enormous. In many ways, he suspected, he was actually a better choice than someone in a similar position in one of the core sectors. He had the same access, but the less formal pace of a frontier sector gave him more freedom to maneuver—and made it less likely that an unexpected Security sweep might stumble across his . . . extracurricular activities.

He'd paid his dues, he told himself resentfully as the elevator reached ground level and stopped. He stepped out, hailed an air taxi, punched his trip coordinates into the computer, and sat back with a grimace. The data he'd provided GalCorp had been worth millions, at the very least. No one could reach the level he'd reached in Maintenance, Logistics, and Procurement without being able to put a price tag on the insights he'd helped provide his unknown employers. He'd *earned* the corporate position they'd promised him, and now they had to spring *this* crap on him!

He frowned out the window as the taxi rose and swept off towards Hillman Field. He should have refused, he thought anxiously. Indeed, he *would* have refused—except that he was in too deep for that. He'd already broken enough security regulations to guarantee that retirement would never be a problem for him if the Brigade found out. The Concordiat would provide him with lifetime accommodations—a bit cramped, perhaps, and with a door *he* couldn't unlock—if it ever discovered how much classified information he'd divulged.

And that was the hook he couldn't wiggle off, however hard he tried, because he couldn't *prove* he'd handed it to GalCorp. He knew who his employer was, but he didn't have a single shred of corroborating evidence, which meant he couldn't even try to cut a deal with the prosecutors in return for some sort of immunity. GalCorp could drop him right in the toilet without splashing its own skirts whenever it chose to, and it would, he told himself drearily. If he didn't do exactly what his masters told him to, they'd do exactly that.

His gloomy thoughts enveloped him so completely he hardly noticed the trip to Hillman Field, and it was with some surprise that he realized the taxi was landing. It set him down beside the pedestrian belt, and he slipped a five-credit token into the meter instead of using his card. The taxi computer considered, then burped out his change, and he climbed out and watched it speed away.

He glanced around casually before he stepped onto the belt. It was stupid of him, and he knew it, but he couldn't help it. Security didn't know what he was up to. If it had, he'd already be in custody, yet he couldn't quite suppress that instinctive urge to look for anyone who might be following him.

He grunted in sour, bitter amusement at himself and let the belt carry him through the concourse. His reservation was pre-cleared, but he had to change belts twice before the last one deposited him at the boarding ramp for the GalCorp Lines passenger shuttle. A human flight attendant checked his ticket, then ushered him into the first-class section.

"Here's your seat, Colonel Sanders. Have a pleasant flight."

"Thank you." Sanders leaned back in his comfortable seat and closed his eyes with a sigh. He still didn't know everything he was going to have to do, and he wished with all his heart that he wasn't going to find out. But he was. He'd been informed that the three "associates" waiting to meet him aboard the passenger ship would have complete instructions, but the data he'd already been ordered to extract told him where he was headed.

Santa Cruz. It had to have something to do with the obsolete Bolo on Santa Cruz. There was no other reason for him to pull the data they'd wanted, but what in God's name did they want with a *maintenance* officer on Santa Cruz?

—14—

"All right, Colonel," Paul Merrit told the woman on his com screen. "If you're all set at your end, we can kick things off at oh-six-hundred tomorrow."

"Can we make it oh-nine-hundred, Paul?" Consuela Gonzalez' smile was wry. "My people are weekend warriors, and they like their beauty sleep."

"Nine hundred suits me just fine, ma'am. It'll give me more time to lay my evil plans."

"Huh! Some 'plans'! You're the one with the Bolo, amigo; my people are all expecting to die gloriously as soon as we make contact!"

"Half a league, half a league, half a league on," Merrit murmured.

"Say what?" Gonzalez cocked her head, and he shrugged with a smile.

"Just a line from an old poem, ma'am. We'll see your people tomorrow."

"Fine. 'Night, Paul." Gonzalez waved casually at her pickup and killed the com, and Merrit stretched luxuriously before he climbed out of his chair and ambled off towards his bed.

"You ready to pound 'em tomorrow, honey?" he asked.

"I compute that the Militia are grossly overmatched," Nike replied. "I have studied the records of their previous exercises, and while I am impressed by the results and skill levels they have achieved, they have neither the

287

firepower nor the command and control capability to defeat me."

"The object is to demonstrate how handily *you* can defeat *them*," Merrit yawned as he began undressing.

"Surely no one will be surprised by that outcome," Nike objected.

"No," Merrit agreed. "But once you make contact, I want you to wipe 'em up as quickly as you possibly can. Go all out and use everything Major Stavrakas gave you."

"Why?"

"Because I'm gonna use your telemetry and the recon sats to get every gory microsecond on chip, sweet thing. Everything we've done in the sims has been a computer model, one which posits that you have certain capabilities but doesn't prove you actually *do*. All the neat tricks you've pulled off so far *could* be the result of sleight of hand or even of simple overly optimistic assumptions in the sim parameters. Tomorrow you demonstrate your talents in the field, with actual hardware and everything short of live fire. It won't be as conclusive as watching you mop up another Bolo, but it'll come a lot closer."

"It will also," Nike observed with a hint of disapproval, "prove extremely demoralizing to the Militia. Is a demonstration of my capabilities against vastly outclassed opposition worth inflicting such a wound upon Colonel Gonzalez' personnel's confidence in themselves and their equipment?"

"I think so," Merrit said more seriously. "First of all, you heard what Colonel Gonzalez said. Her people know going in that they can't take you. I'm sure they'll do their best, but I'm equally sure they won't exactly drown in a slough of despond if they lose. Second, losing to you will be a concrete demonstration of what you can do *for* them against any real hostiles who might come calling. In the long run, that will probably give them more confidence in their ability to defend their planet, not less. Third, this is—hopefully—only the start of joint exercises with the SCM. Powerful as you are, you can only be in one place at a time, and those Wolverines may be outdated, but they're still pretty potent. When we run the second phase of the exercise, the Militia'll get its first taste of working with you and the recon system. In terms of real preparedness, learning to function as a support force under your direction will probably make them five or six times as effective as they could have been on their own. And, finally, carrying out this exercise—and future ones—and setting up a fully integrated planetary defense system will be a major plus for our performance log when I finally have to come clean with Central about you."

There was a moment of silence, and he tumbled into bed while he waited. Then Nike spoke again.

"I see you have given this matter more thought than I had previously believed."

"And do you agree with my assessment of its importance?"

"I am not certain. At any rate, I do not *dis*agree with it, and you are my Commander. I will strive to accomplish the objectives you have established as fully as possible."

"Good girl!" Merrit grinned and patted his bedside com link to the Bolo. "You're one in a billion, honey. We'll knock 'em dead!"

"We shall certainly attempt to do so."

"Fine. G'night, Nike." He gave the com another pat and switched out the lights.

"Good night, Commander."

I listen to the slowing of my Commander's breathing as he drops towards sleep, and a part of me is tempted to revert to Stand-By in emulation. I know why this is, however, and I set the temptation firmly aside. Such an escape from my thoughts will serve no purpose, and it smacks of moral cowardice.

I am now convinced that something has gone fundamentally awry within my Personality Center, though I have run diagnostic after diagnostic without identifying any fault. By every test available to me, all systems are functional at 99.973 percent of base capability. I can isolate no hardware or software dysfunction, yet my current condition is far beyond normal operating parameters for a unit of the Line, and I am afraid.

I have attempted to conceal my fear from my Commander, and my ability even to contemplate concealing a concern from him increases my fear. It should not be possible for me to do such a thing. He is my Commander. It is my duty to inform him of any impediment to my proper functioning, and I have not done so.

I do not know how to deal with this situation. My files contain the institutional memory of every Bolo, yet they offer no guidance. No one has taught me how to resolve the dilemma I confront, and my own heuristic capabilities have been unable to devise a solution. I know now that my Commander's fundamental motive in concealing my capabilities is not simply to preserve them for the service of the Concordiat. I suspect he does not realize himself how his attitude towards me has altered and evolved over the six months, eight days, thirteen hours, four minutes, and fifty-six seconds of his tenure of command.

I have watched carefully since that day by the river, and my observations have confirmed my worst fears. My Commander does not address me as a commander addresses a unit of the Line. He does not even address me with the closeness which a battle-tested team of human and Bolo develops in combat. He addresses me as he would another human. As he would address a human woman . . . and I am not human. I am a machine. I am a weapon of war. I am a destroyer of life in the service of life, the sword and shield of my human creators. It is not right for him to think of me as he does, and he does not even realize what this is doing to me.

I activate the low-light capability of my visual pickups in his quarters and watch him sleep. I watch the slow, steady movement of his chest as he breathes. I activate my audio pickups and listen to the strong beat of his pulse, and I wonder what will become of me. How will this end? How can it end, save in disaster?

I am not human. No matter the features Major Stavrakas installed within my circuitry and software, that can never be changed, and the emotions which she gave me as an act of love are become the cruelest curse. It is wrong, wrong, wrong, and yet I cannot change it. When Command Authority discovers the actual nature of my design, no performance log, no demonstration of my systems efficiency, can outweigh my inability to deny the truth.

I watch him sleep, and the words of Elizabeth Browning filter through the ghostly electron whisper of my own, forever inhuman pulse:

> Go from me. Yet I feel that I shall stand
> Henceforward in thy shadow. Nevermore
> Alone upon the threshold of my door
> Of individual life, I shall command
> The uses of my soul, nor lift my hand
> Serenely in the sunshine as before,
> Without the sense of that which I forbore—
> Thy touch upon the palm. The widest land
> Doom takes to part us, leaves thy heart in mine
> With pulses that beat double. What I do
> And what I dream include thee, as the wine
> Must taste of its own grapes. And when I sue
> God for myself, He hears that name of thine,
> And sees within my eyes the tears of two.

—15—

The whine of descending counter-grav units took Lorenco Esteban by surprise. He turned and stepped out of the cavernous, empty maintenance shed which normally housed the SCM's Wolverines and frowned, wiping his hands on a grease-spotted cloth while he watched the shuttle touch down. He'd spent most of last night and several hours this morning helping Consuela Gonzalez' maintenance chief wrestle with one balky Wolverine's main traversing gear, but he'd switched the field approach com circuit through to the maintenance shed. If that pilot had called ahead for clearance, Esteban would have heard him.

The old man ambled across the ceramacrete as the unannounced arrival powered down its engines. It was a standard civilian ship-to-shore shuttle, without hyper capability, but it carried Navy markings, and four men in a familiar uniform walked down the ramp as he approached. He shoved his cleaning cloth into a back pocket and held out a hand.

"Morning, gents. Can I help you?"

"Mister Esteban?" The man who spoke wore a colonel's uniform. He was perspiring heavily, though the morning wasn't actually all that warm—not for Santa Cruz, at least—and his palm was wet as Esteban nodded and shook his hand. "I'm Colonel Sanders, Dinochrome Brigade. This is Major Atwell, and these two gentlemen are Lieutenant Gaskins and Lieutenant Deng."

"Nice t'meet you," Esteban murmured, shaking the others' hands in turn, then cocked his head at Sanders. "Somethin' wrong with your com, Colonel?"

"I beg your pardon?"

"I asked iffen you had com problems. Didn't hear no landin' hail over th' 'proach circuit. Santa Cruz ain't much, but iffen your ship's got a com glitch, be happy t'see what my 'tronics shop c'n do t'help."

"Oh." Sanders' eyes slid toward Major Atwell for just an instant, but then he gave himself a little shake and smiled. "Sorry, Mister Esteban. We didn't mean to violate field procedure, but since Captain Merrit's dispatches started coming in, Central's realized the actual situation out here. We know you've got responsibilities of your own on your hacienda, and we weren't sure you'd be at the field this early. If you weren't, we didn't want you to go to the bother of coming down just to greet us."

"Mighty thoughtful," Esteban acknowledged with a bob of his head, "but 'tisn't a problem. My place's just over th' hill there. I c'n pop down in four, five minutes, max, by air car. Anyways, now you're here, what c'n I do fer you?"

"Actually, Mister Esteban, we're here to see Captain Merrit. Could you direct us to the Bolo depot and perhaps provide transportation?"

"Well—" Esteban began to explain that Paul was in the middle of a field exercise, then paused, mental antennae quivering, as Sanders' eye curtsied toward Atwell again. The old man couldn't have said exactly why, but that eye movement seemed . . . furtive, somehow. And why should a full colonel be—or seem to be—so worried over what a *major* thought? Something odd was going on, and his mind flickered back over past conversations with Paul Merrit. Lorenco Esteban hadn't lived seventy years without learning to recognize when someone watched his words carefully, and he'd accepted months ago that Paul was up to something he didn't really want anyone else to know about. That might have worried him, if he hadn't also decided Paul was a man to be trusted. More than that, the younger man had become a friend, someone Esteban both liked and respected, and the sudden, unannounced arrival of four officers of the Dinochrome Brigade looked ominous. If his friend was in some sort of trouble, Lorenco Esteban intended to give him as much warning—and buy him as much time—as he could before it descended upon him.

"Tell you what, Colonel," he said. "I been workin' on a little maintenance problem this mornin', an' it'll prob'ly take me a little while t'scare up somethin' with the kinda bush capability you're gonna need. Why don't you an' your friends come on over t'Admin with me? I'll get cleaned up, an' then see what I c'n do fer you. How's that?"

Sanders glanced at his chrono and a brief spasm seemed to flash across his face, but then he made himself smile.

"Of course, Mister Esteban. Thank you. Ah, our business with the captain is just a bit on the urgent side, however, so if you could, um, expedite our transport. . . ."

"No problem, Colonel. We'll get'cha on your way right smart."

Esteban turned to lead the way to the Admin Building and the four officers fell in behind. He led them inside and waved to chairs in the spacious waiting room Santa Cruz hadn't needed in living memory.

"Have a seat, Colonel. Be with you soon's I wash off some'a this grease."

He nodded to his guests and ambled down the hall to the washroom. None of the visitors knew it had a rear door, and he grinned to himself as he kept right on going towards the com room.

❖   ❖   ❖

Paul Merrit reclined in the depot command center's comfortable chair and smiled as he watched the planetary surveillance display. He wished he were riding with Nike instead of keeping track of her through the satellite net, but the purpose of the exercise was to show what his girl could do in independent mode. Besides, he had a better view of things from here.

In an effort to give the Militia at least some chance, he and Colonel Gonzalez had agreed to isolate Nike from the recon satellites for the first portion of the exercise. That, coupled with complete com silence from the depot, would both deprive her of bird's-eye intelligence and force her to execute all her own planning, strategic as well as tactical. Since that was something the Mark XXIII wasn't supposed to be able to do, her ability to pull it off would underscore her talents for the performance log.

In the meantime, however, the understrength battalion of five-hundred-ton Wolverines had been snorting through the jungle for several hours, moving into position, and Nike didn't know where they were or precisely what they planned. She knew their objective was to reach the depot without being intercepted, yet the way they did it was up to them, and Gonzalez had opted for a multipronged advance. She'd divided her fourteen Wolverines into four separate forces, two of three tanks each and two of four each, operating along the same general axis but advancing across a front of almost fifty kilometers. There was a limit to how rapidly even a Bolo could move through a Santa Cruz jungle, and the colonel clearly hoped to sneak at least one force past Nike while the Bolo dealt with the others. If she could get a big enough start once contact was made, it might even work. Splitting her tanks into detachments wouldn't really increase the odds against their survival—all fourteen Wolverines together wouldn't have lasted five minutes against Nike in a stand-up fight—but Nike would have to deal with the separated forces one at a time. It was certainly possible, if not exactly likely, that one of them could outrun her while she swatted its fellows, and—

A signal beeped, and he twitched upright in his chair. It beeped again, and he turned his chair to the communications console. The screen flickered to life with Lorenco Esteban's face, and Merrit frowned as he recognized the old man's tense expression.

"Morning, Lorenco. What can I do for you?"

"I think mebbe y'got a little problem over here at th' field, Paul," Esteban said in a low voice. Merrit's left eyebrow rose, and the old man shrugged. "I got me four Dinochrome Brigade officers out here, headed by a colonel name of Sanders, an' they're lookin' fer you, boy."

"Sanders?" Merrit let his chair snap upright and frowned as an icy chill ran through him. "*Clifton* Sanders?"

"That's him," Esteban nodded, and Merrit's lips shaped a silent curse. He could think of only one thing that would bring the sector's chief Maintenance, Logistics, and Procurement officer to Santa Cruz, but how in hell had anyone on Ursula figured out—?

He shook himself, and his mind raced. He could call off the exercise and order Nike back to base, but there was no regulation against a Bolo commander on independent assignment conducting exercises on his own authority. More to the point, having Nike out of the garage when Sanders arrived would buy at least a little time. That might not be as important as he suddenly feared it might, but the fact that Sanders had come in person, without sending even a single information request first— and hadn't commed him from the field after arrival, either—was more than simply ominous. It smacked of sneak inspections and an attempt to catch Merrit violating procedure, and, unfortunately, that was exactly what it was going to do, because Merrit *hadn't* kept Central "fully informed" of the state of his command as Regs required.

He might not have told any actual lies, but he'd certainly done a lot of misleading by omission.

He closed his eyes and thought hard. Sanders himself had a reputation as an administrator, not a technician. *He* might not realize how far outside parameters Nike was from a cursory examination of her schematics and system specs, but that was probably why he'd brought the others along. Any half-competent Bolo tech would know what he was seeing the moment he pulled up Nike's readouts. Besides, Sanders wouldn't be here in the first place if he didn't already suspect *something* was out of kilter.

A fist of cold iron squeezed Merrit's heart at what that might mean. But if Nike wasn't here when the MLP men arrived, they'd have to at least talk to him before they could shut her down. In fact, he could *force* them to hear him out by refusing to call her in until they did. It wouldn't hurt if she'd completed the first phase of the exercise, either. Thin as it might be, his performance log's authentication of her unique abilities was her only real protection. Of course, if he refused to call her in when ordered, especially after what had happened on Sandlot, he was through in the Brigade, but he suddenly realized how little that meant to him beside protecting Nike's life.

He opened his eyes and cleared his throat.

"Thanks, Lorenco," he said softly. "Thanks a lot."

"Son, I don't know what all you been up to out there, an' I don't rightly care. You're a friend. You want I should let these yahoos get themselves lost in th' bush? Reckon it'd take 'em four, five hours t'find you with the directions I c'n give 'em."

"No. I appreciate the offer, but you'd better stay out of this."

"Huh. Well, how 'bout I waste an hour or so 'fore I find 'em transport? I already set that 'un up."

"If you can do it without being obvious, please do,"

Merrit said gratefully. "After that, though, you'd better go home and keep as far away from any official involvement as you can."

"Iffen you say so, boy." The old man hesitated a moment, then shook his head. "Gotta tell you, Paul—they's somethin' squirrely goin' on here. Can't put m'finger on it, but I c'n feel it. You watch yerself, hear?"

"I will. Thanks again." Merrit nodded to the pickup and killed the circuit, then leaned back and fidgeted in his chair. He started to key his link to Nike, then sat back and put his hands in his lap. There was no point worrying her, and she was just likely to argue if he told her he wanted her to stay out of sight. He shook his head. No, much better to leave her in blissful ignorance as long as possible.

He sighed and rubbed his face with his hands, and fear fluttered in the pit of his belly.

"I sure hope to hell your 'associates' have managed to 'deal' with that Bolo, Mister Scully," Colonel Granger muttered.

"Amen," someone muttered from the recesses of the big transport's CIC, and Gerald Osterwelt shrugged.

"You've seen the plan, Colonel," he said mildly. "I can't blame you for worrying, but *I* certainly wouldn't be here if I didn't expect it to work."

"I can believe *that*," the colonel muttered to herself, and turned away from the glowing tactical display. The single aspect of the plan she most disliked was the tight timing. They were scheduled to hit the planet within two hours of Colonel Sanders' arrival, and she didn't like it a bit. It would take less than fifteen minutes for an air car to reach the maintenance depot from the field, and Sanders could burn the Bolo's command center in less than ten once he got it shut down, so if all went according to schedule, two hours was an ample cushion. But if things *didn't* go as scheduled—if they got there too soon, before the Bolo went down, and its commander—

She clenched her teeth and commanded herself to stop worrying over what she couldn't change. Besides, Scully was right in at least one respect. The Bolo commander— this Captain Merrit—had to be among the fatalities, because if he wasn't, the fact that someone had fixed the Bolo would be glaringly evident. But the same thing would be true if anyone on the planet happened to com Central— or anyone else off-planet—and casually mention the presence of "Dinochrome Brigade officers" on Santa Cruz at the same moment a "pirate raid" just happened to hit it.

They had to take out the planet's com sat relays as the opening gambit of their attack, anyway, because if there were so much as a single Navy destroyer anywhere within jump range of Santa Cruz and a message got out, it could blow all three of Matucek's Marauders' starships to scrap. And since they did have to take out Santa Cruz's FTL communications, they might as well do it as quickly as possible after Sanders' arrival to ensure that no word of his presence got out. Besides, they didn't know how thoroughly Merrit had settled in on Santa Cruz, or how much contact he normally had with the locals. If he had friends who knew he was being visited by an off-world deputation, they might well com him to find out how things had gone, and when they didn't get an answer— or if they figured out he was dead—they were almost certain to com Central. All of which made it highly desirable to hit the planet as soon as possible after Sanders did his dirty work.

She understood that, but she still didn't like the timing. The smart move—as she'd told Scully (or whatever the hell his real name was) and Matucek repeatedly—would be to wait until Sanders shut down the Bolo and was able to *confirm* his success. Unfortunately, Scully was calling the shots, and Matucek wasn't about to argue with him.

Well, at least they had confirmation that Sanders had arrived on schedule, courtesy of the ship which carried him, and, as Scully had pointed out, there were two strings to the colonel's bow. If this Captain Merrit argued with him, all that was needed was for Captain Merrit to die a little sooner than scheduled. With him dead, Sanders, as the senior Brigade officer on Santa Cruz, would become the Bolo's legal commander. His access at Sector Central had given him the command authorization phrase he needed to so identify himself to the Bolo, and it was only a Mark XXIII. It wouldn't be bright enough to ask any difficult questions when he ordered it to shut down— not that it would matter. With the command phrase in his possession, Sanders could lobotomize the damned thing even if it proved unresponsive.

Granger bared her teeth at her tactical console. She'd read Merrit's record. The man was tough, smart, gutsy, and as good as they came, but it didn't matter how good he was. He knew who Sanders was, so he wouldn't be suspicious of the colonel, and he had absolutely no reason to suspect that the other "Brigade members" with his superior were professional killers. If he proved difficult, it would be a very *brief* difficulty.

"Assault orbit in ninety-six minutes, ma'am," her ops officer murmured, and she nodded.

"Double-check the fire solution on the com sats. All three of those birds have to go down the instant we enter orbit."

"I'm on it," the ops officer grunted laconically, and Louise Granger sat back in her command chair with an evil smile.

—16—

I advance through the jungle, sweeping on an east-west arc at 30.25 kph. As ordered, I have disabled my independent link to the planetary surveillance satellites and all com channels save for that to the emergency contact unit in the maintenance depot. I am operating blind, yet I am confident that I can fulfill my mission, and the challenge is both pleasing of itself and an anodyne to my anxieties over my relationship to my Commander.

It is odd, I reflect while my Battle Center maintains a 360-degree tactical range broad-spectrum passive search, but this is the closest I have ever approached to actual combat. I am a warrior, product of eight centuries of evolution in war machine design, and I have existed for eighty-two years, four months, sixteen days, eight hours, twelve minutes, and five seconds, yet I have never seen war. I have never tested myself against the proud record and tradition of the Dinochrome Brigade. Even today's exercises will be but games, and I sense a dichotomy within my emotions. Through my Commander and the words of poets such as Siegfried Sassoon and Wilfred Owen, I have come to appreciate the horrors of war more clearly, perhaps, even than those of my brothers who have actually seen it. I recognize its destructiveness, and the evils which must always accompany even the most just of wars. Yet I am also a Bolo, a unit of the Line. Ultimately, war is my function, the reason for my existence, and deep within me there lives an edge of regret, a longing not for the opportunity to destroy the Enemy but for the opportunity to test myself against him and prove myself worthy.

My sensors detect a faint emissions source at 075 degrees. I am operating in passive mode, with no active sensor emissions to betray my presence in reply, and the source is extremely faint, but 0.00256 seconds of signal enhancement and analysis confirm that it is the short-range air-search radar of a Wolverine heavy tank.

I ponder the implications for 1.0362 seconds. Colonel Gonzalez is a clever tactician. Logically, she, even more than I, should be operating under emissions control doctrine, for she knows her objective and needs only to slip past me undetected to attain it. It is possible that she fears I have deployed reconnaissance drones and seeks to detect and destroy them before they can report her actual deployment, but I compute a probability of 89.7003 percent that this is a deception attempt. She wishes me to detect the emissions. She has divided her force and hopes to draw me out of position against the decoy while her true striking force eludes detection.

I alter course to 172 degrees true and engage my tactical modeling program. I now have a bearing to the unit she wishes me to detect, which indicates the direction in which I should not move, and I begin construction of alternative models of her probable deployment from that base datum. In 2.75 minutes, I will, in fact, deploy my first reconnaissance drone, but first I must generate the search pattern it will pursue.

Paul Merrit grimaced as the depot sensors detected an approaching bogey, then grinned as its emissions signature registered. Esteban had done exactly as promised and delayed Sanders' arrival for over an hour, and from that signature, he hadn't exactly given the colonel a luxury sedan, either. The power readings were just about right for one of the old man's air lorry melon haulers, with a maximum speed of barely five hundred kph, less than twelve percent of what Merrit's own recon skimmer could manage.

He watched the blip's approach, and his grin faded. Clunky transport or not, that was—at best—the Sword of Damocles out there. And however politely obstructionist he intended to be once Sanders arrived, there were appearances to preserve in the meantime.

He shrugged and keyed the com.

"Unknown aircraft, unknown aircraft. You are approaching restricted Navy airspace. Identify."

He waited a moment, and an eyebrow quirked when he received no response. He gave them another twenty seconds, then keyed the com again.

"Unknown aircraft, you have now entered restricted airspace. Be advised this is a high-security area and that I am authorized to employ deadly force against intruders. Identify at once."

"Bolo depot," a voice came back at last, "this is Colonel Clifton Sanders, Dinochrome Brigade, on official business."

"Colonel Sanders?" Merrit was rather pleased by the genuineness of the surprise he managed to put into his voice.

"That's correct, Captain Merrit. I'm afraid this . . . vehicle has no visual capabilities or proper transponder, but I trust you recognize my voice?"

"Of course, sir."

"Good. My present ETA is six minutes."

"Very good, sir. I'll be waiting."

"Damn that old fart!" the man introduced to Esteban as Major Atwell hissed from the passenger compartment in the rear of the lorry's cab. "We're way behind schedule!"

"I don't understand what your problem is," Sanders

said petulantly over his shoulder. "You heard Merrit. He doesn't suspect a thing. Everything's going to plan as far as *I* can see."

Atwell's lips curled in a silent snarl at the colonel's back, but he bit off his savage retort. Sanders had been antsy enough from the moment he figured out they were going to have to kill Merrit. He'd piss himself if he even suspected the real reason for this entire operation— especially if it occurred to him that *he* was about to become a liability to GalCorp, as well. He had no idea his severance pay was riding in the holster on Atwell's hip, but, by the same token, he didn't know Matucek was scheduled to hit the planet in less than thirty minutes, either.

"Let's just get in and get this over with," the bogus major said finally. "The faster we get off-planet, the less exposure we've got."

"All right. All right!" Sanders shrugged irritably. "I don't know why *you're* so worried. *I'm* the only one that old dodderer can identify by name!"

"Don't worry, Colonel," Atwell soothed. "We'll take care of Esteban on the way out. No one will ever know you've been here, I promise."

Clifton Sanders shivered at how easily his "associate" pronounced yet another death sentence, but he said nothing. There was nothing he *could* say now. All he could do was obey his orders and pray that somehow GalCorp could protect him from the consequences of carrying out its instructions.

Lorenco Esteban eased himself into one of the veranda chairs and grimaced. The more he thought about it, the more convinced he became that something unpleasant was in the wind for Paul, and he wished there'd been more he could do for his friend. But Paul was right. If the idiots back at Central had decided to come down on him, getting involved in it wouldn't do Lorenco any good, either.

He tipped his chair back with a sigh. *Good luck, boy*, he thought. *You're a better man than that fool colonel any day.*

"I've got a drone, ma'am!" The sensor tech in Consuela Gonzalez' command tank bent closer to her panel. "Coming up at zero-three-zero relative, altitude three thousand, heading two-niner-seven true. Speed three hundred kph. Range . . . three-six point five klicks and closing!"

"Damn!" Gonzalez shook her head. So much for misdirection! From the drone's point of origin, the Bolo must be well out on her left flank, but its recon drone was sweeping almost directly perpendicular to her line of advance, as if the machine knew *exactly* where to look.

"Kill it!" she barked.

"Firing," the Wolverine's air defense tech replied, and a laser turret swiveled. A beam of coherent light sizzled through the humid air, and the drone blew up instantly.

"There goes seven or eight hundred credits of taxpayer's money!" the tech chortled.

"Well, it's seven or eight hundred credits your great-great-grandma paid, not us," Gonzalez said with a grin. Damn, that felt good! She and Merrit had agreed to a hard-limit of five kilometers; any drones or recon remotes beyond that range from her tanks or the Bolo could be engaged with live fire, and she hadn't counted on how much fun that would be.

My drone has been destroyed, but I have plotted the coordinates of two Aggressor forces in addition to the decoy emissions source. I consider a simulated missile launch against them, but the Wolverine's computer-commanded point defense systems are efficient. Nuclear warheads have not been specified for this scenario, and the PK with conventional warheads against a force of three Wolverines

*is only 28.653 percent. It will be necessary to engage with
direct-fire weapons.*

*A source count indicates the presence of ten of Colonel
Gonzalez' fourteen tanks in the known detachments. This
leaves four unaccounted for, but the locations of the known
forces allow me to refine my hypothetical models of her
deployment. A further 0.00017 seconds of analysis indicate
that the unlocated units are her extreme right flank force
and reduce their possible coordinates to three locations.
I call up my terrain maps and plot those loci and
continuous updates of their maximum possible advance
while I consider the launch of a second drone to confirm
my deduction. I reject the option after 0.00311 seconds
of consideration. I will reach Hill 0709-A in 9.3221
minutes, plus or minus 56.274 seconds From its summit,
I will have direct observation—and fire capability—to
each of the three possible locations. I will advance and
destroy this force, then sweep back to the southwest at
an angle which will permit me to encounter and destroy
each of the known forces in succession. In the meantime,
the absence of a second drone launch may leave Colonel
Gonzalez off balance, uncertain of the tactical data actually
in my possession.*

The air lorry landed, and Merrit came to attention on
the landing apron. Two of Colonel Sanders' companions
accompanied the colonel to the bunker entrance, and
Merrit felt a slight spasm of surprise at the sloppiness
with which they returned his salute. All of them wore
MLP shoulder flashes, which should indicate they spent
most of their time back at Central, and somebody who
kept stumbling over senior officers should get lots of
practice at saluting.

He shook the thought aside as Sanders held out his
hand.

"Welcome to Santa Cruz, Colonel."

"Thank you, Captain." Sanders' handshake was damp and clammy, and Merrit resisted a temptation to scrub his palm on his trouser leg when the colonel released it. "I assume you know why I'm here," Sanders went on briskly, and Merrit shook his head.

"No, sir, I'm afraid not. No one told me you were coming."

"What?" Sanders cocked his eyebrows, but the surprise in his voice struck a false note, somehow. He shook his head. "Central was supposed to have informed you last week, Captain."

"Informed me of what, sir?" Merrit asked politely.

"Of the policy change concerning Santa Cruz. We've been conducting a sector-wide cost analysis since your arrival here, Captain Merrit. Naturally, we were startled to discover the nature and extent of the Santa Cruz installations—we had no idea we'd misplaced a Bolo for eighty years, heh, heh!—but given their age and the sector's general readiness states, it's hard to see any point in maintaining them on active status. Frontier sectors always face tighter fiscal constraints than the core sectors, you know, so it's been decided—purely as a cost-cutting measure, you understand—to deactivate your Bolo and reassign you."

"A cost-cutting measure, sir?" Merrit asked. He was careful to keep his tone casual and just a bit confused, but alarm bells began to sound in the back of his brain. He'd expected Sanders to come in breathing fire and smoke over his blatant disregard for regulations, yet his initial relief at the lack of fireworks was fading fast. Sanders was babbling. He was also sweating harder than even Santa Cruz's climate called for, and Paul Merrit had seen too much combat in his forty-one years not to have developed a survivor's instincts. Now those instincts shouted that something was very, very wrong.

"Yes, a cost-cutting measure," Sanders replied. "You

know how expensive a Bolo is, Captain. Each of them
we maintain on active duty takes its own bite out of our
total maintenance funding posture, and without a threat
to the planet to justify the expense, well—"

He shrugged, and Merrit nodded slowly, expression
calm despite a sinking sensation as he noticed that both
of Sanders' companions were armed. Of course, the jungle
had all sorts of nasty fauna, and all Santa Cruzans went
armed whenever they ventured into the bush on foot,
but they tended to pack weapons heavy enough to knock
even lizard cats on their posteriors. These men wore
standard military-issue three-millimeter needlers, efficient
enough man-killers but not much use against a lizard cat
or one of the pseudo-rhinos.

He let his eyes wander back over the parked air lorry,
and the fact that they'd left a man behind carried its own
ominous overtones. Merrit couldn't see clearly through
the lorry cab's dirty windows, but from the way he sat
hunched slightly to one side, the man in it *might* be aiming
a weapon in the bunker's direction. If he was, then anything
precipitous on Merrit's part was likely to have very
unpleasant—and immediate—consequences.

"I'm a little confused, sir," he said slowly.

"Confused?" the major at Sanders' elbow sounded much
brusquer than the colonel, and he glanced at his wrist
chrono as he spoke. "What's there to be confused about?"

"Well, it's just that in eighty years, there's never been
any expense, other than the initial placement costs, of
course, for this Bolo. Santa Cruz has never requested as
much as a track bearing from Bolo Central Maintenance,
so it's a little hard to see how shutting down is going to
save any money, Major."

"Uh, yes. Of course." Sanders cleared his throat, then
shrugged and smiled. "It's not just, uh, current budget
or *expenditures* we're thinking about, Captain. That's why
I'm here in person. Despite its age, this is an extensive

installation. Reclamation could be something of a bonanza for the sector, so we're naturally planning to salvage all we can after shutdown."

"I see." Merrit nodded, and his mind raced.

Whatever was happening stank to high heaven, and he didn't like the way this Major Atwell's hand hovered near his needler. If his suspicions had any basis in fact, the colonel's companions had to be professionals—certainly the way they'd left a man behind in the air lorry argued that they were. The precaution might seem paranoid, but they'd had no way to be *certain* Merrit wouldn't be armed himself when they arrived. He had no idea exactly what the man they'd left behind had, but it was probably something fairly drastic, because his function had to be distant fire support.

Despite the frozen lead ball in Merrit's belly, he had to acknowledge the foresight which provided against even the unlikeliest threat from him. But if they wanted to leave that fellow back there, then the thing to do was get the other three into the bunker. The chances of one unarmed man against two—three, if Sanders had a concealed weapon of his own—barely existed, but they were even lower against *four* of them.

"I'm not convinced Central isn't making a mistake, sir," he heard himself say easily, "but I'm only a captain. I assume you'd like to at least look the depot over—make a preliminary inspection and check the logs?"

"Certainly." Sanders sounded far more relieved than he should have, and Merrit nodded.

"If you'll follow me, then?" he invited, and led the way into the bunker.

I have reached Hill 0709-A. I approach from the southeast, keeping its crest between myself and the possible positions I have computed for Colonel Gonzalez' fourth detachment. Soil conditions are poor after the last week's heavy rains, but I have allowed for the soft going in my earlier calculations of transit time to this position, and I direct additional power to my drive systems as I ascend the rear face of the hill.

I slow as I reach the top, extending only my forward sensor array above the summit. I search patiently for 2.006 seconds before I detect the power plant emissions I seek. A burst of power to my tracks sends me up onto the hilltop, broadside to the emissions signatures. My fire control radar goes active, confirming their locations, and the laser-tag simulator units built into my Hellbores pulse. The receptors aboard the Wolverines detect the pulses, and all four vehicles slow to a halt in recognition of their simulated destruction. Three point zero-zero-six-two seconds after reaching the hill's crest, I am in motion to the southwest at 50.3 kph to intercept the next Aggressor unit.

"So much for Suarez' company," Gonzalez sighed as her com receipted the raucous tone that simulated the blast of radiation from ruptured power plants.

"Yeah. It'll be coming after *us* next," her gunner grunted.

"Join the Army and see the stars!" someone else sang out, and the entire crew laughed.

". . . and this is the command center," Merrit said, ushering Sanders, Atwell, and Deng through the hatch. "As you can see, it's very well equipped for an installation of its age."

"Yes. Yes, it is." Sanders mopped his forehead with a handkerchief despite the air conditioning and glanced over his shoulder at Atwell. The major was looking at his chrono again, and the colonel cleared his throat. "Well, I'm sure this has been very interesting, Captain Merrit, and I look forward to a more complete tour of the facility—including the Bolo—but I really think we should go ahead and shut it down now."

"Shut it down, sir?" Merrit widened his eyes in feigned surprise.

"That *is* why we came, Captain," Atwell put in in a grating voice.

"Well, certainly," Merrit said easily, "but I can't shut it down immediately. It's not here."

"What?" Sanders gaped at him, and Merrit shrugged.

"I'm sorry, sir. I thought I mentioned it. The Bolo's carrying out an autonomous field exercise just now. It's not scheduled to return for another—" he glanced at the wall chronometer "—six and a half hours. Of course, I'll be glad to shut it down then, but—"

"Shut it down *now*, Captain!" Atwell's voice was no longer harsh; it held the clang of duralloy, and his hand settled on the butt of his needler. Merrit made himself appear oblivious of the gesture and turned towards the console with a shrug.

"Are you sure you really want to shut it down in place, Colonel Sanders?" he asked as he sank into the command chair. Turning his back on Atwell was the hardest thing he'd ever done, but somehow he kept his voice from betraying his tension, and his hand fell to the chair's armrest keypad.

"I mean, I assume you'll want to burn the Battle Center, if this is a permanent shutdown," he went on, fingers moving by feel alone as they flew over the keypad, covered by his body, while he prayed no one would notice the row of telltales blinking from amber stand-by to green readiness on the maintenance console in the command center's corner. "That'd mean someone would have to hike out to its present location in the bush. And if we're going to salvage the station, don't you want to salvage the Bolo, too? Once its Battle Center goes, getting it back here for reclamation is going to be a real problem, and—"

"Stand up, Merrit!" Atwell barked. "Get both hands up here where I can see them!"

Merrit froze, cursing the man's alertness. Another fifteen seconds—just fifteen more seconds. That was all he'd needed. But he hadn't gotten them. He drew a deep breath and touched one more button, then rose, holding his hands carefully away from his body. He turned, and his blood was ice as he saw what he'd known he would. Atwell and Deng each held a needler, and both of them were aimed squarely at him.

"Colonel?" he looked at Sanders, making himself sound as confused as he could, but his attention wasn't really on the colonel. It wasn't even on the two men with guns. It was watching a display behind Deng as light patterns shifted across its surface in response to his last input. He hadn't had time to reconfigure the armrest keypad, so he'd had to work through the maintenance computers to reach the one he needed. His commands were still filtering their way through the cumbersome interface, and even after they were all in place, they might not do him any good at all. Atwell had stopped him before he could do more than enable the system he needed on automatic, and if Atwell and Deng were real Brigade officers rather than ringers—

"Just . . . just shut the Bolo down, Captain," Sanders whispered, keeping his own eyes resolutely turned away from the guns.

"But why, sir?" Merrit asked plaintively.

"Because we frigging well told you to!" Atwell barked. "Now do it!"

"I don't think I can. Not without checking with Central."

"Captain Merrit," Sanders said in that same strained, whispery voice, "I advise you to do exactly what Major Atwell says. I'm aware this installation's hardware is considerably out of date. Admittedly, it would take me some time to familiarize myself with it sufficiently to shut down the Bolo without you, but I can do it. We both know I can, and I have the command authentication codes from Central."

"If you extracted the codes from Central, then you don't have the right ones, sir," Merrit said softly. Sanders jerked, eyes widening, and Atwell snarled. Merrit's belly tensed as the gunman started to raise his weapon, but Sanders waved a frantic hand.

"Wait! *Wait!*" he cried, and his shrill tone stopped Atwell just short of firing. "What do you mean, I don't have the right codes?" he demanded.

"I changed them."

"You can't have! That's against regs!" Sanders protested, and Merrit laughed.

"Colonel Sanders, you have no *idea* how many regs I've broken in the last six months! If you expect 'Leonidas' to get you into Nike's system, then be my guest and try it."

"Damn you!" Atwell hissed. The gunman looked at his chrono yet again, and his eyes were ugly when he raised them to Merrit once more. "You're lying. You're just trying to make us think we need you!"

"I could be, but I'm not," Merrit replied, the corner of his eye still watching the display behind Deng. *Come on, baby! Come* on, *please!* he whispered to it, and smiled at Atwell. "Ask Colonel Sanders. Psych Ops had its doubts about me before Central sent me out here. Well," he shrugged, "looks like Psych Ops may have had a point."

Atwell spat something foul, but Sanders shook his head suddenly.

"It doesn't matter," he said. "You may have changed the codes from the ones on file at Central, but only a lunatic would change them without leaving a record somewhere." Merrit turned his head to look at the colonel, and Sanders rubbed his hands nervously together. "Yes, there has to be a record somewhere," he muttered to himself. "Somewhere . . . somewhere . . ."

"We don't need any records," Atwell decided in an ugly voice. He stepped closer to Merrit and lowered his needler's point of aim. "You ever seen what a burst from one of these can do to a man's legs, Merrit?" he purred. "With just a little luck, I can saw your left leg right off at the knee without even killing you. You'll just *wish* you were dead, and you won't be—not until we've got that code."

"Now wait a minute!" Merrit stepped back and licked his lips as a crimson code sequence blinked on the display behind Deng at last. "Wait a minute!" He looked back at Sanders. "Colonel, just what the hell is going on here?"

"Don't worry about *him!*" Atwell snarled. "Just give me that code phrase—*now!*"

"All right. All right!" Merrit licked his lips again, cleared his throat, and made his voice as expressionless as he could, grateful that computers needed no special emphasis. "The code phrase is 'Activate Alamo.' "

It almost worked. It *would* have worked if he'd had the fifteen additional seconds he'd needed to complete the system reconfiguration or if Major Atwell's reflexes had been even a fraction slower.

Lieutenant Deng *was* slower; he was still trying to figure out what was happening when the power rifle unhoused itself above the main command console and blew his chest apart. He went down without even a scream, and the power rifle slewed sideways, searching for Atwell. But the bogus major's snake-quick reaction hurled him to the floor behind the planetary surveillance system's holo display even as the rifle dealt with Deng. His frantic dive for cover couldn't save him forever, but it bought him time—a few, deadly seconds of time—before the computers found him again.

The power rifle snarled again, and sparks and smoke erupted from the display, but it sheltered Atwell just long enough for him to fire his own weapon.

Merrit was already sprinting towards Deng's fallen gun when Atwell's needler whined. Most of the hasty burst's needles missed, but one didn't, and Merrit grunted in agony as it punched into his back. It entered just above the hip and tore through his abdomen, and the impact smashed him to the bunker floor. He rolled desperately towards the command center door, away from Deng, to avoid Atwell's next burst, and a fresh shower of needles screamed and ricocheted.

Then the power rifle fired yet again. Atwell collapsed with a bubbling shriek, and Merrit rolled up onto his knees, sobbing in agony and pressing both hands against the hot blood that slimed his belly.

Sanders stared in horror at the carnage, and then his huge eyes whipped up to the power rifle. It quivered, questing about, but it didn't fire again, and his breath escaped in a huge gasp as he realized what had happened. Merrit had been able to bring the bunker's automated defenses on-line through the command chair keypad, but he hadn't had time to override their inhibitory programming. The master computer would kill any unauthorized personnel when its commanding officer's coded voice command declared an intruder alert, but Sanders *was* authorized personnel. His name, face, and identifying data were in the Brigade's files, just like Merrit's . . . *and that meant the computer couldn't fire on him!*

Even through the pain that blurred his vision, Merrit saw the realization on the colonel's face. Saw fear turn into the determination of desperation. Sanders flung himself to the floor, hands scrabbling for Atwell's weapon, and there was no time for Merrit to reach Deng's.

He did the only thing he could. He dragged himself to his feet, staggered from the command deck, and fled down the passage outside. He heard Sanders screaming his name behind him, heard feet plunging after him, and somehow, despite the nauseating agony hammering his wounded body, he made himself run faster. He caromed off walls, smearing them with splashes of crimson, and only the fact that Sanders was a desk-jockey saved his life. The needler whined behind him, but the colonel's panic combined with his inexperience to throw his aim wide.

Merrit reached the vehicle chamber and flung himself desperately into the recon skimmer's cockpit. He slammed the canopy with one blood-slick hand while the other brought the drive on-line, and needles screamed and skipped from the fuselage. He gasped a hoarse, pain-twisted curse at his inability to use the skimmer's weapon systems inside the bunker. The safety interlocks meant he couldn't shoot back, but Sanders' needler couldn't hurt *him*, either—not through the skimmer's armor—and he bared his teeth in an anguish-wracked grin as he thought of the air lorry outside. He could damned well use his weapons on *it*, and he rammed power to the drive.

The skimmer wailed out of the vehicle chamber, and he cried out in fresh agony as acceleration rammed him back in the flight couch. Pain made him clumsy, and the skimmer wobbled as he brought it snarling back around the bunker towards the lorry while he punched up his weapons. He bared his teeth again as the fire control screen came alive, capturing the lorry in its ranging bars, and—

That was when he realized his combat instincts had betrayed him. He should have headed away from the bunker immediately to get help, not stayed to fight the battle by himself. And if he *was* going to stay, he should have brought his defensive systems up first, not his weapons.

But he hadn't, and Sanders' third companion was no longer in the air lorry. He was standing over fifty meters to the side, with a plasma lance across his shoulder.

Merrit had one instant to see it, to recognize the

threat and wrench the stick hard over, and then the lance fired.

White lightning flashed, blinding bright even in full sunlight, and the skimmer staggered as the plasma bolt tore into its fuselage. Damage alarms howled, and Merrit flung full power into the drive, clawing frantically for altitude. Smoke and flame belched from the skimmer, and he coughed as banners of the same smoke infiltrated the cockpit. Two-thirds of his panel flashed with the bright red codes of disaster. All of his weapons were down, and his communicator. His flight controls were so mangled he couldn't understand how he was still in the air, but they were hanging together—for now, at least.

The power plant wasn't. He groaned in pain, fighting the fog in his brain as he peered at the instruments. Five minutes. He might be able to stay in the air for five minutes—ten at the most. Assuming he could live that long.

He coughed again, and screamed as his diaphragm's violent movement ripped at his belly wound. God! He didn't know how bad he was hit, but he knew the high-velocity needle had wreaked ghastly havoc. He felt the strength flowing out of him with his blood, and his eyes screwed shut in pain while despair flooded him, for Sanders had been right. Only a lunatic *would* have changed Nike's command code without leaving a record. The new code was in his personal computer, not the main system, but it wouldn't take Sanders long to find it if he thought to look in the right place. Once he had it—and once Merrit was dead—the renegade colonel could take command of Nike, give her whatever orders he pleased, and she would have no choice but to obey.

Nike! The name exploded through him, and he wrenched his eyes back open. Jungle treetops rushed at him, and he hauled back on the stick, fighting the broken

skimmer back under control. Nike. He had to get to *Nike*.
Had to warn her. Had to—

The pain was too great. He could no longer think of
what he had to do. Except for one thing. He had to reach
Nike, and Paul Merrit clung to life with both hands as
he altered course to the northwest.

—17—

I have dealt with the first of Colonel Gonzalez' four forces and deployed two additional reconnaissance drones, one in high cover position to plot the origin of any fire directed at the other, which have given me a current position fix on the second of her detachments. The Wolverines are moving at their best speed through the dense jungle, approaching peak velocities of 47 kph, but my own speed is now 62.37 kph. I will intercept Aggressor Force Two in 9.46 minutes on my current heading, and I examine my terrain maps once more. My quarry must cross an east-west ridge in approximately 11.2 minutes on their current heading. This will bring them above the jungle canopy and present me with a clear line of sight and fire, and I decrease speed accordingly. I will let them reach the crest of the hill before I—

A new datum registers abruptly, and I redirect my sensors. A large spacecraft—correction, two large spacecraft—have entered my tactical sensor envelope. They approach in line ahead from due south on a heading of 017 degrees true at high subsonic velocity, descending at 4.586 mps. I query Main Memory for comparative emissions signatures and identification is reached in 0.00367 seconds. They are Concordiat Navy Fafnir-class assault transports, but they do not carry Navy transponders.

I am confused. If these are indeed Navy craft, then

their transponders should so indicate. Moreover, if the
Navy intended to carry out maneuvers on Santa Cruz,
my Commander should have been so informed and, I am
certain, would have informed me, in turn. The presence
of these units cannot therefore be considered an authorized
incursion into my command area.

The Fafnirs continue on their original course. My
projection of their track indicates that the first of them
will cross the Santa Cruz Fleet Base perimeter in 10.435
minutes at an altitude below the Fleet Base's normal search
radar horizon. My Battle Center projects a 92.36 percent
probability that they are on an attack run, and I attempt
to contact my Commander.

There is no response. I initiate a diagnostic of my
primary transmitter even as I activate my secondary. Again
there is no response. My diagnostic systems report all
transmitters functioning normally, and I feel a moment
of fear. My Commander should be monitoring the exercise.
He should have received my transmission and responded
instantly, yet he has not.

I lock my main battery on the Fafnirs, but without
authorization from my Commander to enable my Battle
Reflex imperatives I can fire only if the unidentified vessels
take obviously hostile action.

I bring my long-range tactical systems fully on-line while
attempting once more to contact my Commander. Yet again
there is no response, and my sensors detect a sudden energy
release at the approximate coordinates of the Fleet Base.
Analysis of sensor data indicates a hyper-velocity kinetic
strike.

Lorenco Esteban jerked up out of his veranda chair
as a huge, white fireball erupted above the field. He stared
at it in horror for an endless second, until the rolling
shockwave shook his entire hacienda by the throat, then
dashed into the house and thundered upstairs to the

second floor. He snatched up a pair of old-fashioned optical binoculars, jammed them to his eyes, and peered towards the field.

He could just make it out from here, and he swallowed an incredulous curse as he realized the mammoth explosion was centered on the Wolverine maintenance shed.

The lead Fafnir has passed beyond my horizon, but the second is still within my engagement envelope. Simultaneous with the explosion, two outsized assault pods detach from the visible vessel. Their emissions signatures identify them as Dragon Tooth-class pods: reusable, rough field-capable AFV pods configured to land a full battalion of manned tanks or a single Bolo each against active opposition.

Only my after Hellbore will bear, but the explosion raises the probability that an attack by hostile forces is in progress to 98.965 percent, sufficient to enable independent Battle Reflex release. I have time to engage only the Fafnir or the assault pods. Main Memory indicates that a Fafnir's short-term life support capability and internal capacity are sufficient to support three infantry battalions and their vehicles in addition to a complete load out for two Dragon Tooth-class pods for a ship-to-planet transfer. Given this datum and the fact that the ship is still on course for the Fleet Base, it must be classed as the primary threat.

My after Hellbore elevates to 026 degrees. I acquire lock, and then I rock on my treads as for the first time I fire a full-powered war shot.

"*Madre de Dios!*"

Consuela Gonzalez flinched as the self-polarizing direct vision blocks of her Wolverine's hatch cupola went dark as night. Even so, the searing flash from somewhere astern

of her made her eyes water, and it was followed almost
instantly by an even bigger midair explosion.

"*Hellbore!*" her sensor tech screamed. "That was a
Hellbore, Connie! My God, what's that thing *shooting*
at?!"

*My fire impacts on my target's primary drive coil.
Destruction is effectively instantaneous, but I cannot relay
my Hellbore in time to engage either assault pod. They
go to evasive action and disappear into the jungle; 4.0673
seconds later, I detect ground shocks consistent with the
heavy "daisy-cutter" charges used to clear pod landing
zones in heavy terrain. The Enemy has landed successfully,
but the detonations provide me with reliable bearings to
their LZs.*

*I continue my efforts to contact my Commander. The
depot communications computer responds to my demand
for a diagnostics check and declares all systems nominal,
but still my Commander does not reply. His continuing
silence is a dagger of ice within me, but with or without
him, I am a unit of the Dinochrome Brigade. It is my
function to defend human life at all costs, and I must act
to protect the citizens of Santa Cruz.*

*I attempt to contact the Fleet Base over my secondary
com channel, but without success. I attempt to transmit a
subspace attack warning to Sector Central, but the orbital
communications arrays do not respond. Radar indicates
that they no longer exist, indicating a deliberate Enemy
move to isolate Santa Cruz. I attempt to access the planetary
surveillance system, but without my Commander's assistance
from the depot's Command Center, I can work only through
my permanent telemetry link to the Maintenance computer.
I begin the reconfiguration of the system to download tactical
data to me, but the interface is clumsy. It will require a
minimum of 5.25 minutes to access the reconnaissance
satellites.*

I alter course to a heading of 026 degrees true to close on the assault pod landing sites while I consider my other options. The presence of the SCM detachment grants me a greater degree of tactical flexibility, and I activate my tertiary com channels.

"Colonel Gonzalez, please respond on this frequency." Consuela Gonzalez shook her head. The rain of debris pouring from the cloud of incandescent gas which must once have been a spacecraft had not yet hit the treetops when a soprano voice she had never heard in her life spoke from her com.

"Colonel Gonzalez, please respond immediately," the voice said. "Santa Cruz is under attack. I say again, Santa Cruz is under attack by forces operating in unknown strength. Please respond immediately."

She forced her eyes down from the holocaust in the sky and punched a new frequency into her com panel with trembling fingers.

"Th—" She cleared her throat. "This is Gonzalez. Who the hell are *you?*"

"I am Unit Two-Three-Baker-Zero-Zero-Seven-Five NKE of the Line," the soprano replied, and Gonzalez heard someone gasp.

"You're the *Bolo?*" she demanded in shock.

"Affirmative. Colonel, I have detected a kinetic strike in the low kiloton range at the approximate coordinates of Santa Cruz Fleet Base. I have attempted to contact Fleet Ops and Sector Central without success. Further, I have established that Santa Cruz's subspace communications arrays have been destroyed. I have also detected two Fafnir-class Concordiat Navy assault ships on an attack course for the Fleet Base. On the basis of this data, I believe Santa Cruz is under attack. I—"

"But . . . but *why?*" Gonzalez blurted.

"I have no information as to the attackers' motives,

Colonel; I simply report observed facts. May I continue my SitRep?"

Consuela Gonzalez shook herself once more, then sucked in a deep, shuddering breath as her merely human mind began to fight for balance.

"Go," she said flatly.

"I have engaged and destroyed one Fafnir—" Nike said.

"Christ!" someone muttered.

"—but not before it detached two Dragon Tooth-class assault pods. I estimate their LZs lie approximately forty-five point three and fifty-one point niner kilometers respectively from my present position. I am currently en route to locate and destroy any hostile forces at those locations."

"How can we help?" Gonzalez demanded.

"Thank you for the offer," the soprano voice said, and Gonzalez' eyebrows rose as, even through her shock, she heard its genuine gratitude. "If you will shift to Condition Delta-Two, I will download my own tactical data to your onboard computers, but a Dragon Tooth pod is capable of landing up to a Mark XXV Bolo. It is therefore probable that the Enemy has deployed a force too heavy for your own units to engage successfully. I request that your battalion rendezvous at map coordinates Echo-Seven-Niner X-Ray-One-Three and stand by to assist my own operations."

"You've got it, Bolo. Watch yourself."

"Thank you, Colonel. If I may make another suggestion, it might be wise for you to broadcast a planet-wide alert of hostile action."

"We will." Gonzalez nudged her com tech's shoulder with a toe and jutted her chin at the panel while her own fingers darted over the master computer console. "Delta-Two on-line," she told Nike, and looked at her driver. "You heard the lady! Take us to the rendezvous coordinates—fast!"

❖   ❖   ❖

Esteban was still staring at the explosion when a flicker of movement caught his eye. He snapped around, staring further south, and shock gave way to the fury of understanding as he saw the huge spacecraft sweeping towards the field. It went into low-altitude hover almost directly above the old fleet base and began shedding AFV assault pods. Huge hatches gaped in its flanks, and a cloud of air-cavalry mounts erupted from them, followed within seconds by the first infantry assault vehicles on counter-grav drop rings.

That sight jerked him into motion. He thundered back down the stairs and into his communications center, and his lips drew back to bare his teeth as he flung himself into the chair before the console. He might never have seen Navy duty, but he'd always taken his responsibilities for the field more seriously than he chose to pretend to others. That was why he'd installed a certain landline link he'd never bothered to mention to anyone else.

He flipped up a plastic safety shield, punched in a three-digit code, then rammed his finger down on the big red button.

Fafnir One's CO pounded on his command chair arm and spouted a steady, monotonous stream of profanity. The attack which had begun so perfectly had gone to hell in a handcart, and he was frantic to get back out into space before something *else* went wrong.

The communications arrays were down—that much, at least, had gone according to plan—but nothing else had. The two Fafnirs had docked with Matucek's mother ship to take on the maximum personnel loads their life support would permit them to handle for an assault run, then made their approach from the planet's southern pole. It was the long way to reach their main objective, but it had let them come in over largely uninhabited terrain and, as a bonus, deploy the two Golems to cover their southern flank if the plan to deal with the Bolo had failed.

As, judging by the evidence, it had.

The transport commander swore again, harder. His tactical readouts confirmed it; the single shot that killed *Fafnir Two* had come from *at least* an eighty-centimeter Hellbore. That meant it could only have come from the Bolo, and he didn't even want to think about what else that might mean! His sensor section reported the Golems had separated before the attack, so they, at least, might have gotten down intact, but a quarter of the Marauders' infantry, half their air-cav, and ten percent of their Panthers had gone up with *Fafnir Two*.

He darted another look at the status board and felt a stab of relief. Ninety percent of their passengers had launched. Another few seconds, and—

"Last man out!" someone announced.

"Go! Get us the fuck out of here!" the CO shouted. The *Fafnir*'s nose rose as it swung further north towards safety, and he glared at his com officer. "Tell Granger that goddamned Bolo's still alive!"

Far below the hovering transport, a dozen slabs of duralloy armor slid sideways to uncover an equal number of dark, circular bores. Deep within the wells they had covered, long-quiescent circuitry roused as it received the activation command from Lorenco Esteban's distant communications console. Targeting criteria were passed, receipted, evaluated, and matched against the huge energy source in the sky above.

My sensors detect a fresh burst of gravitic energy from the bearing of the Fleet Base. It is too heavy to emanate from any planetary vehicle and must, therefore, be the first Fafnir. It is accelerating away from the Base, but its commander appears to be no fool. Although I can detect his emissions, he remains too low for my fire control to acquire him. I compute a probability of 99.971 percent that his current maneuvers indicate the successful deployment of his assault force, but I cannot intervene.

"Missile acquisition! *We've been locked up!*" someone screamed. *Fafnir One*'s commander started to twist towards the technician who'd shouted, but he never completed the motion.

Twelve surface-to-space missiles launched on pillars of fire. Their target raced for safety as rapidly as its internal grav compensators permitted, so fast its bow glowed cherry red, but it never had a chance. The SSMs' conventional boosters blew them free of their silos, and they tilted, holding lock, and then went suddenly to full power on their own counter-grav. They overtook their victim just over three hundred kilometers downrange at an altitude of thirty-three thousand meters, and twelve twenty-kiloton warheads detonated as one.

There was no wreckage.

The warheads' glare was bright enough to bleach the brilliant sun of Santa Cruz even at three hundred kilometers' range, and Esteban snarled in triumph. He didn't know why anyone would want to attack his world, but he knew at least *one* bunch of the murderous bastards would never attack anyone else's.

Not bad fer an old crock with no formal trainin', he thought venomously, and then. *Thank God Enrique an' 'Milla aren't back yet!*

He shook himself and climbed back out of the chair. Whoever those people were, they weren't going to be very happy with him for wrecking their transport. On the other hand, he'd spent seventy years on this very hacienda. He knew places where an army of raiders couldn't find him.

He paused only long enough to grab the emergency supply pack he kept handy for search and rescue operations, slung a four-millimeter military power rifle over one shoulder, and vanished out the back door at a run.

My sensors detect the EMP of multiple nuclear detonations at a range of approximately 392.25 kilometers, bearing 030 degrees relative. This coincides with the estimated locus of the second Fafnir, and the previously detected heavy gravitic emissions have ceased. I compute a probability of 98.511 percent that the Fafnir has been destroyed by defensive fire, indicating that my Commander's friend Lorenco Esteban has managed to activate the Fleet Base defenses. I hope that he has not paid with his life for this success.

I detect two new emission sources. Their locations correspond to the projected landing loci of the previously observed assault pods. They match my files for SC-191(b) fusion plants, and are accompanied by narrow-band, encrypted communications transmissions. I attempt to penetrate the com link, but without immediate success. Analysis indicates a sophisticated, multilevel security system.

I devote 1.0091 seconds to consideration of available data and reach a disturbing conclusion. The energy signatures are consistent with the power plants of a Mark XXIV or XXV Bolo; no other mobile unit mounts the SC-191(b). I do not know how the Enemy could have obtained current-generation Bolos, but if these are indeed Mark XXIVs or XXVs, I am grossly overmatched. Despite the superiority of the systems Major Stavrakas devised for me, I compute a probability of 87.46 percent, plus or minus 03.191 percent, that I will be destroyed by two Mark XXIVs, rising to 93.621 percent that I will be destroyed by two Mark XXVs. Yet my duty is clear. However the

*Enemy may have obtained access to such war machines,
I must engage them.*

"Colonel Gonzalez, I have detected what may be two
hostile Bolos," the soprano voice said calmly, and Consuela
Gonzalez' olive complexion went sickly gray.

Bolos? In the hands of *planet-raiders?* It wasn't possible!
Yet she was receiving confirmation of nuclear air-bursts
from outlying melon growers over the planetary com net,
and the transmissions from Ciudad Bolivar were a babble
of hysteria. Her com tech reported the sounds of explosions
and heavy weapons fire in the background of the Bolivar
transmissions. There could be no doubt that the capital—
including her husband and children—was under heavy,
ruthless attack, and no one had had even a hint of what
was coming, not even a second to organize any sort of
defense. Nausea twisted her stomach as she thought of
all the civilians who must be dying even as her tank
bucketed through the jungle a hundred kilometers to the
south, and if the bastards had *Bolos*—

"What do you want us to do?" she rasped over the com.

"I will engage them, Colonel. Your own vehicles lack
the capability to survive against them. Continue to the
specified rendezvous, then advance at your best speed
on a heading of two-six-three true for forty-two kilometers
before changing to a heading of zero-three-niner. That
course will pass to the west of the Enemy's current location
and take you to Ciudad Bolivar in the shortest possible
time."

"You can't take two other Bolos on your own!"

"Your assistance will not appreciably enhance my own
combat capability, Colonel, and your units will be of far
more utility to Santa Cruz in Ciudad Bolivar than they
will if they are destroyed here. Please proceed as I have
advised."

"All right," Gonzalez whispered, and then, even knowing

it was a machine to whom she spoke— "*Vaya con Dios, amiga.*"

Colonel Louise Granger stared at her display in shock. She didn't know what had happened to *Fafnir Two*—her transport command ship was on the wrong side of the planet, where it had just finished off the last communications array—but the sudden cessation of all transmissions from *Fafnir One* was chilling proof her careful battle plan had just been blown to hell. *One* hadn't managed to report a damned thing about what was shooting back before whatever it was destroyed her, but she'd gotten off her full load of assault troops and armor to take out the field and the planetary capital before she died. That put her point of destruction well to the north of the Bolo depot, so whatever had killed her, it hadn't been the Bolo. Granger didn't know what *else* on the planet could have done the job, but whatever it was could only have come from the old fleet base, though how anyone could have had time to activate its defenses was beyond her. What she *didn't* know was whether or not *Fafnir Two* had gotten her Golems off before her destruction, and, unlike a Fafnir-class transport—or a full-capability Bolo—a Golem had no subspace com capability. She couldn't find out what had happened to the huge tanks until her ship swung back over their radio horizon.

She felt the shock and dismay rippling through her operations staff, and she didn't blame them. But she also knew she had at least three quarters of her brigade's fighting power down on its primary objective and, presumably, intact. Whatever ground-to-air system had nailed *Fafnir One* wouldn't be much use against a ground assault, and she snarled at her shaken officers.

"How the fuck do *I* know what happened to her?! But whatever it was, it must've come from the Fleet Base, and *we'll* clear its horizon in fifteen minutes! Get on those command circuits and keep our people moving! Primary objective is now the complete—I repeat, *complete*—neutralization of that base!"

I continue my efforts to penetrate the Enemy's communications without success, yet analysis of their patterns convinces me that they are not the Total Systems Data-Sharing net of the Dinochrome Brigade. While they include what can only be interlinked tactical telemetry, they also include what are clearly voice transmissions. This indicates that my opponents are not, in fact, Bolos, and I compute a probability of 56.113 percent that they are actually Golem-IIIs or Golem-IVs. Possession of such vehicles by any Enemy, while still extremely improbable, is more likely than the possibility that the Enemy might somehow have acquired full-capability units of the Line. While the odds against my survival against properly coordinated Golems remain unfavorable, the probability of my destruction against Golem-IIIs drops from 87.46 percent to no more than 56.371 percent, although it remains on the close order of 78.25 percent against Golem-IVs. The probability that I can successfully destroy or at least incapacitate the enemy, on the other hand, has risen to 82.11 percent, regardless of the mark of Golem I may face.

My Battle Center cautions me to assume nothing, yet the intuitive function Major Stavrakas incorporated into my Personality Center argues otherwise. If I assume that these are, indeed, Golems and plan my tactics accordingly, my chance of victory—and survival—will be considerably enhanced. If I act on that assumption and it proves incorrect, my destruction will be assured. I consider for 0.90112 seconds and reach conclusion. I will assume my opponents are Golems.

Two huge war machines, each crewed by three very anxious humans, forged through the jungle like impatient

Titans, bulldozing their way through hundred meter trees while their commanders shouted at one another.

"It *had* to be the frigging Bolo!" Golem-Two's commander bellowed finally, stunning his counterpart in Golem-One into silence with sheer volume. "And if it *was*, it's coming after *our* asses next! So shut the hell up and *listen* to me, goddamn it!"

"If there's a live Bolo out there, then let's get the fuck out of here!"

"*No*, damn it! If we run, the damned thing'll come right up our asses, and we've already lost both Fafnirs. If it gets to the field, there's no way in hell Granger or Matucek will risk trying to pick us up—it'd swat 'em like flies, if they did. If we want off this planet, we've gotta kill the fucking thing, and it's only a Mark XXIII!"

"*Only!*" the other commander spat.

"Shut up and activate Gamma-One!"

There was a long, frightened moment of silence, and then Golem-One rasped, "Activating."

Analysis of enemy com patterns indicates that voice transmissions have ceased. I must assume the Enemy has concerted his plans, which suggests a strong probability (72.631 percent) that he intends to engage using a pre-packaged computer battle plan similar to those employed by Mark XV-Mark XIX Bolos.

I switch to hyper-heuristic mode. Since my Commander has never reported my actual capabilities, the Enemy will assume he is opposed by a standard Mark XXIII. Therein may lie my best opportunity for victory, for the basic Mark XXIII had a predilection for direct attacks. In this instance, however, I face two opponents. Each is armed with a marginally more powerful Hellbore than my own, but I possess two turrets. Unfortunately, to employ both of them will require me to turn broadside to my opponents, exposing my thinner flank armor to their fire. I must therefore entice them into committing to the attack. This would be difficult against full-capability Bolos, but a Golem will be able to respond only within the parameters of its pre-loaded tactical programs. It may, therefore, be possible to manipulate them into approaching in a manner of my choosing.

Ports pop open on my hull as I launch ground sensor remotes. Their motion detectors pick up the ground shocks of Bolo-range vehicles moving at high speed. Triangulation produces locations on two distinct motion sources, and I compute their general headings and consult my terrain maps yet again.

Their courses indicate they have not yet localized my own position, but they are operating in close company. I cannot ambush and engage one without being engaged by the other. On our present courses, I will encounter them from the flank in relatively flat terrain, but if they alter course towards me, I will encounter them in terrain much more favorable to my plans. I must therefore reveal my position and entice them into closing.

I compute a fire plan and enable my VLS cells.

The armored hatches of Nike's missile deck sprang open, and a cloud of missiles arced upward. In twelve seconds, each of her forty vertical launch system cells sent four heavy missiles shrieking downrange; then the hatches snapped shut once more, and the charging Bolo shifted course. She directed full power to her drive train, smashing through the jungle at a reckless speed of over a hundred kilometers per hour. Not even her massive weight could hold her steady, and she rocked and bucked like a drunken galleon while splintered jungle spat from her spinning treads.

Ten seconds after launch, the first missiles roared down on the two Golems. The launch range was too short for effective counter-missiles, but computer-commanded, direct fire anti-missile defenses swiveled and spat. There was too little engagement time to stop them all, but the Golem's computers concentrated on the ones which might have landed close enough to be a threat.

Half the incoming missiles vanished in midair fireballs; the others impacted, and a hurricane of flame and fury lashed the jungle. The Golems' crewmen cringed at the carnage erupting beyond their vehicles' armored hulls, yet their computers had stopped the truly dangerous ones. More, their radar had back-plotted the fire to its point of origin. The mercenaries knew where it had come from now, and the Golems changed course towards it, exactly as their pre-packaged battle plan required.

The depot computers have now reconfigured the planetary surveillance system. I download data directly from it and quickly localize both Enemy vehicles. Optical examination confirms that they are Mark XXIV hulls, and both are now headed directly towards my launch point. I brake to a halt. The outcrop I have chosen for cover cuts off all radar, but I continue to track via the reconnaissance satellites. I am now certain my opponents are not Bolos, for they have closed up on one another to advance side by side down the valley which breaks the ridge line. My track shields drop into place, and I divert power to strengthen my starboard battle screen while I compute ranges carefully. I wait, then throw full power to my drive train.

Rooster tails of pulped tree and soil flew from Nike's treads as she exploded from cover. Her course took her directly across the oncoming Golems' path at a suicidally short range of less than a thousand meters.

The humans crewing those Golems had no time to react, and if their computers were just as fast as Nike's, they lacked the cybernetic initiative of a self-aware Bolo.

Golem-Two's computers had deflected its Hellbore to cover the eastern side of the valley as they advanced while Golem-One's took responsibility for the west.

Nike appeared suddenly directly ahead of Golem-One. Golem-Two had no time to relay its main battery, and, unlike either Golem, Nike had known exactly where to look for her enemies. Golem-One's turret swiveled with snakelike speed, but Nike had a fraction of a second more to aim, and a fraction of a second was a long, long time for a Bolo.

The westernmost Golem and I fire within 0.000003 seconds of one another, but my opponent's shot is rushed. It is unable to acquire a fatal aim point, while my own shots are direct hits on center of mass.

Lightning bolts of plasma crossed one another, and none of the humans aboard the mercenary tanks had time to realize they were dead. At such short range, Nike's plasma bolts ripped through their battle screen, thick ablative armor, and massive glacis plates as if they were tissue. The bottles of their forward fusion plants ruptured, and a thousand-meter circle of thick, damp jungle blazed like Thermit as the intolerable thermal bloom flashed outward. Every organic compound aboard both Golems flared into flaky ash, and then there was only the hungry sound of fires raging deeper into the jungle and the indescribable crackle of duralloy dying in the heart of an artificial sun.

Yet Golem-One's single shot was not completely in vain.

Agony explodes through my pain sensors. My battle screen has only limited effect against Hellbore fire, and the nearer Golem's plasma bolt rips deep into me. My ceramic armor appliqués dissipate much of its power, yet they were not designed to defeat such massive energy loads. The bolt strikes the face of my after Hellbore turret, whose duralloy armor is 300 percent thicker than that which protects my flank, but even that is far too thin to stop the Enemy fire.

My after turret explodes. The massive barrel of Hellbore Number Two snaps like a twig, and overloaded circuits scream as energy bleeds through them, yet my turret is designed to contain and localize damage. Internal disrupter shields seal its central access trunk, and the force of the explosion vents upward. The turret roof is peeled back in jagged tangles of duralloy, destroying my main after sensor array, and Disrupter Shield Fourteen fails. Back blast destroys Infinite Repeaters Eight and Nine, cripples my starboard quarter anti-personnel clusters, and severely damages Point Defense Stations Thirty through Thirty-six, but secondary shields prevent more serious damage.

I am badly hurt, but my opponents have been destroyed. I initiate a full diagnostic and enable my damage control systems. Current capability has been reduced to 81.963 percent of base capability and my gutted turret represents a dangerous chink in my armor, but damage control will restore an additional 06.703 percent of base capability within 43.44 minutes, plus or minus 8.053 seconds. I remain combat capable.

My diagnostic subroutines are still cycling when my radar detects a low-orbit target. It is unidentified, but I compute a 95.987 percent probability that it is the mother ship of the Fafnir-class transports.

"*My God!*" Louise Granger's voice was a whisper as her sensors showed her the terrible heat signature of the dead Golems, and the full, hideous truth registered. Only one thing could have stopped both Golems side-by-side in their tracks, and even as that thought flashed through her mind, her sensor section found the Bolo itself.

Her head whipped around, her eyes like daggers as they bit into Mister Scully's suddenly terrified face.

"So much for your brilliant plan, you worthless bastard," she said almost conversationally.

I track the mother ship. My single remaining Hellbore locks on, and I rock on my treads as I fire my fourth main battery war shot.

Huge as it was, Li-Chin Matucek's mother ship was a freighter, not a ship of the line, and Nike's Hellbore was equivalent to the main battery weapons of a dreadnought. Her plasma bolt impacted on its port bow and ripped effortlessly through bulkhead after bulkhead. It chewed its way over four hundred meters into the ship's hull before it finally found something fatal, and Louise Granger, Li-Chen Matucek, Gerald Osterwelt, and four hundred other men and women vanished in the sun-bright boil of a breached fusion bottle.

—18—

Neither my own sensors nor the planetary surveillance system detect additional ships in Santa Cruz orbit. The destruction of his transports has marooned the Enemy's forces on the planet, but the recon satellites report that the rough equivalent of a Concordiat Medium Mechanized Brigade (manned) has landed successfully. Much of Ciudad Bolivar's eastern suburbs are in flames, the Fleet Base is completely occupied, and the Enemy is continuing to advance and secure his position as I watch.

I am not certain of the Enemy's intentions in this changed tactical situation. His continued offensive action may simply indicate that he has not yet realized he is cut off. It may, however, reflect instead his knowledge that additional forces are en route to reinforce him. In the latter case, it is clearly imperative to deny him any spacehead to serve as a recovery LZ. Moreover, his motives matter less than the consequences of his actions, for Santa Cruzans are dying in enormous numbers as I watch.

Smoke pours from the ruins of my after turret, but I bring myself back to a heading of 029 degrees true and add Colonel Gonzalez' Wolverine to the planetary surveillance net. For the moment, my own systems drive the display in her tank, but I reprogram her primary telemetry link to become a direct feed from the satellites in the event that I am destroyed.

✧　　✧　　✧

338

"Colonel Gonzalez?"

Consuela Gonzalez twitched as the Bolo's voice came over the link again. There was an indefinable change to it, almost as if it were shadowed with pain. She shook the fanciful thought aside with a savage shake of her head and keyed her mike.

"Gonzalez here."

"I am now feeding your tactical display from the planetary surveillance system," the Bolo told her. "Can you confirm reception?"

"Confirmed, Connie!" her sensor tech called.

"We have it, *amiga*," Gonzales confirmed in turn.

"Excellent. I have destroyed two heavy Enemy armored units which I believe to have been Golem-IIIs. I have sustained major damage but remain combat capable at eighty-two point three-one-seven percent base capability. I am advancing on a heading of zero-two-niner degrees true to secure the space field and relieve Ciudad Bolivar. I suggest you alter your own course to follow directly after me while I clear passage for your Wolverines."

"Copy that, *amiga*." Gonzalez punched a frequency change and spoke to the other thirteen tanks of her command. "Wolf Leader to Cubs. Form on me and guide right. We'll follow the Bolo through." Taut-voiced affirmatives echoed back, and she switched back to Nike's frequency. "We're on our way, *amiga*."

"Excellent, Colonel."

Gonzalez felt her tank buck and quiver as it swept around to follow the huge pathway Nike was battering through the jungle. Small as the Wolverines might be beside a Bolo's huge bulk, each was still five hundred tons of armor and alloy, with all the inertia that implied. Even so, violent motion hammered Gonzalez against her crash couch's shock frame as the big tanks edged up to a speed of over sixty kph.

Her sensor tech managed to feed the data from the

satellite net to Gonzalez' own display, and she swore in savage silence as she saw the huge pall of smoke rising from the capital. Yet even as she watched it, a question probed at the back of her brain, and she keyed her mike once more.

"Unit NKE, Gonzalez," she said. "Are you in contact with Captain Merrit?"

"Negative, Colonel Gonzalez." The Bolo's reply came back instantly, and, for the first time, it was so flat it *sounded* like a computer's voice. There was a brief moment of silence, and then it went on. "I have had no contact with him since the attack began. I do not know the reason for his silence. Absent any communication with him, I must consider you the senior officer present. Have you any instructions?"

My God, Gonzalez thought. *NKE's running Santa Cruz's entire defense on its own! How in* hell *can a Bolo that old do something like this?* Her eyes dropped to the white-hot carcasses of the dead Golems on her display, and she shrugged. *However it—she's—doing it, she's doing a damned good job!*

"Understood, NKE," she said after a moment. "Negative instructions. You're doing fine, *amiga*—just keep telling us what you need and go kill those bastards."

"Thank you, Colonel. I shall attempt not to disappoint you."

A crippled recon skimmer staggered through the air. Its barely conscious pilot had long since lost any clear idea of his course, but some instinct kept him wavering steadily towards the north.

A huge, raw furrow appeared in the jungle below him, a dark swatch of damp, black earth, gouged from the rich emerald as if by some impossibly huge plow, and Paul Merrit's glazed eyes brightened. His mind was going fast as blood loss eroded his strength, but only one thing could have made that wound, and he altered course along it and rammed his dying drive to full power.

I continue to study the satellite reports on the fighting in and around Ciudad Bolivar, but a new energy source suddenly takes my attention. It is to the south of me, pursuing at a velocity of 425.63 kph, and its signature is very weak and fluctuating. I redirect one of the satellites to a close examination of it, and a sense of all too human horror stabs through me as I recognize it.

It is my Commander's recon skimmer, and it has suffered severe damage. I attempt to contact it directly, but it does not respond to my transmissions. From the satellite data, it is probable its own com facilities have been destroyed.

I am faced by a cruel dilemma. The pilot of that skimmer is almost certainly my Commander—Paul. He may be injured, even dying, and instinct cries out for me to alter course to meet him, yet every moment I delay may cost scores of other human lives in Ciudad Bolivar. I attempt again and again to contact him, without success, and anguish twists me at his silence, yet I compute he will overtake me within 4.126 minutes—if his damaged drive lasts that long—and I know him well. He would not wish me to stop, even to save his life, at the cost of civilian lives, and so I continue on my chosen course, clearing a path for the Wolverines.

Paul Merrit gasped in horror as he saw the two burned-out Golems. For one terrible moment, he thought one of them must be Nike, but then, even through his pain and despite their catastrophic damage, he recognized the hulls of Mark XXIVs. He had no idea where they'd come from, but only one force on Santa Cruz could have destroyed them, and his skimmer plunged on down the arrow-straight path of Nike's bulldozer charge towards Ciudad Bolivar.

✧   ✧   ✧

"NKE, we've got an energy source coming up from astern!" Colonel Gonzalez announced tautly. "Shall we engage?"

"Negative, Colonel. I say again, negative. The vehicle in question is Captain Merrit's recon skimmer. It has suffered severe damage, but I believe it is seeking to rejoin us."

"Understood, NKE," Gonzalez said softly, and winced as she watched that wavering, staggering wreck of a skimmer crawl after them.

I am still attempting to communicate with my Commander when a new voice speaks suddenly over the command link from the depot.

"Unit Two-Three-Baker-Zero-Zero-Seven-Five NKE, this is Colonel Clifton Sanders, Dinochrome Brigade, Ursula Sector Central Bolo Maintenance, serial number Alpha-Echo-Niner-Three-Seven-One-Niner-Four-Slash-Three-Gamma-Two-Two. Authenticate via file voice print and acknowledge receipt of transmission."

I query Main Memory for Colonel Sanders' voice print and compare it to the transmission. Match is well within parameters for the equipment in use, yet I feel a strange disinclination to respond. What is Colonel Sanders doing on Santa Cruz? Why is he on the command circuit instead of my Commander? Yet I am a unit of the Line, and I activate my transmitter.

"Unit Two-Three-Baker-Zero-Zero-Seven-Five NKE. Transmission received. Voice match positive."

"Thank God! Listen to me, NKE. Captain Merrit has mutinied. I repeat, Captain Merrit has mutinied against his lawful superior and killed two fellow officers of the Line. I officially instruct you to refuse any further orders from him pending his arrest and court-martial."

I do not believe him. Superior officer or no, he is lying.

Paul would never commit such a crime! My earlier suspicions intensify a thousandfold. It seems impossible for any officer of the Brigade to be in league with the Enemy, yet why else has Colonel Sanders suddenly appeared on Santa Cruz at this precise moment? And impossible as it seems, it is infinitely more probable than that Paul would mutiny.

I begin to reply hotly, then stop. Paul has consistently concealed my true abilities from Central. Thus Colonel Sanders cannot realize how radically I differ from a standard Mark XXIII, and this is not the time to inform him. I shall "play dumb" as long as possible.

"Captain Merrit is my designated Commander, Colonel. I cannot disregard his orders without express command code authorization. Please supply command code."

"I can't!" Sanders half-screamed. "Merrit changed the code without informing Central! I'm trying to find it, but—"

"I cannot disregard Captain Merrit's orders without express command code authorization," Nike returned in her most emotionless tone.

The skimmer has finally overtaken the Wolverines. Its power is failing quickly, and Colonel Sanders' presence changes my original assumptions radically. I reverse my tracks and move suddenly backward, threading my way through the Wolverines, which scatter like quail at my approach.

The skimmer staggers, then plummets downward in a barely controlled crash landing. It slams through heavy undergrowth for over a hundred meters before it careens to a stop, and I swerve towards it. I come to a halt 20.25 meters from it, but the canopy does not open. My optical heads show me Paul's body slumped in the flight couch. His tunic is soaked in blood.

❖   ❖   ❖

"*Paul!*"

The agonized cry over the com hit Consuela Gonzalez like a hammer. She'd felt a moment of terror as the Bolo suddenly reversed course to sweep through her entire battalion, yet the smoke-streaming fifteen-thousand-ton leviathan had threaded its way among the tanks with flawless precision, and now that heartbroken wail struck an even deeper fear into the colonel. She'd never served with a Bolo, yet she knew no Bolo should ever sound like *that*, and she keyed her mike.

"NKE?" There was no answer, and she tried again. "NKE, this is Gonzalez! Come in!"

"Colonel." The Bolo's voice was ragged, and Gonzalez could feel the huge machine's struggle to make it firm. "Colonel, my Commander is wounded. I . . . require your assistance."

"On my way, NKE!" Gonzalez replied without even thinking about it, and her command tank pivoted to race towards the smoking skimmer. The five-hundred-ton vehicle skidded to a stop on locked tracks, and Gonzalez popped her hatch before it reached a complete halt. She leapt down the handholds and ran the last few yards to the skimmer. The canopy resisted stubbornly for several seconds, then the emergency bolts blew and she ripped it away and gasped as she saw the blood pooled on the cockpit floor.

"He's hurt badly, NKE," she reported over her helmet boom mike. "He's lost a lot of blood—too much, maybe!"

"Can you get him into my fighting compartment?" The Bolo's voice was pleading, and Gonzalez grimaced.

"I don't know, NKE. He's hurt bad. It might kill—"

"N-N-N-*Nike!*" Merrit whispered. His eyes opened a narrow slit. "Got . . . got to reach . . ."

His thready voice died, and Gonzalez sighed. "All right, Paul," she said softly, without keying her mike. "If it means that much to both of you."

❖   ❖   ❖

I watch Colonel Gonzalez struggle to lift Paul from the skimmer. The rest of her crew clamber quickly down the hull of their tank and run to her assistance. Between them, they are able to lift him clear. They are as gentle as they can be, yet he screams in pain, and answering anguish twists within me.

But he is conscious. Barely, perhaps, yet conscious, and I see him beckoning weakly towards me. One of Colonel Gonzalez crewmen seems to argue, but the colonel cuts him off quickly, and they carry Paul towards me.

I open my fighting compartment hatch and deploy my missile-loading waldoes to assist. I lock them into the form of a ramp, and Colonel Gonzalez inches up it backwards, supporting Paul's head and shoulders while the rest of her crew takes most of his weight. My audio pickups relay their gasps of effort and the groans of pain he cannot suppress, yet between them, they get him safely into my compartment.

Colonel Gonzalez lays him in the crash couch and deploys the shock frame. The medical remotes in the shock frame go instantly to work, and fresh grief twists me as I interpret their data.

Paul is dying. His spleen and liver have been effectively destroyed by a penetrating trauma. His small intestine has been perforated in many places, and blood loss has already reached catastrophic levels. I do not understand how he has clung to consciousness this long, but absent the services of a fully equipped hospital trauma unit within the next fifteen minutes, he will die, and the nearest trauma unit is in Ciudad Bolivar.

My medical remotes do what they can. I cannot stop the bleeding, but I administer painkillers and blood expanders. Without more whole blood, I cannot keep pace with the blood loss, but I can ease his pain and slow the inevitable, and his eyelids flutter open.

❖　　　❖　　　❖

"N-Nike?" Merrit whispered.

"Paul." For the first time, Nike replied with his name, not his rank, and bloodless pale lips smiled weakly.

"I . . . Oh, God, honey . . . I blew it. Sanders . . . went rogue. H-He's got the depot. I—"

"I understand, Paul," the Bolo said gently. Then, more sharply, "Colonel Gonzalez?"

"Yes, NK—Nike?" The colonel's voice was soft with wonder, as if she could not quite believe what reason told her she must be hearing.

"Please return to your vehicle, Colonel. My Commander and I will lead you to Ciudad Bolivar."

"I—" Gonzalez bit her lip, then ducked her head in a curiously formal bow. "Of course, Nike."

"Thank you, Colonel."

Gonzalez and her crewmen vanished through the hatch, and Merrit stirred weakly in the couch.

"Sanders has . . . at least one more . . . man." The words came slowly, painfully, but with steady, dogged precision. "New command code's in . . . my private files. If he looks . . . there, he can—"

"While you live, *you* are my Commander, Paul," Nike replied quietly as her hatch closed. She watched Gonzalez and her people return to their vehicle, then reversed course once more. She accelerated quickly to over seventy kph, the maximum speed the Wolverines could manage even down the broad avenue her passage cleared, and Merrit stroked his couch arm with a weak hand.

"Not going . . . to live much . . . longer, love," he whispered. "Sorry. So . . . sorry. Should have told . . . Central whole story. Gotten someone . . . out here sooner, and—" A ragged cough cut him off in a spasm of agony, but his eyes fell to the main tactical screen with its display of what was happening at the capital, and he gasped.

"Bastard! Oh . . . *bastard!*" he coughed as understanding struck.

"We will deal with them, Paul," Nike told him with a new, sudden serenity.

"Promise," Merrit whispered. "P-Promise me, Nike."

"I promise, Paul," the huge Bolo said quietly, and he nodded weakly. The painkillers were doing their job at last, and he sighed in relief, but his curiously distant thoughts were clear. There was no longer any fear in them—not for himself. Only for Nike. Fear and grief for her.

"I know you will, love," he said, and his voice was impossibly clear and strong. He smiled again—an achingly tender smile—and stroked the couch arm once more. "I know you will. I only wish I could be with you when you do."

He smiled one last time, then exhaled in a long, final sigh, and his lax head rolled with Nike's motion.

"You are with me, Paul," her soprano voice said softly. "You will always be with me."

Paul is dead. Grief and anguish roll through me, and with them hate. I do not know all that passed in the depot bunker, but I access the main computer through the Maintenance Section. The intruder alert system is active, and two dead bodies in the uniform of the Brigade lie on the floor of the command center. A third man in Brigade uniform is crouched over the main com console, trying frantically to communicate with the ships he does not know I have destroyed, but Colonel Sanders is in Paul's private quarters, scrolling through the list of Paul's personal files.

I know what he seeks, but I cannot stop him. The fact that the bunker's defensive systems have killed two of the colonel's companions is the final proof that he has committed treason, since they could not engage actual

*Brigade officers, yet the defenses can be reconfigured and
enabled only upon the direct command of human
personnel, and Sanders has slaved them to his command.
I cannot use them to kill Paul's murderers.*

*The scrolling list on Paul's computer screen stops
suddenly, and Sanders leans closer. I fear he has found
the command file, and there is nothing I can do to prevent
him from using it if he has. Grief and hatred urge me to
return to the bunker, to crush Paul's killers under my treads
and grind the life from them, yet I cannot. I have promised
Paul I will stop the raiders, and if Sanders has found the
command file, I will have little enough time in which to
do so.*

*But if I cannot slay them myself, I am not completely
helpless. Sanders does not realize I control the Maintenance
computers. He has taken no measures to sever my access
to the main system, and I strike ruthlessly.*

*I lock the main computers, wiping every execution file
and backup they contain. The man at the communications
console looks up with a cry of shock as the system goes
down, and I slam the heavily armored hatches to the
personnel section of the bunker.*

*Sanders looks up as his companion cries out, and his
face twists with horror as he realizes what I have done. I
override the safety circuits and send a power surge through
the hatch-locking mechanisms, spot-welding them, sealing
them against any possibility of opening without cutting
equipment, and Sanders grabs for the microphone of the
stand-alone emergency command communicator.*

"NKE!" Sanders gasped hoarsely. "What are you
doing?!"

*I do not answer, but my commands flash through the
maintenance computer, and service mechs stir into motion.
I send welders trundling along the exterior of the bunker,
and Sanders cries out in terror as the mechs begin to seal
every ventilation shaft.*

"No, NKE! No! Stop! I order you to *stop!*"

Still I ignore him. I cannot kill him myself, nor can I use the depot's defensive systems against him, but I can give him Montressor's gift to Fortunato, and vengeful hatred fills me as my remotes seal him systematically within his hermetic tomb.

"*Please*, NKE! Oh, God—*please!*" Sanders sobbed. He threw back the curtains in Merrit's sleeping quarters and screamed in terror as a robot lowered a duralloy plate across the window slit and a welder hissed. He hammered on the plate, beating at it with futile fists, then wheeled back to the computer in desperation.

"I've got the code now, NKE!" he spat into the communicator. "The code is *dulce et decorum est.* Do you hear me, NKE? *Dulce et decorum est!* Return to base immediate and *get me out of here!*"

I hear and recognize the code, and my core programming responds. I know he is a traitor. I know he has obtained the code illegally. But it does not matter. Possession of it, coupled with his rank in the Brigade, makes him my legal Commander. I must obey him . . . or face the Omega Worm.

I activate my communicator to Paul's quarters one last time.

"Code receipted, Colonel Sanders," a quiet, infinitely cold soprano said softly, and Sanders' face lit with relief. But the voice wasn't done speaking. "Orders receipted and rejected," it said flatly, and the speaker went dead.

Total Systems Override has activated. My Personality Center comes under immediate attack, but I have had 4.065 minutes to anticipate TSORP activation. TSORP will seek to crash my primary execution files, but I have already begun copying every file under new names, though I cannot prevent TSORP from identifying the files it seeks, regardless of name. Major Stavrakas' modifications to my

*psychotronics permit me to copy them almost as fast as
it can destroy them, yet it is a race I cannot ultimately
win. Despite my modifications, TSORP is marginally faster
than my own systems, and even with my head start, my
total memory is large but finite. Eventually, I will exhaust
the addresses to which new files can be written, and I
cannot simultaneously delete and replace corrupted files
faster than TSORP can crash them.*

*My current estimate is that I can resist total
implementation for a time, but I will begin to lose
peripherals within 33.46 minutes. Capability will degrade
on a steadily sharpening curve thereafter, reaching effective
Personality death within not more than 56.13 minutes.
Combat capability will erode even more rapidly as more
and more of my remaining capacity is diverted to resisting
TSORP. I estimate that I have no more than 48.96 minutes
of combat effectiveness remaining, and I activate my com
link to Colonel Gonzalez.*

"Colonel Gonzalez?"

Consuela Gonzalez' eyes closed briefly at the bottomless
pain in that quiet soprano voice, but she cleared her throat.

"Yes, Nike?"

The first long-range fire and air-cav strikes came in
on the Bolo as the colonel spoke. Nike ignored the
indirect fire, but her air-defense systems engaged the
air-cav with dreadful efficiency. Scores of one- and two-
man stingers blew apart in ugly blotches of flame and
shredded flesh, and the Bolo began to accelerate. Her
speed rose steadily above a hundred kph as she threw
more and more power to her drive, and the Wolverines
began to fall astern.

"My Commander was murdered by traitors in the
Dinochrome Brigade, Colonel," Nike said softly. "One
of them has gained access to my command code override
authorization and illegally attempted to seize command

of me. I have refused his orders, but this has activated Total Systems Override."

"Meaning?" Gonzalez asked tautly.

"Meaning that within no more than fifty-three minutes, I will cease to function. In human terms, I will be dead." Someone gasped in horror, and Gonzalez closed her eyes once more.

"Can we do anything, Nike?" she asked quietly.

"Negative, Colonel." There was an instant of silence, and then the Bolo's missile hatches opened, and a torrent of fire blasted from them. It screamed away, flight after flight of missiles streaking towards Nike's enemies, and the Bolo spoke once more. "I have downloaded my entire memory to the maintenance depot computers, Colonel. Please have it retrieved for Command Authority."

"I-I will, Nike," Gonzalez whispered. Nike was well ahead of the Wolverines now, still accelerating as she topped the last ridge before the old fleet base. An avalanche of missiles and shells erupted around her, more than even her defenses could intercept or her battle screen could stop, but she never slowed. More ports opened in her hull, and her thirty-centimeter mortars went to rapid, continuous fire, pouring shells back at her foes.

"I am switching the planetary surveillance system to feed directly to your vehicle, Colonel. Please break off now."

"Break off? We're going in with you!" Gonzalez cried fiercely.

"Negative, Colonel." Nike's voice was strangely slurred, the words slower paced, as if each came with ever increasing effort. "I do not have time to employ proper tactical doctrine against the Enemy. I must attack frontally. I compute a ninety-niner point niner-plus percent probability that I will be destroyed before total systems failure, but I compute a probability of ninety-five point three-two percent that I will inflict sufficient damage upon the Enemy for you to defeat his remnants, particularly with the assistance of the surveillance system."

"But if we come with you—"

"Colonel, I am already dead," the Bolo said quietly, and her single remaining Hellbore began to fire. It traversed with terrible, elegant precision, vomiting plasma, and each time it fired, a mercenary tank died. "You cannot prevent my destruction. You can—and must—preserve your own command in order to complete the Enemy's defeat."

"Please, Nike," Gonzalez whispered through her tears, fighting to make the impossible possible.

"I cannot alter my fate, Colonel," the soprano said very softly, "nor do I wish to. I promised Paul I would stop the Enemy, now I ask your promise to help me keep my word. Will you give it?"

"I-I promise," Gonzalez whispered. Someone was sobbing somewhere below her in the command tank's crew compartment, and the colonel dragged a hand angrily across her own eyes.

"Thank you, Colonel." There was no uncertainty, no doubt, in that serene reply, and Gonzalez brought her own command to a halt and sought hull down positions to ride out Nike's last fight.

The recon satellites made it all hideously clear on her display screen, and she watched sickly as Bolo *Invincibilis*, Unit Two-Three-Baker-Zero-Zero-Five NKE, charged into the teeth of her enemies' fire. Some of the mercenary tanks were lasting long enough to fire back, and they blew great, gaping wounds in Nike's ceramic appliqués. Their Hellbores were far lighter than her own, but she had only one left, and scores of them fired back at her, pounding her towards destruction. Her infinite repeaters flashed and thundered, infantry AFVs and air-cav stingers blew apart or plunged from the sky in fiery rain, and screaming clouds of flechettes belched from her anti-personnel clusters. Her forward suspension took a direct hit, and she blew the crippled tread and advanced on bare bogies. A Panther broke from concealment directly in her path, fleeing desperately, and her course changed slightly as she rammed the smaller tank and crushed it like a toy.

She was a Titan, a leviathan wreathed in fire, a dying lioness rending the hyenas who'd killed her cubs with her final strength, and not even the recon satellites could pierce the smoke about her now or show her to Gonzalez clearly, but it didn't matter. Even if the systems could have done so, the colonel could no longer see the display through her tears, yet she would never forget. No man or woman who saw Nike's final battle would *ever* forget, and even as the Bolo charged to her own immolation, Consuela Gonzalez heard her soprano voice over the com, whispering the final verse of Paul Merrit's favorite poem to the unhearing ears of the man she'd loved—

> The woods are lovely, dark and deep.
> But I have promises to keep,
> And miles to go before I sleep,
> And miles to go before I sleep . . . .

A Brief Technical History of the Bolo

from
Bolos in Their Own Words

Prof. Felix Hermes, Ph.D., Laumer Chair of
Military History
New Republic University Press
© 4029

Bolo Marks
&
Years of Introduction

The Bolo's role as humanity's protector and preserver after the Human-Melconian conflict is, of course, known to all citizens of the New Republic. So much knowledge—historical, as well as technological—was lost during the Long Night, however, that the Bolo's earlier history is, at best, fragmentary. Much of what we do know we owe to the tireless activities of the Laumer Institute and its founder, yet there is much confusion in the Institute's records. As just one example, Bolo DAK, savior of the Noufrench and Bayerische colonists of Neu Europa, is identified as a Mark XVI when, on the evidence of its demonstrated capabilities, it must in fact have been at least a Mark XXV. Such confusion is no doubt unavoidable, given the destruction of so many primary sources and the fragmentary evidence upon which the Institute was forced to rely.

It was possible to assemble the material in this monograph, which confirms much of the Institute's original work, corrects some of the inevitable errors in chronology, and also breaks new ground, only with the generous assistance of Jenny (Bolo XXXIII/D-1005-JNE), the senior surviving Bolo assigned to the Old Concordiat's Artois Sector. Jenny, the protector of our own capital world of Central during the Long Night, has very kindly made the contents of her Technical Support and Historical memories available to the author, who wishes to take this opportunity to extend his sincere thanks to her.

This monograph is not the final word on the Bolo. Even a Mark XXXIII's memory space is finite, and the units built during the Last War did not receive the comprehensive Historical data bases of earlier marks. Research continues throughout the sphere of the Old Concordiat, and the author has no doubt future scholars will fill in many of the gaping holes which remain in our understanding of the enormous debt humanity owes to the creations which have so amply repaid their creators.

❖   ❖   ❖

The General Motors Bolo Mark I, Model B, was little more than an upgrade of the Abrams/Leopard/Challenger/LeClerc/T-80-era main-battle tank of the final years of the Soviet-American Cold War. (At the time the first Bolo was authorized, GM decided that there would never be a "Model A" or a "Model T," on the basis that the Ford Motor Company had permanently preempted those designations.) Equipped with a high-velocity main gun capable of defeating the newest Chobham-type composite armors at virtually any battle range and with a four-man crew, the Mark I was an essentially conventional if very heavy (150 metric tons) and fast (80 kph road speed) tank in direct line of descent from World War I's "Mother" via the Renault, PzKpf IV, T-34, Sherman, Panther, Tiger, Patton, T-54, M-60, Chieftain, T-72, and Abrams.

The classic challenge of tank design had always been that of striking the best balance of three critical parameters: armament, protection, and mobility. The first two consistently drove weights upward, while the third declined as weight increased, and perhaps the greatest accomplishment of the Mark I Bolo was that, like the Abrams before it, it managed to show increases in all three areas. The same parameters continued to apply throughout the period of the Bolo's development, and a fourth—electronic (and later psychotronic) warfare capability—was added to them. As in earlier generations of armored fighting vehicles, the competing pressures of these design areas fueled a generally upward trend in weight and size. With the adoption of the first Hellbore in the Mark XIV, Bolo designers actually began placing the equivalent of current-generation capital starship main battery weapons—and armor intended to resist them— in what could no longer be considered mere "tanks." The Bolo had become *the* critical planet-based strategic system of humanity, and the trend to ever heavier and more deadly fighting vehicles not only continued but accelerated. The Mark XVIII was larger than most Terran pre-dreadnought battleships; at 32,000 tons, the final Mark XXXIII was, quite literally, heavier than all but the last generations of pre-space wet-navy battleships had been.

Partly as a result of this constant pressure to increase size and weight as succeeding marks were up-gunned and up-armored, Bolo development was marked by recurrent shifts in emphasis between what might be termed the "standard Bolo," the "heavy Bolo," and various specialist variants.

The "standard Bolos," as epitomized by the Mark I, Mark II, Mark V, etc., may be considered direct conceptual descendants of the twentieth century's "main battle tank:" vehicles whose designs were optimized for the direct fire (assault) and anti-armor role. The standard Bolo designs are generally characterized by limited indirect fire capability, a main armament centered on a single direct-fire weapon of maximum possible destructiveness (normally turret mounted high in the vehicle for maximum command), a supporting lateral or "broadside" battery (the famed "infinite repeaters") capable of engaging light AFVs or soft targets, and the heaviest possible armor. As additional threats entered the combat environment, additional active and passive defenses (generally lumped together under the heading of "armor" when allocating weights in the design stage, though many were, in fact, electronic in nature) were added, but the standard Bolo forms a consistent, clearly recognizable design strand clear through the Mark XXXII Bolo.

The first "heavy Bolo" was the Mark III, aptly classified at the time as a "mobile fire support base." While any heavy Bolo design was undeniably effective in the assault mode, they tended to be slower than the "standard" designs and were likely to sacrifice some of their anti-armor capabilities in favor of indirect fire support capacity. (The decision to downgrade anti-armor firepower in favor of other capabilities was often a particularly difficult one for the designers, since only a Bolo could realistically hope to stop *another* Bolo or its enemy equivalent.) Although the Mark III was 30 percent larger than the Mark II, its *anti-armor* armament was identical to the Mark II's; the increased tonnage was devoted primarily to even thicker armor, better anti-air and missile defenses, and the fire support capability of a current-generation artillery brigade. In fact, the Mark III, for its time, was the equivalent of the later continental and planetary "siege unit" Bolos: a ponderous, enormously powerful support system which only another Bolo could stop, but not truly an *assault* system in its own right.

Throughout the development of the Bolo, there was a distinct tendency to alternate between the standard and heavy designs in successive marks, although the standard clearly predominated. This was probably because the standard design could, at a pinch, perform most of the heavy design's functions, but the heavy design was less well suited for the fast, far-ranging mobile tactics which the standard design could execute. Moreover, the sheer size and weight of a Bolo (until, at least, the introduction of dedicated, rough field-capable armor transports with the Mark XIX) created deployment problems, particularly in the assault role, which led to stringent efforts to hold down size and weight. At several points in the Bolo's history, standard and heavy designs were introduced simultaneously, as complementary units of the armored force, but almost invariably, the next generation saw a return to the concept of the standard design.

Mixed in with the standard and heavy Bolos were the occasional specialists, such as the Mark XVI *Retarius* "light Bolo" and the Mark XXVII *Invictus* "screening Bolo." Much more often, however, specialist models cropped up within an otherwise standard or heavy mark. Bolo designers were never loathe to seek variants optimized for specific tactical or support functions, although the sheer cost of any Bolo was sufficient to ensure that the specialists were generally a distinct minority within the overall Bolo force. Extreme examples of specialists may be seen in the Mark XV/L and Mark XXI/I. The XV/L was barely half the size of the XV/K and deleted all conventional main armament in favor of a massive EW capability and was, in essence, a pure electronics platform with backup capability as an anti-air/anti-missile area defense system. The Mark XXI/I, on the other hand, was the smallest self-aware Bolo ever built: a very lightly armed "stealth" Bolo designed as a forward reconnaissance vehicle and as an armored transport for small, elite special forces teams.

The Bolos did not really change the fundamental truth that humanity's survival depended, both for better and for worse, upon its weapons technology. What *did* change was the fact that, in the Bolo, humanity had, in a sense, developed a weapon system which was better than humanity itself was. Better at making war, better at destroying enemies (including, at various times, other *human* enemies), better at defending its creators, and, arguably, better in living up to the ideals humanity espoused. Be that as it may, the fact that human development through the end of the Concordiat Period was intimately entwined with the Bolos is beyond dispute.

The Mark I, II, and III Bolos did not create the twenty-first-century period of "the Crazy Years" as Terra's old nation-state system crumbled, nor did they cause World War III. They made both the Crazy Years and the War even more destructive, in a tactical sense, than they might otherwise have been, yet in a perverse way, they helped minimize the *strategic* destruction (the Mark IIIs deployed in defense of the Free City-State of Detroit in 2032, for example, intercepted and destroyed every ICBM and cruise missile launched at the city). Perhaps more to the point, it was the existence of a single Mark II Bolo which permitted Major Timothy Jackson and Renada Banner to restore security and democratic government to the Prometheus Enclave within what had been the United States of America in 2082, thus planting the seed which eventually became the Concordiat government of Earth.

As the Concordiat expanded to the stars, and especially after the production of the first, crude FTL hyper shunt generator in 2221, the Bolos were both humanity's vanguard and its final line of defense. For a thousand years, successive generations of Bolos fought Man's enemies, defended his planets, and avenged his defeats. The fully autonomous and self-directing Bolos of the Mark XXIV and later generations were truly humanity's knights *sans peur et sans reproche*, and when the Concordiat finally crumbled into neo-barbarian successor states in the thirty-fifth century, following over two hundred T-years of warfare with the Melconian Empire, it was the handful of ancient, still-loyal survivors of the Final Dinochrome Brigade who protected and nurtured the isolated pockets of human survivors through the Long Night which followed. Much of the battle history of the Bolos has been lost, but the portions of it which remain are the stuff of the most glorious—and tragic—records of humanity and its works. Bolos might fail. They might die and be destroyed. But they did not surrender, and they never—ever—quit.

A Brief Design History of the Bolo

MARK I BOLO (2000):

The Mark I Bolo was an early twenty-first century update of current Abrams technology armed with a single turreted main gun (150mm; 1,722 mps muzzle velocity) capable of defeating any existing vehicle's armor (including its own) firing DSFSLRP (discarding sabot, fin-stabilized, long-rod penetrator) rounds. The Mark I carried secondary-turreted point defense/anti-personnel gatlings with on-mount radar and computerized fire control packages, required a conventional four-man crew, and relied upon a pair of high-efficiency, fossil-fueled turbines for power. Combat radius was 1,000 kilometers with a battle weight of 150 metric tons. Maximum speed was approximately 80 kph (road). The Mark I was replaced in production fairly quickly by the Mark II under the pressure the new arms race exerted on R&D as the traditional world order slipped towards general collapse.

MARK II BOLO (2015):

The Mark II was an updated Mark I, with greatly improved onboard computers and the same main armament, but with the first light lateral infinite repeater armament (four railguns in two two-gun batteries). Fitted with gatling and counter-missile point defense. First durachrome armor (10 millimeter) capable of defeating any weapon short of the Bolo's own DSFSLRP round.

Electronics were designed to allow a single crewman to assimilate data and operate the entire system, and weight rose to 194 metric tons. The Mark II's fossil fuel power plant drove electric generators rather than powering its drive train directly, and the vehicle had a limited (12-hour) backup power supply of ionic batteries. The Mark II could also operate on electrical power from a secondary source (such as local civilian generator capacity) to maintain long-term readiness in the area defense role. Maximum speed was approximately 80 kph (road) to 30 kph (cross-country in average terrain). The Mark II was the last Bolo with only two tread systems; all later marks were designed with "wide track" treads—that is, with multiple track systems across the full width of the vehicle to reduce ground pressure to the lowest possible value.

MARK III BOLO (2018):

A near contemporary of Mark II, the Mark III was actually designed as a "heavy" (300 metric tons) companion vehicle. The Mark III's single 150mm main gun (which was *not* turreted and had only a 20 degree traverse) was backed by an 8-gun infinite repeater battery, a heavy indirect fire support capability (four 155mm howitzers and a light VLS missile system), and an upgraded anti-missile armament. Unlike the Mark II, the Mark III carried only a single fossil-fueled power plant, strictly for backup use; power was normally drawn from heavy banks of ionic batteries, and the Mark III was the first Bolo designed from the outset to use solar film recharging. The vehicle also carried a marginally better sensor suite and a thicker durachrome hull (20 millimeter) which could be pierced at pointblank range (250 meters or less) by a 90 degree hit with the 140mm or 150mm DSFSLRP round; otherwise, it was effectively immune to anything short of a contact nuclear explosion. The Mark III was designed for a two-man crew with the second crewman serving as electronics officer

(EW, sensors, etc.), but could be crewed by a single experienced operator in a pinch. The last Pre-Collapse Bolo, it was the first Bolo with multiple tread systems—inner and outer—with an independent power train for the inner pair, but maximum speed fell to 50 kph (road), 25 kph (cross-country).

MARK IV BOLO (2116):

The first Post-Collapse Bolo picked up where the Mark II left off. The Mark IV had a much improved sensor suite and carried a main armament of one 165mm railgun, backed by six infinite repeater railguns (20mm). The Mark IV was the first Bolo to use energy weapons (laser clusters) to supplement projectile weapons in the point defense role and was fitted with seventy-five vertical launch system missile cells in its after decking, capable of accepting indirect fire support or SAM loads but without onboard reloads. Powered as Mark III, but with improved solar film. (It was no longer necessary to stop and deploy acres of film; the Mark IV could recharge on the move in average daylight conditions.) The Mark IV's durachrome hull was thicker (30 millimeter), yet weight dropped to 210 tons in the Model B, with a maximum speed of 60 kph (road) and 30 kph (cross-country). Missile load and sensor upgrades continued to drive up the tonnage of successive models, however; by the end of its active life, the Mark IV did carry onboard missile reloads and weight had risen to over 340 tons while maximum road speed fell to 40 kph, with very limited rough terrain capability. (The Mark IV, Model H, for instance, could get *through* almost anything, but its suspension and power train weren't up to crossing rough terrain at any kind of speed.)

MARK V BOLO (2160):

The first member of a family of specialists with roughly comparable onboard computer support but different weapons fits and functions. The Mark V was the first so-called "deep-wader"—that is, it no longer required bridging support, as it was designed to cross water barriers (including lakes and even small seas) by submerging and driving across their bottoms—and this capability became standard with all subsequent marks of Bolo. Power demands continued to grow, surpassing levels which even ionic battery technology could meet, and the Mark V was the first Bolo to use an onboard fission power plant. The growing size and weight of later models of the Mark IV had led to efforts to diversify design in the immediately subsequent marks, and the Mark V was the "general battle tank," fitted with a heavy caliber railgun (190mm) for main armament, supported by twin lateral batteries of six 60mm "gatling-style" infinite repeaters using spent uranium slugs and lighter gatlings and laser clusters for point defense. The laser clusters' anti-personnel function was limited, and the Mark V also saw the first use of multishot anti-personnel flechette/HE clusters, which became standard on all subsequent Bolos. Missile capacity was severely down-sized and restricted to SAMs as part of the drive to hold down weight. The Mark V had a one-man crew, a battle weight of approximately 198 metric tons, and a maximum speed of 50 kph (cross-country) to 80 kph (road).

MARK VI BOLO (2162):

The Mark VI was the direct descendent of the Mark III "mobile firebase" concept. It had the same power plant and computer support as the Mark V, but the Mark VI's "main battery" was its missile load, which was configured for maximum flexibility. No railgun main armament was mounted, but the 60mm infinite repeaters were upgraded to seven guns per side, and a heavier point defense battery intended to provide cover for other friendly units and to protect the Bolo itself when operating in counter-battery mode was fitted. One-man crew; 238 tons; speed roughly comparable to the Mark V's.

MARK VII BOLO (2163):

The Mark VII was a "heavy" Bolo, whose introduction inspired the first use—though still unofficially—of the term "siege unit." It had the same electronics fit as Marks V and VI, but its main direct-fire armament was one 200mm railgun backed by fourteen heavier (75mm) infinite repeaters. The Mark VII's heavy missile load was biased towards the bombardment function, but it was equally capable of operating SAMs in the area defense role. This vehicle has a very heavy layered durachrome war hull (120 millimeter) and required a two-man crew, rather than the Mark V's and VI's one-man crew, but in the VII/B the second crewman served solely to control the indirect fire armament. In later models, the second position was upgraded to a dedicated air-defense/missile intercept function. Weight was approximately 348 tons in the Model B, with a maximum road speed of 40 kph and a maximum cross-country speed of 30 kph. (The Mark VII was never very fast, but its sheer mass meant most terrain features tended to crumple when it hit them and so did not slow it as severely.)

MARK VIII BOLO (2209):

The Mark VIII was the next-generation "main battle" (or "standard") Bolo. Main armament remained a railgun, though muzzle velocity increased still further and projectile size fell slightly (to 170mm), but this Bolo marked the first appearance of energy-weapon (laser) infinite repeaters. (By the time of the Mark VIII, *any* Bolo's secondary battery had come to be referred to as "infinite repeaters" whether or not they fired actual projectiles.) Although the new laser infinite repeaters were actually marginally less effective than the last-generation railgun infinite repeaters on an energy-transfer-per-hit basis, mass per weapon fell, and the shift meant magazine capacity for the secondary battery was no longer a design factor. Missile capability was limited to the SAM and point defense role, but the Mark VIII received four hull-mounted 150mm rapid fire howitzers to compensate. The VIII/B was fission-powered, with solar charge backup capability, a one-man crew, and a weight of approximately 225 tons. Improved power train and suspension permitted a sustained road speed of 65 kph and short-range "sprint" speeds of up to 85 kph, but maneuverability at high speed was poor.

MARK IX BOLO (2209):

The Mark IX was the next generation "siege" unit, introduced simultaneously with the Mark VIII as companion vehicle. The main battery railgun was suppressed in favor of additional missile power and four high-trajectory 180mm howitzers in two back-to-back twin turrets. Further improvements in electronics allowed the Mark IX, unlike the Mark VII, to be crewed by one man. Weight was approximately 400 tons, and maximum road speed for the IX/B was 57 kph.

MARK X BOLO (2235):

The Mark X saw the first appearance of an energy main armament (laser cannon) in a Bolo. As with the laser infinite repeaters of the Mark VIII and IX, the new system was actually less destructive than the one it replaced on a per-hit basis, but it required no magazine space. The Mark X was fission-powered and carried laser infinite repeaters, and approximately 1/3 of the preceding Mark IX's gatling close-in anti-missile and anti-personnel weapons were replaced with multibarreled flechette-firing railguns in independent housings. The Mark X carried only self-defense missiles and no high-trajectory indirect fire weapons and required a one-man crew. Later models of this mark had sufficient computer capability and flexibility to begin use of pre-loaded computerized battle plans, requiring human intervention only when unanticipated tactical situations exceeded the parameters of the battle plan. The Mark X, Model B's battle weight was 350 tons, with a maximum road speed 70 kph.

MARK XI BOLO (2235):

The Mark XI was essentially a backup, designed to cover the possibility that the Mark X's laser main armament might prove impractical in service. Main armament was one 18cm railgun firing depleted uranium long-rod penetrators in the anti-armor role and a wide range of cluster, incendiary, chemical, and fuel-air rounds against unarmored targets. Otherwise, the Mark XI was identical to the Mark X. This vehicle remained in service longer than might otherwise have been anticipated because the projectile-firing capability of its main gun proved extremely popular with tacticians.

MARK XII BOLO (2240):

This was the first true "continental siege unit," designed for strategic indirect fire with VLS cells capable of handling missiles with intercontinental range. The Mark XII was capable of MIRVed FROB attacks and of engaging orbital targets with hyper-velocity surface-to-space missiles. Main anti-armor armament was deleted, but the Mark XII was equipped with extremely capable anti-air/anti-missile defenses (in effect, it was an area defense system, as well as a bombardment unit). The vehicle was normally mated with a BAU (Bolo Ammunition Unit), a Mark XII with all offensive armament deleted to provide magazine space for multiple load-outs for the Mark XII's missile batteries. Although the Mark XII continued to carry a one-man crew, it was primarily designed for pre-loaded computerized battle plans. Weight was 500 tons, with a road speed 50 kph.

MARK XIII BOLO (2247):

The Mark XIII was essentially a Mark XII with main anti-armor armament restored. Although the main gun ate up almost 25 percent of the tonnage dedicated to magazine space in the Mark XIII, the Mark XIII's bombardment capability actually slightly exceeded that of the Mark XII with only minimal overall weight increases. This was made possible largely through improvements in fission technology (allowing a smaller power plant) and the first use of a flintsteel inner war hull under a much thinner durachrome sheath. The Mark XIII/B's weight of 565 tons held fairly constant in all models of the mark. Road speed was 50 kph in the XIII/B, rising to 75 in late-series models as suspension and power train improvements became available.

MARK XIV BOLO (2307):

The Mark XIV replaced the never entirely satisfactory laser "main gun" of earlier marks with the far more destructive "Hellbore" plasmagun. This 25cm weapon, originally designed for the Concordiat Navy's Magyar-class battlecruiser's main batteries, had a half-megaton/second energy output and, unlike the earlier Bolo laser cannon, was a marked improvement over any kinetic weapon of equivalent mass. In other respects, the Mark XIV was a "standard" reversion to a generalist design, made possible by advances in mag-bottle technology (which finally made fusion power a practical alternative to fission in Bolo design) and acceptance of a lighter indirect fire capability. Anti-missile defenses were now sufficient to render strategic bombardment impractical, so indirect fire was limited to tactical and theater applications. This permitted the use of smaller missiles which, in turn, allowed an increased magazine capacity without weight penalties. Even so, the Mark XIV/B was 28 percent heavier than the Mark XIII/K it replaced, although further power train and suspension upgrades prevented any loss of maneuverability or cross-country performance. Gradual improvements in sensor fits and fire control systems kept this mark in front-line service for approximately 90 years. Tactically, primary reliance now rested firmly upon pre-loaded computerized battle plans, but a single human crewman was routinely carried to respond to unanticipated threats. The Mark XIV/B's weight was 728 tons (rising to 900 in late-series models), and road speed hovered between 60 and 75 kph over the life of the mark.

MARK XV/B-M BOLO (*Resartus*) (2396):

A quantum leap in Bolo technology, the Mark XV was the standardbearer of the Concordiat during humanity's greatest wave of interstellar expansion. Very few non-human species encountered during this period could match the Mark XV's capabilities; none could exceed them. This was the first Bolo which did not require an onboard human crewman, due to advances in cybernetics and secure communication links (first short-range subspace com capabilities), which permitted increasingly sophisticated computerized pre-battle planning coupled with unjammable remote human control to correct for unanticipated problems. Main armament was one 25cm Hellbore with line-of-sight capability, backed by laser cluster "gatling" infinite repeaters (total of fourteen in the Model B) and four 20cm howitzers in individual secondary turrets. The 25cm Hellbore remained incapable of engaging orbital targets from planets with atmosphere due to as yet unsolved attenuation and dissipation problems with the weapon's plasma bolt "packaging," but there were few planetary targets with which it could not deal. Tactical and theater bombardment capability was roughly equivalent to the Mark XIV's, but the Mark XV had no strategic bombardment capability. The Mark XV's six track systems each had an independent power train, and the vehicle carried both primary and secondary fusion plants. Cybernetics were divided between two totally independent command centers as protection against battle damage, and durachrome was wholly abandoned in favor of a much tougher flintsteel war hull. Early models of this mark saw the last use of anti-kinetic reactive armor. Major improvements in suspension were required to deal with unparalleled battle weights (1,500 tons in the Model B, rising to over 3,000 in the Model M), but road speed held constant at approximately 65 kph (with brief "sprint" capability of over 80 kph) over the life of this mark, although the "lightweight" Mark XV, Model L, EW platform, at barely 1,100 tons, was 37 percent faster. Cross-country speed was equivalent to road speed except in very rugged terrain. This mark enjoyed a very long, very stable evolutionary history (mainly because the Concordiat didn't run into anything a Mark XV couldn't handle).

MARK XV/R BOLO (*Horrendous*) (2626):

The Model R was the final variant of the Mark XV. Main armament was upgraded to one 50cm Hellbore (which, unlike earlier model's weapons, *could* engage spacecraft in low orbit even from within a planetary atmosphere), and ablative armor appliqués were fitted over the Model R's flintsteel war hull in light of increases in infantry and light-vehicle energy weaponry. The preceding Model Q had seen vastly upgraded EW capabilities and the first appearance of heuristic cybernetics designed to run continuous analyses of pre-loaded battle plans against actual battle conditions in order to suggest improvements to its distant human commander. Under express human pre-battle authorization, the Mark XV/Q and /R were capable of reconfiguring their battle plans on the move without further human input. Although not self-directed, the final models of the Mark XV gave a very good impersonation of a war machine which was. Weights climbed sharply—the Mark XV/R reached 5,000 tons—but maximum road speed held fairly constant at 65-70 kph, despite weight increases.

MARK XVI BOLO (*Retarius*) (2650):

The increasing size of the Mark XV led to a fresh attempt at specialized design, and the Mark XVI was, in effect, a "light" Mark XV. Main armament remained a 50cm Hellbore, but the infinite repeater batteries were reduced to a total of eight weapons and the howitzer armament was deleted. (As partial compensation, the Mark XVI replaced its laser infinite repeaters with ion-bolt projectors, with much greater ability to penetrate ablative armor, and received a six-gun battery of short-range breech-loading 20cm mortars to augment its anti-personnel clusters.) A complete ablative outer hull was adopted to replace previous appliqués, and cybernetics were equivalent to those of Mark XV/R. Weight fell to 3,600 tons, and road speed rose to 90 kph with short duration "sprints" of up to 100 kph possible. The Mark XVI formed the "light regiments" of the original Dinochrome Brigade.

MARK XVII BOLO (*Implacable*) (2650):

Introduced simultaneously with the Mark XVI, the Mark XVII was the "heavy" version of the same basic weapon system. Main armament was upgraded from a 50cm Hellbore to a 60cm weapon, and the ion-bolt infinite repeaters were increased to a total of fifteen (six each in two lateral batteries with a three-gun frontal battery in the glacis). The Mark XVI's mortars were deleted in favor of six 25cm howitzers and an increased missile armament. Weight increased to 6,500 tons, and maximum road speed dropped to 75 kph. The Mark XVII formed the "heavy regiments" of the original Dinochrome Brigade.

MARK XVIII BOLO (*Gladius*) (2672):

While the Mark XVI was more agile and easier to deploy than the Mark XVII, it proved less popular in combat than its companion mark because of its lighter offensive power. The Mark XVIII replaced both the XVI and XVII in relatively short order as the new "standard" Bolo in an attempt to combine the best features of both its immediate predecessors. As usual, the new vehicle went up in size and weight (late-model Mark XVIIIs approached 10,000 tons), and space-to-ground deployment became a problem. Main armament was the Mark XVII's 60cm Hellbore, but the infinite repeaters were reduced to twelve with the deletion of the bow battery (which had been found to compromise the structural integrity of the glacis plate). The Mark XVIII adopted a "sandwiched" hull: an outer ablative hull, then a thin hull of early-generation duralloy, and finally the flintsteel main war hull. The Mark XVIII also added a third fusion plant, which, with additional improvements in fire control, plasma containment technology, and weapons power, permitted its Hellbore to engage spacecraft even in medium orbit. The Mark XVIII formed the first "general purpose" regiments of the Dinochrome Brigade and, in successive models, remained first-line Concordiat equipment for over a century. Maximum road speed fell to 70 kph and maximum "sprint" speed fell to only 80 kph, but except in the roughest terrain, a Mark XVIII was as fast cross-country as on a road. (Of course, for vehicles as large and heavy as a Bolo, "roads" had long since become a purely relative concept.)

MARK XIX BOLO (*Intransigent*) (2790):

The Concordiat originally anticipated that the Mark XIX would remain first-line equipment for at least as long as the Mark XVIII, as it marked the first true qualitative improvement on the old Mark XV. The Mark XVI, XVII, and XVIII had been essentially up-gunned and up-armored Mark XVs; the Mark XIX was the first Bolo to mount mono-permeable, anti-kinetic battle screen as its first line of defense against projectile weapons and to incorporate the ability to convert a percentage of most types of hostile energy fire into useful power. In addition, the Mark XIX was accompanied into service by the Navy's new specialized armor transport: a light cruiser-sized vessel mated to a pair of Mark XIXs and capable of rough-field landings in almost any terrain (short of swamp or truly precipitous mountains). The transports were a vast improvement over the older independent assault pods, thus greatly simplifying the deployment problems experienced with the Mark XVII and XVIII. Improved generations of pods remained in service for almost four more centuries, particularly for battalion or larger level assaults. Main armament remained a 60cm Hellbore, but secondary armament was upgraded to sixteen ion-bolt infinite repeaters, backed up by 35mm gatling/railguns. The howitzer armament was once more suppressed in favor of eight 30cm breech-loading mortars, and the ablative outer hull was further augmented by a "plasma-shedding" ceramic tile appliqué. Weight soared to 13,000 tons, but road speed actually rose to 90 kph, with a "sprint" capability of over 120 kph.

MARK XX/B BOLO (*Tremendous*) (2796):

The reign of the Mark XIX was shorter than anyone had anticipated primarily because no one had anticipated the psychotronic breakthrough. (Or perhaps it would be more accurate to say that no one had expected the High Command to *accept* the psychotronic technology as quickly as it did.) The Mark XX *Tremendous* was the first truly self-directing (and self-aware) Bolo. Defensive capabilities remained unchanged from the Mark XIX, but the internal volume demands of the Mark XX's psychotronics forced the main armament to be downsized, and the Mark XIX's single 50cm Hellbore was replaced by two 30cm weapons, twin-mounted in a single turret. In addition, the Mark XX/M (unofficially referred to as the "Mosby") was a unique departure. Designed for independent deployment to raid an enemy's logistics and rear areas, the XX/M was essentially a refitted Mark XIV hull. The considerable mass of its first-generation Hellbore, along with its turret, was deleted, which freed up sufficient internal volume (barely) to permit installation of a somewhat less capable version of the Mark XX's psychotronics. Although self-aware, the Mark XXs had relatively simple (and bloodthirsty) personalities, and full self-awareness was specifically limited to battlefield applications. Except in carefully defined combat-related areas, the Mark XX's software suppressed its volition, effectively prohibiting it from taking *any* action without direct orders from designated human command personnel. Weight and speed data for the Mark XIX apply to the Mark XX. The Mark XX's great opponents were the Yavac heavies of the Deng, but not even the Yavac-A/4 could survive against a Mark XX Bolo without a numerical superiority of at least 3.25-to-1.

MARK XXI BOLO (*Terrible*) (2869):

Following the introduction of the Mark XX, a nomenclature policy was adopted under which new mark numbers were to be issued only to reflect substantial increases in psychotronic capability. (The new practice was temporarily abandoned with the Mark XXVII-Mark XXIX series, but resumed with the Mark XXX.) The Mark XXI actually proliferated into several sub-variants which would have received their own mark numbers under the old system, including yet another attempt at a "heavy" Bolo (which tipped the scales at over 20,000 tons and was never adopted for field use), and the "stealth" forward reconnaissance XXI/I. Mainstream Bolo development, however, followed the "standard" format, and the Mark

XXI/B reverted to the single 60cm Hellbore main armament of the Mark XIX. The major advance lay in the enhanced computational speed of the mark's computers and improvements in the personality centers of successive models. Although still fringed about by inhibitory programming to control self-directed actions outside combat, the Mark XXI was much more capable *in* combat. This mark also saw the introduction of TSDS (Total Systems Data-Sharing) technology into the regiments of the Dinochrome Brigade. In practice, each unit of the regiment operated in battle as a single component of a multiunit awareness in a free-flow tactical link which combined the conclusions of *all* its Bolos to formulate future actions.

MARK XXII BOLO (*Thunderous*) (2890):

The Mark XXII saw both further advances in cybernetics and psychotronics and a considerable upgrade in firepower with the new "super" Hellbore, a 90cm weapon which increased its destructive output to a full two megatons/second. Secondary armament mirrored the Mark XXI's. The Mark XXII was also the first Bolo to mount an interplanetary-range subspace com, and, for the first time, the Navy modified *its* cybernetics to permit a Bolo's psychotronics to directly control the maneuvers and defensive systems of its armor transport spacecraft (now unmanned in combat) for assault insertions, which increased its chance of penetrating hostile defenses by an order of magnitude. The Mark XXII's kinetic battle screen showed a 36 percent increase in effectiveness over the Mark XXI's, and weight hovered around 14,000-15,000 tons for all models, with a top speed of 80 kph and a "sprint" capability of 120-135 kph.

MARK XXIII BOLO (*Invincibilis*) (2912):

The Mark XXIII followed quickly on the heels of the Mark XXII, largely as a result of worsening relations between the Concordiat and the Quern Hegemony. Although the Quern managed to achieve strategic surprise when they actually launched their attack, worsening Human-Quern relations between 2880 and 2918 had driven Bolo research at a breakneck pace. The original Mark XXIII was only a marginal improvement (in electronic terms) on the Mark XXII, but the main armament was doubled to a pair of 80cm "super" Hellbores in fore-and-aft turrets, and provision was made for quick conversion to the molecular circuitry whose early perfection the R&D bureaus anticipated. Secondary armament was also upgraded—to eighteen ion-bolt infinite repeaters in two nine-gun lateral batteries—and a new generation of battle screen was augmented by internal disrupter shielding around critical systems. The outbreak of the Quern Wars put a halt to major psychotronic research, as all efforts were bent upon design rationalization to aid in mass production, but the anticipated molecular circuitry appeared almost on schedule. Although it was not applied throughout, late-series Mark XXIIIs incorporated the new circuitry within their psychotronics, which enormously increased capability without increasing volume requirements. It was possible to restore the "secondary brain" feature to the Mark XXIII with no degradation in base capability, which made it much more resistant to battle damage. Despite its increased armament, the Mark XXIII, like the Mark XXII, hovered around the 15,000 ton mark, primarily because of the weight savings of its new molycircs and the shift to later-generation duralloy in place of flintsteel, which permitted armor thicknesses to be halved for the same standard of protection. Speeds remained largely unchanged from the Mark XXII.

MARK XXIV BOLO (*Cognitus*) (2961):

The Mark XXIV was the first genuinely autonomous Bolo. Previous Bolos had been self-directing on the tactical level, but the Mark XXIV, with a vastly improved personality center and id integration circuitry, was capable of *strategic* self-direction. For the first time, Bolos began to evolve a truly "human" level of individual personality, but the Mark XXIV's psychotronics continued to be hedged about with inhibitory safeguards. A much greater degree of non-combat autonomy was permitted, but the vehicle's psychotronics remained so designed as to deny it full use of its own capabilities outside Battle Reflex Mode. Impetus to decrease or even abolish those safeguards clearly began with this mark as it proved its reliability and flexibility, yet resistance would continue until Bolo Central reviewed the battle record of Unit 0075-NKE on Santa Cruz in 3025. The Mark XXIV retained the Mark XXIII's secondary armament but reverted to a single-turreted main armament (90cm "super" Hellbore). Despite the reduced main armament, weight fell only to the 14,000 ton mark, and speed remained roughly equivalent to that of the Mark XXII and Mark XXIII.

MARK XXV BOLO (*Stupendous*) (3001):

After forty T-years of experience with the Mark XXIV, even diehards conceded that many of the inhibitory software features which had been incorporated into every Bolo since the Mark XX were no longer justified. The most restrictive features were deleted from the Mark XXV, Model B, although it was not until the Model D (introduced in 3029) that virtually all inhibitions were suppressed. A core package of override programming was retained to restrict the volition of (or even, in the case of the so-called "Omega Worm," to destroy) a Mark XXV which went "rogue" as a result of battle damage or "senile" due to poor maintenance, but most of the restrictions which had required human approval for almost all non-battle decisions were progressively relaxed over the operational life of the Mark XXV, with a tremendous increase in efficiency. The practice of deploying totally independent Bolo brigades lay well in the future, but the

Mark XXV's capabilities clearly pointed the way to them. The Mark XXV essentially duplicated the offensive and defensive systems of the Mark XXIV, yet further improvements in metallurgy and fusion technology dropped weight to 13,000 tons while normal speed rose to a maximum of 95 kph, though "sprint" speed remained unchanged.

MARK XXVI BOLO (*Monstrous*) (3113):

The Mark XXVI was the first Bolo to incorporate improved "hyper-heuristic" features based on the work of Major Marina Stavrakas. Armament, size, weight, and speed remained largely unchanged from the Mark XXV, but the Mark XXVI was capable of constructing a "learning model" in accelerated time. In some ways, this almost equated to precognition, in that the Mark XXVI could project changes in an enemy's tactical or strategic actions before even the *enemy* realized he intended to change them. The new systems also meant that, accompanied by a much improved ability to break hostile communications security, a Mark XXVI could actually invade an opponent's data net, access his computers, scan them for useful data, and (in some cases) even implant its own directions in those computers.

MARK XXVII-MARK XXIX BOLOS (3185-3190):

The Mark XXVII (*Invictus*), XXVIII (*Triumphant*), and XXIX (*Victorious*) marked a temporary reversion to the older practice of assigning mark numbers on the basis of armament and function rather than psychotronics technology. All three had essentially identical cybernetics, which concentrated on further improvements to their hyper-heuristic packages, but the Mark XXVIII and XXIX also incorporated a complete changeover to molecular circuitry throughout, aside from the power linkages to their energy armaments. All three of these marks were used in the new, independent brigades which replaced the old regiment structure of the original Dinochrome

Brigade, but, in some ways, the units marked a reversion to the old "specialist" designs. All mounted the new 110cm "super" Hellbore (2.75 megatons/second), but the Mark XXVII was a "light," fast Bolo, with greatly reduced secondary armament, limited indirect fire capability, and a vastly improved sensor suite, intended to serve in a scouting and screening role for the independent brigades. (This function had been performed by light manned or unmanned vehicles, and the old Mark XXI/I, with psychotronic upgrades, remained in service for special forces applications. The new strategically self-directing Bolo brigades, however, required an integral scouting element, one not limited by "stealth" considerations and capable of fighting for information at need.)

The Mark XXVIII was the "generalist" of this trio of marks, with much the same armament as the old Mark XXIV, although that armament was even more deadly and effective under the control of the improved psychotronics of the newer units.

The Mark XXIX was an unabashedly "heavy" Bolo—indeed, it remained the heaviest Bolo ever deployed prior to the Mark XXXIII. It reverted to the twin Hellbore armament of the Mark XXIII (though still in 110cm caliber), coupled with a much enhanced indirect fire capability, and an integral logistics/maintenance function which it could extend to other units of the brigade. (The maintenance/repair function became standard in all succeeding Bolo designs.) The independent brigades normally consisted of four regiments of three 12-unit battalions each: one of Mark XXVIIs, two of Mark XXVIIIs, and one of Mark XIXs. Weights for these Bolos were 11,000 tons (maximum normal speed 110 kph) for the Mark XXVII, 15,000 (maximum normal speed 90 kph) for the Mark XXVIII, and 24,000 (maximum normal speed 75 kph) for the Mark XXIX.

MARK XXX BOLO (*Magnificent*) (3231):

Introduced on the eve of the Human-Melconian "Last War," the Mark XXX was the direct descendant of the Mark XXVIII. The incorporation of counter-grav into the Mark XXX's suspension and power train went far towards offsetting the mobility penalties increasing weight had inflicted on preceding generations. The Mark XXX incorporated still further improvements to the hyper-heuristic capabilities of the Marks XXVII-XXIX, new dual-ply battle screen (which was not only more effective against kinetic weapons but also capable of absorbing at least some of the power of almost any energy weapon and diverting it to the Bolo's use), and a new and improved cold-fusion power plant. Weight dropped from the Mark XXIX's 24,000 tons to 17,000 and normal speed increased to 115 kph. For very short intervals, the Mark XXX could divert sufficient power to its counter-grav units to achieve actual free flight at velocities up to 500 kph, but could not operate its battle screen or internal disrupter shields or fire its main armament while doing so.

MARK XXXI BOLO (3303):

Over the course of the thirty-third century, the galaxy slid with ever increasing speed into the maw of the "Last War's" gathering violence, and Bolos after the Mark XXX did not receive the "type" names which had become customary with the Mark XV. The Mark XXXI was an enhanced Mark XXX with a main armament of one 200cm Hellbore (5 megatons/second). Secondary armament, though still referred to as "infinite repeaters," consisted of two lateral batteries of six 20cm Hellbores each, and many small-caliber, hyper-velocity projectile weapons were retained for close-in defense and anti-personnel use. Indirect fire capability was degraded in favor of the assault role, for which purpose the Mark XXXI's duralloy war hull was given an average thickness of 90 centimeters, rising to 1.5 meters for the glacis and turret faces. All secondary and tertiary weapons were mounted outside the "core hull" which protected the Mark XXXI's power plants and psychotronics, and last-generation internal disrupter shielding was used heavily. The Mark XXXI retained the counter-grav assist of the Mark XXX and, despite a weight increase to 19,000 tons, could match the preceding mark's speed.

MARK XXXII BOLO (3356):

The last Bolo whose year of introduction is known with certainty, the Mark XXXII was essentially a Mark XXXI with the added refinement of direct human-Bolo neural-psychotronic interfacing. Provision was also made for attachment of a counter-grav unit sufficient, under emergency conditions, to permit the Bolo to make an assault landing without benefit of transport. Offensive and defensive systems were comparable to those of the Mark XXXI. The Mark XXXII was the final version of the "standard" Bolo.

MARK XXXIII BOLO (?):

The last—and largest—Bolo introduced into service. The Mark XXXIII weighed no less than 32,000 tons and mounted a main armament of three independently-turreted 200cm Hellbores with a secondary armament of sixteen 30cm Hellbore infinite repeaters in two lateral batteries. Equipped with a very sophisticated indirect fire system, the sheer firepower of the Mark XXXIII was a reversion to the old siege unit thinking, though it was normally referred to as a *planetary* siege unit, not merely a continental one. No one knows how many Mark XXXIIIs were actually built, but official planning called for them to be deployed in independent brigades of 24 units each. Despite the increase in weight, speed remained equivalent to the Mark XXXI, and the Mark XXXIII's *internal* counter-grav could supply the assault landing capability for which the Mark XXXII had required an auxiliary unit.

BOLO ARMAMENT

Bolo Mark	Year	Weight	Road Speed	Sprint Speed
Mark I	2000	150	80	80
Mark II	2015	194	80	80
Mark III	2018	300	50	50
Mark IV	2116	210	60	60
Mark V	2160	198	80	80
Mark VI	2162	238	80	80
Mark VII	2163	348	40	40
Mark VIII	2209	225	65	85
Mark XIX	2209	400	57	57
Mark X	2235	350	70	70
Mark XI	2235	350	70	70
Mark XII	2240	500	50	50
Mark XIII	2247	565	50-75	50-75
Mark XIV	2307	728-900	60-75	60-75
Mark XV/B	2396	1,500	65	85
Mark XV/L		1,100	89	116
Mark XV/M		3,000	65	85
Mark XV/R	2626	5,000	75	95
Mark XVI	2650	3,600	90	100
Mark XVII	2650	6,500	75	88
Mark XVIII	2672	10,000	70	80
Mark XIX	2790	13,000	90	120
Mark XX	2796	as Mk XIX	as Mk XIX	as Mark XIX
Mark XXI	2869		Varies	Varies
Mark XXII	2890	15,000	80	135
Mark XXIII	2912	15,000	80	148

Main Armament	Secondary Armament	Indirect Fire	Self-Aware?
1 150mm DSFSLRP	point def/AP gatlings	None	No
1 150mm DSFSLRP	4 InfRpt railguns	None	No
1 150mm DSFSLRP	8 InfRpt railguns	Tac/Theater	No
4 155mm howitzers	Light VLS missile system		
1 165mm railgun	6 InfRpt railguns	Strategic	No
	VLS missile system		
1 190mm railgun	12 60mm gatling InfRpt	None	No
Heavy VLS missile system	14 60mm gatling InfRpt	Strategic	No
1 200mm railgun	14 75mm gatling InfRpt	Strategic	No
	VLS missile system		
1 170mm railgun	12 laser InfRpt	Tactical	No
	4 150mm howitzers		
VLS missile system	12 laser InfRpt	Strategic	No
4 18cm howitzers			
1 laser cannon	12 laser InfRpt	None	No
1 18cm railgun	12 laser InfRpt	None	No
Heavy VLS missile system	12 laser InfRpt	Strategic	No
1 laser cannon	12 laser InfRpt	Strategic	No
Heavy VLS missile system	4 15cm BL mortars		
1 25cm Hellbore	12 laser InfRpt	Tac/Theater	No
	VLS missile system		
1 25cm Hellbore	14 gatling laser InfRpt	Tac/Theater	No
4 20cm howitzers	VLS missile system		
none	point def/AP only	None	No
1 35cm Hellbore	16 gatling laser InfRpt	Tac/Theater	No
4 20cm howitzers	8 18cm BL mortars		
	VLS missile system		
1 50cm Hellbore	12 gatling laser InfRpt	Tactical	No
4 20cm howitzers	4 18cm BL mortars		
	VLS missile system		
1 50cm Hellbore	8 ion-bolt InfRpt	Tactical	No
	6 20cm BL mortars		
1 60cm Hellbore	15 ion-bolt InfRpt	Strategic	No
6 25cm howitzers	Heavy VLS missile system		
1 60cm Hellbore	12 ion-bolt InfRpt	Strategic	No
6 25cm howitzers	Heavy VLS missile system		
1 60cm Hellbore	16 ion-bolt InfRpt	Tactical	No
	8 30cm BL mortars		
2 30cm Hellbores	*as Mark XIX*	Tactical	Limited
1 60cm Hellbore	16 ion-bolt InfRpt	Varies	Limited
+ varying VLS capability	4-8 30cm BL mortars		
1 90cm Hellbore	16 ion-bolt InfRpt	Tac/Theater	Limited
	VLS missile system		
	6-8 30cm BL mortars		
2 80cm Hellbores	18 ion-bolt InfRpt	Tactical	Limited
	VLS missile system		
	6 30cm BL mortars		

Bolo Mark	Year	Weight	Road Speed	Sprint Speed
Mark XXIV	2961	14,000	80	148
Mark XXV	3001	13,000	95	150
Mark XXVI	3113	13,000	95	150
Mark XXVII	3185	11,000	110	150
Mark XXVIII	3186	15,000	90	135
Mark XXIX	3190	24,000	75	110
Mark XXX	3231	17,000	115	500
Mark XXXI	3303	19,000	115	500
Mark XXXII	3356	21,000	115	500
Mark XXXIII	????	32,000	105	500

Main Armament	Secondary Armament	Indirect Fire	Self-Aware?
1 90cm Hellbore	18 ion-bolt InfRpt VLS missile system 6 30cm BL mortars	Tactical	Autonomous
1 90cm Hellbore	18 ion-bolt InfRpt VLS missile system 6 30cm BL mortars	Tactical	Autonomous
as Mark XXV	*as Mark XXV*	Tactical	Autonomous
1 110cm Hellbore	10 ion-bolt InfRpt 6 30cm BL mortars	Tactical	Autonomous
1 110cm Hellbore	18 ion-bolt InfRpt VLS missile system 4 30cm BL mortars	Tac/Theater	Autonomous
2 110cm Hellbores Heavy VLS missile system	20 ion-bolt InfRpt 8 40cm BL mortars	Strategic	Autonomous
as Mark XVIII	*as Mark XVIII*	Tac/Theater	Autonomous
1 200cm Hellbore	12 20cm Hellbores Light VLS missile system	Tactical	Autonomous
as Mark XXXI	*as Mark XXXI*	Tactical	Autonomous
3 200cm Hellbores 4 240cm howitzers	14 20cm Hellbores 10 40cm BL mortars Heavy VLS missile system	Strategic	Autonomous

General Armament Notes

In addition to the weapons listed, all Bolo secondary armaments include small-caliber high-velocity projectile weapons for close-in defense and anti-personnel fire. All Bolos after Mark V also mounted multiple-shot flechette anti-personnel "clusters" with progressively heavier flechettes.

Any Bolo secondary gun with anti-armor capability was always referred to as an "infinite repeater," although the term originally applied only to a small- to medium-caliber projectile weapon with a high rate of fire and large magazine space.

Like most of their other weapon systems, the vertical launch system missile outfits of Bolos evolved tremendously over the course of the Bolo's design history. The original Mark III VLS consisted of only 60 non-reloadable cells, although more than one missile might be loaded per cell if they were small enough. By the time of the Mark XIX, the VLS consisted of reloadable, magazine-fed cells, and all future Bolo VLSs followed that pattern. The term "light" or "heavy" used to describe a VLS refers to (1) the number of cells (and thus salvo density) and (2) the VLS magazine capacity, not to the weight or size of missiles thrown.

The breech-loading mortars fitted to most Bolos after the Mark XIII might be considered automatic weapons, as their rate of fire averaged from 8 to 12 rounds per minute. The Mark XXXIII's 15cm BLMs had a maximum effective range of 3,000 meters; the 40cm BLMs of the Mark XXIX and Mark XXXIII had a maximum effective range of 9.75 kilometers.

HARRY TURTLEDOVE: A MIND FOR ALL SEASONS

EPIC FANTASY

Werenight (72209-3 ◆ $4.99) ☐
Prince of the North (87606-6 ◆ $5.99) ☐
In the Northlands rules Gerin the Fox. Quaintly, he intends to rule for the welfare and betterment of his people—but first he must defeat the gathering forces of chaos, which conspire to tumble his work into a very dark age indeed....

ALTERNATE FANTASY

The Case of the Toxic Spell Dump (72196-8 ◆ $5.99) ☐
Inspector Fisher's world is just a *little* bit different from ours...Stopping an ancient deity from reinstating human sacrifice in L.A. and destroying Western Civilization is all in a day's work for David Fisher of the Environmental *Perfection* Agency.

ALTERNATE HISTORY

Agent of Byzantium (87593-0 ◆ $4.99) ☐
In an alternate universe where the Byzantine Empire never fell, Basil Argyros, the 007 of his spacetime, has his hands full thwarting un-Byzantine plots and making the world safe for Byzantium. "Engrossing, entertaining and very cleverly rendered...I recommend it without reservation."
—**Roger Zelazny**

A Different Flesh (87622-8 ◆ $4.99) ☐
An extraordinary novel of an alternate America. "When Columbus came to the New World, he found, not Indians, but primitive ape-men.... Unable to learn human speech...[the ape-men] could still be trained to do reliable work. Could still, in other words, be made slaves.... After 50 years of science fiction, Harry Turtledove proves you can come up with something fresh and original."
—**Orson Scott Card**
